TEMPTING THE SCOTSMAN

"Collin?" How did she make his name into a caress? She took another step. "I thought . . ." Her hand lifted and inched toward him. "I've seen you watching me," she finally said as her fingers brushed his skin.

He felt his eyes close, felt a groan rumble up his throat and into her hand.

"I thought you wanted me, too," she whispered, the words soft with something close to doubt.

Don't answer her, he told himself. *Just walk away.* But his lips moved of their own accord. "My God, Alexandra. Don't all men want you?" He was reaching for her as he spoke. His hand curled around her nape, the heat of her skin seeping into his palm. He watched her pale neck arch into his grip before his gaze slid to her lips.

"This is a mistake." The words fell from his mouth even as he lowered it to hers.

She sighed, a sweet brush of warmth against his mouth, and then a searing whip of fire when she touched the tip of her tongue to his bottom lip. She shuddered—or he did— and he opened his lips to possess her.

Heat, he thought. She tasted like heat and lust and sweetness. He must be mad. He had to let her go, but he couldn't stop his hand from curving over her waist and pulling her hard against his arousal. Wisps of panic iced his veins, but between her fiery mouth and clutching hand all he could think of was having more of her . . .

BOOK YOUR PLACE ON OUR WEBSITE AND MAKE THE READING CONNECTION!

We've created a customized website just for our very special readers, where you can get the inside scoop on everything that's going on with Zebra, Pinnacle and Kensington books.

When you come online, you'll have the exciting opportunity to:

- View covers of upcoming books
- Read sample chapters
- Learn about our future publishing schedule (listed by publication month *and author*)
- Find out when your favorite authors will be visiting a city near you
- Search for and order backlist books from our online catalog
- Check out author bios and background information
- Send e-mail to your favorite authors
- Meet the Kensington staff online
- Join us in weekly chats with authors, readers and other guests
- Get writing guidelines
- AND MUCH MORE!

**Visit our website at
http://www.kensingtonbooks.com**

To Tempt a Scotsman

Victoria Dahl

ZEBRA BOOKS
Kensington Publishing Corp.
www.kensingtonbooks.com

ZEBRA BOOKS are published by

Kensington Publishing Corp.
850 Third Avenue
New York, NY 10022

All Kensington titles, imprints, and distributed lines are avail-
able at special quantity discounts for bulk purchases for sales
promotion, premiums, fund-raising, educational, or institu-
tional use.

Special book excerpts or customized printings can also be created to fit specific needs. For details, write or phone the office
of the Kensington Special Sales Manager: Attn. Special Sales
Department. Kensington Publishing Corp., 850 Third Avenue,
New York, NY 10022. Phone: 1-800-221-2647.

Zebra and the Z logo Reg. U.S. Pat. & TM Off.

ISBN-13: 978-1-4201-0015-0
ISBN-10: 1-4201-0015-7

First Printing: August 2007
10 9 8 7 6 5 4 3 2 1

Printed in the United States of America

This book is dedicated to my mom, Helen.
I would never have become a writer without you.
Thank you for filling my life with books.

And to the love of my life, Bill.
You've believed in me from the beginning,
and I think you love my stories even more than I do.
You're my husband, my best friend, my biggest fan,
and my hero, all in one.

Thank you to Adam and Ethan for being smart, sweet,
and sometimes quiet.
I love you.

Thank you also to my wonderful agent, Amy Moore-Benson,
for believing in my work, and to Connie Brockway, whose
books inspire me. And special thanks to all my friends:
Amy Jo, the Wild Cards, the Hoydens, and so many others.

Last, but never least,
thank you to my critique partner, Jennifer.
Together we've kept our sanity intact through the many
highs and lows of writing . . . Or have we?

Chapter 1

Yorkshire, June 1844

Lady Alexandra Huntington squinted at the invoice in front of her and breathed out the vilest curse she knew. Unladylike, of course, but then she was sitting at a man's desk, in a man's office, wearing men's riding breeches, and doing a man's job. Her language was likely the least shocking thing about her at the moment.

"Bi . . . Bin . . ." she tried again, glaring at the tangle of scratches that were supposed to be words. "Oh, for God's sake." The miller's writing had always been doubtful, but the man's penmanship had recently taken a turn for the worse. She knew the bill of sale must have something to do with grain, probably oats crushed for the stables, and still she could make neither heads nor tails of it.

It couldn't be helped then. She would have to search out the stable master and compare his recent orders with the few letters she could make out on the invoice. And though the man was polite enough—she was the sister of the duke, after all—he clearly wished she would give up this game of managing her brother's estate.

Alex stood and snatched up the paper. The click of her boots was absorbed by a thick rug as she stepped into the hall, so even though she hurried, the faint echo of an unfamiliar voice still reached her ears.

"You must be mistaken," a man said, as she moved toward the front rooms. The words bounced off the marble walls of Somerhart's entry. "His Grace assured me his sister would be home."

Alex blinked, shocked to hear herself spoken of. Her brother had sent someone from London to see her? It seemed unlikely, however . . . She slowed her pace and paused in the shadow of the side hall to peer toward the front door.

The man stood only a few feet inside the door, tall and dark and glowering at Prescott. That alone was interesting. No one glowered at her brother's butler. Prescott controlled access to a young and powerful duke.

Alexandra felt her prickling interest grow stronger. She edged a little farther into the room.

"If you'd care to leave a card, sir—"

"I do not have a card." The man's eyes flicked toward her, pinned her for a bare moment. He could not suspect who she was in her current attire, with her black hair pulled into a tight knot and the jacket hiding her curves. Still, Alexandra straightened at the brush of that silver gaze, even as it moved back to Prescott. The butler stood silent, not the least affected by the man's coolness. Ten seconds passed. Then twenty.

With a stiff shrug, the stranger finally gave in to the impossibility of intimidating Prescott. "Please tell her I need to speak with her. I'm at the Red Rose."

She watched as he turned, felt the soft tug of her impetuous nature. Who in the world was he? He should have been cowed by the butler's utter indifference, but he looked self-assured to the very fiber of his being even as he was turned away.

His brown hair needed trimming and he appeared to have forgotten his cravat as well as his calling card, but the perfect cut of his brown coat spoke of wealth. And a Scot's burr softened his deep voice—and sped her pulse.

Surely her brother would never speak of her to someone he didn't trust. "Prescott."

Ever unflappable, Prescott simply stepped aside. "My lady. A Mr. Collin Blackburn to see you."

"Thank you, Prescott."

Collin Blackburn froze at the sound of her voice. She watched him turn and step back inside, watched his eyes slide past her to search the corners of the huge entry for a more likely figure, but when he realized who she was, only the barest lift of russet brows betrayed his shock. "Lady Alexandra."

She let him stare a moment, let him take in the oddness of her attire. No gentleman had ever seen her in riding breeches before, none other than her brother. She was dressed inappropriately, indecently even, but it mattered not in the least. She was a fallen woman. She'd earned the freedom to do as she pleased, so she let him look his fill and took the chance to study him as well.

He stood as tall as her brother but wider. Wide shoulders, broad chest. Definitely no padding in that coat. His body wasn't bulky though. He was, in a word, solid.

His face looked purely masculine. Not handsome exactly, but stark and compelling. The slightly crooked nose spoke of an old fight, but his high cheekbones and wide mouth turned the mind to more pleasurable pursuits. She glanced back to the clear gray eyes that studied her so intently and saw his pupils tighten when he met her gaze.

"Thank you for seeing me."

"Prescott, would you have tea brought to the office, please? Mr. Blackburn?" Gesturing back toward the hall, she spun on her heel to lead the way. Her long red coat opened as she turned, and she felt the hem brush against the buff riding breeches that hugged the curve of her thigh and hip. There was no mistaking the widening of his eyes, even at the corner of her vision. He'd had quite the view.

Gritting her teeth against the thrill that chased through her, Alexandra buttoned the coat and hurried toward the door of her cramped office. The morning room would be more appropriate, she supposed, but not dressed like this. Her men's clothes would be a startling sight against a backdrop of flowered upholstery.

Alexandra stepped into the office and waved Blackburn toward a pair of chairs by the window. He waited until she took the chair opposite his, then sat and crossed a booted ankle over his knee.

"What did you wish to discuss with me, Mr. Blackburn?"

He let a heartbeat pass, then another. He watched her and frowned. A lock of hair fell over his brow when he finally inclined his head. "I'm here to ask a few questions."

"Questions?"

"About Damien St. Claire."

The name tightened the muscles of her jaw in a painful bunch. Blood rushed to her ears, roared like crashing waves. She couldn't move for a long moment, couldn't make her throat work. A deep breath forced it open. "I think that you should leave," she said very carefully, very evenly.

Blackburn shook his head, began to protest, but she stood and stabbed a finger at the door. "No. It's obvious my brother did not send you here. Leave. You can find your way out." She pushed past him to the desk and dropped into the seat behind it, hands frantically shuffling papers. A rush of hurt surged in her chest. Why would she think he'd be different from any other man?

Standing with slow purpose, he stepped toward her and leaned to rest his fists on the desktop. His jaw looked as hard as hers felt. "Lady Alexandra, I need to know what happened between you and St. Claire—and John Tibbenham."

"Really? How does it involve you?" Making an obvious show of widening her eyes, she looked up at him with mock dismay. "Oh, I'm sorry. You must have been one of my lovers. I find it so hard to recall them all."

His eyes narrowed as if her words had been a slap, then a sneer twisted his mouth as he leaned close. "Believe me, *my lady*. If I'd been one of your lovers, you'd remember it."

"Truly?" Alexandra let her gaze drift down to rest on the front of his trousers.

His fists tightened to rock on her desk. "Dinna think—" he began, but she cut him off again.

"You are not the first man to come here on the scent of easy prey. A ruined woman who just happens to be an heiress? Is that what you were thinking? Not very original, Mr. Blackburn. Please get out of my home."

"John Tibbenham was my brother."

Alexandra stared at him for a moment, rage trapped like ice in her chest, cracking against her ribs. When his words sunk past the roar of blood in her ears, she flinched and looked down, back to her rumpled papers, away from the hate in his eyes. The heat that had rushed to her cheeks drained away.

John's brother. He had mentioned a half brother once, as they'd trotted through a long country dance. Not the night he'd died. Perhaps the night before.

"I'm so sorry," she breathed and braved a glance at him. "I didn't realize."

He only stared at her until she couldn't hold his gaze any longer, until she flinched in shame. Her fingers smoothed the corner of a letter over and over again. "I am so sorry about your brother," she said more loudly and clasped her hands tight together to cease their movement.

"I'm looking for St. Claire. I would see him brought to justice."

"I don't know where he is."

"The man murdered my brother."

Alexandra took a deep breath and tried to gather her courage. She was not a cringing woman. It was just this one thing, this one night, that shamed her. Straightening her spine, she forced herself to look him in the eye. "His death was terrible. The duel was ridiculous. Still, your brother was the one who issued the challenge. I have no idea what happened afterward, but John challenged St. Claire."

"Regardless of your opinion, St. Claire is a criminal. Killing a man in a duel is still killing."

"I can't help you. I don't know where he is. It's been . . . It's been more than a year."

The office door opened and a maid poked her capped head inside, nodding toward the tea tray she held. The interruption should have been a relief, but Alexandra could not bear to extend this visit even a moment longer than necessary. She waved the tea away, and the thud of the closing door drummed against the silence of the room.

"You are telling me that this man was your . . . *special* friend, that he fought a duel over you—a duel that left him a fugitive—and he has *never once* contacted you?"

Was there any blood at all left in her veins? Her heart fluttered desperately. "Yes."

"St. Claire arranged for my brother to walk in on the two of you."

"What?"

"He wanted to be caught in an indecent position with you."

She blinked several times, felt the twist of her heart regaining its strength, and shook her head. "That's absurd."

"My brother was in the middle of a game of faro when he told his friends he had to meet St. Claire. William Bunting said John went straight to that study. He did not just happen upon you."

"But . . . That cannot be true."

"St. Claire used you."

Alexandra clutched the edge of her desk and surged unsteadily to her feet.

"He told my brother to meet him because he wanted to be caught with a hand up your skirts. It's the truth. John's father looked into this quite thoroughly, I assure you. You needn't protect St. Claire. He is a man without scruples."

Oh God, that was far too easy to believe. She'd been so young when she'd met him, only seventeen, and so thrilled to be running with a fast crowd. A true gentleman would never have accommodated her, but that had been the point, hadn't it? To dance on the edge of respectability?

"I did not wish to involve you in this. Your brother and John's father were both quite clear that I leave you out of it. But I've been after him for nine months and all my leads have run out."

Alexandra shook her head. She could not do this. How could he throw these foul ideas at her, then expect her help? "I'm sorry."

She looked past him, past the dark wood walls of the office, and focused on the brightness of the sun in the window. A full minute passed before his rough sigh filled the room.

"I'll be at the Red Rose tonight. I'd appreciate a note if you're willing to help."

Tipping her head in a nod, Alex lowered herself to her chair.

His hand pushed the door open before he turned back to her, an expression like hate on his face. "My brother was only twenty. He was twenty when Damien St. Claire shot him through the head."

A memory of John laughing brought tears to her eyes. She closed them. "I am sorry, Mr. Blackburn. He was a kind young man. A good man." The door clicked softly closed before she'd spoken the last word.

Thor flew over the hard-packed dirt, black hooves pounding out his eagerness to run the two miles to the inn. Collin needed the run as well. She knew something, was hiding something. Idiot girl. She'd probably believed whatever sweet-nothings St. Claire had whispered to her as he tossed up her skirts.

Still, young as she was, she was no innocent. She'd played two men against each other just for the sport of it, and her game had ruined her and killed John. And just because she was a tiny thing with great blue eyes didn't mean she wasn't a whore as well.

His brother had been madly in love with her even as she took another man to her bed. There was no telling who else had been there. She'd even admitted it herself, for God's sake. And after one quick view of the shape of those thighs, Collin knew she must've attracted men in droves. John had never stood a chance.

Collin cracked a bitter smile at the thought. If he'd met the girl at twenty, he'd have been panting after her, too. Her black hair and bright eyes were a potent combination. And the contrast of her delicate size and compact curves, the innocence of that heart-shaped face and the boldness of her clothing . . . lovely. Not lovely enough to die for though. Apparently his brother hadn't realized that, damn him for a fool. And damn their father too, for extracting this promise from Collin. Who the hell could deny an old man his dying wish?

He was meant to be in Scotland, on his farm, oversee-ing the work on his new home, getting the horses ready for fair. Instead he gallivanted about England and France, gathering information and chasing after criminals like a runner . . . And now he had to convince a spoiled English lightskirt to help him.

She was the cause of this, she and her lover. So, saint or sinner, Alexandra Huntington would help, whether she willed it or no.

The edges of the letters dug into the damp skin of Alexandra's palm. Forehead pressed to the glass of her bedroom window, she crumpled the papers, willed them to disappear, to never have existed, but the strokes and spikes of Damien's arrogant handwriting failed to fade.

She had wept over these letters once. Cried over the first one when he asked her to come to France and marry him. And the second, when he'd set aside his pride and begged for money to survive in exile. She had sent a generous amount, thinking it the least she could do for him.

She had sent money once more, after one last request, though she'd hesitated that time, thinking of John. And after Blackburn's hard words, Damien's stories of hardship seemed blatantly crafted to inspire guilt. Her guilt.

She tried to imagine her brother writing a letter to a

woman, begging help. Or her cousin George Tate, or even
Collin Blackburn. Impossible. She could not picture one
of those men pouring out the details of their troubles and
laying them at a lady's feet. Still, even if Damien wasn't as
good a man as he should be, that didn't mean he was a
murderer. Only weak and scared.

Hands shaking, Alexandra dropped the letters to the
floor and stripped off the boy's clothes she wore for estate
work. Her gray riding habit already lay on the bed, dull
against the ice blue coverlet. The wool was too heavy for
summer, too dark, but she couldn't present herself to this
man, this man who must hate her, in some frippery of
yellow and green silk.

She would see Blackburn. She would give him what he
asked for, not because of what he'd said, not out of guilt,
but because she knew something. Something she had tried
to push aside ever since the morning of John's death.

Damien had hated John Tibbenham.

She'd thought nothing of it before that terrible night.
Men were prickly about their competition. She'd assumed
it was only jealousy, though she'd told Damien many times
that John was only a friend.

But when John had opened that door and seen them,
when he'd looked at her with stark pain in his eyes and
challenged Damien to a duel, there had been a moment—
just a beat of her heart—when she'd looked into Damien's
face and seen satisfaction. It had disturbed her, that look
of pleasure, but she'd dismissed it in the aftermath. John,
after all, had been the one to issue the challenge. And both
men had refused to back down.

She'd told herself that they had all contributed to the
tragedy. But now . . . to think everything had been planned.
Planned by Damien.

*Just come in here for a moment, my sweet. I'll die if I
don't touch you tonight.* The excitement of flirting with
danger. The thrill of Damien's hands on her, pushing her
skirts to her hips. And then . . . John and his anguished gaze.

Alexandra clenched her eyes shut and pushed the memory

away. She had no doubt she'd relive that night over and over before she slept, but she didn't have time to think about it now.

She would do this thing, turn her lover over to Collin Blackburn, because if what he said were true—and it was painfully easy to believe—then she had been ruined, and her family humiliated, and sweet John Tibbenham had been killed, *purposefully.*

And if it weren't true?

Alexandra pressed her fingers hard into her temples, remembered that look on Damien's face, remembered how quickly, how easily he'd accepted the challenge. Oh, it all made sense now, though Damien's motive escaped her. It certainly hadn't been love.

She grabbed the letters from the floor and stuffed them back into the dresser, under the ruffled petticoats that she rarely bothered wearing anymore, then called her maid to help her finish dressing. Once dressed, she rushed from the room, desperate to get the meeting over with, but not desperate enough to simply send a note 'round. She had been called many things in her life, but never a coward.

Word had already been sent for Brinn to be saddled, and the groom stood waiting at the front steps. Alexandra mounted and let Brinn lead the way, mind blanking as it always did when the bay mare moved smoothly into a run. The world narrowed to the path ahead and the feel of wind and force and muscle.

She could forget, for a moment, that she traveled to meet a man whose eyes flashed with honesty and scorn. Life was just the horse beneath her and the ground ahead. A quarter hour flew by in seconds, and the yard of the inn loomed suddenly, too soon.

Alexandra dismounted, throwing the reins to the stable boy before she could change her mind. Her footsteps faltered at the sight of the red door.

"Please walk the horse," she murmured. "This will only take a moment."

With one last deep breath, she stepped up onto the

threshold and through the doorway. The great room seemed dim after the sun, but even in shadow it was hard to miss Collin Blackburn. He sat relaxed, perusing a stack of papers, pint of ale in hand. He was very still, she realized. He did not bounce his knee or tap the table as he read. No, he held his long body quiet, as if his movements were valuable to him, a resource not to be wasted. She could not keep still for a moment when she worked the ledgers. A meaningful difference between them, perhaps.

A curl of hair escaped over the edge of his collar, the softness such a contrast to his hard face. There was something about him, something in his eyes that spoke of nobility and honor. Something unyielding.

"Lady Alexandra!" the proprietor's voice boomed across the room. "Welcome, welcome. Will you have dinner this evening?"

Blackburn's eyes jerked from his papers to lock with hers. "No, Mr. Sims," she answered without looking away from the man she'd come to see. "I have business to attend."

Blackburn stood to pull back a chair when she walked toward him. "Lady Alexandra."

Ignoring the proffered seat, she handed him the note. He opened it, looked back to her, his expression unreadable.

"The last direction is from two months ago," she explained past stiff lips.

"Thank you."

"I'm sorry about everything." She started to turn, but he placed his hand on her arm—not a grip . . . a touch.

"This was a shock to you. I'm sorry I lost my temper."

"You have every right to be angry."

"Still. I was harsh."

"I understand what you must think of me. How could you not?" She gave him what she hoped was a light smile. "I appreciate that you did not involve me until you had to. I wish you luck." She turned again, needing to leave, to flee the sharpness of his eyes but, again, she was stopped by his voice.

His words were low, soft, and not the least bit kind. "*What am I supposed to think of you?*"

Jaw set, Alexandra pivoted, anger giving her the will to meet his gaze. It hurt to be around people who knew nothing of her but the lowest moment of her life. Hurt even more to be near a man who seemed so solid and unpretentious and who must hold her in such contempt. What did he want her to say? What did anyone want her to say?

"I did not come here to explain myself to you. You asked for something and I've given it to you. That's the end of it."

"Will you contact me if he writes you again?"

"Why would he write again?"

"You sent him money."

Blood rose to her face, giving her away. "Should I tell you I did, so you can truly hate me?"

His eyes flashed something hot, then traveled about the room, measuring each face before he took her arm and guided her toward the door. "People are watching."

She let him lead her only because it meant she'd be that much closer to leaving. As soon as they stepped out the door, as soon as her foot touched the dirt yard, she edged away, putting distance between them. "Thank you for escorting me out. Have a good journey." The stable boy nodded at her gesture and led Brinn toward the mounting steps, but before Alexandra could follow him, Blackburn's soft words touched her ear.

"You are not what I thought you would be, Lady Alexandra."

She glanced back at him, taking in the angled planes of his face and the flint of his gray eyes. *He was a hard man,* she thought, *but fair.* He'd apologized. Still, he did not like her or, at the very least, did not want to. He was just like the rest of them in that way.

She gave him her back and spoke into the soft breeze. "You do not know the first thing about me, Mr. Blackburn."

She ignored the painful pounding of her heart and stepped to her horse. The mare's ears pricked for a bare moment as Alexandra mounted, whispering of speed before she'd even secured her seat. Brinn wheeled about, forcing the boy back a step, snorting wildly over the sound of Blackburn's curse.

Alexandra did not look back; she simply rode, flying toward home. The journey seemed to take an hour this time, the ride no longer a haven from thought. The moment Brinn's hooves clattered against the stone drive of Somerhart, Alexandra tossed the reins to a groom and slid from the saddle, then ran inside and up the stairs to the sanctuary of her bedchamber.

"Bastard," she huffed and threw her riding crop across the room in a high arc. She would not cry, she told herself again, sniffing against tears and dragging a sleeve across her eyes.

The man was a stranger. It did not matter what he thought of her. He was not the first person to look at her as if she were a pile of rubbish, and he would not be the last.

It was all so ridiculous. Her brother ran around as if he were Bacchus incarnate and all anyone could think was what a fine, strong, eligible man he was. But she gets caught in one tiny indiscretion and what results? Death, destruction, mayhem.

The heels of her hands caught her tears. She could live with it. She would. A man had died, and she would have that sorrow on her heart for the rest of her life, but she was only nineteen and it could not be the end of her. She'd done nothing more than men did every hour of every day.

Fingers trembling, Alexandra jerked the bellpull, then tugged at her jacket, wincing when a button broke loose under her clumsy fingers and bounced across the floor.

A bath was in order. A hot bath and a glass of wine before dinner. Her brother was in London and she would dine alone, but she would take pleasure in dressing. She might be a fallen woman, a harlot who lured men to their deaths, but she was alive and able and that was something.

And tomorrow she would work until she was too sore to think, and, please God, too tired to feel.

* * *

Collin Blackburn decided to leave the woman be for a fortnight. His men in France had flushed St. Claire out of his hole three weeks ago, and the man had left all his possessions behind, including the letters from one Lady Alexandra.

St. Claire had nothing now. He would write soon, begging for money. Collin could simply swoop in to retrieve the whereabouts of that bastard and he'd never have to see the girl again.

His head still spun from their meeting the night before. From glancing up to find her standing there, pale and lovely and somehow younger in her respectable gray. No breeches to distract him from her smallness, no bright red coat to add color to her cheeks. She'd looked vulnerable, and that vulnerability had angered him.

The note had been a surprise, or the honesty of it at least. St. Claire had used all three French locations, including the one he'd fled most recently.

Why such forthrightness? Guilt. It dulled her eyes, those damned eyes that pricked his conscience with their glimpses of hurt and defiance. Well, this mess wasn't his fault. She'd made her own bed.

Collin packed his bag and stowed his breakfast of bread and cheese for the journey. He could make it to his cousin's home before dark if he didn't tarry. Lucy would be happy to have him for a week or two, had, in fact, threatened to box his ears if he ever ventured near her home and didn't visit.

So he rode out at dawn, chewing his breakfast, making a very good effort not to think of the young Alexandra Huntington. He could measure his trip now in days-till-home. As long as he made it back to Scotland within the month, he'd get to the first horse fair. Past time to choose which of his stock would go up for sale, but things were running smoothly in his absence—no mares sick, no foals lost. Of course, if the girl did provide new information on St. Claire, Collin would be away longer. A detour to France would take weeks.

Coming around a slow bend in the road, Collin glanced up to a rise in the west. Workmen labored next to a low wall, large stones strewn at their feet. There in their midst stood a slender figure, red coat ablaze in the rising sun. Alexandra Huntington. It had to be her. She gestured widely with the spade she held, appearing to shout, though the distance stole the words. Collin stopped his horse to watch.

He'd known she acted as her brother's manager, a rare position for a nobleman much less a gently bred woman, but he'd assumed it was merely an amusement for her. A novelty, an excuse to be scandalous and wear men's clothes. He should have known better after glimpsing that simmering will in her eyes. She looked to be more involved than most managers would be.

How vulnerable she appeared, standing among the hulking laborers, weighing half of even the smallest of them. But, to a man, they stood still as she spoke, some of them nodding at her words.

One of the group inclined his head and she turned to stare down the hill. She went still, probably shocked at finding herself watched, then took a step in his direction. Just one. Collin wondered at her expression as he raised a hand in farewell, and felt a moment's regret that she didn't return the gesture. She stood like a statue, stiff and proud in the pink light, her face unreadable. Then she turned back to the men with a sharp word that set them all in motion.

She'd dismissed him. Just as well. She'd be unhappy with him regardless when he returned to demand further information. No point calling a truce now.

As he urged Thor to a brisk pace, Collin felt a small curl of anticipation in his stomach at the thought of another visit, but he tamped the feeling down with cool efficiency. The woman was intriguing, dangerously so, and definitely not someone he should get to know better. Someone he should avoid at all costs, even. But she was also very likely his only chance at fulfilling this damned promise to his father.

Chapter 2

"Collin, are you coming down?"

A smile stole over Collin's face at the sound of his cousin's shout echoing up the stairway and through the open library door.

"Collin?"

"Be right there."

Tossing the book back onto the chair where he'd found it, Collin stepped out of the library and made a careful survey of the angled hall before choosing the stone archway to his left. Lucy's home was massive and rambling, having been added onto at least a dozen times, and visitors often found themselves lost. Collin had been here for three days and he had yet to get his bearings.

"Oh, my word! Oh, I can't believe it!"

He rolled his eyes at Lucy's echo. She had never been the perfect example of a gentlewoman, perhaps because she was not very gently bred. No telling what had excited her into shouting this time, there were so many possibilities. A new kitten, a letter from a friend . . . perhaps even a tempting biscuit. Still chuckling when he found the stairs, Collin descended to the landing, looked down, and felt his tongue freeze to the roof of his mouth at the sight of Lucy's latest thrill.

"Oh, you naughty thing!" Lucy sang, her red curls bouncing. "What are you doing here?"

Naughty thing indeed. Below him, radiant in a rumpled gown of aquamarine silk, stood the naughty Lady Alexandra herself.

"Good God," Collin breathed, or perhaps just thought, he couldn't be sure. His brain had stuttered at the unexpected sight of her. He watched his cousin hug her, coo over her, then made himself walk down the rest of the stairs. "Lady Alexandra," he murmured when he reached the first floor.

She snapped around with a sharp gasp. "Blackburn!"

"But . . . You know each other?" Lucy asked, wariness tightening her voice.

"Aye," Collin said just as Alexandra shook her head.

She shot a hot look in his direction. "I think 'know' is too strong a word."

Lucy frowned, but before she could question them further, George walked in and swept Alexandra into his arms to twirl her about the hall.

"Put me down!" she ordered, though a hint of laughter bubbled through.

"Sorry. Forgot the wife was here," George said, leering comically as he set her on her feet.

"Ha! You say that very convincingly for a man who hasn't noticed another woman in ten years."

George winked just before he spied Collin. A narrow look of worry descended over his face as he cleared his throat and turned Alexandra around.

"Lady Alexandra, may I present Collin Blackburn? He is Lucy's cousin by marriage."

"We've met," she said evenly, then, "I didn't mean to intrude."

"Oh, no, no, no," Lucy chattered, plump cheeks reddening. "You're both family. Why shouldn't you have a nice visit? Um . . . There's no reason . . ."

George smiled a sick smile and took his wife's hand. "Alexandra is my second cousin, Collin."

"Ah." What else could he say?

George cleared his throat, obviously aware of the tension in the room and the reason for it. He'd sent a deeply sympathetic letter at John's death, but he'd never told Collin of his connection to Alexandra. Of course, there'd been no mention of her role in the incident, not in polite company.

"Yes, well," George boomed with a clap of his thin hands. "We were about to take Collin out for a ride to the village. Will you accompany us, Alex?"

Her eyes flitted from face to face and she looked so miserable that even Collin wanted to grimace.

"I do believe I'd rather stay and catch up with Alex," Lucy said breezily. "You two go talk about manly things like fields and horses and fishing. We'll get her settled and rested before dinner."

George, nodding vigorously, had turned to the door before his wife had finished speaking.

Collin tried to catch Alexandra's eye, though he didn't know why. *Only to read her,* he told himself, *not to reassure her*. He owed her nothing.

She did not look at him, just let Lucy take her arm and guide her away without a glance in his direction. The set of her jaw bespoke anger, at him or the situation or both.

Collin glared at her back as she walked away, resenting the guilt that burned his gut. He'd done nothing wrong, certainly hadn't known she'd be coming here. And now he would have to speak with her, try to make peace because they were both guests in George's home. He didn't want to make friends with the woman. He wanted to shake her.

"Collin?" George stuck his head back inside.

"Coming," he muttered and followed his miserable host out to the waiting horses.

"Well, then. That was a little tense." Lucy closed the door of the bedchamber with a soft click.

Alex groaned and threw herself face down on the bed. "What is he doing here?"

"Oh, Alex, he's my cousin! Or not really. His aunt married my uncle . . ."

"I know. I mean, that is . . . I didn't know. Lucy, why didn't you ever tell me you were related to John?" She pushed herself up, miserable and fighting tears of frustration.

"I'm not. He and Collin were half brothers. I never even met John."

"This is terrible! I should just go back to Somerhart."

"No, I absolutely forbid it."

She fell back upon the bed, covering her face with her hands. She had come here for comfort, for company and distraction, anything to avoid the regret that had fallen over her after Blackburn's visit.

"Alex, what is it? Has he been cruel to you? I may have to stand on a chair to do it, but I'm not afraid to box his ears."

A surprised laugh bubbled up from her throat at the image. "Really?"

"Please tell me what's going on."

"Oh, it's nothing that terrible. I'm just overwrought. I only met him three days ago. He wished to speak with me about his brother's death."

"Why?"

She could almost hear her friend frowning. Sighing, Alex sat up, wondering if she looked like a melodramatic marionette as she flopped about on the bed. "He's looking for St. Claire. Naturally, he wanted to speak with me. I gave him what I could and he left. The end."

"Did he know you were coming here?"

"No, and I certainly did not know he would be here."

"We never mentioned . . . That is . . . I could ask him to go."

"No! No, of course not. He's done nothing wrong. I believe that distinction belongs to me."

"Oh, Alex, don't say that, please. Men are solely responsible for those stupid games of honor that they play. That duel was between those two men and likely had little enough to do with you."

That struck a little close to home. "You may be more right than you think."

"Alex—"

A soft knock on the door saved her from explanation. A young footman entered, toting her trunk as if it weighed nothing. Alexandra stood, put a smile on her face.

"Don't worry, Lucy. I was only surprised to see him. I'll be fine. And next time I'll inquire before coming to visit."

"But—"

"No, no. Don't think of it again." She put her arm around Lucy's shoulders—an awkward task as the woman was several inches taller—and managed to steer her toward the door. "I'll see you at dinner."

Lucy narrowed her eyes at the obviousness of the action, but she left, followed closely by the footman. As soon as the door closed, Alex stomped her foot hard into the carpet.

She wanted to fly down the stairs and back to her carriage, have the driver whip the horses on till she saw the gates of home. But Blackburn would know she ran from him. Would it still be obvious if she waited until morning to flee?

A growl rose in her throat. She'd come here for refuge from her own thoughts and now she was confronted with the very cause of her turmoil. A cousin by marriage, indeed.

Shock had rippled through her body at the sight of him, standing there where she least expected. Worse yet was the realization that she had not been entirely dismayed. In that first instant of recognition her body had responded with pleasure, then her brain had scrambled to catch up, and the thrill flooding her veins had changed to instant anxiety.

Damn him, why did he have to be so appealing? His visit to her home had stirred up more than just the old nightmares of John and his freshly dug grave. Since then, she'd been haunted by dreams about a large Scotsman and unyielding arms that demanded she soothe his hurt. More than once she'd awakened with that hot ache upon her body. The pain of her want seemed worse than her sorrow now.

Clenching her jaw, she blew air through her teeth and sat down to await her maid. Danielle could get her out of this wrinkled dress and brush out the braid that now seemed woven just to give her a headache. Then she would prepare for dinner. Prepare to dine with the first man she'd found attractive in a long while. A man who looked at her and saw the death of his brother.

Collin watched Lady Alexandra step from her room, brow furrowed with thought or worry as she turned to head for the stairs. When her eyes touched him they flew wide in surprise.

"What do you want?"

He pushed away from the wall. "I thought we should speak privately before dinner."

"Why ever would you think that?"

A maid stepped out of a room a few doors down and spared them a quick glance before rushing away. Lady Alexandra stared after her, tight-jawed, as if she wished it were herself escaping. "What do you want, Blackburn?"

"I'm not here to torment you. My father's deathbed wish was that I find St. Claire and bring him back to England for trial. I cannot just forget about him, much as I'd like to."

She finally met his gaze then, her eyes unreadable in the flickering light of the hallway. "It's not that I resent what you're doing. I'm sure I would not walk away from such a thing if my brother were killed, but that doesn't mean I enjoy your company. I can't pretend to feel comfortable with you just because I understand your contempt."

He stared at her for a long moment, torn between the weariness in her voice and his anger at what she had done to his brother. This unexpected sympathy served to renew his rage. "My brother was in love with you," he finally said, "and your complete disregard for his feelings led to his death."

The girl stared at him, expression seeping from wariness to horror before she shook her head. "That is simply not true."

"Oh, please," he spat, lashing out against the softness of her reply.

"No. John and I were friends. He was not in love with me."

Those big blue eyes looked up at him, awash with confusion and innocence. My God, the woman was a consummate actress. How could she deny it right to his face? Everyone in London had expected them to marry.

"He wrote me a week before his death, confessing his love for you, vowing to ask for your hand before the Season was out. He called you an angel, said you were kind and lovely and decent. I got that letter the day after I learned he'd been killed in a duel over your dubious honor. Just days after he found you mounting St. Claire."

Her mouth fell open. No sound emerged. Collin ground his teeth together at the stark pain in her eyes. She couldn't be innocent, couldn't have been so blind to his brother's feelings.

A tear fell, caught on black lashes, trembled there. He heard the wheeze of air straining in her throat and closed his eyes. God, please let her be acting.

One deep breath, and he opened his eyes to find her face frozen, closed off, impassive. Her hands were behind her, fumbling blindly for the doorknob as she stared at him. Fingernails clawed over the wood, searching, but the knob eluded her grasp. Her skin paled to an alarming white.

"Lady Alexandra?" he managed.

"No. Just leave me alone."

He heard the rattle of her hand closing over the doorknob, the sound quickly swallowed by her gasp of relief.

Collin watched as she pushed the door open, as she spun in an awkward turn, moving as though her legs refused to budge. Before he could think to catch her, she fell to her knees on the carpet, amber skirts crumpling like paper.

"Christ," he muttered, and reached for her. Ignoring her slight struggle and her panted "no," he lifted her easily in his arms and stepped into her room. He'd barely made it to the wide expanse of white coverlet when she thrashed and rolled from his grip, landing on her knees on the bed. He expected her to sob. She glared.

"Do not touch me again." Her lips drew back in a snarl. "Do you know what it's been like for me these past days? You come to my home, tell me that Damien used me as a weapon, as a tool to murder John. Now you tell me John loved me?" The last words rose to a shout, but the tears were finally there. Collin found he now had no wish to see them.

"I was frustrated," he said with care. "I shouldn't have put it so bluntly."

She held her breath, silent in an obvious attempt to control herself. Tears pooled in her eyes, turning them liquid.

Collin shook his head. "I just . . . I need to know what happened. Why he died. Why St. Claire wanted him dead."

She did not answer for long minutes, only breathed steadily and slowly, ribs rising and falling in silent struggle. He'd begun to think he should call for Lucy when she swallowed and spoke.

"I can understand that." She blinked, and two fat tears snaked down pale cheeks. She ignored them. Collin wondered if he should give her a handkerchief, wondered if she would strangle him with it.

"Your brother gave me no indication of his feelings. We were friends, John and I. He would tease me about the men I danced with, make a game of always having sordid information about a suitor." A shudder of air left her lungs, seeming to deflate her. "He never, ever told me of his feelings. I would not have led him on, not if I knew. We were friends. I thought him in love with Beatrice Wimbledon. He *let* me think that, I swear."

The line of her neck stayed straight and tense as she sank down to sit on the mattress. Collin realized he had no reason not to believe her. His brother had been young and perhaps not confident enough to declare his love to a girl like Lady Alexandra. Hell, many grown men wouldn't be. He was reaching for her arm when she began to shake.

Flinching in shame, he laid a hand on her elbow and felt her freeze at his touch. "I assumed the worst of you and I had no right to."

"Go away. I don't want to talk to you anymore."

"I was wrong. I'm sorry. Again."

"Again." Her small body trembled, but she sneered at his words before she turned away from him, curling onto her side to face the wall.

Collin's gut burned with sharp regret. He'd meant to wound her, thinking she deserved it. In truth, he hadn't wanted to see her as a victim. It interfered with the easy idea of her guilt. But perhaps she wasn't guilty of anything more than reckless lust and the indiscretions of youth.

Now he wanted to comfort her, knew he must, just as he knew he should not touch her.

"Hush," he breathed in the same voice he used to calm frightened horses. "Dinna cry."

"I don't cry," she hissed.

"Of course not." But he reached out to touch her just the same. His fingers moved over the silken curl of her hair, smoothed the waves of black. She stiffened, ready to lash out, but even when he repeated the touch, she did not move away. When he cupped the back of her head in his palm, her body softened.

"I'm sorry about John. I am."

"I believe you."

"Do you?" She rolled toward him, onto her back, and Collin found his hand trapped beneath her. "Do you believe me?"

He watched her for a long moment, exploring her eyes and her mouth and her creamy skin in the dim light of the room as he leaned over her like a lover. He was surprised at the truth of his answer. "Yes, I believe you."

And he no longer felt comforting. The clean smell of her, the warmth of her neck on his fingers, her breasts pushing high against the smooth amber-gold bodice of her dress—these things crystallized in his mind and pricked sharply at his senses. Fighting the urge to jerk away, he disentangled his fingers from her hair and slid his hand from under her heat.

"Can we start over, do you think?" Her voice came soft and husky now, and he wondered if she'd felt the change in him.

Could he start over? Treat her as if she were a friend of his cousin's and not an accessory to a crime? She was only a girl, after all. And it was true that she'd been used as a weapon. She'd been hardly more than a victim herself, it seemed.

"For the sake of our hosts," he agreed, glad when she smiled at his paltry joke.

"You are a hard man, Collin Blackburn."

He choked, for she was very nearly right. To his horror, a blush crept up her cheeks, warming her skin into a temptation. He stood and stumbled a step back from the bed. "I'll see you at dinner."

Her blue gaze burned into his back as he fled, slamming the door behind him.

Chapter 3

"Collin."

Collin nearly tumbled down the stairs, heart in his throat. Catching the banister, he turned to see George stepping down from the other wing of the house. "George," he said too loudly.

"I'd like a word with you, if you don't mind."

Christ, surely George couldn't know that he'd just snuck out of Alexandra's room. Unless the maid had alerted him . . .

George stepped heavily down the oak steps, but his face was weighted by sadness, not anger. "Would you come to my office for a moment?"

"Of course."

"I know we already spoke of this, but . . ." George glanced about as they descended, nodded his head to the right when they reached the bottom of the stairs. Collin followed him into the study, ducking beneath the low hang of the crooked little door. The study was spacious, but worn and oddly shaped, one wall stretching on for twenty feet, the other angling, following the line of an older section of the house. George paced to a large chair and leaned against its back.

"I feel I didn't adequately express myself earlier . . . regarding Alexandra."

"George, I—"

"No, I was shocked when she arrived and I wanted to explain. You said you're convinced St. Claire was out to murder your brother. I did not speak plainly earlier, but I feel the need to defend my cousin. You have every reason to dislike her, or resent her, but please bear in mind her youth."

"There's really—"

George held up a hand, eyes pleading, and Collin fell silent.

"All I ask is that you try to feel some sympathy for her in this. If St. Claire did arrange this incident, think how dreadfully he used my cousin, a young girl just out in society. My God, she very likely loved the man and he abused her in the worst possible way."

"George, I understand that."

His friend sighed, his thin chest seeming to collapse. "I'm glad to hear that. I know she must seem mannish and bold to you."

"Mannish," Collin croaked, thinking of her delicate beauty, but George nodded solemnly.

"She grew up nearly without a mother, eventually without a father too. And Somerhart was left to raise her alone, though he didn't have to. He could have sent her off to an aunt or some such but preferred to keep her close."

"An ideal brother."

"Perhaps, but not an ideal parent, you understand. And after this happened . . ." He waved a circle to encompass the tragedy. "He was concerned for her. She was not really herself, and even a duke could not make it right."

"No, I suppose not." Collin thought of the stiffness in her face when he'd wounded her.

"So you may look at her and see a hoyden, an unnatural girl who works her brother's estate and attracts scandal like a magnet, but she is more than that. She is . . ." He waved again, frowning as he searched for words.

"George. You don't have to defend her. I won't deny that

I thought little enough of her when I arrived here, but you're right. She's young. She did not mean to injure John."

"No. No, I can assure you of that. She's a kind girl and always has been. A bit spoiled, mind you, but we're all to blame. Motherless child and all that."

He smiled at the gruff love in George's voice. "I should like to see a portrait of her as a child."

"By God, I'm sure I have one around here somewhere." George turned to scan the dozens of bookcases lining the long wall, relief sinking his shoulders. "Somerhart must have sent us a new miniature every half-year."

Collin smiled as he recalled the great Duke of Somerhart— an icy, intelligent man with a razor-sharp wit. Who would have thought the duke such a soft touch for an orphaned child?

The real Alexandra Huntington made her debut in the formal dining room. Here was the confident woman who'd enchanted the ton; the sparkling, dark beauty the men spoke of, some with wistful looks, some with lust. Collin had not fully understood their admiration, not until this night.

She flushed a little as they greeted each other, but with each course that passed over their plates, Alexandra relaxed a fraction more. She did not seem selfish or thoughtless. She did not even seem particularly spoiled. And she had freckles on her nose.

Ridiculous, of course, but as Collin sat there in the yellow-walled dining room, eating goose and salmon and Yorkshire pudding, he stared at her—at her wild, dark curls and big eyes and those nearly invisible freckles sprinkled across her nose—and he realized: *This woman is no whore.*

And more surprising than that? He wanted her.

Impossible. She was only nineteen. She was English. And the sister of a duke. Practically a damned English princess, for God's sake. Regardless of her past, she was not a woman to have a tryst with. She was royalty.

His torturous thoughts were interrupted by George's sigh. "Women and their money talk. It quite makes my head spin."

Alexandra stopped her chatter about expenses and grinned at them, wrinkling her nose at her cousin before she turned back to Lucy. "And Hart has given permission to expand his stables, so I'll no doubt spend some time at the horse fairs this summer."

"Perhaps Collin can assist you."

Collin caught the confused glance she threw in his direction.

"He breeds horses," Lucy added helpfully.

"Oh, I didn't realize. Blackburn?" Brow furrowed in thought, she looked again to Collin. "I don't think I've heard of you."

George chuckled, obviously enjoying Collin's anonymity. "Collin does not use his title. He is Baron Westmore."

"Oh? Oh, of course!" Her face brightened. "The Westmore stables. Your horses are coveted."

He smiled at the sheer regard in her voice. "They are fine animals."

She nodded at that, but her grin faded, the frown returned. Collin could almost hear the click of her mind turning over some troubling detail. "Your surname is different than John's . . . I'd assumed you had a different father, but you said something—"

"I'm a bastard."

Her eyes widened at the blunt words, and Collin caught George's cringe at the edge of his vision. He waited to see what the duke's daughter would think of dining with a bastard. Blue eyes narrowed and Collin felt his eyes narrow in turn, but then she smiled—a smile that widened as the seconds ticked past.

"Oh, my. A *bastard*. However did you become a baron?"

"My father purchased a Scottish barony in a fit of guilt. I'm not the least bit respectable."

"Well, you are in good company then. A bastard, a harlot, and a witch. I'm afraid that George is the only truly respectable one at the table."

Lucy tried to smother a laugh and snorted instead.

Collin raised an eyebrow at the indiscreet sound. "Cousin, I had no idea you were a witch." Lucy's eyes flew wide and her husband's chuckle ended on an alarmingly choked cough. Collin's brow tightened at the feeling he'd misstepped.

Dessert arrived in the form of glazed berries and cream. The servants retreated. Silence hung heavy over the room.

Then Alexandra smiled sweetly across the table, adding to Collin's unease. "Now, my dear Lord Westmore," she said, hands spreading to gesture around the table, "whoever said that I was the harlot?"

The air grew stifling and drew heat that spread in a tingling burn over his cheeks. Christ, he'd just called the woman a whore at the supper table. His mouth fell open of its own accord; nothing emerged. He closed it, tried to think of something—anything—to say. Alexandra's mask of innocence suddenly dissolved into a fit of laughter.

Lucy snorted again. "Really, Alex, that was quite cruel."

"His face." She gestured toward Collin.

Surely he couldn't get any more red. The heat spread to his ears. "I suppose I deserved that."

"Oh, you did!" she laughed, leaning toward him. Despite everything, the shadow of her cleavage still caught his attention. He clenched his teeth, wondered if it would be bad form to flee the room as he'd fled her bedchamber. He grabbed his wine instead and raised the glass toward her before draining it.

"Oh, that was well worth any grudge you may hold against me now."

"No grudge," Collin conceded. "What I implied was inexcusable."

George's smile was sympathetic if a little weak. "These two are too quick for the male mind to follow, but really, you waltzed into that one."

Collin tipped his head in agreement, gave a helpless shrug. "Well, Cousin, whether you are a witch or a harlot, I would hear the story."

"I am the witch, or was. But there is no harlot here, and I will hear no more talk of it."

Alexandra rolled her eyes and grinned.

"When George and I married, Alex was only eight—"

"Nine!" she called.

"Pardon me. Lady Alexandra Huntington was a mature young woman of nine."

She chuckled, the sound brushing Collin's spine.

"She had a rather fierce crush on George—"

"My grown cousin!"

"—and she found it difficult to like me. In fact, I believe to this very day that she plotted my murder."

"Not true. I only wanted to run you off."

"Well, thankfully I'd said my vows just before I met her, or I may very well have abandoned him." Lucy flashed her husband a tender smile that belied her words.

"So what did you do, Lady Alexandra?" Collin asked. Her naughty smile made him want to groan.

"I only played a prank. Lucy didn't find it amusing."

"She put a mouse in my bridal bed!"

Alexandra and George collapsed into laughter.

"You should have seen her, Collin," George gasped. "So delightfully shy and pink, then shrieking about the room without a stitch, all modesty out the window!"

"George!" But his wife laughed too, and Collin couldn't help but chuckle.

"That must have been a sight for a new bridegroom."

"Oh, it was. I was so enthused that she accused me of planting the rodent myself. I will say I wasn't quite as upset with Alex as I should have been."

"We didn't know who'd done it, of course, or even if it'd been happenstance . . . until our farewell breakfast the next morning. In walks little Alex, looking quite pleased with herself, until she spots me and howls, 'Why are you still here?'"

"Oh, I'd convinced myself she'd hie back to wherever she'd come from, and I'd have George all to my own again."

"Well, I knew immediately it was her, and I dragged her

by her ear out to the garden to give her a stern talking to. The girl never even blinked. She had no fear."

Collin wasn't surprised. She'd likely never been denied a thing in her life. "So you told her you were a witch?"

"I did." Lucy still looked smug, ten years later. "I was only seventeen, you know. But you'll remember my family, Collin. Children crawling from every nook and cranny. I knew I had to put a fear in her. So I told her I'd already roasted the mouse and cut off its tail and ears. Told her all I had to do was mash them up with a little blood of a bat and slip that into her porridge . . . She'd turn into a mouse before the next full moon."

"And what did you say, Lady Alexandra?"

She turned pink when his eyes locked with hers. "I told Lucy to eat horse dung and ran to find my nurse." Her smile went naughty again, tightening the muscles of his stomach. "Then I decided that George was not my true love after all."

"I made an impression on her. She didn't come near me for two years."

George reached out to pat Alexandra's hand with a proud smile. "Not the most trouble you've ever caused, but—" As soon as the words left his mouth, his face paled. "I meant . . ."

"Come now, George," Alex murmured. "None of that. Not among friends." She raised her glass of wine. "A toast. To memories of old times!"

Lucy laughed and drank with her. "She says that so convincingly for a girl no more than nineteen."

"To memories," George added, slanting a sly grin at his wife.

Collin raised his glass and smiled at Alexandra's hearty, "Here, here!" Her eyes sparkled with laughter and her cheeks were flushed from the wine. She glowed.

She glanced his way and he watched her eyes dart away from his stare. But only a heartbeat passed before they slid back to him. Her mouth smiled a softer smile. He drank in the sight of her pink cheeks and pinker lips. He watched her gaze fall to his mouth and felt his blood rush low in response. Not good. Not good at all.

George cleared his throat, jerking Collin's eyes away from her lovely face to meet the speculative look. Collin shifted, coughed, tried not to feel guilty.

"When are you returning home, Collin?" Lucy asked with a lightness he didn't trust.

Unsure of the answer, he shrugged. "Within a few weeks. I still have some business here in England."

A movement drew his eye back to Alexandra, and he found her stiff now, the smile fading from her face. "What kind of business?"

"Oh, various things. As manager of Somerhart, you must understand how tedious these matters can be."

She watched him carefully for a moment, then seemed to blink away her suspicions. "Yes, but I don't find the work tedious at all. I find it invigorating."

He couldn't help a disgusted grunt. "I would rather work the horses."

"Well, we all have our passions, I suppose."

His eyes locked with hers, seemed to draw the color back to her cheeks. "Aye," he agreed finally, and wondered why she was becoming one of his.

Alex stepped into the dim morning light of the court-yard, announcing her arrival with a wistful sigh. She'd hung about in the breakfast room for almost an hour, straightening at every sound that filtered in from the hall. She'd even trailed about the library for a while, hoping to run into Collin Blackburn.

The man had disappeared early last night, staying no more than half an hour in the drawing room before mur-muring his goodnights. He hadn't appeared since.

Lucy claimed not to know where he'd hidden himself and had found her own words oddly amusing. Alexandra decided on a tour of the horse yard. At worst she'd walk off some tension. At best, she'd run into him.

Hurrying toward the stables, she chastised herself for this sudden *tendre* she'd developed. She hardly knew the man. And what he knew of her, he didn't like.

The hazy light of the stable enfolded her as she stepped through the door, an apple held idly against her skirt. The golden dance of dust motes caught her eye first, then a slow movement in the closest stall . . .

Alex's muscles locked, her heart stopped beating, her mind creaked to a shuddering halt. Here he was. Collin Blackburn. Right under her nose and wearing nothing more than breeches and boots.

She devoured the sight of his naked back as he groomed a pitch-black horse. Muscles tightened and bunched and stretched as he brushed. Drops of sweat gathered like liquid crystals at his neck, then dripped in a warm slide down his spine, tracking a path to the waist of his tight gray breeches. She watched each drop dissolve into damp fabric.

Surely she'd never seen anything so lovely in her life. Her fingers curled into the palms of her hands and her lips went so dry she had to lick them. Oh, she'd seen men remove their shirts before, laborers and noblemen alike, but nothing had ever moved her like this. Nothing had set her nerves to a hum.

Blackburn crouched down and ran a careful hand over the stallion's hind leg, checking for soreness. Alex thought of his hands running over her like that, and a frightening jolt of heat swept through her belly. Oh, God. Would that he'd check her for tender spots. He'd find them.

She must have made some small sound, must have sighed, because he was suddenly on his feet and spinning around to face her.

"Christ!" he barked, turning to jerk his shirt up from a stool and wrestle his arms into it. He stared at her as he buttoned it, eyes narrowing as the seconds passed.

She couldn't speak, could only watch in sorrow as the muscles of his chest disappeared beneath white linen.

"What do you want?"

She blinked and met his eyes again, flushing with the thought of just what she wanted. "I . . . I want . . ."

Collin growled a low curse and grabbed his coat.

"I—" Her brain clanked back to working order as his body disappeared beneath too many layers of cloth. "Brinn! I brought an apple for my mare."

He did not say a word, only put his tools away and shut the stall door before edging carefully past her toward the yard. "I must send a letter to my manager."

"Such an urgent one?"

"Aye," he threw over his shoulder.

"I thought we had reached a truce." Her words slowed him to a halt, until he stood silent in the bright square of the door. "Mr. Blackburn?"

He turned, reluctance punctuating the movement. "Forgive me, Lady—"

"Call me Alexandra. We are very nearly cousins."

He slanted a look at the door. "Very well. Alexandra. It is nothing to do with you. I've just remembered something important."

"Your dislike of me?"

"Of course not."

She stared at him, trying to read his shuttered face. He did not blink under her gaze, but his jaw softened and ceased to tic.

"It's not that I dislike you." The hard glint left his eyes and the silver began to warm to gray. "You are a very interesting woman." And with that, he spun on his heel and left.

Alex huffed her outrage, growling out a foul name as the stable door swung shut and plunged her into twilight. But there was no true anger behind the curse. Indeed, the word sounded a great deal like a sigh, even to her own jaded ears.

A sigh, because Collin Blackburn *liked* her.

He could be as rude as he wanted, but she wasn't some silly young girl who didn't know when a man wanted her. He had come close to kissing her in her bedroom yesterday.

She had wanted him to, had been surprisingly desperate for it, but he'd fled the room instead.

That moment had passed so quickly she'd begun to think it imagined. But just now . . . Oh, he'd been disturbed all right. Almost as disturbed as she. She wanted Collin Blackburn, and he wanted her.

It wasn't that she thought it would be right to take a lover. No, it would certainly not be *right*. It would just be . . . lovely. A momentary joy. She'd lost so many friends that night in London, so many connections. And though she was satisfied, even happy with her life as it was now, she also felt very alone. And the great advantage of her fall from grace was that she could not fall again. She was free to take what risks she would, and Collin was undoubtedly a risk worth taking.

Interesting, he'd called her, as if she were a new animal. "Ha!" Alexandra huffed. Interesting indeed. He would find out just how interesting she could be. And how much trouble. They hadn't named her The Errant Heiress for nothing.

Chapter 4

Collin adjusted the girth of Thor's saddle and patted the stallion's shoulder. He tried to quiet his mind to match the silence of the dawning day, the peace of the deserted stable. Only the soft shift and snort of horses disturbed the morning.

He'd slept badly last night and woke before dawn, restless and edgy with a need he refused to acknowledge. Even as he pushed the thought of that woman from his mind, Thor's ears pricked, warning of an intruder.

"Collin!"

A heartfelt curse lurched to the tip of his tongue. He froze to gather his self-control, bit back the curse, and turned to look at her. "Lady Alexandra."

"Just Alexandra, please. May I join you for a ride this morning?"

He tried to wither her with his glare, but her pretty face smiled back, undaunted. "I'm not out for a leisurely ride. Thor needs a good run today."

"Wonderful."

"You'll have to keep up."

Her eyes glinted, but she nodded and smiled.

Collin wracked his mind for a better excuse to leave her behind, but a drowsy stable boy hurried in, no doubt awakened by their voices, and led Alexandra's mare from her stall.

He really couldn't avoid riding with her without being unconscionably rude. He didn't want to hurt her, he just wanted to avoid the temptation of being around her. Still, she would leave the next day—he'd announced as much at dinner with a sly look in his direction. Surely he was mature enough to spend one day with her without succumbing to his lust.

He led Thor out and mounted, then made sure to look impatient as he waited. She ignored his show, chatting with the now-lively stable hand and sending Collin only the occasional glance.

She looked like a dream in the early morning light. Fresh and lovely and impossibly young. Her dark, unruly hair had been tamed into a shiny black braid that fell nearly to her waist. Still, nothing could keep the curls completely under control. Several strands had already escaped to float against her cheeks, teasing the dimples that were nearly always in evidence.

She wore a royal blue riding habit that mirrored the color of her eyes. Her tiny hat seemed constructed only of net and ribbon; it reminded him of the freckles on her nose and how different she was from other women, never worrying over keeping her skin fair and perfect. Perhaps she was too rich to worry over white skin.

The boy led her horse to the block and she mounted her mare as she did everything—with grace and ease. The way she moved through the world pulled at him and he couldn't keep his eyes from watching her.

She would leave tomorrow, he reminded himself, and the gods be praised.

"Ready?" he grumbled.

In answer, she urged her horse out of the yard at a trot. Collin smiled at the beauty of the mare's gait and followed.

He rode behind her for a long while but found it torturous to watch her small body move so fluidly in the saddle. Worse, she kept turning to flash him a delighted smile that caught at his breath. So when they came to a wide, grassy meadow, he urged Thor to his full speed and quickly passed her by.

He stayed just ahead of her and they rode for miles in silence. They cut over to the coast and followed it, sometimes at a run and sometimes at a more gentle pace, until the sun shone bright and hot above them. The sea wind whipped salt air over their skin until he could taste it on his lips, and the water glinted blue and white as far as he could see. When Thor slowed to a walk, Alexandra pulled Brinn next to him.

Collin looked unwillingly in her direction. "There's a copse of trees just ahead. Would you like to stop? Have a drink?"

Her eyes beamed as she nodded, the bright blue soaking in the sparkle of the water's shine.

Thor snorted and nudged the mare roughly. "I'll need to tether him a good distance away. I think he's gotten her scent."

She looked at Thor and then up at him. "Yes, I think he has," she said simply, but heat crept into his face and Collin was relieved when she pulled away to ride toward the small grove of trees. Collin led Thor a good thirty yards away before he walked back to join her.

"Water?" He held out the skin and looked over the sea as she drank her fill. "You're a fine rider," he finally said, uncomfortable with the silence.

"Thank you." She smiled and gave no hint of false modesty. He looked back to the glinting waves.

"Collin." She touched his arm.

He cringed at the soft sound of his name on her lips and took the water from her. But as he reached for it, their fingers brushed and his eyes traveled inexorably to her mouth. A tiny drop of moisture clung to her bottom lip and he had the overwhelming urge to lean down and brush it away with a kiss. A moment passed, then two. The flick of her pink tongue licked the drop away and set fire to Collin's blood.

With a muttered curse and a few sharp, silent words for himself, he tipped the skin up to his mouth, praying the cold, sweet water would tamp the heat in his body. He swallowed and swallowed, desperate to ignore her. But she refused to be ignored, damn her, and her warm fingers were suddenly on him, stroking down his neck.

He jerked from the caress, choking, and bent over at the waist to cough, strangling on shock and water. She started to slap his back, but he stood and stepped away from her as soon as her palm hit his body.

"What are you doing?" he gasped.

"Trying to help."

"No, not that! The other . . ."

She shrugged and sent him the first shy smile he'd seen cross her lips. "I couldn't help it."

"Couldn't help what?"

"Touching you."

He drew back from her, took another panicked step away and held up a hand to ward her off, but he only received a fierce frown in return.

"You needn't look so horrified."

"Lady Alexandra," he started, cringing at the desperate edge of his voice.

"I was under the impression that my interest was returned."

"My God, girl, you're the sister of a duke!"

"Well, what does that have to do with anything?"

He stared at her open-mouthed, incredulous. "I am a Scotsman, a bastard."

"Well, I'm a fallen woman—a whore as far as society is concerned." She shrugged. "The idea is only enhanced by my brother's title."

Unable to think of anything to say to that, he threw his hands in the air, rolling his eyes in disgust.

Her eyes narrowed at him, seemed to threaten something as she took a purposeful step forward. His body tensed to jump away, but he forced himself to be still. She was just a wee girl, after all.

"Collin?" How did she make his name into a caress? She took another step. "I thought . . ." Her hand lifted and inched toward him. He wanted to shy like a wild, wary horse as he followed its inexorable progress toward his neck. "I've seen you watching me," she finally said as her fingers brushed his skin.

He felt his eyes close, felt a groan rumble up his throat and into her hand.

"I thought you wanted me, too," she whispered, the words soft with something close to doubt.

Don't answer her, he told himself. *Just walk away*. But his lips moved of their own accord. "My God, Alexandra. Don't all men want you?"

"No, of course not. No. Even if they did, it wouldn't matter to me. But you . . . You're so lovely."

His eyes flew open and locked with hers. "That's ridiculous," he rasped, but he was reaching for her as he spoke. His hand curled around her nape, the heat of her skin seeping into his palm. He watched her pale neck arch into his grip before his gaze slid to her lips.

"This is a mistake." The words fell from his mouth even as he lowered it to hers.

She sighed, a sweet brush of warmth against his mouth, and then a searing whip of fire when she touched the tip of her tongue to his bottom lip. She shuddered—or he did—and he opened his lips to possess her.

Heat, he thought. She tasted like heat and lust and sweetness. Her small hand smoothed from his neck to the curls of hair just above his collar and clutched him there, and Collin felt his cock swell.

Jesus, he must be mad. He had to let her go, but he couldn't stop his hand from curving over her waist and pulling her hard against his arousal. Wisps of panic iced his veins, but between her fiery mouth and clutching hand all he could think of was having more of her.

The roundness of her backside tempted the edge of his palm. Even as he thought of exploring it, he realized he'd already swept his arm down, and now he found her gorgeous bottom cupped in his hand, the perfect shape to fill it.

A small sound vibrated into his mouth. A tantalizing sound, something between a purr and a moan. Searing lust shot through him like fire, banishing his alarm, and he groaned and pressed his hips against her belly.

The sun shone hot on them, and Collin felt her hand slide up under his coat and then the shock of her fingers pressing into his back. Even through his linen shirt, the feel of her touching him was so unexpected that it gave him the strength to try to pull away, but she pressed small kisses to his jaw and throat and murmured his name. When he felt the sharpness of her teeth against his skin, he jumped and set her apart from him.

"We canna do this," he panted.

"What? Why?"

He could only answer her confusion with a pained laugh.

"Collin," she moaned, "please." Her tongue flicked out to lick her lips. She stared at his mouth like it might save her from some dire danger.

She needed to be startled to her senses just as he had been. "Think about this, Alex. Do you want me to take you here? Right here in the open, on the ground?" He threw the words at her in a growl—an insult, a threat—but they had the opposite effect he'd intended.

Instead of drawing herself up in outrage, instead of slapping his face with the flat of her hand, she parted her flushed lips and sighed, and her eyes flared with blue desire. "Oh, yes," she breathed. "Would you please?"

"Oh, God." He didn't recall moving toward her, but she was in his arms. He lifted her, carried her to a soft patch of grass sheltered beneath a tree, and laid her gently on the ground.

"You canna expect me to ignore a pretty request like that," he murmured, pressing his mouth to the salt-damp skin of her neck. Her delighted laugh sealed his fate, and Collin lost his hard-fought battle with lust.

Alex arched her neck to give him full access to that sensitive spot just below her ear. She felt the press of one of his hard thighs between her legs and scooted her knees farther apart as he kissed and nipped at her skin, and the muscles of her belly tightened at the feel of his body between her legs.

She couldn't keep from humming in pleasure and was thrilled when her sighs excited him further, excited him until he kissed her so deeply her body ached with it.

Urging him on, pushing him further, she eased her hands beneath the shoulders of his coat and slid the fabric back as far as she could. He broke away from her mouth, rising up to tear off his coat in one great shrug. Before she could manage to even pull his shirt past his breeches, he had framed her face with his hands and kissed her again, more carefully, nearly gently.

That gentleness stopped the press of her need for an instant, brushing against her heart instead of her body. She almost pulled her mouth from his, almost pressed a hand to his chest to end this mad embrace. She almost tried to reason with her selfish body. Almost. But when he groaned and slicked his tongue over hers, she let her conscience sink back to its hiding place beneath her lust.

The sea breeze caressed her, tried to cool her skin but didn't succeed. She felt the brush of air on her thigh, and knew that his knee had pushed higher, raising her skirts up her legs. His hand left her face to skim down her body, down to her knee, then up to push her skirt higher so he could slide the calloused pads of his fingers over the skin just above her stocking.

A terrible and wonderful tension coiled in her belly. She'd certainly been touched before, but the simple brush of a man's fingers over skin had never affected her like this. His mouth moved over hers with such delicious skill, but all she could do was close her eyes and wonder at the effect his hand had on her body. His fingers brushed over her thigh, rising slowly up, closer to that place where everything tightened to a shuddering pulse. The anticipation built to torment, and she cried out before his hand had even traveled halfway up her thigh.

A growl sprang from his mouth to hers, and his hand gripped her leg in a tight hold for a moment before he slid his palm up the last few inches of her thigh. He stroked just the barest touch against the curls between her legs, and she jerked her mouth from his, gasping and straining, then crying out when his hand lifted to hover over her, a cruel torment.

Desperate, she opened her clenched eyes to slits to see him. His face looked carved from stone, it was edged so sharply, but his jaw jumped in time with her own pulse. Fearing he would change his mind and cry off, she squirmed beneath him, pushed her hips up till his hand was flush against her. He lowered his mouth to hers again and curled his fingers into the wetness.

"Collin!" His name flew from her lips as he slid one finger into her slick seam, then farther, until he was snug inside her body and so, so deep. She wanted to tremble, wanted to buck beneath him, but she held herself still, waiting. His finger slid out, out, then slipped to trace tiny circles around a little nub of sensation.

"Oh," she moaned, turning her face away. "Oh, yes."

It felt like torture, like she would die from the pleasure and pressure curling deep in her belly. She'd wanted so badly to be calm and irresistible and enticing to this man and all she could do was push herself against him and try not to scream as he rubbed and thrust and stroked.

Tiny shivers took her body, starting somewhere in her knees and working up, up, up till even her chin shook.

"Alex."

She heard her name against her throat just before her back arched and her hips jerked so hard that she sobbed. Every feeling in her body rose and spun and thrummed through her until it spiraled tight and exploded, and she finally grew limp against him.

"Oh, Collin," she sighed one last time and let her head fall back to the green ground.

* * *

Collin's smile nearly split his face. A man could live his whole life and never hear his name spoken with that kind of reverence.

He'd lost any will to resist her long minutes before. She wanted him and he certainly wanted her and they were both adults. Young as she was, she was no innocent, there was no reason to protect her from her wants.

Now he was simply fighting not to throw her skirts over her head and push roughly into that tight heat.

He squeezed his eyes shut, took several deep breaths. Her response had shattered his control. She'd reacted to even the simplest touch with such unbridled pleasure that he worried he would hurt her in his eagerness. Not that she wasn't ready. Not that she wasn't so slippery that his mouth watered. Still, he had yet to even undress her.

Slowly, missing the warmth of her already, he slid his finger out of her limp body. "I hope you're not planning to sleep now."

A soft smile played over her lips as he unbuttoned her jacket. "No. No, I couldn't bear to miss a thing."

Finished with the jacket, he went to work on the buttons of her demure white shirt. Alex's drowsy eyes met his as he reached the last button and his hand smoothed the fabric away from her. Her corset was cut low, and her breasts rose above it, covered by only the thinnest linen of her shift.

His eyes fell to the tiny bows that held the chemise together, and he watched as his callused brown fingers pulled at the blue bows. The linen parted in a slow revelation. He felt her eyes on his face as he slid the fabric down and his fingers brushed over bare skin. She was small and perfect, the warm rise of her just fitting into his palm.

He felt curiously unhurried now, though his cock strained at the tightness of his breeches. He let his hand rest still against her hot skin a moment, absorbed the hard thud of her heart into his palm before he slid it aside and lowered his mouth. His tongue circled the pink tip of her breast, felt it harden and peak against him. Alex sighed and her fingers curled into his hair. He took the hard pebble of her nipple into his mouth and laved his tongue against her until he felt her hands tighten to fists.

Urgency came upon him again, and he shifted and bared her other breast to taste that one as well. She moaned and raised her knees into a V that cradled him between her thighs. His clothes were suddenly the roughest wool cloth against his skin.

Collin knelt between those raised legs, tugged at his cravat, and tore his fingers down the buttons of his shirt. Her flushed face stared up at him, her small, beautiful breasts heaved with the force of her breath.

An unwelcome sound floated to his ears over the thump of his heart and the steady rush of the sea. He froze, shifting his eyes to a place above her body.

"Collin, what—?"

He raised a hand for silence, but she groaned when the clear jingle of a harness chimed from the west.

Hands already closing his shirt, he stood to retrieve his coat and laid it over her nakedness. "A rider. Stay here."

Throwing her hands over her eyes, Alexandra blew out a loud sigh that followed him as he walked away.

Collin slipped into the trees, then worked his way back toward Thor. The jingling of the harness grew louder with each step.

By the time he reached Thor, he'd spotted the wheel ruts of a much-used trail twenty yards away. It seemed to follow the western edge of the wooded area. Looking back to where Alex lay, he was relieved to see no sign of her. He couldn't even see Brinn from here.

He stayed in the shadows, unwilling to take the risk of some friendly traveler stopping for a long chat. He was not in the mood. Still, he wasn't in quite the same mood he had been a bare minute ago.

His blood had definitely cooled, he realized with some disappointment as he watched a tinker's cart emerge from the copse of trees and rumble past. The tinker himself looked to be asleep at the reins. Collin watched for a good ten minutes to be sure that the cart continued on its way, then sighed with no small amount of sorrow as he turned to work his way back to the lovely Alexandra.

His brain had sprung back to vigilant attention. Damn. She was by far the most responsive woman he'd ever had the pleasure of touching. Holding her had been like holding a living fire in his arms, a fire that threatened to burn out of control at any moment.

A few minutes ago he'd thought he would die if he didn't slide himself into the core of her. Now, mourning the loss of that pleasure, he would have to help her back into her clothes and escort her home.

Why had he been cursed with a mother who'd browbeaten him into responsibility?

He approached their makeshift bed and saw her still lying on the grass. As he drew closer, his scowl relaxed into a smile. She'd fallen asleep. Despite the danger of being spied by a traveler, she hadn't even bothered to dress. She'd only pulled down her skirts and drawn his coat close before curling onto her side.

As quietly as he could, Collin sat on the grass next to her, arms resting on his bent knees. He watched her, studied her face, turned as it was toward the shade. Her lovely pink mouth had relaxed in sleep, lips parted slightly and curved just the tiniest bit into a smile.

By God, she was a beauty. Her heart-shaped face was delicate—the perfect foil for those huge blue eyes. Her black hair contrasted deliciously with pale skin, especially the pale skin of her belly and thighs.

No, he told himself sternly. *Do not think of that.*

Even her imperfections were perfect. The freckles made her seem real. And the too-strong jut of her chin matured what might have been a child-like face.

Still, she looked young and fragile, a fairy princess caught in a nap.

The soft breeze picked up a stray curl and it whispered over her cheek to caress her lip. Collin gently brushed it away and leaned in to replace it with a kiss. Those blue eyes of hers peeked out beneath heavy lids.

"Collin," she breathed and he remembered very clearly how he had lost himself in that mouth so easily. But he only smiled down at her.

"Do you feel as lovely as you look?"

Her smile turned to a grin as she rolled to her back and stretched like a well-fed kitten, shirt gaping open to reveal one shell-pink nipple. Collin took a deep breath and reached toward her—he couldn't help himself—but he forced his twitching fingers to draw the shirt together. Her naughty smile faltered when he began to refasten the buttons.

"What are you doing?"

Collin fought the urge to laugh out loud. Any other young miss would have spoken those words if he had had the gall to try to *un*button her blouse.

"I'm fixing your clothes," he finally replied.

"But you . . . I mean . . . We are not *done!*"

He did laugh then, as he moved on to the next button. "I think we'd best be done after all."

Alex gasped and slapped his hands away from her half-open shirt. "No! Stop that!"

His smile gentled at the confusion in her eyes. "Alex. We can't do this."

"I was under the impression that we were doing it quite successfully before we were interrupted."

He didn't know now whether to laugh or cry at her outrageous statement. He had keen memories of just how nicely it had been going.

"Alexandra, you are—"

She cut him off with a frantic wave of her hand, eyes flashing danger at him. "If you dare to bring up my brother's title again, I will hurt you."

"Your social status is nothing to be scoffed at. However—" he held up a hand when he saw her lips part—"I was going to say that you are George's cousin and a friend to Lucy and it would be unconscionable for me to take advantage of their friendship by . . . by taking advantage of you."

Her luscious mouth thinned to a hard line of displeasure. "I had not planned to run back and announce what we'd done. And I'd hardly call it taking advantage."

His hand felt rough when he ran it over his face, and his throat felt rougher when he spoke. "I'm sorry, Alex. Believe me. I am sorry. But this cannot be."

She blinked, looked away from him. That stubborn jaw worked hard to clench and unclench her teeth. High spots of red burned her cheeks.

"Fine, Blackburn. You obviously have your reasons. Shall we return to the house then?"

He watched her hurriedly fasten the last three buttons of her shirt and stand. She adjusted her skirts with rough twitches and tucked in her shirt, all without meeting his eyes. He saw the exact moment her face cleared of all emotion.

When she turned to look about for her discarded jacket, he reached to take her hand. "Alex, please don't."

"Don't what, Mr. Blackburn?"

"I'm trying to do the right thing by you. Don't look past me like that."

She finally met his eyes and he saw them warm to just above freezing. "It is a rather uncomfortable situation, is it not?"

"It does not have to be. It was a surpassingly lovely morning."

Her lips quirked. "I did enjoy myself."

"Well, lassie,"—he couldn't resist pressing a quick peck to her mouth—"so did I."

Alex glanced away and forced a wider smile. He was very sweet to lie to her like that. It was part of the problem, this extreme likeability of his.

"We should head back," she murmured. "We will miss luncheon."

Her not-quite lover nodded and bent to retrieve his coat.

He gave her a searching look before he walked away toward Thor.

When he'd gone, she put her hands to her face and groaned. How embarrassing this all was. She should have learned her lesson the last time she'd been humiliated by her baser needs. Of course, that time had been nothing like this. No, this time had been very nearly worth any amount of embarrassment.

Nearly. It had taken her a few awkward moments to realize he was rejecting her. She'd offered herself to him like the harlot she was, and he had, very politely, turned her down. She didn't even know that men would *do* that.

He must find her wanting in some way. She almost smiled at the thought, despite her rising humiliation. Oh, she was wanting all right.

Not waiting for help from him, she scrambled onto Brinn's back and stared out at the sea until she heard the soft sound of hooves behind her. When she turned, she found Collin watching her intently and smiled for his benefit. No need to make him feel guilty for something she had forced between them.

During the long ride back, Alex made every effort to keep some distance between their horses, trying, simultaneously, not to make it obvious. But as they drew closer to the manor, Collin pulled his horse next to hers and said her name.

She sent him a vacuous smile.

"Alexandra, I wanted to ask you . . ."

"Yes?"

"Will you contact me if St. Claire writes again?"

She frowned, blinked. She had not expected to hear him speak of it again.

"I . . . But what of the information I gave you?"

He shook his head. "Old."

"Oh." More humiliation to add to his account. "You didn't tell me."

He had the grace, at least, to shift in his saddle. "When I left Somerhart, I left with the intention of coming back in two weeks to see if you'd received additional letters. But I thought, now, considering the circumstances, perhaps it would be better if you simply sent me notice next time."

Her spine stiffened. What did he mean by "the circumstances?" And had he shown interest in her just to secure her cooperation?

She glared at him, and he looked back, mouth flat and miserable, but his eyes did not avoid hers. No. No, he hadn't used her. He seemed more noble than any nobleman she'd ever met. And anyway, he hadn't bothered to cement their relationship nearly as tightly as he could have. The very uncomfortable "circumstance" he'd referred to, no doubt.

"I'll send the direction," she said simply.

When they reached the manor, she tossed her reins to a groom while Collin led his own horse to the stables. She hurried into the house and up the stairs and told herself she had no reason to be mad at him for rejecting her when she was the woman who'd betrayed his brother so vilely. She should be thankful he could be kind to her, be friendly. But as she closed her bedroom door with a firm thud, thankfulness was the least of her emotions.

Chapter 5

She'll be gone in the morning.

Collin told himself this every time his eye fell on Alexandra Huntington.

Don't worry. She'll be gone soon.

She looked beautiful, of course, in a fluff of red dress that accentuated her alabaster skin and the smallness of her waist. The dress also rather successfully drew the eye to the soft rise of her breasts. It was not daring by society standards, but the bodice curved more than low enough to offer a tantalizing glimpse of her firm breasts. Collin did what he could to stop himself staring. Not an easy task when he could picture perfectly the shape and shade of them beneath his hand.

Perhaps more maddening than his fascination with her bosom was the way her eyes slid away from his every time he looked at her. Even when he'd greeted her before dinner she'd stared at his collar. Now she stared at the wineglass that had not left her hand since the first course was served.

"How is your head?"

She blinked as if drawn from a deep thought. "Pardon me?"

"Your head. That is why you missed luncheon? A headache?"

"Oh. Yes. My head is better, thank you."

"I hope it was not the strenuous ride today that discomposed you." Oh, her eyes flew to meet his then.

Collin kept his face straight—very straight—and raised an innocent, inquiring brow. Her cheeks flamed.

"It was not the ride, Mr. Blackburn," she bit out. "I am an experienced rider, after all."

Ouch. Her behavior was so demure this evening that he'd forgotten that kittens' claws were not only tiny but also devastatingly sharp.

"Of course." This time, when she looked away, he slumped back into the chair to glare at his bowl of stewed fruit.

"My word," Lucy injected into the silence that followed. "Our guests are quiet this evening, George. I do believe we're boring them to death with our rusticating ways."

They both muttered something negative. Lucy's eyes narrowed.

"You two rode together this morning?"

"Yes," Alex squeaked and sat up straighter.

Collin felt the hair on his nape rise at his cousin's suspicious look. A sudden memory of naked thighs assaulted him.

"Did you argue? Collin, were you bothering her about London again?"

"No. No, we did not argue. Absolutely not."

"Alex?"

"Of course not, Lucy. Perhaps we only went too far, after all. I'm exhausted."

Went too far. Oh, she was clever. So clever he wanted to shake her. My God, you'd think he'd ravished an innocent the way she treated him as if he had the plague. Hadn't he been admirably restrained? Hadn't he saved her from making a dire mistake?

Her words pierced the fog of his resentment. "I believe I shall retire now. I don't wish to be rude, but—"

"Oh, but it's your last night here!"

"I know, Lucy. I know. But I must leave early. I'd hoped to make it back to Somerhart by tomorrow evening."

"You can sleep in the carriage."

Alex laughed and shook her head. "No. I'm going to ride Brinn and have the carriage follow. I'll make better time."

"But—"

"Stop!" She cried out, laughing at Lucy's pout. "I'll see you in a month, after all, before your trip to the Continent."

Lucy sighed and let her shoulders slump in melodramatic defeat. "All right. I suppose if you're tired, you're tired. But do not leave in the morning without saying good-bye."

"I promise." Alex quickly drained the dregs of her wine and stood. She kissed Lucy's cheek, hugged George, and spared Collin the barest nod before fleeing the room.

A violent jolt of anger shot through him. Did she think that she could just dismiss him, just walk away with nothing but a nod? By God, he wasn't one of her London playthings.

"Collin?"

Lucy and George had retaken their seats and now sat gaping up at him while he stood and stared at the empty doorway.

"Are you quite well? I don't know what's happened between you two, but—"

"Excuse me," he interrupted.

Lucy's laughter followed him when he stalked from the room.

Alex frowned when she spotted Danielle dozing on a chair by her open trunk. She couldn't help but wonder if her maid had also spent an exhausting morning being humiliated by a man.

"Danielle, darling, wake up and go get some dinner."

Her brown eyes popped wide in shock. "*Merde*, I'm sorry! The packing is finished."

"Thank you. Now go and feed yourself and don't forget to go to bed tonight."

The maid's sly smile answered her curiosity. Not an embarrassing morning then, but an adventurous night. Danielle was so delightfully French. Only she had dismissed Alex's terrible scandal with a shrug and sniff. "Was it worth it?" had been all she'd asked. Her companionship had been just what Alex needed in the time since.

She closed the door on her maid's saucy grin and, with a deep sigh, leaned against the ancient wood. She felt so tired. She should not have had those extra glasses of wine with dinner. She should not have skipped luncheon either, but it had taken her all day just to screw up her courage and face him.

It wasn't just the rejection. It was the letter that had been waiting in her room when she'd returned from her unsuccessful tryst. If only Prescott had ignored her instructions to forward personal mail.

The sharp knock she'd been half-expecting rattled the door against her back.

"Good God," Alex muttered, pressing a hand to her stuttering heart. She knew who it was. He'd glared daggers into her just moments before when she'd said her goodbyes. What the hell did he want from her?

Steeling herself against the coming confrontation, she stepped away from the door and opened it just a crack.

"Alexandra," he said in a suspiciously even voice. "Might I speak with you?"

"Yes."

His mouth tightened. "Will you open the door?"

She stared at him for a long moment just to be difficult, then let the door swing open. "What is it?"

She pretended not to notice his anger, but she did back a few steps away from him as he slipped in and shut the door.

"Why are you acting like this?"

"What do you mean?"

"Like I've done something terrible."

"I'm not acting that way at all."

"You won't speak to me. You won't even look at me. You're leaving tomorrow and all you can manage for me is a nod of your damned head?"

Oh, this was ridiculous. "I can't imagine why you'd care."

Collin growled, hands crumpling to fists. "You think I wouldn't even care to say a proper good-bye to you?"

Her temper ruled her, off-balance as she was from a combination of his overwhelming presence and the wine she'd consumed. "I think that you had every reason not to like me when we met, and I think you do not like me now. I, I offered myself to you like a . . ." She pulled herself straight and refused to say it. "And you didn't want me."

"That's absolutely not true."

"Of course it is." She looked down at the floor, unable to meet his suddenly understanding gaze. "You're simply too nice to say it."

"Come here."

"No." She shook her head to emphasize the word. She heard a step and saw his boots come into her line of vision.

"Alex," he said more softly.

She shook her head again, wishing he'd go away, wishing she didn't feel so uncertain. She felt his hand beneath her chin and let him raise her face to his gaze.

"Surely you know when a man wants you."

"Apparently not."

"Alex." She heard the laughter in the word, his amusement at her pouting. And then his breath touched her lips. And then his mouth was against hers and she was sighing and opening to him.

The kiss was so soft, so hesitant that, though her heart leapt at the touch, it only confirmed what she feared. He did not want her as she wanted him. He didn't kiss her hard and hot. He didn't push her to the bed and strip her naked and slake his need. He only held her, licked gently at her bottom lip.

She wanted his tongue. She wanted his arousal.

She broke away, swiped at the warmth that lingered on her mouth. "Don't lie to me, Collin." Ignoring his shocked eyes, she spun and jerked open the corner drawer of her dresser.

"Here." She thrust the stiff paper into his hands, pushing it away from her. "Take it. Leave."

He just stared at her a moment, looking almost hurt.

Finally, he glanced down, brow furrowed as he turned the paper over in his hands. "What is it?"

"What do you think it is?"

The paper snapped, it unfolded so quickly beneath his fingers. His face blanked, then flushed. Alex turned to her trunk and smoothed the already neat bundles of clothing.

She'd given it to him in anger, and already her hand itched to snatch it back. Damien's note was passionate and flirtatious, and she'd only wanted to show Collin that someone didn't think her too low to desire. Now she felt foolish. Used.

"It came this afternoon," she muttered. The letter was brief. Surely he'd finished it.

"I thank you for the information. And the titillation."

A glance over her shoulder found him holding it out toward her. She sniffed. "Shouldn't you keep it? It's what you wanted, after all."

"Oh, I wouldn't deprive you of such a tender keepsake. Surely you treasure his vivid remembrance of that evening in the rose garden. It is all that keeps him going, after all."

Alex snatched it back from him as she should have done before he'd read it. A hard toss sent it floating into the chest and she slammed the lid against the sight of it.

"Good-bye, Mr. Blackburn. Let me know if I can be of assistance to you in the future." The silence behind her stretched her nerves thin. "What?"

A shush of fabric as he shifted. Then nothing.

"*What?*"

"I did not kiss you, or . . . I did not make love to you as a means to get information."

"Really?"

He cursed. It sounded like a curse, anyway, though it wasn't English. Gaelic, she guessed. Of course, she didn't really think he'd used her, but better he think that the cause of her anger than injured pride and hurt feelings.

"I realize you do not know me well," he murmured from close behind her. "But I would never do that. I meant to not touch you at all, but I could not help myself."

A shiver of pleasure slid over her spine at the honest heat in his voice.

"I am not a man who often loses control."

"And so you did not."

"I did. If not for that ill-timed cart I would have happily buried myself between your legs and damn the consequences."

The shiver turned to a stroke of hot lust. Oh, God, she could picture him rocking against her, his naked hips pressed against her own.

His hand reached from behind to circle her wrist. He pulled her around to face him. "Is this a habit of yours? Collecting confessions of lust from men who can't have you?"

"I . . ." His nearness, the savage light in his eyes . . . She had to breathe deep to clear her head. "You could have me."

"You are not the type of woman a man simply beds."

That surprised a sharp laugh out of her. "I am exactly that type of woman."

"Don't speak that way of yourself," he growled. "It's not true. I knew the moment I met you it wasn't true."

"But . . ." she choked out, confused and oddly hurt by his words.

"We all do stupid things when we're young, Alex. Do not let past indiscretions dictate the rest of your life. You are a fine woman—smart and kind."

"Oh, Collin," she sighed and pulled her hand from his. "Don't be naïve. I'm truly ruined. The Errant Heiress, they call me. The Duke's Despair."

"You are rich and beautiful and the sister of a duke. Don't tell me you haven't had men clamoring to marry you even since the scandal."

She shrugged, sullen in the face of the truth. "Not the kind of men I'd marry."

"One day there will be. And you should not damage yourself further because of past mistakes."

This was almost comical. Was he really turning her away out of some misguided morality? She did not want to be fine and good. She wanted to be happy.

"Good-bye, Alexandra. It was truly a pleasure."

My God, he was really going. She set aside her pride for later. "A kiss good-bye, at least?"

He hesitated, but only for the barest moment. "Aye. Of course."

Reaching high on her tiptoes, she pressed her mouth to his before he could change his mind. He kissed her tenderly and thoroughly—and held her body an inch from his. Undaunted, she pressed her palms to his chest and felt him shift toward her. Good. Good. He was saying farewell and she would likely never see him again and he would damn well think of her when he was gone.

She couldn't stop the small, sad sound she made as he closed the space between them.

His hand curled into her hair. His mouth left hers. He pulled her back and stared down at her, eyes sliding over her eyes, her neck, her parted lips. Then his hands slipped out of her hair and he stepped away.

"Good-bye," she whispered, hating the feel of his heat seeping away from her.

Collin Blackburn opened the door of her room and walked silently out of her life.

Chapter 6

"Julia will be coming out next Season?"

"Oh, yes." Aunt Augusta fairly vibrated with excitement. "And she has finally shed her baby fat, Alex! You cannot imagine how excited she is!"

Alexandra forced a smile. Of course she could. She had felt that same excitement not two years before.

"We are taking her to Madame Desante for her wardrobe, of course."

"Of course."

"She says that the coming styles are perfect for Julia."

"That's wonderful, Aunt Augusta. And Justine? Is she thirteen now?"

"Oh, yes. And as wild as her little brother." A tired sigh made her cheeks quiver. "We shall see about that one."

Alex couldn't help but smile a little more widely. "She will outgrow it, I'm sure. And you have only Julia to think about now."

"Oh, and she will be lovely. You must come to her ball, Alexandra. She would miss your not being there."

"Perhaps," she lied. She had absolutely no intention of slinking back to London with her tail between her legs, and she certainly would not taint her cousin's coming out.

When Augusta turned to speak to Mr. Covington, Alex swept her gaze around the table, then glanced up to her brother to watch as he raised a subtle toast in her direction. She grinned, aware that she was lucky to have such a wonderful brother. He made her comfortable life possible. If he'd been anyone else she'd have been married to a fortune hunter by now. Someone more than willing to overlook her scandalous past for the chance of shaping her into the perfect rich wife.

Her eye caught on Robert Dixon then, smiling at her from mid-table. She smiled back.

He was a cousin of some sort, though God knew how distant. She'd met him twice before. He was very handsome, in a polished, blond sort of way, and he had been subtly flirting with her since dinner began.

Letting her eyes fall away from his, she continued her sweep of the table. Hart had planned this party to coincide with her twentieth birthday, and no more than two dozen handpicked guests had been invited—only the friends and relatives who'd treated her kindly after the scandal. No one else would find themselves close to the handsome Duke of Somerhart anytime soon.

George and Lucy had sailed to France not a week ago, however, and she found herself oddly nervous without their support. And still lonely, despite her brother's intention to cheer her up.

Loneliness had settled upon her over the past weeks, cold and suffocating, like a muffling blanket of snow that shrouded her happiness. It wasn't just the loss of Collin Blackburn, though that was certainly a part of it. She was, quite simply, alone. There were no other women like her, not that she knew of. Women who worked the land and the books. Women who were blessed with the luxury of playing at manly pursuits. And thank God she had that, for hard work was the only pleasure she had.

Laughter swelled briefly around her, and Alex laughed too, making sure that none of the guests could see her distraction. The increasing volume of the chatter signaled the winding down of dinner, and Alex nodded toward Hart and stood.

"Gentlemen. Please stay for a few moments to enjoy your port. Ladies?"

They stood around her in a flutter of silks and satins, each bright butterfly wing of gown separated from the next by the stark black of the men's jackets until the women stepped away to file out. Alexandra followed, murmuring pleasantries to the men she passed, and very aware of Robert Dixon's eyes on her.

A quarter hour passed. Fifteen minutes of torturous talk of babies and tatting and husbands and fashion. Alex spoke of gardens and thought of Collin. She laughed at a joke about waltzing and imagined his hand as it gripped her thigh.

She could not make herself forget him.

The men wandered out of the dining room in groups or pairs, trailing the scent of cigars and providing her with a distraction. She made her eyes look at Robert Dixon, made herself study him at his post near the door.

Aside from being handsome, he was cultured and polite, though his smile spoke of a steel will. And he would inherit the title of Viscount Landry from his father. In short, he was a man she would have found attractive during her Season. Regardless, he did not send any sparks racing through her veins. Had Collin ruined her for other men? Perhaps Mr. Dixon could help her find out.

His eyes met hers across the room and he moved immediately toward her.

"Mr. Dixon."

"Lady Alexandra. You look very . . . happy tonight."

She laughed at his choice of words. "You expected me to be withering away in exile?"

He smiled with an endearing touch of embarrassment. "Not withering away, certainly, but you seem almost content."

"I am. My life is much fuller now that it consists of more than dresses and parties."

"Surely you enjoyed life in London? You certainly seemed to."

"Yes. Of course I enjoyed London." His smile disappeared at her flat words.

"I'm sorry. That was a stupid thing to say."

"Nonsense, Mr. Dixon." She set her hand boldly on his sleeve. "I am not so fragile as that."

His hazel eyes warmed at her touch, and she blushed a little and removed her hand. She didn't want to lead him on, didn't want to deceive him, but she needed to *know*.

His shoulders eased the slightest bit closer to her as if he would speak softly, and Alex felt her heart speed. She had flirted entire days away in London, but now it felt unnatural, as if she were in danger. As his head dipped toward her ear, she spied Hart approaching from over his shoulder and nearly jumped with relief.

"Your Grace!" Robert sounded more than surprised to Alex's ears as he pushed to his feet. "Have you come to rescue your sister from my company?"

Hart smiled easily and took her hand. He kissed her cheek before looking down at his friend. "I only came to check on her, but seeing you here, I am now sure that she is near death from boredom."

She rolled her eyes. "Absolutely untrue, Hart. Don't be cruel."

Robert smiled ruefully as he bowed. "I'll leave you to your brother's attention, Lady Alexandra. I can see he wishes to speak with you."

"He seems like a nice young man," Alex offered as soon as he'd moved out of earshot.

Her brother glanced distractedly at his retreating back and shrugged. "Nice enough, I suppose. I wanted to see how you were doing."

She fought the urge to roll her eyes again. Hart was overprotective now. His guardianship in early years had been characterized by a marked disinterest in details. "I am fine, Hart."

"Are you sure?"

"You know, I was very good at this before. Chatting

with people isn't difficult, even for someone of my limited intelligence and delicate health."

A wide smile spread across his face. The kind of smile, she suspected, that many women would swoon to see directed at them. "No, I suppose it isn't."

She gave in and rolled her eyes. "Really, Hart, there is nothing to worry about."

His blue gaze held her own for a long moment, the smile fading away, then he placed her hand on his arm and led her across the room to the open patio doors. She frowned up at him when he stopped to face her just outside the light that spilled from the house.

"You've been quiet the past few weeks, Alex." His words were soft as down.

She shook her head automatically. "No, I've only had a lot on my mind." His hand came up to cup her cheek, and Alex fought back the urge to confess her obsession with Collin Blackburn.

"Pet, you know that you are free to marry at any time. All I ask is that you inform me of any suitors. There are always those men who'd pursue you for your fortune, Alex, and I would look into anyone who caught your interest."

"Don't—"

"But you are a lovely woman and you are sure to find someone. I worry that you're lonely."

Oh, I am *lonely,* she wanted to cry out, but she only swallowed and shook her head in the dark. "There have been no suitors, Hart. But I think that's probably best for a while, don't you?"

"I would see you happy."

Really? she stopped herself from asking. *Would you bring me a large Scotsman then, to be my lover?* "I am happy, if only because of my indulgent big brother."

"It is not indulgence. This will all be yours for as long as you want it, Alex. Somerhart is your home as much as mine."

She loved him so much, she thought, wrapping her arms around his waist so she could press her cheek to his beating heart. "I love you, brother. You're the only man for me. Now let us get back to our guests."

He held on a moment longer, his chest expanding as if he would speak, but he did not. Instead, he pressed a hard kiss to her head and led her back toward the doors. Before they'd even stepped through, she watched him transform himself back into the perfect host. He was painfully handsome and the most elegant man she'd ever known. No one suspected that beneath his aloof exterior lurked a caring man.

The thought brought a smile to her mouth. Surely someday he'd fall in love. She couldn't wait to see it. The smile froze on her face. Love. Was that what she suffered from? Surely not. No. Absolutely not. She would not let it be love.

The second day of the party tumbled by, rushed and seemingly endless. Alex discovered that she'd grown quite used to her solitary life in the country. Having so many people underfoot overwhelmed her when it had seemed a delightful thing a few years ago.

But now . . . Now it was just too much. Breakfast, then riding, then luncheon. A stroll around the grounds, teatime, a short rest in her room. Finally, dinner and a small musical show. She managed to avoid a private conversation with Robert Dixon, though he made every effort to edge her away from the crowd. She could not imagine why she was avoiding him.

Hadn't she kissed every man who'd ever caught her eye? Well, perhaps not every man, but given the opportunity, she hadn't shied away from the excitement of a flirtation.

Confusion weighed her down by the time she fell into her bed at two in the morning. She was exhausted, but her mind buzzed with the remnants of meaningless conversations, so she lay in bed and played absently with the end of her braid, trying to puzzle out her new attitude.

Collin Blackburn had to be the cause. What else could it be?

She pressed her hands to hot cheeks. Collin. She had hoped her reaction to him had only been something to do with her own body, some new maturity that gave her greater pleasure in men and their touches. But that couldn't be the case. Just being near Collin had felt different than being close to other men. He'd tainted her blood.

She knew Robert Dixon to be attractive, but he did not attract *her*.

So she wanted only Collin, and he lived God knew how many miles away and was determined *not* to be had. He'd only written once after all, and not a personal word to be found in the whole letter. And perhaps "letter" was the wrong word altogether. Paragraph. That was it.

He eluded us again, by mere minutes. If he suspects you, he likely won't write again. My appreciation for your help.

"Blackburn," he'd signed it. No closing. Not one personal word. She'd spent ceaseless nights fantasizing about him and he'd revealed nothing.

He was not pining for her, why should she waste her time? Time to set thoughts of him aside.

But at night . . . At night, she couldn't help remembering his mouth, his hands, the silky steel of his body. She relived that tension and that release, that release that nothing in life had prepared her for. She wanted more.

It was beginning to annoy her, really. Why did it have to be him? Or maybe she had an affinity for Scotsmen. Maybe she should travel north to explore the possibility. The thought pulled her eyes open.

Scotland. Hmm.

No, she told herself, *absolutely not.*

Alex punched her pillow several times, laid her head back onto the lumpiness, then groaned in frustration. The pillow hit the far wall with a soft thump which was followed immediately by a delicate scratching.

Scratching? Alex sat up and stared at the white shape of her pillow on the floor. Had it grown fingers? The scratching again, not from that direction. The door, not the pillow.

She slid from the bed and padded to her door, aware now of the shadow of feet beneath it. "Yes?"

"Mr. James, missus," a girl whispered. "He says to tell you that the mare is taking food again."

Alex yanked the door open, surprising the maid into a jump. The girl's hair had started to escape from her sleeping cap, her eyes were heavy despite the surprise.

"Did he say anything else?"

"Just that she may recover after all, milady."

"Thank you."

"Shall I call your maid?"

"No, no . . . I'm fine. Get to bed."

Alex closed the door and leaned against it. *Queenie was recovering*. The poor thing had been in steady decline since she'd delivered a stillborn foal at the end of spring. The stable master had wanted to put her down, but Alex had ordered that he wait for one more week to see if she could recover from the infection. But she had not held out much hope.

She allowed herself a smile, then headed for her wardrobe to pull out an old pair of breeches. Tonight, at least, would not be spent thinking of Collin Blackburn.

"Are you a ghost?"

Alex froze, heart like a trapped animal in her throat. Her eyes flew over the dark, picking out familiar shadows until they caught on the fiery tip of a cigar.

She hovered, uncertain what to do. The red spot moved, bobbed closer until she could hear footsteps against the grass.

"Not a ghost, I suppose. I can hear you breathing."

Her mind finally placed the man's voice and her chest ceased to strangle her. "Mr. Dixon."

"Lady Alexandra? Whatever are you doing outside at this small hour?"

"I . . ." She stuttered, caught her breath. "I have business to see to."

"Business?"

Alex clutched her cloak tight at her throat and glanced toward her destination. This was exactly what she'd hoped to avoid, being spied in her scandalous attire. But she couldn't wear dinner dress into a horse stall.

"Lady Alexandra, I fear I have interfered with a . . . a private meeting. Forgive me."

She could just make him out now, still dressed for the party. His dark coat turned away from her.

"No," she whispered, then with more ease, "No, of course not. One of my mares is sick. I'd like to see her myself. There is no rendezvous, I assure you."

He drew a little closer at her words. She watched the bright spark of his cigar die beneath a boot heel. "Do you not fear for your safety, out alone in the dark?"

"This is my home."

"Yes, of course."

"I   "

"Allow me to escort you to the stables, at least."

"Oh, I don't know. I mean, I suppose . . ." He held out his arm. She wanted to refuse him, claim that it wouldn't be proper, but it wasn't precisely decent to be out alone, after all.

So she slid a hand out from under the folds of her cloak and took his arm. His teeth flashed white in the moonlight when he smiled. "Are you often called to your duties at odd hours?"

"Not often. Actually, I'm sure the stable master would rather I stay away, but I am not easily dissuaded."

"Your brother despairs of your strong will."

"Does he?"

"A little, only."

Alex pushed aside the prick of hurt. Why shouldn't he despair? "Well, I *am* strong-willed. I'm sure that comes as no surprise."

"No. But some men do not mind a bold woman."

"Oh?" Alex hesitated. "Do you mean yourself?"

"I do."

When he stopped, Alex tensed. She'd been kissed often enough in London to read the signs of desire. Even as she was trying to decide whether to allow it, he leaned forward. His lips were firm and warm against hers, his technique measured and pleasant. Alex's nerves did not even twitch.

His did, it seemed. He sighed and kissed her harder, easing one arm around her as he coaxed her mouth to open to his tongue. It tasted of cigars.

Ignoring the ashy smell, she tried to muster the interest to kiss him back, tried to give him a fair chance, and succeeded in her pretending, apparently. The arm around her waist tightened and pulled her into his body until she could feel him harden against her stomach.

His mouth pulled away with a gasp that echoed her own. "What . . . What are you wearing?"

Alex blinked up at him, hands trapped against his chest, and realized that his fingers had stolen under her cape. He folded back the fabric before she could stop him and stared in disbelief at the boy's clothes she wore. Even before his eyes cleared and sharpened, his fingers swept down to cup her bottom.

"My God," he moaned and yanked her back to the press of his body.

"Wait," she said into his mouth, but his tongue had slipped between her lips again, stabbed, really, until the force of the kiss smothered her breath.

Alex pushed against his muscles, arms straining to win a few inches, but her arched back pressed her harder into his erection, and he moaned and gripped her bottom with bruising force. His hand left her as quickly as it squeezed, but her relief was short-lived. Her shirt tugged and slid against her skin, pulled from her breeches as he tried to find a way beneath her clothing. His smothering mouth sucked at her—pulling, taking.

A fizz of panic bubbled into her veins, burned through her limbs. She was aware in a way she'd never been before of her small stature, and of the muscles that corded a man's arms with strength. He could take her here, drag her to the ground and cover her mouth and push himself inside her, and she could fight with all her will and not damage him in the least.

Just as his hand slid beneath her shirt, she managed to twist her face away from his assault.

"Don't! What are you doing?"

"Oh, God," he groaned again, words wet against her jaw.

She shuddered, tried to think. She could scream, but she could not be caught like this again, not by a guest, not by one of the men who worked for her.

"Mr. Dixon, please. Let me go."

"I knew you were a hot piece, but I had no idea." His hand swept over her naked back as he spoke, then slithered around to rub her breast in a shock of clammy cool.

"Let me go," she hissed and shoved as hard as she could. He stumbled, still wrapped around her, jerking her back toward him until her legs gave way and she fell to her knees. She felt the hard cushion of the earth, felt the sting of his button where it had scratched her face, then a breeze touched her chest, colder than his hand.

His dark shape loomed, fingers still clutching the raised hem of her shirt, eyes glazed, as shocked by the sight of her breasts as she was to have them exposed. Alexandra recovered first, grabbing the fabric with both hands to jerk it from his fist. That sudden jolt released him from his trance and he nodded, reached to unbutton his trousers.

"Yes, take off the shirt, Alexandra. I want to suckle those tits."

"You are mad," she whispered, wishing her voice sharp instead of scared.

She pitched to the side and crawled away, pushed to her feet just as his hand snagged her braid.

"Where are you going?"

"To my brother."

"Your brother?" His hand fell away, letting her lurch back from the sight of his open trousers. Robert Dixon gaped. "You can't mean to leave me like this?"

Alex caught a glimpse of hair and hard red flesh before she retreated further into the night. Anger fought to replace her fear. Her voice hissed instead of shaking. "I granted you a kiss. You . . . You attacked me."

"I attacked you? You are sneaking about by yourself at three in the morning. You flirted with the first man you came across, and . . . and you're wearing breeches! Do not play coy now. You're not even wearing a shift!"

"I . . ." Alex shook her head, prayed that the rustle of cloth was Mr. Dixon putting himself away. "I was seeing to my horse. I hardly sought you out."

He moved closer and she fought the impulse to cringe and bolt. This was her land, her home. And she held the power here, for if she did tell her brother, Mr. Dixon would wish himself dead.

"You should take care in the future, miss, not to offer your lips to a man in privacy of the blackest night. Any man would assume you invited more."

"A gentleman would have waited for an actual invitation."

"A gentlewoman would never find herself in the position of pondering this question."

The breeze came again, cooling her skin as her blood boiled. "Do not chastise me. I offered you nothing more scandalous than a kiss. You disgraced yourself."

"Ha. You dare speak of disgrace."

"Mr. Dixon, I do not want you near me. I would suggest you find an excuse to depart in the morning lest I take this debate to my brother. Let him decide what was invited and what taken."

She heard the growl of his frustrated sigh, the slap of hand striking leg.

"Fine." His boots still muffled by the grass, his step drew closer until the white of his bared teeth passed her by. "But let me warn you again. Be careful whom you toy with in the future. Men are not designed to stop once they are started."

"Perhaps you speak of boys."

"You shall find out some day soon, I do not doubt." With

that insult, he stomped toward the house, hopefully to wake his valet and prepare his packing.

She prayed he spent a few years, at least, harboring the fear that she would tell the duke. Perhaps he would sweat each time he greeted her brother, waiting for the cut. It was her only consolation. She had no doubt he would speak ill of her to all of England.

Alex toed the short grass with her boot, kicked at it with her heel. Guilt tensed her shoulders, then frustration that his words could wound her. True, the rules of society helped to protect women from the baser instincts of men. If she hadn't been wandering alone in the night, she certainly wouldn't have stumbled over Mr. Dixon, wouldn't have tempted him to drop his pants in a maelstrom of lust. But really, she had enough work controlling her own impulses, why should it be her responsibility to help men control theirs as well?

He was wrong. They all were. Men must take responsibility for their own transgressions. Real men did. Real men like Collin Blackburn. He hadn't pounced on her, hadn't grabbed her like a piece of meat fallen into a dog pen.

And she was not fooled by her words to Robert Dixon. Many men would've behaved exactly as he had. None had ever been quite so aggressive, but she'd heard that tone that he'd used on her. That ring of arrogance and victory. *I knew you were a hot piece*. That pride in exposing a woman for her dark nature—a whore, a vessel for their lust. It was almost a need they had, to destroy a woman with the wants of her body. Or theirs.

But not Collin. No, when he'd spoken in lust, whispered it against her skin, he'd sounded reverent, awed. He'd sounded perfect.

Muttering curses, Alex tucked in her rumpled shirt and glanced back and forth between two choices. The stable, where sense and duty waited, or the house, to plot and plan a trap for the man she wanted.

Her legs felt weak and boneless as the last of her fear dissolved. She jerked her cloak back around her body and turned to her decision. She'd do what she'd come here to do, see to her horse . . . then on to more impractical things. More delicious, impractical, and utterly disgraceful things.

Craven gentlemen of society be damned. She was going to catch herself a bastard.

Chapter 7

Her hands trembled with excitement as the curricle bounced along the wide Edinburgh road. The city was beautiful, the air fresh and warm and tinged with the scent of summer flowers, but Alexandra felt only the stifling weight of worry.

Too much of this plan hinged on chance. The chance that Collin would attend the horse fair himself, the chance that he'd spy her across the crowd, and the biggest chance of all . . . that he'd care enough to hunt her down.

"Stop that," Danielle ordered. "You'll hardly entice him with a frown."

True, but they hadn't reached the grounds of the fair yet, and he was unlikely to be hanging about on a street corner. But just as she found the will to relax her face into a pleasant smile, the driver turned onto a wide lane that headed into a warren of stables and outbuildings and cordoned-off parade areas. Horses were everywhere, being ridden or walked on dirt and trampled patches of grass.

This was surely a ridiculous plan, but she didn't want to walk right up to Collin Blackburn. Didn't want him to think she'd travel to Scotland just to see him, true as it was. No, she wanted to be pursued. Wanted him just as anxious for it as she had become over these two weeks of planning.

They hadn't traveled a quarter of the way through the

grounds when she spotted him. They wouldn't even have to leave the carriage.

"There he is." The air grew thick around her, far too thick to breathe.

Danielle twisted in the high seat of the curricle. "Where?"

"Don't look. He'll see you!"

"*Merde*. He won't see anything in this crush."

The thought of failure squared Alexandra's shoulders. She had nothing to fear. If she failed in this, suffered complete humiliation, she could simply retreat to her brother's estate and never see Collin Blackburn again. Simple.

"He's next to the red building on the right, about fifty yards ahead. Do you see?"

"*Oui*. I'd forgotten how positively magnificent he is."

"Isn't he?" Alex let herself take him in for a moment. She watched as he crossed his arms and nodded to the shorter man at his side. Collin was dressed more casually than she'd ever seen him. No jacket, no cravat, his cream-colored shirt open at the collar in a V of dark skin. The sight made her fingers curl.

Oh, she couldn't back down now. The memory of him like this, handsome and work-worn, would haunt her.

The carriage inched forward, parting a way through the crowd. They had plenty of time. Perhaps too much. If he spotted them too soon he could simply walk right over and stop them. No, she wanted him to stew for a day or so; to wonder where the hell she was and what she was doing in Edinburgh. Assuming, of course, that he didn't simply shrug his shoulders and go about his work.

Danielle winked and lowered the gauze veil that dipped down from her hat. "Are you ready, *Mademoiselle?*"

They'd almost drawn abreast of him now. He stood less than ten yards to her right, still speaking somberly to his companion, still unaware of her presence.

Alexandra took a deep breath, turned back to Danielle and nodded.

Danielle laughed aloud, a joyful, throaty laugh that

brought several men's heads swiveling toward them even before she spoke. "Really, Lady Alexandra," she trilled, her English accent impeccable. "You can't convince me that you will actually enter the horse yards."

Alex felt a genuine grin steal over her face at her maid's choice of topic. "I will," she replied, letting go the tension that had crouched in her chest since she'd awakened that morning. "Scandalous, I know."

"Surely the duke doesn't allow you to run so free." Danielle's eyes widened as she spoke, and her head bobbed in the barest of nods.

Exhilaration rushed through Alexandra's veins. He was looking. She tossed her head, triumph warming her skin as she turned to look straight ahead, tilted her face up to the sun and smiled widely.

"Indeed, I am quite free. One can only be ruined once."

Danielle laughed again, an honest laugh, and Alex joined her, fighting the urge to look for Collin. Was he shocked, stunned, *thrilled* to see her?

Her companion leaned in close. "Mr. Blackburn is thunderstruck."

Alex felt her heart skip.

"He's moving this way."

Pulse stuttering in wild excitement, she glared at the carriage ahead, cursing it silently to move, move, move. Seconds ticked by, sweat dampened the palms of her gloves. Their wheels crunched slowly over gravel, then turned faster, until the whole line of vehicles ahead of them began to move at a quick walk. They rolled along, picking up speed until they passed through the fair and into the green outskirts of the city.

"Oh. Oh, my." She inhaled the dusty, grassy scent of the countryside and trembled in disbelief. "Oh, my. I think we did it."

"He was dumbstruck, *Mademoiselle*. Pale with shock."

"Oh, Danielle." She pulled her maid into a happy hug.

"He'll work himself into a frenzy by Saturday night."

"A frenzy?"

"*Oui.*"

"A frenzy. I like that."

"Wouldn't we all?"

Alexandra slumped against the seat, sure and happy, almost the same feeling she'd had after Collin had brought her to that long ago peak. "You were marvelous, Danielle. Perfect."

"It is not so very hard to fool a man."

Closing her eyes against the sun, Alex let the wind sweep the warmth of anxiety from her skin. She'd tossed and turned the night away and her body reminded her of that as the excitement ebbed away. "Well, the fooling is done. I'll be on my own for the rest of it."

"I'll make you as enticing as possible. He won't be able to resist."

"Ha. He resisted quite easily a few weeks ago."

"Oh, no. Not easily."

She rolled her eyes behind closed lids. "What could you know of it? You saw him all of two times."

"True, but you'll remember that your cousin loaned him a manservant?"

"Mm."

"The boy assured me that your Mr. Blackburn slept not a wink the night before you left, and not so well the rest of his nights either."

"Really?" She opened one eye.

"Really."

She tried not to smile. "It was likely something else bothering him."

Danielle snorted in French disdain. "We will solve that mystery soon enough."

Collin tore the wrinkled cloth from his neck and hurled it across the room. The fine linen floated to the floor, landing with a disappointing whisper that tempted him to kick it for good measure.

"Need some assistance?"

"Where the hell have you been?"

Fergus stepped cheerfully through the door and bowed deeply. "Only following yer instructions, sir. We are here to sell horses, after all."

"Fuck off."

"I canna wait to meet the lassie's got you so tied up in knots."

"Well, don't hold your breath, you shit. She's not likely to come visit, is she?"

"I've nae idea. Is she?"

Collin ignored him and jerked a freshly pressed cravat from the bureau. "Did he sign it?"

"Happily. The wait to breed with Devil is now three years out."

"And well worth it," he grunted, staring down at the evil strip of starched cloth. "He's a fine one." Fergus's hand reached into his vision to pluck it from his grasp.

"Turn 'round."

"I can tie my own—"

"Just shut up and turn around. I've ne'er seen a man with such a sad inability to tie a cravat."

Collin turned slowly, crossing his arms over his chest, and glared at his manager. One of the downsides to being a lord was the dependence on another person to help you dress. Oh, he was happy to let someone polish his boots and press his shirts, but to stand like a child and be helped into jackets and shoes and cravats . . . Why not slip into shortpants and a smock for good measure?

Fergus flashed him a grin, making clear he enjoyed Collin's discomfort. The man knew horseflesh and he was a fearsome negotiator, but he took an inordinate interest in clothing and the latest styles. His blond hair and beard were always neatly trimmed, his coats cut from the finest cloth. And even the Frenchmen who came to Westmore complimented him on his intricate cravats. The French-women complimented him also, and looked stricken when they realized that Lord Westmore was actually the big brute in rough trousers and shirtsleeves.

"There. What do ye think?"

Collin was shoved around to scowl at his reflection. "It's fine."

"Fine? It's perfect."

"Perfect. Whatever." Collin squinted at the tumbling folds of cloth. "Why is there something *sparkling* at me?"

"It's a pin, Collin. Ye think a creation that beautiful can hold itself together?"

"It's a diamond, and I think I've made myself clear—"

"Good night. I'm off to my own enjoyment."

"Fergus!" Collin shouted after him, but the door was already slamming shut. He was now adorned in jewels. If he removed the pin, the tie would be ruined and he'd be even later to the ball. Jesus, even if Alexandra was there, she could have left to attend another party by now. If she was still in Edinburgh at all.

"Damn," he muttered, glaring at the winking flash of the diamond. He pinched a small bit of fabric between his fingers and tried to tug it down to cover the pin, but it popped back up when he let go. A bloody masterpiece of a cravat.

Resigned, he slid into his coat and stalked out the door, scowling at the thought of the carriage waiting below. He couldn't even ride his own horse for fear his black trousers would get dusty. Ridiculous.

The ride to the ball was slow and maddening. He itched to jump down and find his way on foot, but he couldn't very well arrive with muck and mud on his shoes. No, he was stuck in the coach with muscles that ached with tension and a brain that wouldn't stop twitching and turning. Because of her.

"She won't be there," he growled, meaning to flatten the hope that rose in his chest. She hadn't been at any of the dances or dinners or parties he'd hunted through last night. Granted, the MacDrummond ball was the premiere event of the fair, but invitations were hard to come by. Add to that the possibility that she was still hiding from society, and there was almost no chance she would be there. Yet she had to be.

He'd lived like a starving man for weeks. He had so

nobly sent her on her way in England, with hardly more than a kiss on the cheek and a friendly wave, and had cursed himself every night afterward. She crept into his bed each evening, bodice gaping, fine blue skirt pushed up to her hips. She lay on his twisted sheets and asked him to take her, to mount her. His dreams were so vivid, he awoke with the scent of her arousal like a taste in his mouth. Jesus, he hadn't even had the chance to taste her.

He had thought half a dozen times of riding down to Somerhart and claiming her, had picked up a quill more times than that to write a real letter. He'd had an excuse, could've asked about St. Claire, but then she might have taken insult. She'd given her word, after all, to pass on new information.

The lust would fade, he'd told himself. He'd had the strength to walk away from her ready body, he could wait for this too to pass. And it *had* begun to fade, just barely, over the past few weeks. And then he'd heard her voice yesterday, above the din of the fair crowd. He'd swept the lines of people and saw her face, lit up by the sun and her own glow. He would have thought her an illusion if he hadn't heard her name, a laughing censure from the woman beside her.

And now he couldn't find a damned trace of her. And he needed to find her. He was done with being responsible. He'd measure her by the same standard he'd measured his other lovers. If his seed caught, could he stand to marry her? Aye, he could.

Bastard born, he would not leave a child of his to be raised without a father, so he never slept with a woman whose companionship would be unbearable. But Alexandra would be far from unbearable. Ach, if he'd seen the girl walking to market in Scotland, he'd have had her in the church within a fortnight. But she was a far cry from a simple Scottish lass, and he was little more than a stable boy . . . had, in fact, been a stable boy at one time. No, he did not fancy himself good enough to marry her, but good enough to go to her bed?

Collin smiled humorlessly at the thought. She had assured

him he was good enough for that; he'd only needed time to convince himself.

Thousands of candles glittered above, magnified by the sparkling crystal of the chandeliers and drawing a smile to Alex's face. The light threw off heat, and there existed the startling danger of burning drops of wax, but she much preferred candles to gas, especially at a ball. Balls were meant to be magic and she desperately needed a little magic tonight. The candles were a good omen.

Anxiety bubbled through her veins like champagne. Champagne bubbled in her veins also, but it didn't seem to be helping to calm her. No, now she just felt a little sick. She would certainly get Collin's attention if she vomited at first sight of him.

But she truly wanted to relax and enjoy herself. This was her first evening out since the scandal and her first foray into Scottish society. The murmur of voices riding the air had a slightly different rhythm, the barest twist of cadence that spoke of the Scots burr.

Not that all the guests were Scottish, by any means, but she hadn't yet seen anyone she knew. Nor was she likely to. The Season was in full swing in London. The ton did not travel to Scotland for balls, not during the Season.

"Lady Alexandra."

Alexandra jumped, grateful her glass was empty when she spun awkwardly toward the woman's voice. "Oh, Lady MacDrummond. Thank you again for the invitation."

"My pleasure, dear. And may I say what a beautiful dress that is? Far more in the French fashion than most young Englishwomen have the sense for."

"My mother was French, you know. Perhaps it is something I learned at her knee."

The woman nodded, the blood rubies in her ears sparking with the movement. "Well, do not let that French blood get you into any more trouble."

Alex's eyes flew wide in surprise. Before she could

think what to say, Lady MacDrummond winked in sly conspiracy.

"Oh, I am aware of your little indiscretion in London, my dear, but we all have our indiscretions, private or public. I would not hold it against you."

Alexandra wondered if her eyes were in danger of falling from her head. She blinked hard. "Thank you."

The grandmotherly woman leaned in, scarlet skirts brushing against Alex's blue dress. "If it had been a Scotsman, dearie, he would've thought to lock the door."

"Oh," she murmured dumbly. "Of course."

Lady MacDrummond glided away in a cloud of laughter, skirt swinging around her, while Alex was left to wipe her sweaty gloves against the striped silk of her dress. The narrow strips of periwinkle and royal blue made her seem taller and she certainly needed help with that. It was one reason she preferred the French fashion. The wider English skirts did not suit her—she looked rather like a giant pudding sliding about.

Raising her eyes to scan the crowd, she wondered if she should move. The ballroom was an ingenious design, circular and ringed entirely by a low, wide balcony that rose no more than two feet above the ballroom floor. The elevation provided just enough height to give everyone a good view of the dancing and suited her purpose perfectly. She could see past the crowds to watch for Collin, but she was torn between the compulsion to search him out and the desire to appear naturally occupied.

She wavered for a good quarter hour, watching the entrance, feigning nonchalance. He had to come to the MacDrummond's. If he had any desire to see her at all, he would put in an appearance at this ball on this night. Please let him come.

Alexandra smiled briefly at a man who nodded in her direction before shifting her eyes away. She couldn't simply approach a strange man without an introduction, and the only women around her were chaperones and matrons.

Better to have Collin see her alone and dignified than cloistered with the elderly. Or was it?

Just as she took a step away from the railing, she spotted a young woman walking toward her, then, beyond the girl's head, a man's large form darkened the main door. Collin. Oh my.

She turned her back to the door even as his appearance crystallized in her mind. He wore full formal dress, of course. A shiver touched her legs and settled in her knees.

The woman on the balcony drew even with Alex. She was pretty in the way that the luckier redheads were—skin pale and almost fragile. Her thinness furthered the air of delicacy, though a generous bosom ensured that one did not think her too thin. She began to pass, smiling uncertainly at Alex's stare.

The nape of her neck prickled and tightened, raising tiny hairs. Collin was watching.

"Hello," she boomed, startling the girl into a jump. "Have we met somewhere before?"

"No, I . . ." She blinked, pale-green eyes wide with surprise. "I don't think so. I'm sure I would remember."

"I'm sorry. My mistake. May I introduce myself? I'm Alexandra Huntington. It's a pleasure to meet you." Smiling brightly, she waited, hoping the girl wouldn't bolt.

"Yes, um . . . I'm Jeannie. Jeannie Kirkland."

The girl's burr was lovely, the soft words soothing to her frayed nerves. "Miss Kirkland, I am so glad I mistook you for someone else, though I don't know how I could have. I daresay I've never met a woman with such beautiful hair."

Jeannie blushed, touching her hair with nervous fingers. "Oh, no. That canna be right. My brothers have assured me my whole life that I've hair the color of pumpkin innards."

Alexandra laughed in genuine amusement, but the sound hiccupped into a rather breathless cackle. Jeannie's hand rose to touch just one finger to Alex's bare arm, her face drawn into a concerned frown. Then her eyes shifted, drawn to some movement over Alex's shoulder. The confusion fell from her face in an instant, chased away by amused understanding.

"He is headed this way with a rather ferocious scowl. Shall I intercept him?"

"No," Alex whispered, shutting her eyes against the suspense. "No, let him come."

Jeannie chuckled and Alexandra opened her eyes to watch the girl wave cheerfully. She had no choice but to turn, not if she wanted to seem unaware. So she turned and saw him, standing not a dozen feet away, and found that she did not have to feign her reaction. Her breath left her in a rush past numb lips, and she stared at Collin Blackburn.

She'd never seen him like this, dressed impeccably, his cravat a snowy sculpture at his dark throat, his black coat a sharp outline of the strength of his shoulders. And his hair was so short, just cut, like a sweet young boy dressed for a portrait. How could he look so intimidating and so touchable at the same time?

His eyes pierced her, nearly black in that fierce face, and so full of questions that she almost abandoned her plan of coyness. But she was better than that.

Alex made her mouth smile, made her hands relax and uncurl, and took a step toward him. "Lord Westmore. What an unexpected pleasure." And the hunt was on.

Chapter 8

Here she was. This little slip of a thing who'd made him so miserable. Here she was. Now what the hell to do with her?

She drew closer, a vision of black hair and cream skin, close enough that Collin could just make out those freckles on her nose. Two more steps and she would be so close he could lean down and kiss them. She stopped at one.

"Lord Westmore," Jeannie Kirkland said from her side. "I see you've already met my friend."

Collin shot her a quick glare, this girl he'd known his whole life. "Your friend."

She flushed a little, pointed chin inching up. "My new friend. She's very nice."

"Yes. She is." He let his eyes swing back to Alexandra, their natural resting place when she was near. "Lady Alexandra, whatever are you doing here?" Her rosy lips parted, and he thought of them pressing into his skin.

"Why, I am here to buy horses, of course."

"Of course."

She licked those lips, her tongue a pink surprise, then drew a breath that tested the modesty of her gown. "It is wonderful to see you."

Collin stared at her, took her in, her beauty, her spark . . . stared until Jeannie cleared her throat.

"Collin, I will speak with you later." She narrowed her eyes meaningfully, then smiled at Alex. "*Lady* Alexandra, it was a pleasure to meet you."

She must have left, because the next time he glanced away from Alex's face he found they were standing alone, the party flowing around them like a babbling stream.

"Would you walk with me outside, my lady?"

She watched him, seemed to measure him through the sooty veil of her lashes as a smile spread slowly over her face, a smile that lit her up and heated his blood.

She didn't speak, only slid her arm through his and let him lead her to the wall of doors, then out into the moon-bright garden below. A cool wind swept over them, green and light. She shivered at his side as he pulled her into the deep shade of a tree.

Reaching to unbutton his coat, Collin began to shrug it off, but she made a low sound of distress that stayed his hands. "What is it?"

"Don't. Don't take off your coat. You look so . . ." Her hand caressed the air in front of him. "Magnificent."

"Magnificent?" His body stuttered to a halt. When he could move again, he found his fingers reaching to rebutton the coat. Her husky laugh sent blood racing to his face as well as to the lower reaches of his body. She seemed to have some torturous gift for arousing and embarrassing him simultaneously, a siren with a wicked wit.

How could this woman, this vision, be attracted to him? It confused him, put him on the defensive and touched him somewhere deep inside. And she was still attracted, he wasn't blind. She devoured him with her eyes, touching each part of him, lingering on his mouth. When she slipped off a glove and reached a small hand up to stroke the hair behind his ear, Collin pulled her against him and kissed her with all the need he'd been tamping down for months. He pressed her lips open with his own and slipped into her wet warmth.

Her hand tightened, tried to grab his hair, slid downward to clutch at his neck. Not in outrage, no. She fell into the kiss, plunged into it, raised onto her toes and pushed herself at him. More than willing to oblige, he pulled her up off her feet to line their bodies up. She smelled of flowers and tasted like wine, and oh God, how he wished she were wearing her boy's clothes now, wished he could feel the softness of her breasts and the hard press of her pelvic bone against his cock.

She stroked his tongue with a rhythm that drew a shudder through his body and melted his mind. He had no wish to resist her this time and prayed this was an invitation to escort her home. He was done resisting, couldn't think why he ever had.

The sharp bite of her nails stung his neck, thrilling him, pushing him over the edge of reason. He jerked her skirts up in bunches, inches at a time, trying to expose her body with his one free hand, trying to reach the center of her.

"Good God!" a hard voice exclaimed, spiking Collin's arousal with fear. Sweeping Alexandra around to hide her, he placed her carefully back on the ground.

"Did she actually invite Roxbury?"

"Surely he snuck in!"

Alex melted in his arms. They hadn't been spotted. Collin eased her backward, deeper into the shadows of the flowering branches. Tiny petals floated down as his head brushed the leaves, landing in her dark curls, in the shadow of her breasts, white spots of fragrance.

"Alex," he breathed, framing her heart-shaped face between rough hands. "Why did you come here?"

She smiled at his tortured words, mouth red as a rose from his kisses. "I've missed you, Collin."

"Missed me? Surely you've forgotten me by now."

Something close to pain froze his blood when she pulled away from his hands to press her face into his skin, nuzzling the place beneath his ear. A yearning rose up in him, more than lust or want, and her hair spilled around his hands, pins flying away at his clutching fingers. She smelled like flowers and rain and the underlying spice of need. Need for him.

"Oh, Collin. I wish I could forget you." The fierce whisper burned his neck.

He growled in dark humor. "I understand exactly."

She pressed her lips hard to his throat, trailed kisses up his jaw until he caught her with his mouth and kissed her again. Gentler, this time, and tinged with sadness and his own loneliness. She sighed into him, a deep, broken sound, and his sanity returned.

"I'm sorry." He touched her arms, held her away from him. "I'm sorry to fall upon you like a starving beast."

One of her dark eyebrows arched high. "You are easily appeased for a starving beast."

"Not appeased. Not at all."

"No? You are a perverse man, Collin. Always so in control."

"If I were in control, I wouldn't have spent the past two days dashing to every damned social function in the city."

The eyebrow dropped. "Pardon me?"

"I saw you at the fair, riding by, and nearly had a fit of the vapors."

Her laugh stroked his body, warmed his blood. A sudden vision made him ache—Alexandra, above him, riding his shaft, a delighted laugh spilling from her mouth. One of the many fantasies he'd indulged in over the past months. She was a damned affliction and a painful one at that.

"I'm sorry you've been tormented. Still, it only serves you right."

"Oh?"

"Don't forget who walked away."

"I rarely do."

Grinning, she grabbed his hand and pulled him out onto the path, out of their leafy alcove and back into the world. Collin tried not to groan as she turned them for a stroll into the darkest part of the garden.

"We could have already satisfied our curiosity and gotten over each other by now."

"You think so?"

When she shrugged, the small mounds of her breasts rose against her dress as Collin watched with avid interest.

"Perhaps. Surely it's the anticipation, the wondering, that's made me so . . ." She shrugged again.

Collin swallowed. "So what?"

A frown tugged at her brow as her left hand drifted up to brush low against her belly. "So hungry."

His breath hissed out between his teeth, drawing her sparkling eyes.

"You have undone me, Collin Blackburn." She smiled a little when he didn't respond, shook her head sadly. "I'm leaving tomorrow afternoon."

"Tomorrow?" Panic tumbled his gut. "Why?"

"I'm going home. Let's not pretend you would invite me to stay."

"No," he said without thought and cursed himself when she smirked and looked away.

"You searched me out here, pulled me into the garden, fell upon me, as you say. What do you want, Collin? Certainly not a strolling companion."

"No."

"No?" She shot back, pulling her hand from his to cross her arms.

"No, you know what I want."

"Hardly. I know what *I* want. I want you in my bed. If you wanted the same thing, we would've already been there."

"Jesus, do you want me to come and have you tonight? To slake my thirst and sneak out the window before the hour's out?"

"No."

"Then perhaps you'd be happy if I took you behind the hedge here and stood you against the wall?"

"No."

"No?" Collin swallowed hard, fighting the urge to shout at her.

"I want you to come back to England."

Growling, cursing, he threw his hands in the air, wondering how she always drove him to such frustration.

"Listen, Collin. I'm to go away next week. There's a

small house outside my brother's land. It's mine, passed to me by my mother. Meet me there."

He stared at her, dumbfounded. Her chest rose and fell in rapid rhythm, excitement or anger, he couldn't tell. "Meet you."

"Yes. Stay with me. A week. Two. Long enough to ease this need we've roused between us."

His mind raced, weaving disastrous outcomes with his memories of her naked thighs. *Stay with her.* God, it was a terrible idea and a grand one, and every reason he'd ever had for not making love to her still applied. He no longer cared. He wasn't a damned saint.

"Where is this house?"

Alex smiled, then grinned, then squealed like a child and jumped into his arms to rain kisses over his face.

"I haven't agreed yet," he protested futilely before opening his mouth and kissing her back as her tongue stroked his. His body hardened and pulsed, aware, despite his words, that there was no turning back from this. He would have her finally, or she would have him.

"Tonight," he whispered fiercely. "Here. Stay here in Edinburgh."

When she shook her head, Collin felt suddenly sure he'd burn to ash if he didn't bury himself inside her soon.

"No." She gasped the word as he set his teeth to her neck. "Oh, God. No, not here. I want to be alone with you. No neighbors, no servants, just you." A moan. "The cottage is perfect. In the forest. No one will know."

Anger slashed him, sudden and sharp. "You've done this before."

"No!" She drew away, stumbling a little. "Of course not. I've only been there once. With my family."

God, he wanted to believe her. Wanted to be an exception in her life, not just one more indiscretion along the way, but she was so alive in his arms, not a woman to live staid and quiet as a spinster. He wasn't her first, but would he be her third or fourth or fifth? It shouldn't matter.

"Never mind." Her words were low, almost lost in the rustle of wind-blown trees. "Never mind."

"No, Alex. No . . . I'm sorry. I shouldn't have said that."

"Well, you did. And why shouldn't you?"

"Forgive me. It was jealousy, nothing more. Not logic."

"Of course not." She shrugged, smiled, but her eyes shone too bright.

"That won't happen again, I swear. God knows I'm not a virgin either. Shall I tell you of my sins so you can use them against me in the future?" She laughed, happy again, and Collin's gut unwound.

"Maybe just one sin."

"A little one?"

She shook her head, resumed her stroll, skirts a swaying seduction.

"A big one, hmm?" He stepped to join her, boots crunching on the shell path, and sifted through his embarrassments. One in particular was excavated rather easily.

"Thought of something, have you?"

"I've never told anyone."

"Oh, perfect! A secret sin."

Grimacing, he tried to think how to phrase it, how to make it sound better. No luck. "My first time. She was a married woman."

"Why, Collin Blackburn, isn't adultery a mortal sin in the Catholic Church?"

He rolled his eyes at her mock distress. "I'm not Catholic."

"Oh."

"Still, it was wrong, and I was ashamed. After it was done, at any rate."

"I believe that's how it normally works."

"Mm. In my defense, I was very young and a little eager to discover the joys of women. She was happy to teach me."

"I'd imagine so. Well, I can assure you I've never sinned with a married woman."

Collin choked, shook his head. "No?"

"What? How could I even—? I mean, how could a

woman—?" She blushed fiercely, pink even in the moon-light. "Never mind. I don't want to know."

"Are you sure?" As her shock grew to mortification, Collin laughed aloud. "I'm teasing, Alex. You are scandalous enough without adding women to the plot."

"I didn't know they could be added," she muttered.

"They can't. Forget I mentioned it. Really."

"Hm."

"Have you been well?"

"I have. And you? Any word about St. Claire?"

"No. I'm not even sure he's still in France. He fled out a back window when we found his apartment."

"You went yourself?"

"Yes, for what good it did. The man's as slippery as an eel. I expect you'll never hear from him again. I'm sure he knows you turned the information over to me."

The path curved again, heading back to the well-lit patio. Collin watched her walk, memorized her neck, her bare arms, the tumble of wild hair.

"Is there some way I can help with your hair?"

"My hair?" Her fingers reached to inspect. "Oh." Her freckled nose wrinkled. "Oh."

"Beyond repair?"

"I think so."

"Shall I sneak you out the back then, and take you home?"

She sighed, huffed really. "I had hoped to dance with you."

Collin was shaking his head before she'd finished the sentence. "I don't dance." She opened her mouth to argue, but he rushed on. "I'm a bastard. I lived in a two room cottage until I was twelve. I don't dance. I don't know how."

"I could teach you."

"Perhaps you could, but not tonight."

"No, I suppose not . . . But you will let me teach you?" She'd brightened again, looking so young he felt perverted.

"We will negotiate the terms of my surrender at your cottage."

"Ooo, I like that. I shall have to draw up a list."

Her happy leer made him chuckle, then laugh aloud. There were so few people who made him laugh, but he couldn't avoid it with Alexandra. She threw off humor like sparks. Her eyes glittered and gleamed, pleased with his laugh. Finally giving himself over to the inevitable, Collin leaned down, aimed straight for her nose, and placed a chaste kiss on his very favorite freckle.

"Write a long list. If I'm going to hell, I want to be sure I earn my place."

"My philosophy exactly . . . in case you hadn't noticed."

His laugh boomed through the garden and echoed off the stone walls of the house.

Jeannie Kirkland had learned patience from her saint of a mother and it paid off in spades tonight. She waited and waited, not taking her eyes from the patio doors. Waited until she was sure he had snuck out the back gate. Finally, nearly an hour after he'd disappeared with Alexandra Huntington, Collin Blackburn slipped back into the ball.

He was a changed man, no longer radiating tension like a horse in a summer storm. No, now he looked tired and almost happy. Jeannie blinked. Surely he hadn't . . .

Oh, he was already edging toward the front door, that sneaky dog. She pushed away from the column she'd been supporting for the past hour and glided toward him. He didn't see her coming, didn't give a thought to her until she slid her arm through his and steered him toward the next set of doors. A hallway. Perfect.

He drew back when she released him, pulling in his chin to watch her with wary eyes. She took her time looking him over, noting every button undone and every hair out of place.

"Collin Blackburn, are those lilac petals in your hair?"

"What?" Both his hands flew up as if to cover the evidence.

"Been doing a bit of gardening this fine even'?"

"Now, Jeannie—"

"I am verra, verra surprised at ye, me fine lad." She

imitated the thick burr of her incorrigible grandmother, a woman who'd buried three husbands and claimed to have ridden them all to their deaths. "And ye, such an upstanding citizen, sae right in all ye do. Ach, 'tis a shock to me puir wee heart."

"Jeannie—"

"My God, Collin. Tell me everything. Who is she?"

"Who is she? She's *your* friend, isn't she?"

"Oh, give over. Is she still out there? I should tell you, Collin, that when you have an assignation with a lady in the garden, you are supposed to let her return first, then you follow a few minutes later. It's rude to leave her skulking about outside in the—"

"Your brother is right. You do read too much."

"'Your brother' he says, as if I didn't have eight. And never mind them. Where is she?"

"She's gone."

"Gone? Gone where?" Jeannie clapped a hand over her mouth in shock, then leaned up toward his blushing face. "Is she to meet you in your rooms then?"

"Jeannie Kirkland, you should be ashamed of yourself."

"Not as ashamed as you, I'd say. Your coat is all askew."

"What?" He drew back again, running hands over buttons and lapels. "What's wrong with it?"

"Well, it's misbuttoned for one. And it's dusted with flower petals just like your hair."

Grinning, she watched him refasten his coat and brush at it with violent strokes. When he'd finished, he glanced about the bright hallway before pulling her into the broad recess of a doorway. "You smell pretty," she crooned.

"You must not speak of this to anyone, Jeannie. She's a fine lady and I'll not have her name bandied about."

"Bah. Do you think me an idiot as well as a gossip?"

"No, I . . . No, of course not."

"I think she's very nice and I would love for a woman like her to live nearby. Do you know how long it's been since I've had a woman friend at hand?"

He stared blankly, reminding her of her brothers.

"A wife, Collin. It's plain you're in love with the girl. I've never seen you so bothered."

His blankness hardened quickly into outrage. "I am certainly not in love. She's a friend, is all."

"*I* am a friend, and I daresay you've never dragged me into a dark garden to make love. And you've certainly never worn diamonds for me." She poked a finger at his cravat.

"Listen to me," he whispered harshly, taking her wrist in a firm grip. "She is the sister of a duke. I did not make love to her in the garden and I am certainly not going to ask for her hand." He glared until she shrugged, then huffed, "A wife."

Jeannie tugged on her arm, stuck out her tongue when he released it. "Fine, deny it. And as long as you don't love her, I suppose it doesn't matter in the least."

"It does not."

"Perfect. May I have her direction?"

"What? Why?"

"I wish to write her."

His gray eyes bore into her, studying her wide-eyed gaze. "I think not."

"All right. I shall get it somewhere else then." Turning away to flounce off, she heard his deep, weary sigh and smiled.

"She's at Somerhart in Yorkshire. Please do not try to match-make."

"I wouldn't dream of it, *Lord Westmore*. Honest." Fingers crossed, she bounced back into the party with not an ounce of pity for her favorite neighbor.

Chapter 9

Four hours. Four hours more and she'd be at her cottage, and surely Collin would arrive soon after. Alex shifted on the seat, already crawling with restlessness after just the first hour in the carriage.

"I think I'll ride for a bit." She reached up to tap the roof.

Danielle waved sleepily. "Do not tire yourself out, *Mademoiselle*."

Alex let the driver hand her out and waited as he untied Brinn. As she mounted and settled into the saddle, her eyes swept the rolling countryside. This was so much better than sitting inside the shadowed carriage. She could distract herself out here, or at least feel the fresh air while she obsessed over Collin.

The carriage rolled on and, as Alex turned to follow, she spied movement at the crest of the hill they'd just descended. A rider, moving in their direction. Whoever he was, he was too far away to see, but the notion struck her that it could be Collin. Her heart quickened that he might be so near, but it was a ridiculous notion, surely. Just her overactive imagination. Alex forced her thoughts back to tonight and what they would do.

If he made it by tonight. She couldn't bear the thought of spending her first night in the cottage without him, but he was coming from far away, and there were so many ways to be delayed. Still, she had the hope that if she wished hard enough, the man would appear just when she wanted him to.

A half hour later they rounded a long curve, and Alex caught site of the lone rider through the trees. He seemed slightly closer, but she couldn't quite make him out past the leaves.

Perhaps it *was* Collin. It would be just like the man to arrive early and follow her carriage to be sure of her safety. She slowed her horse a little and let the carriage roll ahead. If it was him—*oh, let it be*—she planned to give him every opportunity to approach.

The distance between her and the carriage grew to forty feet, then eighty. Hoofbeats thumped faintly from behind and drew a smile to her lips even as she wondered if she looked road-worn and dusty.

She drew the cuff of her jacket over her brow, then rubbed it across her mouth before she glanced back . . . and caught the unexpected glint of sunshine off bright blond hair. *Not him*, her brain squeaked. *Not Collin.* Five hard heartbeats passed. She made herself look again.

The rider was close enough now that Alex could see the line of a hard-set, narrow jaw that shocked in its familiarity. By the time the man raised a hand in an elegant wave, Alex was sure who had followed her from Somerhart. Damien. Damien St. Claire. Here, in England.

Oh, God. She twisted in the saddle, taking in her surroundings as quickly as possible. Brinn danced sideways and snorted her displeasure, but Alex ignored it.

There was no one about. No one. Not even a rise of smoke in the distance. They were alone, she and her maid and the driver. Will carried a pistol, she knew that, but she also knew that Damien was desperate and on the run and probably armed to the teeth. And if Will drew him down . . . Well, Damien had already proved himself an accurate shot. Alex couldn't let that happen.

She pulled her mare to a stop. *I'm sure he knows*, Collin had said. Damien must know that she'd passed his location on to Collin. He must know and he must want his revenge. Alex took a deep breath and wheeled Brinn around to face him.

From twenty yards away, she watched his mouth spring from a snarl to a smile. His brown eyes stayed blank.

"Damien!" she called, because he would expect it. He barreled toward her and yanked his mount to a stop not a foot from Brinn's nose.

"My dear Lady Alexandra!" His words held more than a hint of ice, but Alex pretended not to notice.

"Damien, I can't believe it's really you! I thought my eyes had tricked me. Whatever are you doing here? Has everything . . . ?"

The carriage wheels quieted on the road ahead. She looked to see her driver standing atop his post. He nodded when she stretched up her hand, and Damien's smile was slightly more genuine when he met her eyes.

She tried her best to look relieved. "Has everything worked out then?"

"Everything?"

"You are home, Damien, so all must be well."

His eyes narrowed. He didn't bother to hide his suspicion. Anxiety inched through her nerves, but even over her fear she could still hear her mind marveling that she'd once found this man so attractive. His hair was far too light, his jaw too weak, shoulders too narrow. And there was not a glimmer of decency in his eyes.

"Your naiveté is refreshing," he finally answered. "But no, all is not well, my darling Alexandra."

"But you are here."

"Yes."

"Then . . . Then you are in danger!" He did not seem to mind her overacting. In fact, he puffed up as she gasped and pressed a hand to her mouth.

"I am. And you are my only hope of safety."

"Oh, Damien!"

"'Tis true. Have you ever made the acquaintance of a Collin Blackburn?"

"Collin . . ." Alex summoned up the last dregs of her acting skills. "I do not think so, though I daresay I've heard the name."

"Well, I am relieved you've never suffered his presence. The man is no more than a thug. But are you quite sure? He's a big Scottish brute, dark and rough-mannered."

"Do not tell me that such a man is after you?"

"He is."

"But that is terrible! You could be hurt."

Her gut churned, telling her she was overdoing it, but her nerves were stretched too tight to grant her subtlety. Still, Damien seemed to find it easy to believe her a simpleton. He nodded solemnly, cold eyes wide.

"I'm sure I could defend myself against a more honorable man, but this one . . . I fear that I will be murdered in my bed."

"Oh!"

"I need your help, Alexandra. *Darling*."

"Of course."

"I had always hoped . . ." He heaved a great sigh and shifted his eyes to the horizon. "I had always hoped that one day, this catastrophe would resolve itself, and I could make an offer for your hand. A decent, civilized offer."

When his narrowed eyes cut back to her, she gave the barest nod.

"I understand why you could not accept my recent proposal. Though I *was* heartbroken."

"I . . ."

"But I hope you will see fit to help me build a new life for myself. A good life. I plan to go to America, you see."

"America! That is so far."

"Yes. And I'm afraid I must prostrate myself before you again. I will repay you, of course, once I am settled."

Alex's mind raced and strained to find a solution. She could not turn around and go home. Hart would not return from London for another day; she'd made sure of that before she'd arranged her deception.

The local magistrate was a pleasant man, but surely no

match for Damien, and Alex was damned determined that she would not give the man money again. No, she wanted him caught, wanted to turn him over to Collin . . .

"I have twenty-five pounds in my luggage. Would that be enough?" she asked him, knowing it would not. Predictably, his face drew up in a snarl.

"Twenty-five pounds? That would not buy me a bunk in the hold."

"Oh, I . . . Of course. It is such a long journey, I can't imagine. But, you see, my brother . . ."

"Your brother?"

"He somehow found out that I'd sent you funds before. He has cut off my allowance."

"I see. Your brother has found you out. That makes sense, then. Where are you going?"

"Me? Oh, I am going shopping in Greendale. There is the most wonderful little millinery there, and Hart has already sent them a note to vouch for my credit. I shall—"

"You must go back home, and access your household accounts."

"Oh, but Hart has declared that he must approve everything! And he is not there. He's gone to London. I don't . . . maybe . . ."

"Yes?"

"No, that would take too long."

"What?" Damien pressed, eyes glinting like cut topaz.

"I could write him a note, send it as soon as I reach Greendale. He promised me a new phaeton, Damien, and two high-flyers! Can you imagine me racing down the drive of Somerhart? If I told him I'd found the perfect matched set of whites and the most wonderful little carriage . . . Do you think a thousand quid would be enough, Damien?"

Those eyes flashed. "I will pay you back."

"But then I shall have to give up my phaeton, I suppose."

"I'll make it up to you," he said flatly. "And I'm sure your dear brother will forgive you."

"Oh, I suppose. All right. Shall I meet you back here

then? On Saturday perhaps? It would take a few days to get his response, but I'd think that a week would—"

"Yes. Saturday. There is an inn about five miles ahead. I'll meet you in the orchards next to it."

Alex raised her eyebrows. "Must you stay hidden, Damien?"

"I must."

"Damien . . . I . . . Hart said the most awful thing about you. He said that you wanted John Tibbenham dead. That cannot be true, though. I told him it wasn't." Bile rose in her throat as she watched a glow of triumph light his face.

"Of course not, my dear. It was all a terrible misunderstanding. If I could take it back . . ."

"I know," she made herself say, and thought of how pleased she would be to offer him up to Collin on a platter. A week with Collin—what she'd wanted so much for so long—and then she could give Collin just what *he'd* been waiting for.

Alex sprang from the chair, padding quickly on bare feet to peer out the window. Again. She propped her arms on the sill and her chin on her wrists and breathed in the smell of old wood and vinegar, the scent she'd been breathing on and off for two hours.

He would come. He had to.

Swaying a little on the balls of her feet, swinging her hips in the air, she imagined herself a simple farm girl waiting for her strapping young beau. Her skirt brushed against bare legs, her hair hung unrestrained down her back, curling over the bright white cotton and lace of the dressing gown.

A simple farm girl. Well, she worked the stables sometimes, didn't she? And certainly crops were grown on her brother's land. And Collin was nothing if not strapping.

Pressing her cheek to the glass, she could just make out the dark wood of the stable. Hmm. If they were going to live out a fantasy, she would do her best to seduce Collin into taking her in there. In the closeness of the afternoon heat, on a bed of clean blankets and fresh hay, as dust motes danced over their heads. Every farm girl made love at least once in a barn, didn't she?

Her smile was a soft echo of the anticipation growing between her legs. She wanted him with such fierceness that she walked through her days with weak thighs and a hard ache deep in her belly. Her nervousness today only made her lust more keen.

She had no doubt he was regretting this agreement they'd come to, had no doubt he'd like to change his mind, but he wouldn't. He would not leave her sitting in this house like an undressed courtesan pining for her protector. At worst, he would arrive and try to talk her out of it. She had ways of dealing with such resistance. She had chased him, after all. If she had made a fool of herself, she would at least have his body as appeasement.

Someone rode into view. Alexandra froze, terrified that Damien had followed her here despite her cautiousness. But the horse drew closer, down the long lane that curved through the trees, and she saw the rider's face.

Oh, here was reality. Collin scowled, thoughtful and tense, and Alex smiled. Yes, he thought this a very poor plan indeed. Too bad for him.

Humming a little through her wide grin, she danced to the door, counted to twenty and stepped into the sunshine to corner her prey.

Collin slanted an annoyed glance at the small stable, wondering if it were clean. The cottage itself looked sturdy enough, well tended, even welcoming. He should turn around and ride away before he complicated both their lives. He dismounted instead.

The small blue door opened just as he gathered the reins to lead his mount to the stable. Collin's lungs seized for a long second, and before he could manage to take her in—or draw another breath—she skipped out the door to run to him.

Catching her midair, he swung her around and away from the shying horse, assuring himself that the thrill crashing over his body was fear for her safety.

"Welcome to our rendezvous," she cried, arching her whole body back, counting on Collin to hold her secure. She grinned up at him with flashing eyes, and he couldn't stop his answering smile.

"Rendezvous, eh? Have I stepped into the middle of an outdoor drama then?"

"Yes," she responded with a lift of her chin. "It's called *Hell in a Handcart*. I hope you enjoy it."

Throwing back his head, Collin laughed and let his trepidation slide away. His heart lightened, broke free of its doubts and denials, and he pulled her up, curved her into him and held her an inch away from his mouth. She closed her eyes and waited.

"I can't kiss you yet, or Samson will likely spend a week here in the yard."

She nodded, eyes still closed, just-parted lips curved in a small smile. Collin groaned and set her a safe distance away.

"Come. Tell me about this love nest while I tend the horses."

"Brinn has already been seen to," she said breezily as she swung along beside him, hand curled in his.

"You brought a groom?"

"I did not!"

Her bare toes peeked beneath her skirt as she walked, catching his eye.

"Really, Collin, do you think yourself the only person who can care for a horse?"

He arched a doubtful glance at her and shook his head. "You groom your own horse?"

"Well, not every day. But I am in the stables constantly and I'm not a raging idiot."

"Perhaps not." He dodged a small, well-aimed foot.

"Come now. What other noblewoman do you know who can do that? My surprise is warranted."

She sniffed, but she wasn't truly offended. He could see not a smidgen of tension in that jaw. And he'd seen it hard as steel often enough.

"Catherine the Great."

"What?"

"Catherine the Great. A noblewoman who personally cared for her horses."

Collin stopped at the stable door to gape at her. She couldn't possibly mean . . . Then she tilted her face up and smiled with a boldness that left no question.

"She was quite the horsewoman, I understand." She slipped into the dim of the stable, leaving him shaking his head that he'd even doubted what she meant.

"I'm beginning to think you a fraud. A tavern wench masquerading as a duke's sister."

"Not a tavern wench," she called, stroking her mare's flank. "A saucy farmer's daughter."

Collin snorted and led his horse to the far stall. He'd ridden a sturdy gelding this time, knowing Thor wouldn't stand a week in a small stable with such a lovely mare as Brinn. He saw to Samson's brushing and feeding, hiding the looks he sent toward Brinn, not wanting to reveal he was checking Alex's work. She'd done a fine job.

Alex lounged against the rough wood wall, watching his hands and explaining the arrangements she'd made.

"So you'll cook for us?"

"Oho, aren't you a funny one? The woman I hired to clean in the mornings will also prepare a full day's worth of food before she leaves. She promised to be gone by nine every day, so we shan't even see her."

"You have a devious mind, young woman."

She shrugged, eyes sparkling with self-satisfaction. "I trained in London."

"Well, hopefully there are still some Scottish skills I can pass on." He watched as she wiggled a little under his gaze.

"My governess was adamant that there is always room to further one's education."

Samson turned to nudge Collin away from the spot he'd been brushing for nigh on two minutes. With a sigh, he set his mind to the task at hand. His chores would be complete within a quarter hour, and they had the whole of a week before them. He tried not to look at her again. Tried and failed.

When he'd finally toted the last bucket of water from the spring, he found he'd misplaced one rosy-cheeked woman. He discovered her inside the house, frowning in puzzlement at a large plate of red mush on the kitchen table.

"Making my dinner, dearest?"

Alexandra jumped and looked toward him with alarmed eyes. "She said to leave the pie in the window to cool."

"Well, it looks cool." Collin squinted toward the shadowed sill of the kitchen window. Red tracks wove over the wood in a serpentine pattern. "Cool enough for a crow anyway."

She stared down at the cherry mess of ruined pie and blinked. "What a terrible kitchen maid I'd make."

"Well, I've worked as a kitchen maid and I'll be happy to serve you."

"Really?" She blinked her shock away and looked him over with a crooked smile. "It must take yards of wool to make a dress your size."

"As luck would have it, my mother did not require me to dress the part."

Her giggle was a little high-pitched. Collin hadn't realized she was nervous, and perhaps she hadn't been earlier, but now he saw that her hands plucked at her skirt as she looked over the room, that her teeth worried the full curve of her bottom lip. It was easy to forget, especially in this circumstance, that the girl was only nineteen . . . no, twenty now. Twenty and usually so very sure of herself.

He stepped close to press a kiss to her nose. "I'll light the lamps. It'll be dark soon."

She avoided his eyes, let her gaze touch everything in the kitchen but him. "I should set the table. Get you some dinner."

"I'm not hungry."

"No?" Her gaze finally settled on his boots. "Thirsty then?"

"Aye," he conceded, tilting up her chin with one callused finger. "I could do with a touch of wine." She brightened with relief and moved quickly to the table, so urgent that her hair trailed out on a breeze behind her.

The cottage was simple and small, and he took in the whole of the first floor with a sweeping glance. Stairs at the back of the kitchen led up to what must be the bedroom. Everything was neat and clean, stone and wood and fine rugs to protect against the hard oak floor.

He wondered who had lived here before. Perhaps no one, perhaps it had always been a trysting place, a hideaway. It was certainly secluded enough. The dimming light of the sun filtered though a canopy of leaves, casting dusk an hour early. Collin moved to light the lamps.

He laid out a small fire for good measure and was trying to decide whether to light it when her shadow fell over his shoulder. Turning from the hearth, he found Alexandra standing a few feet away with a tremulous smile and two glasses of deep red wine.

His mouth watered.

"The wine." Her voice was soft, a little husky, almost a question.

"Yes," he answered, eyes on her mouth. She licked her lips, a gesture he recognized now . . . and appreciated. Smiling, he took the glass she offered and delighted in the blush that stained her cheeks. She didn't seem to know what to do with him now that she had him in her clutches, and Collin was relieved to finally be the seducer.

Sipping his wine, he watched her gulp hers before she turned and retreated to the kitchen to refill her glass. When she wandered back, she did not walk to him, but stopped to stare nonchalantly out the window at the dimness of leaves and shadow.

A wave of heat prickled his nerves and stiffened his cock, an anticipation like the scent of prey. The lust had always been there, always at the surface, but now it was tinged with the chase, the challenge of arousing her beyond her hesitation. He moved toward her with narrow-eyed focus, leaving his wine glass on the table as he passed.

The line of her shoulders was hard beneath the cotton of her gown. She heard him approach, perhaps even saw him reflected in the window, but she pretended not to notice, frozen like a rabbit in the hunt. His smile widened.

Chest no more than a hand's-breadth from the curve of her back, he stopped and breathed in the sweet, flowered smell of her hair. His shaft swelled.

A gasp flew from her throat when his hand touched her hair to sweep it away from her neck. She hissed out a breath when he leaned close enough to kiss her. He didn't though. He only inhaled, savoring the scent that had haunted his nights for months, wanting more of it, the smell of her skin and her arousal, the smell of sex.

She stood still beneath him, holding her breath, waiting. Collin closed his eyes, put his mouth to her neck just as he spread his fingers wide over the curve of her waist.

He wished that he was a beast then, when she shook and gasped. Wished he had sharp teeth to sink into her flesh, that he could press her against the wall and plunge into her from behind like a dog, like an animal.

She thought him so controlled, when he was everything but controlled with her. He wanted to punish her for that, to hurt her the way it hurt him to be near her, but not now. Not like this. Still . . . He was wild and the most he could offer her was pleasure in that wildness.

Stepping away from her, he wrenched off his dusty coat. She turned to watch, no longer blushing, but flushed with desire. She shone with it, eyes glinting in the lamplight.

"I canna promise you finesse this time, Alex."

She shook her head. "No."

"Tomorrow, perhaps."

Her mouth softened a little, smiled, but her eyes

dropped to his chest as he reached for the buttons of his shirt. Her lips parted as she watched his movements, avid and heavy-eyed. When Collin jerked the shirt from his breeches, she stepped forward to push the linen up.

His muscles jumped and strained at the sweep of her fingers. She pressed both hands to his ribs, slid them over his chest and up to slip the shirt from his body. Collin threw his head back, overwhelmed by her roaming touch and the fascination on her beautiful face. That she could look upon him with such fervor . . .

"You can't know how much I've wanted to do this, Collin. Since that day in the stables . . . I've spent hours dreaming of your body. Days."

He felt her palms surveying him, lingering over his nipples, the hair that curled in the middle of his chest.

A growl of need flooded his throat, and he laid his hands over hers to still them. "You will unman me before we even start." When he opened his eyes again, she grinned up at him with delight. So much for the hunter being the hunted.

Collin smiled at the thought, chuckled.

"What?"

"Nothing. I overreached myself is all."

She blinked in puzzlement, but her smile never faltered, even as she backed away and began to unfasten her simple dress. Collin's laugh regressed to a growl.

The tiny ribbons of her bodice opened beneath her fingers at a maddeningly slow rate. Dozens of them trailed down the cotton, a line of restraint that ended below her waist, and his fingers itched to help. By the time she had reached the bows at the middle of her belly, Collin realized she wore nothing beneath and lost his fight for patience. She gasped when he reached for the collar and spread it wide, sliding it down over her arms till she was naked to the waist. She did not try to stop him.

"Jesus God," he whispered and kissed her finally, drank in her taste of wine and heat, and nearly spent himself at the warm press of her breasts against his body. A groan fell from her throat and Collin's hands shook as he buried them in her loose hair.

"God," he whispered again, pulling away from her mouth and dropping to his knees before her. Her small, high breasts rose and fell just above his eyes, lifted by her panting chest.

Reverent, fierce, he gazed up at her, almost afraid to touch that soft curve of flesh, afraid to give himself over to her power. She watched him, waiting as he set his hands at her waist and pushed the dress down, letting it fall away from her.

The fabric slithered into a pile and left silence in its wake. He couldn't breathe, couldn't speak. Alexandra stood before him, naked and glorious and unashamed, and Collin's heart twisted with a pop of pain.

"Alex," he moaned, hands smoothing a line from her hips to her waist, to the hard curve of her ribs. "How can you be so beautiful?"

He pressed his face to her belly, to the twitch of strong muscle and satin skin. He dragged his lips over the texture of silk and the scent of woman. Bit lightly at the first rib he found so that her legs gave out and he had to hold her, so that her body fell far enough that the pearl pink tip of one nipple slid right into his mouth.

She arched into him with a cry and a plea. He sucked and she wept. Nipped and she screamed. Then she wrapped herself around him, trapped him within the circle of her legs and pressed her wet heat against his belly.

They both panted, both pressed hard into the other as he fell back on his haunches and slid her onto his lap.

Her mouth fell upon his, and he thrust into her with his tongue as he longed to do with his cock, slipped his hands down to clutch the round firmness of her buttocks, and cursed the painful confinement of his breeches. His hands refused to relinquish their prize long enough to set her aside and tear them off, but he was going to explode before he ever got inside her if he didn't hurry. He'd been waiting so damn long.

Alex rocked against him, sucking his tongue, and Collin

forgot his breeches and slipped one hand further down, along the seam of her body and into her slick core.

Rearing up, she cried out as his fingertips pressed in, screamed when he slid them further along to the hard nub of her pleasure. She was already peaking, he realized in shock, even as he circled her again, even as he pushed a finger deep inside her. Her body squeezed him, tight and so soft he wanted to weep in desperation, wanted to cry out with her as she pushed and rocked against his hand.

Waiting till the last spasm shook her, Collin laid her back against the burgundy rug and tore at the buttons of his riding breeches. His eyes took in her panting mouth, her tight nipples, before they settled on her center, pink and wet and spread before him.

"I willna last long, *mo caitein*. No longer than you. I'm sorry." She trembled a little as he finally slipped free of his damned clothes.

Her hand rose, and Collin tried to stop her, tried to stay her movement, but her fingers brushed his erection before he could manage a word. Looking down, unable to help himself, he saw her small hand, her delicate fingers trying to wrap around him, to grasp him. The sight of that hand, nearly too small to circle the whole of his shaft, sent him over the edge. He pulled out of her reach, braced his knees against the ground, and slid the tip of himself inside her.

His body was already straining, already drawing itself up to explode, and he knew he could not hesitate or it would be over before it began.

"I'm sorry," he growled again and thrust deep and hard, sinking himself to the hilt.

His release was upon him even as she screamed, even as he felt the sudden resistance that was even more suddenly gone, even as he realized with a horrible shock that something was very wrong.

His muscles clenched. His seed spilled into her, and her small white hands pushed at his shoulders, trying to free her body from his.

Chapter 10

The room began to right itself, slowly inching back into place. Collin reared back, still tight inside her, and stared into her wide eyes. He felt the beginnings of a thought, felt his brain begin to ease back to reality, and tried to deny what it was telling him.

Absolutely not. He had not taken her maidenhead.

But she was shaking beneath him, trembling, her face tight and pale. "Please," she bleated, hands pressed into her own stomach.

He withdrew with a grimace and stared in disbelief at the bright smear of blood on his flesh. Blinking hard, he shook his head, rose to his feet. His mind stirred anew as he padded into the kitchen and wet a cloth with cold water. He delivered it to Alexandra, tossed her his shirt to cover herself, and turned to find his breeches.

"I'm sorry," she said from behind him.

"Sorry." He fastened his buttons with numb fingers. "Yes."

He swung about to find her still huddled on the floor, his shirt clutched tight to her body. Her chin inched up, and he was shocked by the urge to slap her. "That's it?"

"What?"

"Is that the whole of your apology?"

"I . . ." She swallowed, glanced around at her scattered clothing. "I would like to explain."

"Oh, *explain*! Explain what? That you are a liar and a cheat? That you tricked me into coming here? Explain that I will have to do the honorable thing and marry you because I'm now covered in your virgin's blood? Good God, is there someone hiding in the broom closet, waiting to give witness?"

Her jaw tightened, flexed to rock. "Don't be ridiculous."

Collin choked, coughing on his rage. "What the hell have you done, Alexandra?"

Her eyes jerked around the room again. "Could you please turn around so I can dress?"

"Turn around?" Collin could hear himself shouting and cared not a whit. "Turn around? For God's sake, woman, I just plowed through ye!"

She drew herself up straight, red spots of rage bright on her pale cheeks. "Fine." Standing, she crumpled his shirt and threw it at his face. Collin glimpsed a pink drop of fluid snaking down her thigh before he turned his back to her.

Rustling cloth and soft curses reached his ears as she dressed. Collin's heart began to stutter with panic as the reality of the situation sunk in. She would be his wife now. His wife.

Jeannie Kirkland would be pleased, at least.

"I didn't come here to trick you into marriage," Alex spit at his back when she finally felt covered enough. The words spun him around.

"Well, it's too late to cry off now."

"No, Collin, listen. I don't want to marry you, I just—"

He cut her off with a snort, spreading his hands wide. "It's too late."

Alex resisted the urge to press her hands to the ache between her legs.

"You are despicable. To trap me into a marriage that I never once encouraged. Jesus, you're English. An English princess. What the hell am I supposed to do with you at a horse farm? *God damn it!*" A small stool flew across the floor, propelled by his bare foot.

She gasped, struck by hurt and sudden alarm. She had known he wouldn't be happy, but she hadn't thought he'd be quite so *mad*. What did it matter anyway, if he was the first or the tenth?

"You were a virgin. You could have married anyone. Why do this to me?"

She blinked back tears and the urge to hit him. "Don't be stupid," she yelled instead of slapping. "Why would I want to marry you?" He didn't even look her way, simply kept pacing and panting, enraged because he might have to suffer her presence for the rest of his life.

"I am the daughter of a duke. I am rich, richer than you'll ever be, Collin Blackburn. What the hell makes you think I would deign to marry a Scots bastard who breeds horses for money?" That got his attention, froze him in his tracks. "I wasn't looking for marriage, you idiot. I was looking to get 'plowed' as you so eloquently put it. Really, what's the point of being a whore if you can't enjoy yourself once in a while?"

"'*Enjoy yourself.*'"

The rush of her anger drained away at the hatred in his eyes. When he took a step, she backed away.

"Ye wee selfish *bitch*. You've been handed everything your whole life. Everything and still it wasn't enough. You had to ruin your brother's life and your own. My brother too. And now me.

"I was one of those shiny things you wanted, eh? Another toy to entertain you? Well, you've had me. Was it as good as you expected, spreading your legs for a low-born Scot?"

Her chin shook, giving her away. She clenched her teeth and glared. "No," she answered, very clearly. "No, it wasn't nearly as good as I'd hoped."

She had thought him angry enough, but her reckless, spiteful words goaded him into fury. The skin of his face tightened and paled, and his silver eyes glittered. She took another step back, actually flinched when he raised his arm. She stared at his large hand, waiting for it to strike her, but he only ran it through his hair, gaping in disgust at her fear.

"Do you think me an animal, Alex? Is that why you wanted me? The danger of a man who might strike you when you need it?"

"No, I . . ." Her throat closed up with tears that she refused to let out. "I just wanted to be with you."

"You knew I would not want this. You knew I would never have done this if I'd known."

"I did," she answered with false bravado. "But I never lied to you. You just assumed."

Collin shook his head and the sadness on his face thickened the tears in her throat. "I did assume. You're right. And you will marry me now, whether you will it or no."

"I won't."

"I'll go to your brother and tell him what's happened."

"No. I'll deny it . . . that I was a virgin. I'll tell him you're after my fortune."

He drew back, taking her in with cold eyes this time, eyes that measured her and found her less than he'd expected. "You'd truly do that?"

"I would."

His face turned from her. He looked out the window, at nothing, at darkness. She watched the anger drain from him, watched his shoulders slump.

"I tried hard not to dishonor you when I thought you a harlot. To be the one to make you into that . . ." The sound of his choking laugh made her ache. "You knew it would hurt me."

"I'm sorry," she whispered, as one tear finally escaped her control. "I'm sorry. I wanted you, you're right. But it's not fair. If I were a man—"

"But you're not a man. You're a woman—a girl, it seems."

"I don't want to marry," she cried out, frustrated and

hurt. "You or anyone else. My life is more now than it ever was. I am free to do as I please."

"Don't be childish," he spat. "You are not free. Where are all your friends? Where are your loyal suitors? You are free to dress as a boy and roust about with laborers, but what of a husband? What of children?"

"I don't want—"

"And your brother will marry one day, have a wife and a family. Will she be happy to have you hanging about, running her estate, crowding her responsibilities?"

Alex sneered at him, outraged that he would try to take apart her life. "My brother would never marry a woman who did not welcome me."

"I'm glad you don't mind so limiting his choice of mate."

When she raised a hand to push a stray curl off her forehead, she was frightened to see how badly it shook. Collin didn't notice. He was staring at the floor now, hard, as if it had gotten him into this mess. His breath jumped out in a great huff and he glanced at her, then away as he moved to grab his boots.

"I need to think."

Staring at him, afraid to speak, she wondered if he was leaving, if he would just resaddle his horse and ride away. As she watched, he tucked in his shirt, fastened his buttons, pulled on his boots and coat. He did not once look at her, did not say a word before he turned and walked out the door, shutting it with a quiet thump.

Alex let her weak knees give and sat down hard on the floor, on the exact spot where she'd just been deflowered. He was so angry. She hadn't thought he'd be so angry.

Weren't men supposed to be honored by being the first? Surely he was just the tiniest bit thrilled.

"Blast!" She fell back onto the rug with a moan. "Stupid, stupid!" This was not going as planned. She'd finally managed to get rid of this damned burden of a maidenhead and now she sat alone on the floor, bleeding and sore and teary-eyed. Worst of all, she felt guilty.

He hated her now. She had led him astray, tempted him

into ignoring his morals. She should have known better. Anyone who'd ever heard the story of Adam and Eve should have known better. The woman is always to blame for sin.

Still, she couldn't pout herself into believing him unreasonable. She had misled him, knowing exactly how he'd feel if he knew the truth, knowing he'd be shamed. And it hadn't even been worth it. After that first experience with him months ago, she'd been so impatient to complete the act, had been so sure after that prelude that the finale would be so much *more*.

She'd even been hopeful he wouldn't notice, had begun to wonder if she was still a virgin after all the fumbling with Damien. And Danielle had assured her that virginity could be faked, so she'd thought it must be a subtle thing, like the difference between one vintage wine and the next.

It had not been subtle at all. She'd felt like a fish squirming on a spear and was surprised there wasn't a pool of blood widening beneath her.

Curious, she eased the wet cloth under her skirt and pressed it between her legs. The cold was shocking and heavenly. When she drew it away, only a few spots of blood stained the white. Utterly undramatic.

Well, she knew now. And all those whispers of a woman's burden and wifely duties were apparently true. The act itself must be strictly for the man's satisfaction. But the *before*. That was something. Perhaps even worth the after. Certainly no woman would do it otherwise.

Sighing, Alex pushed herself up to her knees and stood with slow care. She'd assumed he would offer marriage if he discovered the truth, but she had planned to explain reasonably, gently, that she had no wish to marry. She hadn't expected that he would be so opposed to marrying her. Selfish English bitch, indeed. She was no more selfish than he. He had not saved himself for marriage, had he?

Wondering if he'd abandoned her, she tiptoed to the front door and opened it a crack. Nothing. She stuck her head out in the green-scented air. It was true dark now, and quiet. She waited for her eyes to adjust, hoping Collin wasn't standing a few feet away watching her gawk about like a startled cow. She found the yard empty and peered toward the stable. No light, no sound but the soft snort of a sleepy horse.

Muttering a curse, she crept off the step and snuck across the leaf-strewn grass toward the darker square of the open stable door. A prayer tumbled silently from her lips as she drew closer. If Collin was inside, what would she say? *Oh, hello. You're still here. Just checking.* And if he wanted to yell at her for a few more minutes . . . Wouldn't that be fun?

But he wasn't inside, unless he crouched in one of the black corners. No, he wasn't there, but his horse was. He hadn't abandoned her.

Tears filled her eyes and spilled over to leave hot trails across her cheeks. Alex swiped them away with a hard flick of her hand and sniffed loudly, startling Collin's horse into a nicker.

"Sorry," she whispered and hurried out, across the cool grass and back to the warm glow of the house.

Where in the world was he? The closest village was a mile away and it had been almost dark when he'd left. He'd grown up in the country though, free to roam and explore, day or night. Perhaps it was nothing to him to wander on strange roads after dark.

Alex shivered at the thought and closed the door, briefly considered latching it and chose not to. She thought about dinner also, but her stomach roiled with something more sinister than hunger. No dinner then, just bed. And she was tired enough to sleep despite the horrible turn of the day. After extinguishing most of the lamps, she took a candle up the stairs, cringing only occasionally at her soreness.

I should be glad he wants nothing to do with me, she told herself. Better than being impaled again, certainly. Though, God, she would miss the rest of it. And she'd had no time to explore his body. The sad thought made her sigh.

She undressed more slowly and with less climactic results than earlier in the evening. Instead of pressing herself into the warmth of a naked man, she sponged herself off with tepid water and slipped on a linen shift. The bed was cold and unfamiliar and she lay in it alone, alternating between self-pity and worry for Collin. The moon rose bright in the window just before her eyes closed, and she fell asleep to dream of dark hands running over her skin and the pleasure of a hard kiss.

A groan woke him to a dazzling agony of sunlight. Raising his head, Collin rubbed his palms over a scratchy jaw and heard the groan again. His own. Too many pints of ale last night and not a drop of whisky to be found. The memory reminded him of where he was, what had happened the night before, and he let his head fall back with a thump.

"I've straightened the bedroom, sir. I'd like to start on the kitchen, if you don't mind."

Collin opened one eye against his better judgment, closed it. He didn't have to look to know it wasn't Alex. Aside from the fact she'd never uttered a phrase like that in her life, this woman's voice was noticeably deeper than hers.

"Cup of tea, sir?"

"No," he rasped, then "yes."

The invisible woman snorted and approached in a quick whoosh of skirts, her shadow relieving his eyelids from the merciless light.

"Thank you."

She sniffed. "There's a spring out past the stable if you'd care to clean up."

Collin opened both his eyes, taking in the dark shape of the woman standing over him. She retreated a little when he took the cup of tea and he could make out her blond hair and long face. Younger than he'd expected. Thirty at most. She slanted him a wary frown and moved away, glancing back at him only once.

"Thank you," he called again as she began to bang around in the other room. He swung his legs onto the floor and grimaced at the mud that spattered his clothes. He hoped it was mud, anyway.

The tea nearly scalded his tongue, but he drank it as quickly as possible. The promise of a dip in a cold pond prodded him to hurry. The water would hopefully ease his aching back and clear the ale fog from his head, and he didn't particularly care to argue with Alexandra reeking of sweat and mud and maybe worse.

"There's towels and such upstairs," the woman said when he brought the cup to the kitchen to set it on the oak table.

"Oh?" He threw a glance at the stairs, not even considering going up them.

"She's not here."

"Hm?"

"The lady's not here."

He watched her brow lower in concern, realized the coolness seeping down his cheeks was the feeling of blood draining from his face. She had gone. Grown angry and disappeared with the same wretched suddenness with which she'd appeared in his life.

"When did she leave?"

"Sunrise, same as when I got here. She needed help dressing. But she's not gone, you understand. Only went for a ride."

"A ride." He looked to the closed door as if it could confirm this. "You're sure?"

"Oh, yes." She smiled then, wide enough to reveal a gap where she'd lost a back tooth. Her brown eyes twinkled. "Had a bit of a row, did you?"

"A bit, yes."

With a chuckle, she turned back to the pot of water where she rinsed a wineglass before looking about the kitchen for more dishes. Her gaze fell on the ruined pie. "There are plates and knives in the cupboard, you know."

"Plates?" Collin stared at the pie with her, mind still reeling with the shock of thinking Alex had run off. "Oh. A crow got to it before we could."

"Hm. I thought perhaps she'd smashed your face in it."

He narrowed his eyes at her, a look that had terrified many a stable boy, but she only snorted again and went back to her chores, humming some jaunty tune as she moved about the room.

Collin spun on his heel and headed for the stairs. There were two rooms above, he found—one small room tucked in beneath the eaves at the end of the hallway. The door to the larger room stood open also, revealing a massive four-post bed and a bright yellow bedspread, mottled by the leafy light pouring through the window.

Spotting a wardrobe, Collin strode in and threw open the doors, searching for towels and soap. Instead, he found thin shifts and vividly colored dresses. He closed it with a snap. The dresser then.

The first drawer was empty. The second yielded a tangle of white lace and silk that startled him even more than her dresses had. He slammed it shut with a force that rattled the doors of the wardrobe.

Vowing to retreat without the towels if he encountered her stockings, he jerked open the bottom drawer.

"Finally." Linen sheets and soap in hand, he rushed out the door and back down the stairs.

"Have a good swim," a voice called.

"Thank you, um . . ." Collin turned to look at her, the edge of the front door gripped in his hand.

"Betsy."

"Betsy. My thanks."

Chapter 11

Collin trudged back up to the cottage with a scowl, wishing he were anywhere else. He was clean and clear-headed, but he still did not want to talk to Alexandra, didn't know what he would say to her. Anger prickled his nerves, though he felt more angry at himself than he had the night before. He'd known better than to come here. He'd known the first time he met the woman that she would cause him immeasurable amounts of trouble. Then he'd walked right into it with a smile. And a cockstand.

He tossed his bab back into the stable where he'd left it last night, relieved to see her horsestill gone. She'd be home soon though, and likely as hungry as he. May as well set out breakfast. They couldn't speak if they were chewing.

The counter was clean again, the offending pie removed and replaced with meat pasties and fruit. Collin laid out plates and added a jug of fresh milk he found in a cold box. He sliced bread and cheese, put out the platter of meat pies and the bowl of cherries. When the work-smoothed table overflowed with food, Collin hovered over it, uncertain what to do with himself, refusing to pace to the window and watch for her. He strained his ears though, until the silence of the house roared. Just as he cursed, as he took a step toward the window, a horse whinnied. Not Samson.

The door cracked open and there she stood, a shadow

against the light. Seconds passed and Collin's heart raced, anger and anxiety fighting to rule him. When he couldn't take the silence any longer, he gestured with a jerk toward the table. "Are you hungry?"

She didn't move, didn't answer, and Collin felt nervousness join the mix of bad humor in his blood.

"Alex?"

"Yes," she finally said. "I am hungry."

Moving inside with rough speed, she went straight to the table, sat in the closest chair. When he joined her, she blinked in surprise.

"This is lovely. Thank you."

The first thing he noticed was her riding habit—the same one she'd worn at her cousin's. Had she brought it to remind him of that day? Thinking how close she'd come to losing her virginity in a seaside meadow to a virtual stranger, Collin scowled. Alex didn't notice, she stared hard at the jug of milk as she ate.

Her face was pale, the freckles on her nose stark against unnaturally white skin. Dark circles of exhaustion bruised the delicate flesh beneath her eyes. Collin swallowed his curse.

He hadn't given her feelings much thought the night before. He'd been wounded and raging and had needed to be away from her. But now, looking at her, he was suddenly reminded that she had lain with a man for the first time and then spent the night absolutely alone.

And she was young. Younger than he'd realized.

"Alex." She jumped at his voice. "I'm sorry for leaving. I needed to be alone."

"Of course. I must apologize too. I did deceive you and I'm sorry for it." Her eyes never left the piece of buttered bread she held.

"Sorry you deceived me, but not sorry you arranged this?" Collin watched her jaw edge out, watched her pink mouth tighten.

"No," she answered, meeting his eyes at last. "No,

I'm not sorry about that. Were you sorry when you lost your virginity?"

"Alexandra . . ."

She raised her arching brows high, waiting in vicious anticipation for whatever he had to offer. Collin retreated, shaking his head.

"I truly don't want to marry, Collin. It has nothing to do with you. I knew my whole life that my future lay in marriage, as every woman does, but I never thought about it, never dreamed of who my husband would be. And my Season . . ." She shrugged, a weary movement. "I just wanted to live. It felt like a short reprieve before execution. I wanted to experience everything—drink and cigars, Covent Gardens and gambling, illicit love."

Collin cringed, and she smiled in real amusement before her face sobered again. "When I was caught, I had to wonder if that was the outcome I'd hoped for."

"But don't you want children? A home?"

"Don't you?"

"I—" He choked in surprise. "I . . . Of course. Someday."

"Exactly. Perhaps someday I will too. I'm not nearly as old as you, you know."

With a roll of his eyes, he leaned back in his chair, stretched his legs out in front of him. "Are you trying to tell me you're no different than I?"

"Do you think you could bear to marry a woman who expected you to do nothing more than ride and shop and visit with friends?"

"Of course not."

"Of course not. I am never happier than when I am helping run my brother's estate. How can I go from that to wife?"

"You would have a household to run."

She speared him with a look of disgust. "I can plan a dinner for thirty in my sleep. It's not so difficult."

Collin rubbed a hard hand over his face.

"I have the life I want, for now at any rate. But it is lonely sometimes. That is where you came in."

"Like a rabbit into a wolf's den."

She snorted and the sound brought a smile to his lips. Her eyes brightened, and his anger dissolved like mist before the sun, proving just how stupid he was for this woman.

"You should not have misled me." Even he recognized it for a pitiful reproach.

"I know and I understand that you'll leave now. I will not hold it against you."

"I should leave. And so should you. But I don't necessarily want to."

Her eyes blinked at him. Twice. Then she stared. Collin pulled his feet under him and stood, held out his hand to her. "Why don't we go for a walk? I noticed a trail through the woods."

"Oh. Yes, all right." With a small shake of her head, she stood also, eyes wide. "I'd like to change first, if you don't mind waiting."

"Not at all."

She flashed a nervous smile and darted from the room and up the stairs.

Frowning, Collin stared at the ceiling, listening to the click of her boots above him and wondering what the hell he was doing.

He might stay?

Alex stripped off her clothes and threw them on the floor before remembering she had to keep them clean and unwrinkled herself. She'd brought only a satchel, after all. So she picked up the riding habit, brushed it with a hasty slap, and hung it carefully in the wardrobe before stepping back to stare at the other choices. Three simple dresses she could wear over her loosened corset. A light wrap. She hadn't thought she'd have much use for any of them. Shrugging, Alex pulled out the lilac dress, dug a shift from a drawer, and began to dress, trying not to imagine what Collin was planning.

He might stay. Apprehension and excitement fizzed in

her chest. She hadn't thought of him staying and now she wondered if she even wanted him to. How could she possibly tell him she had no wish to . . . to . . . take him inside her again?

A sigh of frustration escaped her mouth. What a mess she'd made of this. Perhaps he'd been right after all. Perhaps she wasn't the type of woman who could carry on a casual affair. Still, she felt like that kind of woman.

A quick glance at her reflection made her cringe. She didn't look like a mistress, she looked tired and pale, and the knot she'd pulled her hair into didn't help. She jerked out the pins and did her best to smooth out the tangled curls, then lifted her skirt to her ankles to frown at her boots. They weren't made for walking, but neither were the one pair of silk slippers she'd shoved into her bag. Her rump hit the floor with a smack, and she tugged off the black riding boots. Barefoot again. That seemed best. But she'd have to ask Collin to fasten the back of her dress.

Torn between stalling and hurrying, she finally stood and left the room. Below, she found Collin already outside, his brown hair glinting copper in the sun.

Her chest tightened at the sight of him, so straight and stern. She felt like weeping, though she didn't know why . . . relief that he was no longer so angry with her maybe. Or something more?

Curls flying with a quick shake of her head, Alexandra straightened her spine and pushed away the thought of loving him. He'd made it clear how he felt about her—liked her well enough, she supposed, but not so well as to trust her. And the chance of the man ever declaring undying love to anyone brought a smile to her lips. Her staid, serious Scotsman. Far too in control to love beyond reason. Fine, then. She would not love him either. And she certainly wouldn't try mating with him again.

They strolled along the path, heading toward the green archway of trees past the stable. She was conscious of the foot of space between them, conscious that they should have been holding hands or walking so close as to brush the other's clothing. Instead, they went awkward and uneasy, silence a boulder between them.

She vowed she would not start the conversation, regardless that the quiet made her itch. What could she say? *Please stay. Stay and make love to me, but keep that thing to yourself, if you don't mind.* No, that would probably be the beginning of a bad end between them. My God, who would've thought she'd be half-hoping for him to leave on their second day together?

"I should leave," he said suddenly, with such darkness she thought he must be talking to himself. "I should leave," he repeated, looking to her this time. "But I do believe some of your pragmatism is rubbing off on me."

"My pragmatism?" Her distracted mind noticed the glint of water through the trees just over his shoulder.

"I'm angry on one hand, but on the other . . ." He ran a hand through his hair. "A little voice in my head whispers, 'It is done now. Where is the harm?'"

"And what do you say to that little voice?"

His bitter chuckle tickled her belly. "I say nothing. I tremble before it."

Oh, God. "Collin, I . . ." She stumbled over words and wrapped shaking hands in her skirts to hide them. His brows rose in question. "I don't . . . I don't think we fit."

"We don't fit? You mean we don't get on?"

"No, I . . ." God. Oh, God. Maybe she should just pretend to like it so she wouldn't have to have this conversation.

"Alex?"

"You-are-far-too-big-and-I-think-you-should-go-home."

"What?" He blinked at her, lips moving as he deciphered her spewed words.

She saw his understanding in the darkening of his face, in the thinning of his lips. She stopped dead in the path, to cover her eyes and hide.

"Alexandra, you were a virgin—"

"I know! I *know* it hurts most the first time but, Collin,

look at me. I can't think why I didn't consider it before. I am small!" She dared a peek through her fingers. "You are . . . not!"

"You cannot think to judge me, to judge the pleasure I can give you based on that. If I'd known . . . Yes, it is painful for a virgin, but there are ways of easing that. You can't . . . You can't think to send me away like *that*."

Alex groaned into her hands. "I can't do it again, Collin, please."

He cursed, a string of Scottish words, their meaning quite clear though she didn't understand a one. She peeked again. He looked up to the sky, to the patch of blue stretching through the leaves. His lips moved as if in prayer.

His face tilted down suddenly and he caught her watching, smiled past the strain on his face. "I guess the decision is made then."

Alex felt relieved and terribly, terribly sad. "I'm sorry. I—"

"I must stay."

"Stay?"

"I can hardly pass up a chance to be the seducer, can I?"

"Seducer?" He'd reduced her to a dumb child, repeating simple words in hopes the repetition would reveal their meaning.

"You know you're being ridiculous, Alex. You are an intelligent woman and a passionate one. You know that women must enjoy it, at least some of the time."

"Only the things that come before!" she cried, finally pushing away her cowardice and letting her hands fall. "You are . . . I know you are too large. You're far bigger than—" She pressed a hand to her lips, too wise to continue.

An incongruous mix of emotions played over Collin's face: amusement, horror, pride. The amusement finally won out. "I've never received any complaints in that area, as to being too small or too big. No. None."

She could only stare, afraid to open her mouth again.

"I'm sure I am quite normal. And how exactly would you know anything about the range of sizes, Lady Alexandra?"

"I was a virgin," she hissed, "not a nun."

"Really? I could've sworn you were convent raised."

"How can you find this so amusing?"

"Well, it is either that or fly back to the alehouse to drink myself to a shameful death."

"'Tis nothing to be ashamed of, Collin. Everything else was lovely. More than lovely! It's not your fault. We are simply mismatched."

"Trust me."

Trust him? She had no reason not to . . . "I don't know. I don't want to." She glanced at him, at his angled face and curling hair and, oh, she wanted him to stay. Wanted to have the time to stroke his hair and kiss his neck. Wanted to play with his body the way he'd played with hers.

"Oh, all right," she conceded. "All right. I am willing to try it, but only once more."

Collin nodded, one dip of his chin, and moved away, resuming the walk. She hurried to catch up.

"You must understand that if there is a babe, we will marry. I should have made that clear in Edinburgh." He took her hand loosely in his. "I will not have a child raised a bastard."

"No. I understand that. Will there . . . ? Will there be a child?" Hand cradled in his, she felt the tiny jolt of shock run through his fingers.

"I didn't think to ask, Alex, but you do know that what we did . . . the part you didn't like . . . that is how women conceive?"

A stunned laugh bounced from her throat. "Of course I know that. My God."

"Well, you're apparently more innocent than you seem, *caitein*. I wanted to be sure."

"Yes, I know that. But my maid said you would know a way to lessen the chance."

"Um, yes." He squirmed a little at her questioning look. "Yes, there is a way to help prevent it, but I forgot myself last night. Still, it's not proof against children, else so many girls wouldn't be rushed to the altar."

"How is it done?"

Collin coughed and laughed, ears reddening at the tips. "I should not have spilled my seed inside you."

"Oh." She answered very solemnly. "It's a matter of timing then."

"Yes, timing." He watched her then, as they walked, kept glancing at her until she blushed. His teeth suddenly appeared, framed by a wolfish smile, and even his eyes flashed like a beast's, caught in a ray of bright sun. Alex swallowed hard. That couldn't be right though. Her Collin? A wolf? Impossible.

"This is too much work."

"Nonsense." Collin set the pail of steaming water next to the tub and wiped a hand over his brow. "Check the temperature."

Alex swept her fingers through the half-filled tub. "Just a touch more and it will be perfect."

She stood as he poured the bucket in, pressed her lips together nervously when he rose next to her "Thank you, Collin."

He reached for the back of her dress.

"You're going to stay in the room?"

"I'm going to do more than stay. I'm going to bathe you."

"Oh." She didn't protest, didn't pretend any modesty, though her hands fluttered toward his. "Shall I help, or . . . ?"

"No. Let me." He watched his brown fingers against the pale fabric, watched the tiny hooks fall open under his hands. The skin of her face was a little tanned, but here, as the material parted, alabaster skin was revealed, just a shade darker than white. She wore a shift this time, a soft wisp of gauze that covered nothing. When he slid the dress low and turned her, he found a pale pink corset that pushed her breasts high, rounding them.

Her head bent as he looked, as if she would see what he saw. They both watched his work-rough hands etch a line over her collarbone, over the front of her shoulder and down the inside of her arm to her wrist.

"You are so finely wrought," he breathed. "Like a new child."

Even as she shook at his words, his hands stole down to push her dress off. She unhooked her corset, and the shift was her only garment now, a veil that skimmed over her stomach and hips, hiding nothing of the dark triangle at the juncture of her thighs.

Collin kept the distance between them, caressed her with his eyes, drank in the beauty of her body veiled like a virgin bride. But how could he ever have suspected her of virginity?

Even as he watched she became more aroused, her breath stuttering to a pant. She responded to him like a mare kept from her stallion too long, just the scent of him enough to rouse her. Her lust called his beast, raised in him a need to dominate and subdue, to ravish her into surrender. Of course, she would not surrender. Not for more than a moment. Then it would start again.

Setting his jaw, Collin touched his thumbs to the thin ribbons of lace at her shoulders and pushed them aside. When the slip of fabric had slithered down her body and left her naked, she raised her head and smiled.

"Into the tub." His gruff words caressed her.

Alex brushed past him as she walked, letting her arm rub against his shirt, against the solid mass of his chest beneath it. She loved the effect she had on this man, loved that she could control his very breath. Make him gasp or pant or stop breathing altogether.

She stepped over the edge, sunk one foot into stinging-hot water.

Collin watched, seeming fascinated by the water lapping at her knee. She pulled her other leg in and slid down. When she touched bottom, the water came just to her ribs, tiny waves sloshed against the underside of her breasts. Collin stared.

His gaze heated her nipples, seemed to scrape against them until something twisted in her belly, something almost painful and as hot and liquid as the water that swirled about her. When his eyes slid up to lock with hers, the silver wildness of them caught her breath and deepened the pain in her belly.

She'd never seen his eyes like this, glinting gray on black, hot and icy cold at once. She suddenly felt in danger of being burned by the fire she'd so recklessly tended. He was not a plaything; he was a man, a man she'd pushed to the limits of temper and control. Alex shivered in the hot water and closed her eyes against the danger.

The cool air of the room shifted. He was moving, circling her. Her muscles vibrated in anxious tension as she waited for a touch, for anything.

"Lean forward."

She jerked, felt the water rippling against her skin as the light weight of her hair was lifted from her back. She felt him dip a hand into the water, heard the slippery squish of wet soap and then those slick fingers took her in their grip, trailing a cloud of steamy lavender.

His hands pressed into her shoulders, slipped to her neck and then down, over her chest, over the high rise of her breasts. His fingers separated, opened to let her nipples slide between them, to rub those sensitive peaks until they caught at the start of his palm.

Alex gasped, then whimpered as he pressed his fingers together to squeeze a delicious pressure into her nerves. His hold turned. His thumbs flicked over the hard pebbles, pushing past and back again in twin circles that brought her to a squirm.

"Collin!"

"Mm."

At the sound of his chest rumbling near her ear, Alex threw back her head and pressed it into that solidness.

His thumbs finally left her nipples. His palms, instead,

caressed her, cupped the whole of her breasts. Her body pressed into those hands, wishing they could cover all of her skin at once.

"Shh," his deep voice soothed, and she sighed at the departure of his touch.

Alex heard the water, the soap again, and then he cleaned her. He soaped her arms, her hands, her armpits. He diligently washed her, stroked each rib, each notch of her spine, his skin slick against her, like a tongue that licked at every space on her body.

He lifted her hair, poured fresh warm water over her shoulders and arms.

"Stand." The order was curt but so warm it burned her. She stood.

More soap on his hands and then her waist, her belly. Alex couldn't stop the trembling that took her body. Her belly twitched at the pass of his hands, jerking away from the too-wonderful touch.

He still knelt behind her, and she could feel his breath cool the dampness at the small of her back. She tried to picture him there, his mouth easing closer to her skin as his hands slicked down the curve of her belly and into the dripping curls of hair. A choking gasp clawed its way up her throat. She wanted him to kiss her, to bite her hip and curl his fingers up and inside her, but he only washed, only pushed the soap into that triangle of hair, then pulled away to wet his hands again.

Roughness tinged his grasp when he returned to his task. His fingers gripped her hips tight, held on for a moment, then let go to slide down her thighs. He pushed up again, toward the swell of her bottom, and seemed to push with him all the feeling in her legs, so that her feet and knees and thighs numbed and sent all their nerves to that hollow between her legs. A pulse took up the beat of her heart, a pulse that throbbed at the opening to her womb, a drum to call him.

Collin cupped the round halves of her bottom, spread his fingers wide and slipped his thumbs into the crease, sliding along it and back down, slowly, slowly. He caressed again and again, teasing closer to her core with every pass. Alex shook and burned and moaned when she felt his hands slide apart and down her hips, spreading her buttocks, then letting her slide free again as he soaped her legs.

"Lift your leg." Oh, he tried to sound detached, but his throat wouldn't loosen enough to let him. Alex wanted to tease him, but her own mouth was too busy holding back a plea, so she raised her left leg and perched her foot on the edge of the tub.

Turning her head, she saw his pupils dilate, saw his eyes turn to black as he gazed at her, open and slick with soap and woman's need. He squeezed the soap, twisted viciously until it jumped from his hands and into the water with a plop.

His shoulder brushed her as he lifted her foot. The movement unbalanced her so she had to grab his hair to steady herself. He didn't seem to notice, and she found she needed the feel of him.

His fingers rubbed her toes, between them, into the arch and up her heel. He pressed both hands together, an erotic vise that squeezed her ankle, her calf, the bend of her knee. The pads of his fingers touched, then slid apart as he eased up, over the curve of her thigh, higher to the dip just below the dark curls of her sex.

Alex's body tightened, the pulse beat sharp and painful as she waited for him to touch her, finally—to ease her. She was so close.

"Please, Collin. I'm—"

"No." His hands stilled.

"Please. I'm almost—"

"No. Not yet. Wait."

Shaking her head, she twisted her fingers in his hair.

"Yes, *caitein*. You'll wait." And he moved away, away from her center, denying her, destroying her.

Alex squirmed and shifted her own hand from her side, reached to touch herself since he would not.

"If you'd prefer to do it yourself, Alex, I've no idea why I'm here in England."

"I'd prefer you!"

"You've another foot needs washing."

Growling, glaring, she splashed her foot down and spun to face him. She lifted her right foot to where her left had perched and opened herself before him.

"Do it," she whispered, wondering if she begged.

His eyes caught hers, held for a moment before falling to the sight she'd presented him. He leaned closer, closer, till her breath squeezed from her chest and ruffled the mess of his hair. But he was only searching for the soap. He drew away when he had it in his grasp.

I might beg him, she realized as he sat back. *I might.* But then she saw his fingers shake as he reached for her foot and knew she wouldn't have to.

He soaped this foot more slowly, no doubt a punishment for the interruption, but Alex didn't complain. She could wait. She could wait now that she knew he shook with need as well. It appeased something between her legs even as it tightened her there, tightened until she felt her body draw up and open for him. He just might fit. The prospect of penetration lost its terror.

They stared, together, at his hands. She wondered if he watched as she did, looking beyond the hard sweep of his fingers to what they would do to her minutes from now. Again he proved more patient. By the time he reached the start of her thigh, her hips were twitching, easing forward in a blatant attempt to claim his attention. His eyes strayed from his hands, caught by the sight.

Triumph blurred the edges of her vision until his face was all she could see, his face as he leaned in, his mouth as her hips drew him. That cool breath again, this time against her belly and the flesh beneath it. His hands, forgotten for a moment, gripped one thigh and then the other, even as he pressed his lips into the dark shadow of her sex.

Her hands—her whole body—shook at the picture

before her . . . his dark hair mussed against her bare belly, his shoulders square beneath her hands.

"Alexandra." The word rumbled through her fingers, through her stomach and the bones of her pelvis, up to her spine. "You smell of everything right in the world."

A laugh caught in her chest, thickened into something close to tears.

"You taste of everything I've ever wanted."

Yes, she wanted to scream. *I love you*, she needed to cry. But she only growled wordlessly, because she knew never to confuse lust with love, no matter that it felt more. It wasn't love, not even when he pressed small kisses to the wet seam of her body. Not even when he raised his head and searched her face with night-black eyes. Not even when his fingers finally found her.

She cried out then, but not of love.

He traced the shape of her with a touch as light as fur. More twitching from her shameless hips until she pushed at him, not begging with words, but pleading nonetheless. Finally . . . Finally he stroked into the wet, rubbing the side of one long, callused finger into her folds. He laved her, worsened her need, forced a hum past her mouth.

He still refused to enter her, but he pushed farther, sweeping the thick edge of his hand along her, back to front and back again. A soft abrasion over that little nub of nerves, over her opening, farther still to the crease of her backside. *Oh, please*, she thought.

"Sit."

Alex clenched her thighs, trapping his hand as she squirmed. He slipped away.

"Sit."

"Bastard," she huffed as she fell into the water, happy to splash him as she rinsed.

Collin laughed a growl. "Yes."

But she had little time for resentment. He plucked her from the tub, soaking up the water with his own clothes as he bounded up the stairs to the bed that waited above. She didn't even have time to shiver before he stripped off his sodden clothes and covered her with his body.

The weight of him was just right, regardless that it set the bed ropes creaking. The hard, jutting length of him pressing into her thigh, warm and smooth against her, was the perfect weight as well.

Collin's mouth fell upon hers and she opened to him, opened to the strong stroke of his tongue and the taste of hot need. She couldn't stop her hands from feeling him. Hungry, starving, they ran over his back, his waist, his shoulders and neck. She skipped over his ribs like piano keys, grasped his buttocks to test their give. He seemed to like that, pressing himself firmly to her hip and kissing her with a deeper thrust. So she did it again and dared to run her fingers into the crease of his bottom as he'd done to her. Collin gasped and reared back.

"Please tell me you're not afraid."

"No. No, I want it. Please."

He'd shifted his weight as he spoke, freed a hand to smooth down her belly to cup that whole throbbing-soft place between her legs. A small shudder flew through her as his fingers pressed gently.

"Are you tender?"

She shook her head, frantic.

"What about here?" One long finger eased into her body.

"Oh!" Alex squirmed hard against the heel of his hand. "No!"

"And this?"

"Oh," she repeated as a second finger pressed against her, urged her flesh to give way. Her body took him snugly in with the slightest twinge of discomfort. "Just a little."

"Mm. And here?" He smiled as he asked, smiled as he rubbed his hand in a firm circle that rolled her eyes in her skull.

Wet heat touched her breast and her eyes popped open to find his head bent over her nipple, to see the flick of his tongue as he teased her.

"Oh, God," she moaned as tendrils of sharp heat squeezed through her body, flickering up and down on invisible threads that linked her breasts to her womb.

His mouth left her, his fingers too. She moaned a protest, but was held speechless by the continuing sparks of pleasure. A soft touch urged her legs apart, and when she opened her heavy eyes he was poised above her, face fierce and edged with that wildness. A firm length rubbed her, sent sparks flying again, then he was stretching her, filling her with one slow push of his hips.

Alexandra's mouth fell open to suck in air. The pressure was tremendous, a little uncomfortable, but good in a way she couldn't have imagined. He eased something deep inside her, pushed her wide and open, making a place for himself inside her body that she hadn't known was there.

His hips finally sat tight in the curve of her thighs. There. There. He did fit. Tears filled her eyes. She arched her head away to hide them but heard his sharp breath all the same.

"Alex?" he started to lift up.

"Yes," she gasped and clasped her hands behind his neck.

His whole body heaved with a sigh before he curved into her and kissed her deeply. The tug of his body sliding out made her writhe until he thrust back in, less gently this time. Another withdrawal. He eased further up her body then, shifted his hips and this time, this time, when he thrust he rubbed against a spot that sent pleasure breaking along her skin like cracks in weakening glass.

A high croak jumped from her throat.

"Ah," Collin moaned, a pleased sound.

Oh, God, he moved again, pushing and rubbing and filling until she screamed. In and out and in again, so smoothly that it all blended together into one long assault of pleasure twisting her insides into knots of joy.

Some small part of her mind felt the skin of his shoulders give under her nails and reveled in his hiss of pain. His hurt got tied up somehow in her pleasure and she knew she should stop and couldn't. Couldn't let go her grip on him, and the harder she clutched the harder he thrust, until the tight coil in her belly finally sprung loose, overwhelming her as nothing ever had.

Alex screamed, screamed till her throat hurt and the sound died, but she still gasped and sobbed into his neck because he didn't stop. He kept driving into her and it came again, exploding waves that jerked her hips even under his weight.

She couldn't bear any more, almost asked him to stop, but she opened her clenched eyes and the sight of his face stilled her words. He was beautiful, strained and stark and blind with pleasure. The tendons of his neck stood out like metal under flesh. His cheekbones pushed against his skin. And then she saw it coming over him even as it built again in her. As she closed her eyes and opened herself, he quickened and roughened and shuddered. When he slipped out of her body, she wanted to weep, but clasped him to her instead, holding tight as she could while pleasure wracked him.

The world swirled around their bed, settling and stilling as the minutes passed. Alexandra stared in disbelief at the timbers of the ceiling above.

"You were . . ." She swallowed her hoarseness. "You were right. We fit splendidly."

Collin's body shook above her. She took it to be laughter, but he didn't make a sound. He pressed a kiss to her shoulder. "I've never fit quite so well in my life."

"No?" A pleased warmth swept over her, coaxing a grin.

His weight lightened as he raised to his elbows to peer at her smile. He smiled back. "No."

Alex threw her arms around his neck and laughed aloud.

Chapter 12

When Collin woke, the evening sun fell across their bodies in a hot line. Alex had thrown aside the blankets so her naked body glowed a soft peach in the light.

Collin turned onto his back. He didn't need to watch her, couldn't bear to. A few days more, a week, that's all he had. And he'd already memorized every slow curve, every hollow.

Her soft thigh pressed against his in a line of damp heat, so that he felt her waking long before she stretched.

"Dinner." Her stretch ended with a tantalizing wiggle of her bottom as she burrowed into the sheets. Collin smiled at the ceiling and pressed his hip more firmly against her arse.

"I took care of breakfast. Isn't it your turn to serve?"

A hand emerged from the linens to wave him away. "Hungry. Food."

He shook his head and decided to indulge her. Better to have her in his debt for the rest of the evening. There were far more tantalizing things than food she could present to him. His body pulsed to life at the idea.

Collin slipped from the bed and padded naked to the kitchen. He gathered up food and plate, wine and water, more wine. By the time he returned to the room, Alex was smiling sleepily in his direction.

"Good evening, Mr. Blackburn," she purred, her words a glide of satin over his bare skin. "Are you going to serve me in bed?" Her bold words were in delicious contrast to the blush that fired her cheeks. Everything about her was delicious and contrary.

"Aye," he answered, approaching with the oak tray. "I am obedient in all things."

"Oh, not true, sir. You are willful. Insolent, even."

Collin filled a glass to the brim with wine and held it carefully out. "I am only looking out for your good, Mistress. You are known to be rash and hurried in some arenas."

"Mm. I'll concede that. You were exceedingly instructive today."

"Perhaps you shall promote me to tutor."

Alexandra took a long sip from her wine. Collin watched the slide and swallow of her white throat. When she licked an errant drop from her lips, her eyes fell, caught by the swelling of his body. "A tutor. I should like that very much." Collin felt his skin stretching. "Will you teach me how to please you, then?" She licked her lips again, glanced up through lashes to gauge his reaction.

"My God," he laughed. "You are shameless." His tone and his tumescence left little doubt where he stood on the issue. Her shamelessness aroused him completely. "Eat your dinner, *caitein*. We'll continue this discussion later."

She sighed as if in grief, then set to her food with an enthusiasm that belied her acting. Her sheet fell away, exposing those small breasts that had branded his hands. Collin watched with sheer appreciation as he sat down on the bed, the tray a temporary barrier between them. The woman had not a stitch of modesty. She sat there, naked, and dined with him as if she attended nude dinner parties on a regular basis. Even the most experienced of women he'd bedded had always developed an odd consciousness of their bodies after the lust wore off. Not Alexandra. She buttered her bread and raised her glass with nothing more than a friendly sparkle in his direction. Her breasts bobbed with each motion, utterly distracting him.

"Aren't you going to eat?" she asked at one point.

"Of course," he answered and fed himself without tasting a morsel.

By God, she was lovely. And what was he to do with her? She'd return to Somerhart soon, and then what? Find another lover? She couldn't remain chaste. Even as a virgin, she'd been pulsing with sensuality; now that she'd discovered the workings of her body . . . His jaw popped in the quiet room.

Alexandra didn't notice. She'd discovered a peach tart and was biting into it, eyes closed in pleasure. Her tangled mess of curls swept against her shoulders and down over the smooth arch of her back. Her movements stirred the scent of lavender and sex that clung to her.

Fear spiked his blood, and Collin drained his goblet in defense. He should marry her, wealth and standing be damned. He didn't want her to ever take another lover, but he did not want her waking every morning alone either. He wanted to slip between her thighs as she slept, wake her each day to the feel of his cock sliding deep and true into her body.

She caught his gaze and her eyes widened in surprise. Collin looked away to hide the sharpness of his passion. "More wine?"

As soon as he'd lifted the bottle, she grabbed the tray and hauled it off the bed, staggering a little under its weight. She held out her glass when she returned, watching while he poured the wine.

Glass full again, she sauntered away to stand at the window, watching the coming dark. Collin devoured the sight of her, framed against the haunting blue of dusk.

"This is my favorite time of day," she murmured. "No matter where you are, the world looks beautiful."

"You're beautiful."

She tossed him a surprisingly demure smile. "You don't think I look like a boy?"

Wine stung his throat, wrenching a cough from his lungs. "A boy?" he croaked.

"I've no breasts to speak of, no hips." She shrugged, turning to lean her back against the window sill.

"You've perfect breasts, Alex. And precious hips." She rolled her eyes. "And your arse alone could make a man weep with joy."

"What?"

"Oh, yes. You've a backside like two halves of a melon, sweet and firm and tasting of nectar."

"Ha!" She laughed at his words but glanced back as if to weigh their truth.

"Do ye no' believe me?" He growled playfully and stood. Her eyes fell to take in his reaction.

"I suppose I must."

"*Trobhad, caitein.*"

"Oh, my tutelage begins with Gaelic. What does that mean? '*Caitein*'?"

"It means cat, kitten. That's what you remind me of, sleek and small and canny."

"I like that." Her eyes roamed over him, warm with approval at the sight he provided. Collin stood before her and let her look. "And what's that called?"

Collin looked down. "*Coileach.* Cock."

Alexandra slid toward him, touched one finger to the tip. He hissed and grasped her wrist.

"I want you more than life itself, *caitein*, but you're surely too tender."

"Mm. I will admit to a certain soreness."

He held her wrist, but couldn't summon the will to move her hand. Her finger stroked, circled the ridge of his head.

"But I was not raised in a nunnery, if you'll recall. And I've heard tell that men enjoy any number of pleasures." Her fingers danced a sizzling path up his shaft.

"As do women," Collin growled, letting go his hold. Those fingers wrapped around him, cool against his heat, and firmed with the barest pressure.

Alexandra leaned close, rubbed her cheek against his chest as if she were the cat he'd named her. Her breath touched his nipple. "I am obedient in all things, my lord."

* * *

Collin shifted in a dark haze of sleep, tried to move away from the heat that seared his side. Sweat dampened the bedsheets, and he kicked them away, twisting to lie on his stomach.

Better. Fresh air settled over him, cooling the damp. His mind stirred a touch, waking him to frown into the pillow. He was missing something.

Ah. His woman.

The sheet wrapped persistently around his arm when he pulled. He untangled himself with a grumble and reached blindly for some part of her. His hand touched fire.

"Shit," he croaked and jerked away to push himself up to his elbows. Blinking around, he tried to orient his eyes to the moonlight. There was Alex, sprawled in all her glory across the other side of the bed. He stared, afraid. His brain roused itself another notch and told him to stop acting a fool.

Collin pushed one hand forward through the fog of his anxiety to lay a hand on her arm.

"My God," he breathed at the feel of her skin. She burned. She burned so hot it brought his heart to his throat. "Alex?" Her name did not rouse her, even loud and edged with panic as it was.

His body froze, half-raised. If he didn't move, didn't rise to light a lamp, perhaps he could just go back to sleep and leave this dream to the night. He took his fingers from the hot iron of her skin and trailed them through her hair.

"*Caitein*, wake up. Please." Not even a whimper touched the dark room. "Christ."

Collin sprang from the bed, ran to her side to set match to lamp. Even as the wick sputtered, he clasped her burning face between his hands. Her skin gleamed white, grew whiter as the flame caught and grew. Even her freckles seemed gone, burned off by the heat. Two streaks of crimson scalded her cheeks, mocking the flush of good health and turning her ghastly.

Collin held his breath and cupped her cheeks in his palms. "Oh, Alex." No one could burn like this and survive, certainly not this slip of a woman. She would die.

He surged to his feet and rushed about the room, scrambling into clothes and boots. He wet a towel in the basin and approached her again, not wanting to, hating to see her slack face. When he stroked the water over her skin, she stirred a tiny bit, moaning against his wrist.

"*Caitein*, listen to me." Her eyes rolled behind their lids. "Listen. You must be strong. Please? I'll get you to a doctor." The water seemed to dry before he'd even moved the towel away. It had taken some of the heat from her though; the linen steamed in his hand. "Alex?"

Not even her eyes stirred this time.

Terror seized his gut. They were alone here. Alone with naught more than a tiny village to run to. There could be no doctor there, likely they went to an herb woman for care. Still, she'd only just fallen ill. Surely there was time to think. People did not die from the fever in hours. No, it took days at least.

The thought of her death spurred him back to action. Wisps of silk fluttered through the air as he tore through the dresser drawers, searching for some garment to cover her nakedness. He had to take her with him, he couldn't run to the village and leave her here alone. What if . . . ?

Collin looked blindly down at the frothy pile of undergarments at his feet. What could be done for a fever anyway? A doctor would check her eyes and pulse, tell him to give her broth and pray for the best. *Prepare for the worst*, he'd say. *Pray for the best. It is in God's hands*. How many times had he heard that as a child? He had to get her home to Somerhart.

He bounded to the wardrobe, pulled out a dress and threw it on the bed. Water splashed over his hands and clothes as he hurried the basin to her side to sponge again over her pale lips and bright cheeks, down to her breasts and belly and arms. Somerhart. It was south of here, he knew that. South through the village down the road. Perhaps someone there knew the fastest way.

Collin dressed her with as much care as he could manage, cringing at her whimpers, whispering to soothe her. When she was decently covered, he pulled the quilt from the foot of the bed and wrapped her in that too, before he carried her from the room and downstairs.

"All right, Alex," he breathed, laying her on the couch. "All right. I need to get the horses. I'll be right back."

He sprinted toward the door, rocked back to a halt as he glanced at the kitchen and back to her, torn. His arms ached with fear and the need to keep her close. But the horses needed to be readied and what of the tending she needed before they left?

"Christ," he cursed, whipping open the door. Even as he lifted a foot over the threshold, he cursed again and spun around to stalk back to the kitchen.

"Drink," he crooned to her a moment later, pressing a glass to her open lips. Her throat worked for a moment, but she swallowed no more than a teaspoon before a terrible choking cough tore from her body.

She cried out, reaching for her throat as the glass shattered with a frightening noise against the wood floor. He started to snatch her up, thinking she was choking, but she turned her head and vomited, purging the meal they'd eaten just a few hours before.

"Oh, Jesus," he groaned, and smoothed her hair back with a shaking hand. If she couldn't keep down even water, what was he to do for her? "Oh, God."

He wasted no time then. He cleaned up the mess as best he could, then bounded out the door to saddle both horses, praying he could keep them from going lame if he switched them often enough. Still, dark roads and an extra rider . . . Things could go badly. The horses snorted and stomped as he brought them out, disturbed by his agitation and their strange awakening. Collin had no time to comfort them. He bundled Alex up and mounted Samson on the second try.

"Don't worry, *caitein*. I'll see you safe." He did not dare to think whether his promise could be kept.

The thick wood door boomed beneath his fist, the sound echoing like thunder through the dark lane.

"Ach. Calm yerself!" a grizzled voice shouted from within. The door flew open to frame a portly man in a nightshirt.

"I need assistance. Can you tell me the way to Somerhart?"

"Summer what? Do ye know what time 'tis?"

"Aye. Past midnight. Do you not know Somerhart? The duke's home?"

"What the hell would I have to do with a duke?"

Collin held back a growl. "Where does Mistress Betsy live?"

"Who?"

"Damn it—"

"She's down the row, two houses in," a voice shouted from the next doorway.

Collin raised a hand in thanks and whirled around to carry Alex into the darkness. The second house in was wide and rambling and very, very old. Betsy herself answered.

"Betsy," Collin huffed. "The lady is ill. A fever. There is no doctor about?"

"No. No," she answered, a tremble breaking her voice. "What is it?"

"I don't know. She's hot as Hades and can't keep even water down."

Betsy blinked several times and took a step away. "The putrid sore throat. Some children had it the next town over."

"Do you know the way to Somerhart? The fastest route?"

She shook her head, looking as helpless as Collin felt. "There's a fork in the road two miles out. Take the east road, that's all I know. But it's hours away."

"I know. If anyone comes for her, you must tell them I've taken her home, understand? Her maid or driver . . ."

She edged the door closed, murmuring, "Of course. God keep you."

Chapter 13

The hours passed so slowly that Collin began to feel mad, began to wonder if he'd slipped into some nightmare where dawn did not exist. He was forced to go carefully; even his panic could not make him run the horses on the strange road. Then there were the frequent stops, to change mounts, to urge a few drops of water past Alex's dried lips. Sometimes she was sick. Sometimes she kept it down. Once, she even opened her eyes, such a shock that he nearly dropped her.

"Whatever are we doing?" she'd croaked. Before hope could surge in his chest, she'd tumbled back into sleep. Finally, finally, just as he began to wonder if he'd ridden off the edge of the earth, the black lightened to gray, then to no color at all, and he could see.

He switched horses immediately, urged Samson to a tired run, murmuring promises of oats and hay all the while. He recognized the waking town he came to and knew it was only a few more miles to her home.

He did not waste time with wondering how to explain himself, but repeated the same questions over and over in his mind. Was the duke in residence? Did he keep a reliable doctor close by? Or would Alexandra die under the care of a leech, without even her brother to comfort her?

Another hour passed before he spied the Red Rose.

Only a quarter hour more. A small weight fell from his shoulders. He could get her home at least. Get her into her own bed.

He reined in suddenly at the sight of a familiar face. The innkeeper. "Mr. Sims," he called across the road.

"Aye?"

"Is there a physician in town? Someone who tends the duke's family?"

Sims crept closer, suspicion wrinkling his red brow. He swept a searching look over Collin, tried to peer into the blanket. "Aye. There's Maddox. He's seen to them several times." He craned his neck.

"Send him up to the house, if you please. It's urgent."

Sims nodded, eyes still straining as Collin kicked the horse back to a run. Samson tossed his head in irritation, but he leapt to speed and delivered his riders to Somerhart with no more complaint.

Collin slid from the saddle before even the quickest groom had appeared.

"Somerhart!" He shouted as he crashed through the door. A hue and cry answered him, as several servants rushed for the entry. "Is the duke here?" he asked the man he recognized from his last visit.

"I beg your pardon—"

Collin threw back the blanket to reveal his fevered burden. The butler gaped at the swath of white skin revealed above her soiled dress. A maid gasped, loud and shrill.

"Your mistress is gravely ill."

"Jones," the butler barked to some invisible person. "His Grace is riding. Track him down. Bridget. Show this gentleman the way to her chambers." He glanced around, still dignified, but burning with purpose. "Where is Thom? He must be sent for the doctor."

"The doctor's on his way. I left word in town."

The maid began to scurry toward the stairs. Collin followed her, leaving behind a racket of whispers and urgent hisses. He flew up the soft carpet of the stairs, Alex lighter than she should be in his tired arms. When he laid her on her bed his muscles tingled and jumped at the strangeness of having nothing to hold.

Bridget hovered, darting panicked glances between her mistress and the stranger. "Get some water," he barked. "A towel."

"I'll take care of that."

Collin turned to the scrape of that voice and found himself face to face with six feet of outraged housekeeper. She shouldered Collin to the side and began to wash Alexandra's face, her arms and feet, clucking and shaking her head with every pass of the rag. Collin backed away, wondered what to do with himself.

"She took ill around midnight," he finally contributed. The woman pierced him with green eyes. "High fever. She can't keep even water down most of the time." Collin looked away from her to Alexandra's face. Her teeth began to chatter, each shiver sending ice into his veins.

"Get out! I need to see her properly dressed."

Collin backed from the room, knowing he had no right to be there and desperately wanting to stay. He hovered just outside the chamber door and gazed dazedly around her sitting room, noticing only the oddest things . . . The rearing jade horse perched on the mantle, the small circle of a bright red pillow canted against a chairback. One yellowing glove lay on a table next to the window, beginning to crack with age. A keepsake, no doubt.

The hall door opened to a maid who bustled by, weighted down by a tray. Collin caught the faint spice of tea. He followed her back into the bedchamber.

The women ignored him, allowed him to stare down at their charge. It had been hours since he'd seen her in good light. Surely her cheekbones had been just as prominent earlier, surely the skin around her mouth was always so pale. She couldn't be so ill, so quickly. He'd made love to her not twelve hours before.

A sudden shift in the room caught Collin's attention. Both servants straightened and stared at a point somewhere over his shoulder. The maid bobbed a curtsy.

The Duke of Somerhart moved past without a glance in his direction. He rushed to his sister's side, pressed a hand to her cheek with grave care. "Alex?"

There was no response. Collin watched the man reach beneath the crisp sheets to pull her hand out. Their coloring was the same, black hair and blue eyes. There the similarities ended. Somerhart was tall and whip-hard, and his usual expression of idle contempt could cut glass. His face was even sharper than that now. He squeezed her hand, stroked her fingers with his thumb, and then he turned cold blue eyes to Collin.

"What the fuck are you doing with my sister?"

"She—"

"I made it clear you were to stay away from her."

"I can't defend myself."

"Is this your revenge?"

"No."

Somerhart turned his eyes back to Alexandra, apparently done with Collin for the moment. He sat gently on the bed and pressed her slack fingers to his mouth, then bent to murmur something close to her ear. She stirred a little at the words, but her eyelids only fluttered.

"Move back."

Collin took a step back, assuming he was being ordered from the room. When a short man dressed in severe black brushed past, he realized the doctor was speaking to the room in general. The man was a small package of efficient energy as he situated his equipment and bent to his task. He briskly examined Alexandra, peering into her eyes, her throat, her ears, checking her pulse and her breathing. He even unbuttoned the woolen nightdress she'd been dressed in. Collin looked away. He felt weakness vibrate up from his knees. *The doctor has come,* was all he could think.

"Scarletina," the man's voice cracked. "See the rash starting here?"

Somerhart rumbled a low answer.

"You must get some water into her. Willow bark tea if you can." He pulled a jar from his bag, opened the lid. "Try to keep her comfortable. Keep her warm." He pressed a leech to her neck. "Marrow broth if she keeps down the tea."

Bile burned the back of Collin's throat at the sight of the writhing leech dark against her skin. It was obscene, that thing burrowing into her white flesh, sucking her precious blood. Another one squirmed on her wrist, then another at the crook of her arm.

"Blackburn." Collin's name fell like a fist from the duke's lips. "Get out. See yourself to my library."

Collin hesitated, wondering if this were the last time he'd see her. But now was not the time for tender goodbyes. He had apologies to make and explanations to give. And if Somerhart refused to allow him near her, he would scale the walls.

Forcing his feet to move, he turned away from her, left her behind in the care of others. He wandered down the stairs and was directed to the library with a jerk of the butler's head. He was not surprised when refreshments failed to appear.

The air seemed to thicken with rage when the duke stepped inside the library and pinned him with a glare.

"I came to see your sister. After you ordered me not to."

"That was months ago."

"Yes. We spoke only briefly. We happened upon each other again at your cousin's home. George Tate is married to my cousin, Lucy."

"Yes. I am aware of that." Somerhart stalked to the sideboard and poured himself a drink. He did not offer one to Collin.

"We became better acquainted."

"You seduced her, you mean?"

"No, that's not what I mean. We were . . ." Collin rubbed a fist against his brow, trying to free his rusty brain from its exhaustion. "We engaged in a flirtation."

"A flirtation. And did you mean to wound her? To punish her?"

"Of course not. I do not hold her responsible for my brother's death."

"Don't lie to me," Somerhart growled, jaw set with desperate anger. "I could see it clearly on your face when we spoke. You held her in contempt."

"I did. Then. After I met her . . ." His shrug sent pain dancing down his arms.

"So how did she end up half-dead and in your care?"

"She . . . She came to Edinburgh, came to the fair. When I saw her there, we . . ." He could not say the truth, could not tell him that his little sister had propositioned a man. "We arranged to meet. For a week at her cottage."

"For a week." Somerhart placed the glass carefully on the marble top of a table. "So there was no doubt of your intention."

"No. None. I meant to have her."

Collin did not step away when her brother approached, he did not flinch at the sight of his fist. He was ready for the impact. Still, it propelled him backward, flung him off his feet to land with a thump onto the floor. His jaw rang with pain, a vibration that traveled at gleeful speed to his head and set off a sympathetic ache there.

He was dimly surprised that Somerhart did not leap upon him and pummel him into the rug. He only stood over him, fists clenched, panting with suppressed violence.

Collin rubbed his sore face and staggered to his feet, waited for the room to right itself. The dim clink of glass informed him that Somerhart had moved away.

"She is not a whore, you bastard. She is a girl, barely a woman."

"She was a virgin."

Collin watched the man's hand still, watched his jaw jump and clench. "What?" That one word was razor sharp and cut into Collin's conscience with ease.

"She was a virgin."

"Was."

"Aye. By the time I realized, it was too late."

"You mean by the time you penetrated her. My baby sister." Collin felt it was wiser not to respond to that.

Somerhart's eyes rose from his drink to sweep him with a contemptuous sneer.

"I suppose you expect to marry her now, a woman of high rank, a woman with an income twice yours, I don't doubt."

"I proposed immediately. She refused in like time."

"She refused?"

"She says she is not looking for a husband."

"What the hell is she looking for then?"

Collin cleared his throat, not knowing how to answer, but Somerhart stared at him, waiting. "She wants no more than what you have, I suppose. Freedom to do as she wants."

"She's had as much freedom as she's going to get."

"I'd imagine so."

Somerhart's arm jerked in a blur of motion and Collin heard crystal explode against the far wall in a great cacophony of glass and liquid. "God damn it to hell!" the duke growled, his face suddenly savage, brutal with frustration. No, not frustration, Collin realized. Fear.

"She will pull through this." Collin wondered at the certainty in his words. "She must. The scarlet fever is a childhood illness. Surely she's strong enough to withstand it."

"When was she last conscious?"

"Last night. Last night around ten. I woke at midnight and found her as she is now."

"Have you mistreated her?"

Collin tried not to take offense. It was a legitimate question considering the circumstances. "No. Though I was angry at her deception. I would never have, that is . . . I suppose it makes little difference, but I would never have taken her maidenhead, and she knew that." He felt pinned under the duke's glare but met his eyes without flinching. "I care for your sister. I would not have seen her harmed."

"And you did not think it harmful to tryst with an unmarried young girl, regardless of her respectability?"

"I did not feel it was right, and still I did it. There is no excuse for my actions."

Those icy eyes narrowed, studied him for a moment.

"Oh, there's an excuse, I'll wager. Alex has been known to be ruthless in her enthusiasms."

Collin coughed, cleared his throat, and fought the flush that heated his skin.

"When she was sixteen, she insisted she needed a stallion for riding. She said a mare or gelding would not do. I resisted her, but it was rough going for several months. Her will has not been tempered in the meantime."

"No." Collin shifted, ran a hand through his hair. "I'll ask for her hand again when she recovers. She seemed quite adamant in her refusal, but perhaps I can change her mind."

"I'm not sure I'd want you to."

"Hardly a surprise. I'm quite beneath her, as you've said."

"Yes." But he studied Collin with an assessing gleam that any horseman could recognize. "You are not given to excess though. You're straightforward, intelligent. I've never heard a word said against you."

"I am seldom in London, Your Grace."

"Don't start with the 'Your Graces' now. It's a little late for that considering you've defiled my sister."

Collin inclined his head, trying not to betray his newly hatched irritation. He could hardly protest the treatment.

"Would you have offered for her in any case? Virgin or not?"

He opened his mouth to answer honestly and found he could not. *No*, he meant to say, but hadn't he thought of it, briefly, during that visit to Lucy's? Thought of it and dismissed it out of hand? And again at the cottage? But even if she hadn't been a virgin, could he have spent a week in her bed and given her up with naught more than a farewell kiss?

"Your silence speaks for itself."

"No, actually. I'm not sure of my answer. If I'd meant to marry her, I wouldn't have met her as I did, but as to how I would have felt afterward? I can't say. She's a remarkable woman, a woman to be proud of."

"You think so?" His words were a genuine question, not a reproach for Alexandra.

"If she had not been your sister, if she'd been born no more than a Scottish seamstress, I would have offered for her, virgin or not."

"Hm." Those eyes swept Collin again, chilling in their appraisal. "Thank you for bringing her home. You did not abandon her to her sickness, at the very least."

Collin's irritation pitched forward into anger. "Do not insult me."

One elegant black brow rose in mock surprise. "What should I have expected from you, do you think?"

"As much as you'd expect from any Scotsman. A sense of decency."

"Well, I believe you've just insulted my countrymen, but you're an improvement over her English lover, by any measure."

"He wasn't her lover," Collin spat.

"No," the man smiled humorlessly at Collin's ire. "He was something to her, but not her lover, it seems. Again, I appreciate her safekeeping. I will notify you of her health."

Collin drew himself up, tried to release the muscles of his jaw enough to speak. "You can't think I mean to drop her at your doorstep and flee. I'll not leave before she's well again."

"No?" The eyes flashed with something less than icy for the barest moment. "Fine. I'll allow you to stay until she's well. But you will not reside under my roof. There's an inn—"

"I know it."

"Right. I'd forgotten you'd been to my home before. You know the way out."

And with that, he stalked from the room, and left Collin alone with a heart hollowed out by fear.

The fever has broken.

The note did not change over the full minute that he stared.

The fever has broken.

Five days. Five days she'd been suffering, delirious and wracked with pain. Collin pressed his hands against hot eyes. Thank God. Thank God she was not dead.

"Is it . . ." The hesitant voice of the innkeeper's wife barely penetrated the rushing in his ears. "Is it bad news, then?"

"No." He swallowed the raw edge of his relief. "No. Her fever broke. I must go."

A rush of boots over the wood floor. Their boy gone to saddle Samson, no doubt. Collin rubbed hard at his face and pushed back from the table. Opening his eyes, he found himself the recipient of the first kind look he'd gotten from the plump woman who brought his ale and tended his laundry.

"Will you break your fast before you go?"

"No."

Collin bounded up the stairs. He changed his worn clothes and shaved with cold water, rushed through his washing. He would not come to her sickroom stinking of smoke and whisky, would not give the duke an excuse to kick him out.

Finally presentable, he stalked downstairs and out the door to ride for Somerhart. He'd only been allowed to see her twice, both times with her brother standing sentinel, watching every move. So he'd held her limp hand and whispered in Gaelic, speaking of her body and her soul, commanding her to heal herself. Somerhart's eyes had glinted when she soothed under Collin's touch, his icy gaze turning from angry to measuring.

She had even whispered his name once, so softly that he still did not know if he'd imagined it. That murmur had lifted his heart with hope . . . And then she'd begun thrashing and trembling on the pillows and her brother had jerked his head toward the door with a withering glare, and he had not seen her again.

A groom stood waiting for him at the front steps, a shadow of blue against the glaring white façade of the house. The moment Collin's foot touched the ground, he was assailed with anxiety. Was she awake? Would her eyes widen in horror at the sight of him among her family? She might not even know what had happened, might not know that their secret lay exposed.

Collin gave a polite greeting to the butler, instead of rushing past him as he had done before. The man was cool . . . Cooler than he was to anyone else, Collin could not say.

"His Grace awaits you in the library," the man intoned, taking his hat before he turned to lead the way.

Collin stared at the balcony above and did not curse. The library first. Fine. Alexandra was out of danger. He could stand to wait a moment.

When the library doors opened, when he saw Somerhart standing in the window, fear spiked his blood. Something was wrong. The always impeccable man was disheveled, his face tired and creased with worry.

"What is it?"

Somerhart blinked at him, hand tight around the handle of a porcelain cup. His frown was blank, as if he couldn't quite place this strange man in his home.

Collin's chest twisted. "She's worse."

"No. No. She's resting. She's better. I, on the other hand, am exhausted."

Collin's shoulders slumped with relief, his knees too, forcing him to collapse into the nearest chair.

"I must look even worse than I feel."

"Can I see her then?"

"I just left her. She's just fallen asleep."

Dryness burned his eyes. They felt large, swollen till they pressed against their lids, scraping the flesh. Collin rubbed them carefully, heard the whoosh of her brother dropping into a chair close by.

"She nearly died last night. I nearly lost her."

"But the fever has broken?"

"Yes. At three this morning. She finally quieted and her skin cooled. I thought she had died, you see. I thought she was dead and growing cold with it. But it was only the fever breaking."

The pain in Collin's eyes eased, and when he opened them he realized they were wet. Somerhart's face twisted, as if he too would weep, but his eyes were dry. Dry and sunken.

"You may ask for her hand, if that's what you plan to do. But I will not force her to anything. She is alive and that's my only care. She may do what she wishes. She may move to town and wear her breeches to balls and have my blessing."

"I would not want a wife who didn't come willingly."

"Well, good luck to you then."

Collin stared at the duke's hand, at his fingers looped carelessly in the handle of a teacup. The cup was empty. Collin felt almost as empty inside. He wouldn't be at ease until he saw for himself that she was out of danger. Leaning forward to rise, he was stopped by a sudden, sharp glance from Somerhart's bloodshot eyes.

"You had best be sure you can make her happy if you mean to marry her. I will kill you if you break her."

Collin nodded. "She would not settle for anything less than happiness."

The duke seemed to measure him, seemed to try to draw something out of him with his gaze. Whatever he found must have been enough, because he leaned back with a nod. "Well, do your best then. I wouldn't start measuring for a new jacket just yet though."

"No. But I am at an advantage. She is weak and not in her right mind."

Somerhart's rusty laughter followed him from the room.

Chapter 14

Do not let Collin fool you with his scowls and curses. I have never seen him enamored before, so I can only guess that this is the cause of his current mood.

And imagine how excited I was to learn that you are a scandalous woman. What better neighbor could I hope for? Please consider accepting Collin's proposal, whether he has made it or not. We are sadly in need of interesting women here in my part of the Lowlands. And, of course, Collin would make as fine a husband as a man can. Faint praise, I suppose, but I feel certain you are well aware of his best qualities.

Alex tucked the letter back under her pillow with a crooked smile. What a character Jeannie Kirkland was, and what a perfect friend she would be.

Collin had not proposed yet, not again, at any rate, but she was rigid with the knowledge that he would. He would certainly not be lurking about her brother's home if he did not intend to do the honorable thing.

Yes, Mr. Blackburn, please come in. Shall we leave you two alone for a spot of bedplay, then?

Alex smothered a giggle. This was not the time for lightness. She had to focus. She'd been utterly unprepared for his visit this morning, as no one had seen fit to inform her that he'd not only stayed in town but had actually been admitted to Somerhart itself. Nobody had mentioned one word about him, actually, and she'd been afraid to ask. Then his voice had rumbled just outside her door, answered by a maid's low murmur, and Alex had burrowed into her pillow like a squirrel seeking cover. Why her first inclination had been to hide, she couldn't guess, but hide she did, pulling the covers up to her nose and her braid over her cheek.

That bit of cowardice made her glad now, for even after an hour she couldn't begin to think what to say to him. An apology, certainly. There was no possible pleasant scenario she could conjure of his welcome to her home. At best, he'd been shamed by his own conscience, at worst her brother had done him violence.

And now he would have to propose again, and a refusal would not come so easy this time. There was Collin to think of, his pride and honor, and the shame he would suffer to be known as a debaucher of women, something so truly at odds with his character that it hurt her chest to think of it.

Her brother must be considered too. He could not help but be ashamed of her now. She'd lied to him, sullied the Huntington honor in selfish disregard of his feelings. She could've claimed naiveté as a defense the first time; now she had no excuse but her own slatternly nature. So there were two men who would suffer for her refusal of Collin's offer.

And she herself, would she suffer? She thought of Collin's presence in her room, of the scent and shape that was his alone, of the shiver that took her skin even as he stood in the doorway. And when he'd smoothed his fingers over her cheek, when he'd leaned in close and whispered a prayer of gratitude over her head . . . Oh, she'd almost thrown her arms around him and wept in happiness that he was hers. So, yes. Yes, she would be injured too, if she sent him away, possibly more than anyone. She loved him. She loved him, and how could she not?

But she was a pragmatic girl, or so Collin had told her. He did not love her and might never love her. And what of her freedom? What of her precious independence?

Alex reached for her tea and nearly spilled it with the clumsy lurch. My God, she was weak as a newborn foal. And probably looked something like one too.

The cup cracked sharp against the saucer when she set it down to grab the tiny bell beside it. Danielle flew in from the dressing room before she'd even finished the first peal.

"*Mademoiselle?*" Her deep curtsy dizzied Alex's tired eyes.

"Oh, would you please stop that? It's my brother who's angry with you, not I."

"Your brother pays my wage."

"Well, I will pay it myself if your security would be improved. You'll not be dismissed. I don't even have to argue for you. Hart knows that I placed you in an untenable position."

"He did not seem so understanding yesterday."

"He was only worried for me."

"And so were we all." She gathered brush and ribbon and jerked the bell pull in passing. "It was a close thing, you know. His Grace had lost hope."

"Well, the problem I pose cannot be gotten rid of so easily, I'm afraid. And you did not tell me that Collin had been here."

"I did not know myself. No one is speaking to me."

"I am sorry, Danielle. Things did not go as I'd planned."

"It's fine. I did enjoy my week, though it was not worth risking your very life."

"Mine was." She settled against the pillows with a sigh, enjoying both her memories and the soothing whisper of the brush over her hair. A quick peek revealed her maid's sparkling look.

"That good, was he?"

"Oh, you have no idea. I did not, at the very least."

"Will you marry him then?"

Alex's happiness trailed away, the loss punctuated by a snarl the maid caught with the brush. "I am considering it." She thought of his hands slicking over her naked skin. "I am sorely tempted. What do you think?"

"I think if Scottish footmen look like your Mr. Blackburn I would be content to move north."

"Ha."

"And I think that if a man can tempt *you* to marriage, then you'd be wise to marry him. You've never been tempted before, not that I can recall."

"No." She thought of Collin again. Of him older, hair graying. Thought of him cradling a tiny child in those muscled arms. Her heart warmed, melted a little, the heat of it dripping down to pool in her belly. "He's a good man. He would be a good father, a good husband." She thought of his dignity and honor. "I don't think he'd be unfaithful."

"And you love him, do you not?"

A smile trembled over her lips. "He is easy to love."

"That is the best kind of man."

"Have you ever been in love, Danielle?"

Her maid's pert nose wrinkled. "Definitely not."

"Not even a little?"

"Hmph," she sniffed, nose now raised in the air. "And who am I to fall in love with a pale English boy? I loved my father and I was rather fond of that chef your brother hired just before we left London, but he kissed like a farmer despite his airs."

"Like a farmer?" Alex laughed. "Whatever does that mean?"

"He kissed like a man who must hurry back to the fields, not a man who has time to savor."

"Ah."

"And your Scotsman? How does he kiss?"

Alex closed her eyes, imagined his mouth falling to hers. "He kisses like . . . He kisses like a man who knows what he wants and will never have it again." She bit her lip, body already tight with the memory of pleasure.

When her eyes slid open, Danielle's wicked smile made her blush. "He loves you, *Mademoiselle*. Marry him."

"I wish it were that simple."

"He is poor, no?"

"I don't care if he's poor. I have money enough. The problem is his pride, a worse fault by far. And he doesn't . . . He doesn't truly want to marry me."

"Pah. Men cannot be depended upon to know these things. You do what you want and he'll follow along easily enough . . . If you keep him pleasured."

"Well." Alex felt a blush creep up her skin, though it wasn't embarrassment. Awareness, more likely. "Well, I would do my best, certainly."

Her maid smoothed the dark curls up to the back of Alex's head and began to braid just as a young maid rushed in to curtsy, cheeks flushed pink before the scandalous Lady Alexandra.

"Bring a bowl of hot water. Some soap and towels."

"Oh, a bath, please," Alex interrupted.

"*Non*. Tomorrow, maybe. The doctor has ordered that you not be chilled."

The girl bobbed at the maid's narrow look and rushed from the room. Danielle coiled the braid and pinned it before heading toward the sitting room. She returned with an armful of lace and linen.

"Something pretty, I think. Blackburn is still below."

Her heart fluttered so, Alex wondered if the fever had made a sudden return. But no, strength rushed to her shaky limbs as the seconds ticked by. Oh, it was a fever, but it was no illness.

"Is he waiting then?"

"That's my understanding."

"I would imagine my brother cannot have made him too comfortable. Hurry and get me out of this gown."

A quarter hour later found her scrubbed and tidied as well as she could be. The barest touch of rouge dispelled the

sickly pallor from her cheeks and lips, and Danielle had pow-
dered her face to help conceal the dark hollows beneath her
eyes. She no longer resembled a day-old corpse at any rate.

Her brother came to her room first, carrying a tray for
her, of all things. His blue eyes seemed soft with sadness,
though he smiled when she greeted him.

Alex could count on one hand the number of times she'd
felt uncomfortable with her brother. This was one of them.
She'd seen him only briefly this morning and had been too
tired to consider what he might think of her, but now . . .
Now there was no ignoring it.

"You look splendid, Alexandra. How are you feeling?"

"Well."

He leaned close, arranging the tray on a side table and
moving closer still to press a firm kiss to her head. "You
must never scare me like that again, pet. You stole a decade
from my life, at least."

When he sat on the bed, hip pressed to hers, she saw the
marks of exhaustion on his handsome face.

"I promise never to fall ill again," she said with a solemn
smile.

He did not return it, not until his eyes had studied her
face for long seconds, then he relented, white teeth flashing. "Well, this deadly fever was an excellent ploy to distract me from your recent misstep." Alex's heart throbbed
in a hollow chest, but he still smiled. "It worked. I am not
half as angry as I should be."

"No?" Tears burned hot in her eyes.

"No, not half. Do you love him or was this a lark?"

"I . . . I'm not sure. I think I may. Love him, I mean."

"He claims he offered marriage and you declined."

"He did, and I did."

"But you say you might love him? Is it his standing
then? His pedigree?"

"No, no. None of that."

"What then?"

"He did not truly want to marry me, Hart. He only proposed after . . . after . . ."

"After what?"

Alex shrugged and looked down to her hands, so that the two tears that fell wouldn't leave tracks in her powder.

"What he said was true? You were a virgin?"

She let her silence answer. What could she say? She had never dreamed she would be discussing her deflowering with her brother.

Hart took her hand and cradled it in the warmth of his long fingers. "Why did you let him think the worst of you, Alexandra? Why did you let me?"

She blinked the last of the wetness from her eyes, a familiar anger burning them dry. "No one even asked me. No one ever asked if I was a strumpet or just playing at being one. Well, I was only playing at it, but once I was caught, I . . . I was almost relieved."

"Alex, how—"

"Can you imagine being set loose in London for the first time—to dance and drink and flirt and laugh—set free to have the best time of your life and knowing all the while that you must find a mate and put it to an end? I daresay you've never been tempted to marry; why should you have been? I wanted to have everything. Everything that you take for granted."

His mouth fell open and stayed there, as if he had lost whatever word was set to emerge. He blinked and closed it. "I had no idea you were unhappy."

"I wasn't unhappy, really. Or I didn't know I was. I just wanted something that I couldn't put a name to."

"Sex?"

A nervous cough choked her. "No, not that exactly. A reprieve, I suppose."

"Alex, you were free to take your time. Two Seasons, three or four. I wouldn't have cared."

"Oh, I had planned on two at least. But I ended up with only a half. A reprieve indeed. A full commutation from the sentence of marriage."

"And is that what you wanted?"

Alex smoothed her hands over the pale blue of her bed,

trying to find her words, her thoughts. "I've been happy since then, I think. Useful. But now . . . Now I find myself wanting more than just usefulness."

"Blackburn seems a good sort, or he did before he turned up on the doorstep with my little sister in his arms."

"Is that how it happened?" She blushed at the tight set of his mouth.

"You remember nothing, I suppose?"

Her blush heated and spread down her neck. "Not after a certain point."

Hart's scowl seemed to warm the air. "Well, luckily, I do not know those details, but Blackburn says you took feverish in the middle of the night. He carried you here on horseback, afraid to trust your health to a midwife or herbalist. He brought you here and refused to leave."

"You let him stay?"

"Not under my roof."

"No, I wouldn't think so. And how long was I ill?"

"Five days. Five nights."

A shock of horror jolted through her. "Five nights? What day is it?"

"Sunday."

"Sunday? Oh, no!" *Damien.* She should have told Collin at the beginning. Perhaps he wouldn't have left the cottage immediately. And now he would hate her.

"What is it, pet?"

"Oh, I . . . Surely he . . . Collin . . . Surely he needs to return home."

"I gather that he had planned to visit your cottage for several days at least."

"Um. Yes, I guess he did." She plucked at the bedspread, mind buzzing, unable to think of anything more to say.

"Well, I'll send him up then. I don't doubt he will propose, but I did not ask him to, mind you. I would not force either of you to marriage, you understand?"

She nodded.

"You are free to do what you will. Do not marry him unless you think you will be happy. It is your decision."

"Yes, Hart."

"I mean it."

She nodded, then twitched in surprise when he swooped in to hug her.

"I love you like no other, Alexandra. And I understand you. We are too much alike, you and I."

"Ha!" She forced a laugh past her tight throat, pressing her face to his familiar shoulder. "Do not insult me."

"Watch yourself. I still owe you a thrashing."

His arms slipped away, leaving her laughing, but her laughter faded as he stalked from the room. Was Collin waiting outside the door? Did she have only a moment to prepare herself or half an hour? The answer arrived immediately.

"Alex."

She could read nothing in him but tension, but she remembered the words he'd whispered over her that morning and forced a smile. Perhaps he would not hate her. Perhaps she could make this right.

"Collin." Just saying his name gave her a happy jolt, or maybe it was his body, large and male and *in her bedroom*. She felt a real smile bloom.

Something lightened in him too, as he drew closer, as he watched her smile, and Alex was shocked to realize he was nervous. He stopped a few feet from her bed.

"How do you feel, Alex?"

"Well."

"You look well. Impossibly so."

"Thank you. Won't you come sit with me?" He blinked, looked at her bed, and she realized that he was about to say no and rushed on to stop him. "No one would be shocked to find you here."

Ah, there was that hard jaw she knew so well. "No, I don't suppose they would be."

"I'm sorry, Collin. I'm sorry to have gotten you into this mess." She noticed the green cast on one side of his chin and cringed. Still, a bruised jaw was better than a broken nose.

He stepped closer then, bringing the scent of rain. When he sat beside her, she could not resist the urge to wrap her fingers into his hand. Collin watched this, staring as he stroked his thumb over her knuckles, a warm rasp of skin on skin. His eyes finally revealed something, a hot, fierce pain that startled her, even as she saw him leaning in to kiss her.

"Alex." Her name whispered over her lips as he pressed his mouth to hers. When his palm came up to cradle her cheek, she felt her heart break open and shine, so that she almost cried out *yes!* before he'd even asked for her hand.

His mouth slid from her lips to press kisses over her cheeks, her eyelids, her nose. "You scared me to death, ye wee brat."

"You sound just like my brother."

Grunting, he pulled back to sweep her face with his eyes, taking her in until she touched fingers to his jaw.

"I'm sorry he hit you."

"He had a right to it." His thumb traced her eyebrow, then her cheek, trailing sparks that swirled into her veins and down to her belly.

"Would you have missed me if I'd died?"

His thumb stilled, his hand firmed against her chin and that bright hurt lit his eyes again, fading her smile. "Aye. I had plenty of time to think how much I'd miss you."

Tears pricked her eyes, and, wanting to soothe his pain and her own love, she reached to curl her hand around the back of his neck, sliding her fingers beneath the collar of his shirt to the hot skin beneath. He leaned in when she pulled him close, and she kissed him, harder, more fiercely than he'd kissed her.

Collin tried to gentle it, but she opened her mouth and licked at his bottom lip, pressed between his lips with her tongue until he groaned and cursed and kissed her back.

She couldn't help a small laugh of triumph, a laugh that was caught by his questing mouth. Oh, his tongue was so hot, sliding over hers, and he tasted of tea and something sweet and of the man she wanted so much. She thought of that tongue and what it could do to her and moaned so roughly that he kissed her harder, till she sank back into the pillows and pulled his body atop hers.

When his hand wandered down to slide over her nipple, she cried out, high and loud, and startled him away from her.

"Ah, Christ," he groaned, pulling back till her hands fell away.

Alex pouted.

"I've insulted you and your brother enough. I meant not to touch you again."

"Ever?" Panic pierced her heart, but her pulse quieted at his quick smile.

"Not till we're married at any rate."

"Married?"

"Aye. Will ye have me, *caitein?* I cannot give you the life you're accustomed to, but I can provide. I've a home and servants. I own more horses than you'd care to ride."

"Yes."

"And I believe that— Yes?"

"Yes. I will have you, Collin Blackburn."

"You will?"

"If you really want me."

"Oh, I want you."

"And not just to soothe your honor?"

"Ha." His hand rose to smooth her hair. "I'm finding it hard not to maul you in your sickbed. That has little enough to do with honor. And you? Would you marry me to honor your family?"

"Oh, you know me better than that, my lord. I care not a whit for honor."

His silver eyes narrowed at her, searching for an answer, urging her to offer him a reason, but she kept her lips tight together. Oh, she loved him, but she wasn't such a fool that she'd offer him that. He did not love her and, regardless what he'd said, his honor was the crux of this proposal. Still, he wanted her, and he liked her more than a little and that was enough. She would love him so well, be such a good wife, that he would fall in love with her before the year was out, she was sure of it.

If she could make this right.

"Collin . . ."

His lightness faded into worry. "Aye?"

"I must tell you something first, before this goes further."

"Ominous words, *caitein*. What is it?"

"I . . . I meant this to turn out well."

"And so it will."

She tried to smile, but couldn't manage it, and stared at her hands instead.

"Alex?"

"I saw Damien St. Claire. On my way to meet you. I convinced him to meet me later. I thought to send you to him, but not until after . . . well, afterward. And then I was ill."

She looked up to see his shock. "I was to meet him at an inn on Saturday. And now he must be gone. I am sorry."

He did not look furious, exactly. "And you did not tell me?"

"No." She shook her head. "I wanted to keep you with me. And I did not see the harm. But it was wrong, of course. Selfish."

"Selfish."

"I'm sorry."

"Did he hurt you, Alex? Threaten you? If he—"

"No. I was scared, but he believed me when I acted as if I knew nothing."

Collin sighed, a deep exhalation that ruffled her hair. Then he offered her the last thing she expected: a smile. Strained, at best, but beautiful all the same. "Well, I'd like to strangle you, I suppose, but it's probably an unlucky way to seal a betrothal. And you are still weak."

"Collin?"

"Perhaps he's heard you are sick. He may still be hanging about."

"And perhaps he's heard that I was in the care of a Scotsman named Blackburn."

"Perhaps." He leaned in to kiss her nose. "But you are alive, Alexandra. And he cannot stay hidden forever. Now tell me about this inn."

The warmth in his gaze melted her heart and wet her eyes, so she sat up and buried her face in his shirt, breathing in the scent of her lover and husband. "I am so sorry. But I'll be a better wife than I've been a lover. I promise."

His laugh rumbled through her. "Do not make threats, *caitein*. Anything better would surely kill me."

Chapter 15

"And the Northumberland parcel? That should pass to a daughter, should it not?"

Collin blinked, trying not to doze, lulled as he was by the droning of the solicitors. Jewels, land, income, furniture. All of it had to be accounted for and documented. All of her wealth and he wanted none of it. Her money would remain hers. It would pass to any children, as would her jewels and land. The furniture . . . Ah, that had proved a sticky question. In the end, the furniture she brought to his home would belong to Collin. He would also be the proud new owner of a coach and four. He'd never owned a carriage before, but he couldn't expect his wife and offspring to travel on horseback and camp beneath the stars. So . . . a coach, some furniture, and a wife.

Still it went on. Collin had no idea what they were speaking of now, but at each utterance of the word *children* or *offspring*, a strange flutter buffeted his chest. Children . . . babies . . . Alexandra round and firm and huge with his child. *Flutter. Flutter.*

It was anticipation, certainly—warm and wonderful. But it was fear also. She was so tiny, how could she possibly carry a child of his? He supposed it was done. His own mother was only two inches taller than Alex, after all, and he'd turned out to be a great brute.

And what a mother Alex would be—

"You can wake up now. They're gone."

He opened his eyes to find the duke smirking down at him, blessedly possessed of two glasses of whisky.

"Is it over?"

"Yes. My sister has been successfully broken down into legal parcels and those parcels distributed accordingly. The final papers will be drawn up tomorrow."

Collin gratefully took the offered glass and drank a healthy portion of it.

"You are better off than you let on, Lord Westmore."

"Collin. We are to be brothers, after all."

He waited for a sneer or a barb, but Somerhart merely nodded. "Collin. Well, you must call me Hart then, though I'll ask you not to use any of Alex's nicknames for me."

"Ah, no. Hart it is."

"You're avoiding the question."

"Which question?"

"Does Alex know just how comfortable you are?"

"My assets are less than hers."

"Hers are substantial."

Collin shrugged, finishing his whisky with one final gulp.

"You were unusually generous in the marriage contract."

"I will not have Alex or anyone else wondering if I've married her for money."

Hart raised his glass, offering Collin a toast and a quirk of his brow. "It is more than I'd hoped for her, frankly, even before the scandal."

"Surely you jest. Alex had her pick of the damned empire."

"Yes, she is lovely and intelligent and yes, men want her. But she is also an heiress and the daughter of a duke. A prize. Certain men might have been desperate to have her. Men worse than St. Claire." Hart's hand clenched, white knuckles a contrast to the amber liquid in his glass. "I should be shot for not guarding her more closely."

"She was chaperoned, surely?"

"Yes, but by a companion she herself chose. Cousin Merriweather turned out to be a sickly, self-indulgent chaperone, no doubt just as Alex planned. Of course, I was not willing to endure the marriage mart to supervise her personally, and she paid the price for that."

Collin winced, absolutely understanding the man's guilt. The woman had brought him to a very similar place. "Well, as you said, she can be ruthless in her enthusiasm. If she had determined to ruin herself, she would have got to it eventually."

Hart grunted into his glass as he finished his whisky. He did not shatter the glass against the wall this time, only set it firmly on the table beside him and frowned at it.

"Still nothing?"

"No." Collin had spent the past week scouring the countryside for any hint of St. Claire, but the man was gone or well-hidden. There had been several cold campgrounds near the inn where he'd meant to meet Alex though. Apparently St. Claire had grown too wary to show himself in public.

He hadn't been afraid to send a note to Alexandra though, the vicious dog. *You have betrayed me, darling bitch. I will not forget this.* No explicit threat, but Collin would kill the man all the same, just for the look on Alex's face as she'd read it.

Collin snarled in frustration. "I still have the next week before the wedding. He's gone to ground, but I'll find him if he so much as twitches."

"I should have gone after him myself," Hart murmured. "I did not, because Alex begged me to show mercy. She pled with me, took all the blame on herself. I wanted to kill him, of course, but she . . ."

He shrugged, shoulders eloquent in their self-directed scorn. "When you told me that she'd been used as a pawn, I realized I should never have promised her anything."

"You wanted to protect her."

"Well, I was wrong. I thought it was nothing more than what it appeared—a game of flirtation gone awry. But I looked into it after you came to me, Collin. Asked around.

You know that he and your brother were classmates at Harrow."

"Yes. They were supposed to have been friends."

"I think they were, but at some point St. Claire began to resent your brother—his money, his future title . . . something. He lost a great deal of money to him one night and John forgave it, returned his notes to him. St. Claire apparently lost his temper, began raging about disrespect and arrogance and the whole damned system of noble rank."

"When was this?" Collin sat forward, grimly eager to have this mystery of motive solved.

"Years before the duel. Five years ago maybe."

"Could that be it? A stupid argument between two young bucks?" He rubbed his suddenly aching head. "He would risk his life just for revenge against John's *kindness* to him?"

"It was the only solid thing I could come up with. St. Claire made clear that he did not consider your brother a friend after that incident, though John was obviously the injured party."

"So . . . What? He simply resented his wealth?" Collin shook his head in disgust. Oh, he'd had reason himself to resent many a wealthy man, but he had pride, for God's sake. He had taken his resentment and built himself a business, a life. He'd determined to make his money off the very men who would look down on him for his mother's blood. And now he would marry one of the finest daughters of the realm. Sweet justice indeed, if he wanted it. But he didn't want that, not in his bed.

"A rumor circulated," Hart added, his words carefully spaced.

"About?"

"I couldn't confirm it, but there was talk that St. Claire had taken up cards again . . . and that he lost another fortune to John."

"Just before the duel?"

"Two months."

Collin leaned his head back over the top of the wing chair, stared at the elaborate relief sculpted in the plaster of the ceiling. Cherubs peeked from behind plaster clouds, every tiny curl on their heads accounted for. Cherubs in the library. Oh, Alex would be very disappointed with her new home.

"Collin?"

"I guess . . . I guess that must be it then. St. Claire thought to beat him and regain his pride. And when he was beaten again, he compromised the woman John loved. I wonder if he knew that John would challenge him, or if killing him was just a bonus."

"I'll do everything I can to help find him. And when he's caught, he will be prosecuted."

"I'm not sure anything more can be done. My men in France are watching for his return. I've bribed his solicitor. It's a waiting game."

He glanced to Hart to find the man staring at the ceiling as well. Perhaps the cherubs were functional, a distraction from troubling thoughts.

"Your Grace?"

They both jumped and looked toward the door to find Prescott standing at the threshold, his clothing more lordlike than anything Collin even owned. The man was impeccable, as always, while Collin looked exactly like a man who'd spent a week in the saddle.

"Lady Alexandra has requested—"

Prescott shifted quite abruptly to the left, displaced by an outraged vision in lace and lawn.

"Hart, I don't need to stay in bed anymore. The doctor made quite clear— Collin!" She flew across the room, impossibly alive for a girl only days out of her deathbed.

Collin could not get his knees straight before she was on him, her dressing robe flying apart to reveal the less conservative nightgown beneath. Her warm bottom landed squarely on his lap as he hit his chair with a grunt, but Alex did not grant him a moment's reprieve.

"How long have you been here? Why haven't you come

up? I'm dying of boredom, I tell you." She leaned closer and pressed her lips to his ear. "You look in need of a bath, and I do have that debt to repay."

"Your brother is sitting not three feet away," he responded as quietly as he could.

"So?"

"Alex . . ."

"Your loss," she countered, and bounced to her feet. She flashed Hart a sassy smile and sauntered across the room. "Just what are you boys up to?"

Collin gave his future brother-in-law a wary look, but Hart shrugged back at him and stood.

"We're negotiating your marriage contract, pet. Your assets must be assigned."

"Oh?" The hot wariness in her gaze burned through Collin's skin. "Well, it must be done I suppose."

"I think you'll find your new husband to be the soul of generosity."

"Of course," she answered, but he could see the relief that cooled her eyes.

God, he hated this whole situation. Why couldn't she have been a tavern keeper's daughter or the sister of a squire? Why had he fallen for a princess?

Her hand trailed over the large table, sliding over one of the working drafts of the contract. She stopped and straightened, then leaned in to peer closely at the words. Collin stiffened.

"What's this?"

He felt his jaw clench. He didn't want her to look at the numbers, felt as if his life had been laid bare on those papers, lined up to be judged. She had the right though. Of course she did.

"MacTibbenham?"

Collin cleared his throat, but not before he heard a distinct snort from Hart's direction.

"MacTibbenham Collin Blackburn? That's your name?"

"Ah . . ."

Hart coughed, raising a ridiculous commotion.

"I'm not sure if my mother meant to honor the man or shame him, but it seems she was determined to give me his name."

"She certainly was." He watched her closely, but she did not even smirk, much less giggle.

"I've never—"

"May I shorten it to Mac? I don't know if I can quite get my tongue around—"

"You may call me Collin."

"All right. Collin." Her lips twitched, lifted.

"I would suggest you hold your laughter or I will be tempted to give our first son his father's name."

She made a good show of feigning absolute terror, and even Collin felt his lips curl into a smile as she begged him not to curse their child with such an unspeakable burden.

"If you'd care to go up and dress yourself, Alex," Hart interjected, "I was about to ring for tea."

"Really? I could have sworn I smelled whisky in this room. I thought perhaps you'd begun teatime without me."

It was Collin's turn to snort this time. Hart simply wrapped a hand around her braid and tugged her toward the door. "Come along. If you can make yourself decent, I'll let you have a few minutes alone with your betrothed."

"How many?"

"Five."

"Fifteen!" came her reply as she was towed into the hall-way. Collin leaned his head back and smiled at the nearest cherub, wondering just what those fifteen minutes would entail and looking forward to every one.

"Wife." Alex tried the word just to feel it on her lips. "Mrs. Collin Blackburn."

Collin's smile flashed across the dim carriage.

"Mrs. Blackburn. Lady Westmore. Do you never use your title, Collin?"

"No, wife—"

She giggled.

"—I only use it when it comes in handy for selling horses. But if you'd prefer it—"

"No! I like Blackburn. It's so wonderfully Scottish."

"So it is." His teeth flashed again.

"So are you," she ventured, wondering at the way he kept his distance.

"Well." He added nothing more.

Alex slumped back into the deeply cushioned seat and pushed a curtain open with a petulant shove. She'd closed them all as soon as the carriage rolled away from Somerhart, as soon as she'd waved her last good-bye to the small crowd of wedding guests. She had closed the curtains in anticipation, had waited impatiently to be taken by her groom.

A half hour had since passed in near silence. But she would not chase him this time; her chasing days were over. She—

"Oh, what is wrong?" she cried out.

Collin chuckled and shifted his knee to sink into her voluminous skirts. "Whatever do you mean, wife?"

Alex flashed him a quick smile, then let her lips fall back to pouting.

"Are you sitting there, thinking what you'd like me to do to you?"

She crossed her arms and shrugged, refusing to let him see the way his simple words made her shiver.

"Are you wondering why I haven't kissed you, or why I haven't slipped my hand beneath your skirts just to see if you're already wet for me?"

Her chin stiffened with the effort to stay silent.

"Are you, wife? Are you wet for me?"

"I . . ." When she licked her tingling lips, he chuckled again. The sound sent spiraling tremors down her legs. All the moisture had left her mouth, but there was plenty of it elsewhere, just as he suspected. Alex squirmed.

"You could tempt a saint, Mrs. Blackburn, and I'll not pretend I'm not aching to sink inside you, but it's your wedding day—the only one you'll have, I hope—and we'll not consummate it in a carriage."

"Please?"

He laughed outright then and ran a shaking hand through his hair; the sight of it cheered her a little. "By God, I'd like to. I'd like to set you on your knees and—" He broke off to clear his throat. "But you're mine now, Alex, and I can stand to wait until I have you in a proper bed."

Her insides clenched and clenched again, but if he could stand to wait, she supposed she could too. His reasoning escaped her though. Really, what more romantic place to consummate their marriage than on the drive away from the wedding breakfast? Perhaps he simply didn't understand romance. Too bad he had such a thorough understanding of control. It was almost a character flaw.

"Fine. I am not a slave to my lust. What shall we do to pass the time?"

"A slave to your lust," Collin laughed, irritating her further. "I suppose I wouldn't mind if you were."

"Well, I'm not. Now what?"

Who could have known the man grinned so much? She told herself not to kick him. Really, that was not the story she wanted to tell her grandchildren. Well, not much of this story could be told at any rate, but the wedding had gone off smoothly. There had been no shouted objections in the church. Her breasts had not popped from her bodice at any time. And she had not once been discovered in a compromising position, primarily because Collin refused to indulge her. Propriety. Control. What had she gotten herself into?

"Have I told you how lovely you are today?"

Alex started, surprised from her brooding thoughts. Collin's eyes glowed with warmth as they swept over the daffodil-yellow length of her dress. Her irritation melted away.

"And you are the most handsome man I've ever married."

"Really?"

"Truly."

"Witch."

She tossed her head, pleased with her small revenge. "Since you refuse to do your husbandly duty, I suppose we must talk."

"I suppose."

"Will you tell me about my new home? About your family?"

"Hmm." His brow furrowed and he glanced out the window to the cloudy skies above. Alex was rather surprised to realize that he was truly thinking what to tell her. "Westmore is very old. It's large and the lands are lovely, but it's a wild place. Not what you're used to at all."

"I shall love it, I'm sure."

His mouth flattened. "We'll see. As to family . . . I have none, really. My mother has lived in Dundee these five years. She's married now and I see her rarely, though I'm certain she will be curious to come meet you."

"Have you told her?"

"I wrote her immediately, to tell her I'd found a bride. She'll be pleased."

"But did you tell her I'm English?"

"Aye." His mouth relaxed, and Alex felt some anxiety leave her shoulders when his eyes touched hers. "She will not mind, *caitein*. She encouraged me to embrace my father's blood. We had many fights about that over the years."

"Why?"

"My father paid little enough attention to his bastard at first, though he always sent an allowance. More than most men would do, I suppose. He had a change of heart after John was born. A fit of conscience. So when I was nine, my life changed drastically. I was suddenly besieged by tutors, then he offered to send me to school. I was horrified at the thought, scared really, but my mother insisted, so off I went to Edinburgh."

"Against your will?"

"Oh, aye. They didn't drag me away in chains, of course, but I offered some choice words for both my parents. And at school, I spoke only Gaelic for the first few weeks and suffered for it. Thank God my father didn't insist on an English school. I would have run off to be a sailor before moving to England."

Alex winced a little at that, but Collin didn't notice. He was smiling at some memory.

"My mother is a fine woman."

"What is she like?"

"She is kind and witty. Bold and generous to a fault. I always wondered whether it was her boldness or her generosity that led her to be my father's mistress. A little of both, I suppose."

Alex laughed with him, glad to know he felt so warmly toward his mother. She imagined that some men would hold a woman accountable for their low beginnings, but Collin spoke of her with love.

"She is a weaver, a skilled one. She was not a chambermaid caught by a visiting noble or some such thing. She always made clear that my father was a good man who'd left her with fond memories."

"That's wonderful."

He threw her a surprised glance. "Thank you."

"And your father? He would visit?"

"He came to meet me when I was ten. He visited every year afterward and brought John sometimes. He said we were brothers and were to treat each other as such."

Alex tried to blink back the tears that suddenly wet her eyes. "He sounds like a lovely man."

"Really, Alex," Collin snorted and handed her a handkerchief. "It's not so romantic as all that. The man drank too much and he was a terrible horseman. And he would roar curses at me if I spoke like a Scotsman in front of him. Between him and that school it's a wonder I didn't lose my burr entirely."

She nodded, but couldn't keep from sniffling one last time.

"And when he handed me the deed to Westmore, when he told me he'd purchased this dead title and it was mine . . .

Oh, I wanted to knock him down. I wanted to curse him and run away and never set eyes on him again."

"Why?"

He shrugged his broad shoulders and looked back to the window, knee sliding away from hers. "I did not want to become the thing I'd always resented. But I knew Westmore. I'd grown up not an hour from it, and I knew its empty stables and the lush pasture and, God, I wanted to breed horses more than anything."

"It's no more than your birthright, Collin."

"No, Alex, it is not. Bastards have a right to nothing. You know that."

"But you are his son. And he must have loved you, must have respected you to have done this."

"I suppose he did, in his way. Regardless, I took the deed and I took the title. I vowed not to use it, but I realized it was good business, after all, and so I do."

"That's nothing to be ashamed of. Many men purchase titles for less noble reasons than that."

His eyes hardened and struck out at her. "I am not ashamed."

"No," she answered, startled by his sudden anger. "I didn't mean—"

"My blood may not be as exalted as yours, but—"

"Stop it."

"What?" The hardness left his face, but his mouth stayed tight and flat.

"You cannot throw my family in my face at every turn. I cannot help where I come from anymore than you."

His eyes did not waver from her face. He did not move a muscle. Alex felt a tight anxiety creep from her neck to her shoulders. This was a starting point for them. An indication of how this marriage would go. She felt afraid for the first time that he might not be the husband she'd imagined.

Then he blinked. "You are right, of course."

Her breath shook from her throat.

"I apologize for my anger."

"You do not have to apologize," she offered with a smile.

Her mood bounced back to its previous high. "I suspect we will exchange words on occasion."

"Oh, do you?"

"Yes."

A smile softened his face, even as his eyes glinted with something hot. "As long as you understand that your disrespect will be punished with spankings."

Alex couldn't keep her jaw from dropping open at the picture that formed in her mind. A very naughty book was secreted away in her luggage, a book some friend of her brother's had left in the library long ago. She was suddenly curious as to its accuracy. Some of the illustrations had struck her as silly and impossible, but she now wondered at the extent of the adventures she could attempt with her new husband. This marriage business could turn out to be interesting indeed.

"*Caitein*, I didn't mean to shock you. It was a joke."

"Oh! Um, of course . . ." Alex dipped her head to hide the light in her eyes. She thought of a particularly detailed drawing of a man standing, his—

"Alex." Her husband's hand interrupted her thoughts, touching her lightly on the cheek. "I forget, sometimes, how innocent you are. I would never strike you, *caitein*."

"Oh, I am not so innocent," she offered past a giggle.

"You are. But it is one of the incongruities in you that I treasure."

Ha! she laughed to herself, taking Collin's hand in hers. She wouldn't be innocent for long, not once they reached her cottage. Once there, she would recreate page twenty-six from that naughty book and see what her husband thought of her innocence then.

Chapter 16

Naught but a few miles lay between his wife and Westmore, and each inch closer ratcheted Collin's shoulders to a new level of tension. Westmore was a castle, he supposed, but not a castle meant for a princess. It was a keep, built to house soldiers and knights, and now fit more for moaning ghosts and hibernating squirrels. A ruin. A wreck.

Constructed early in the fourteenth century, its stone walls and slate roof had stood the test of time and the onslaught of Alexandra's ancestors, but the place had been uninhabited for fifty years at least before he'd moved in. No one had ever bothered with improvements.

Westmore had no gaslight, no piped water, no elegant rooms. Not even glass in what few windows there were, just shutters to close against the cold and wet. Drafts howled through even during the summer.

Truly, it was a castle of the oldest sort. The first floor consisted entirely of the kitchen and one giant, echoing great hall. Everyone ate meals there. Together.

Collin blinked. My God, he hadn't even considered that. The Lady Alexandra—*Mrs. Blackburn*, he reminded himself—the grand mistress of Somerhart, dining among the stable hands and grooms. Ah, God.

He should warn her. He should. Just as he should explain that he was building a new home—a lovely, modern home—just over the hill. A home with real windows and real rooms . . . even a few luxuries like a marble bath.

He wanted to tell her. He opened his mouth to do it. And closed it again.

This was his way of testing her. He knew that just as certainly as he knew it was wrong. Still, the miles rolled past with no word passing his lips.

Alex spent the last few miles perched on the edge of her seat, fairly vibrating with excitement. Her eyes, wide and shining, drank in the countryside as if she could embrace her new home with only her gaze.

"It smells so lovely. Like autumn already!"

Collin grunted, more irritated by her pleasure than he would have been by hesitance. Yes, it was autumn already, in mid-September, and snow would likely fall within the month. And then? Nothing but months of cold and dark and a drafty keep to occupy the lovely Alexandra. What would she think of her home then?

"How far now, Collin?" The happy glance she aimed his way stabbed into his conscience. He should have explained everything, described his life in detail *before* this marriage. Before he'd even asked for her hand. It was too late now, really. An explanation would sound like an apology for who he was.

"A few minutes," he answered. "No more."

"Really?" His wife literally bounced in her seat. Then, unable to contain herself, she finally thrust her head through the open window and craned her neck to see past the horses.

"Oh, we're coming to the top of the hill! Is Westmore on the other side?"

"No. There's one more hill yet."

"It's so beautiful here." Her head reappeared, curls tousled against the vista of crag and hill, boulder and tree. "Will you take me exploring right away?"

"I expect I will have a lot of work awaiting me."

Those great blue eyes blinked. Her black brows frowned a little, then smoothed out to perfect arches again. "Of course. I did not mean to be flip. You've been away from home too long."

"Yes."

Collin met her eyes evenly, though it cost him a small piece of his heart to watch the worry etch itself over her face. A wariness entered her eyes before she looked away.

He'd let himself forget their differences over the past few days. He'd set aside his concerns about this marriage for the sheer joy of his bride's body and spirit. But they could not spend all the hours of their days together in bed. There would be no escaping that he had brought her low with this marriage. Best for her to realize it now. And if she wanted to leave, at least he would know immediately.

"Will they accept me, do you think?"

"Hmm?" He frowned at the familiar landscape rolling past the window.

"Do you think people will be upset that I'm English?"

"Which people?"

"I don't know."

Pulling himself from his dark thoughts, he saw that she had sobered to a great degree and fought the urge to fold her into his arms. "I'm sure everyone is surprised by the news. But Fergus—my manager—he will not care one whit about your English blood. And the Kirklands are my closest neighbors. You remember Jeannie, she already likes you. Did she write?"

A faint tinge of pink crept up her cheeks. "Yes."

Collin saw her intention to say more and held up a hand. "Pray, don't tell me what she said. I'd prefer to remain ignorant."

A bright smile returned.

"Other than those two—I cannot really speak for the servants and workers, but I can't imagine they'd care one way or the other."

"You'd be surprised."

A low shout filtered to his ears over the rumbling drone of the coach wheels, and he glanced out to see the ridge that faced Westmore. One of the horses snorted loudly, obviously catching the scent of so many brethren gathered in the stables below.

He could've sworn that Alex's ears pricked, and she vaulted across the small space to hang out the window. At least the Westmore folk would not think her stiff and haughty.

Her body stilled, and Collin could just make out the curve of her jaw and her half-open mouth as she gaped ahead.

Picturing his home, he tried to see it through her eyes, to think what she would notice. First, the old stone stables at the base of Westmore's hill, the thatched roofs golden and prickly. Then the newer, larger stables stretching out at an angle to the original stalls, wooden walls painted white so they glowed in the lowering light.

From there, a well-worn road wound up to the outbuildings: a smithy, a hayrick, several square sheds. All were built from the old stone of the original bailey wall.

The moat had been filled in, thank God, so the road rose unimpeded the rest of the way up the hill, to the ancient square monstrosity that crouched atop it.

Her body slipped slowly back into the carriage. "It's a castle," she whispered, eyes wide again.

"A keep," he insisted.

"I didn't expect . . ." She shook herself, curls trembling around her shoulders. "How exciting!"

Collin bit back a laugh. Her words were genuine, but she had not yet seen the interior. Whatever romantic notions she had about ancient castles would crumble when she stepped through the door. The damned place was dark as Hades—

"Do you sleep in the tower?"

The smile finally overwhelmed his frown. "No. But the room I thought to give you is adjoined by a small turret."

"Am I not to share your room?"

The crumbled ruins of the old spring house slipped past them, distracting him from the conversation. Just a few bare moments—

"Collin? Are we to have separate beds?"

"No. No! The chambers are small and I doubt we could manage to fit your wardrobe into mine. We could share your larger room and I will keep my room for dressing and bathing. I am usually covered in muck by the end of the day. I should not like to drag manure into your sitting room."

"Well, that's a lovely thought then. I wouldn't . . . I wouldn't want to sleep alone at night."

He managed a weak smile, despite that they were driving alongside the stones of the old stable walls. The long black nose of his best stud poked itself from the shadows over a stall door.

"Look at him, Collin!"

"That's Othello," he muttered.

"Oh, isn't he fine? Will you show me the horses tomorrow, at least? I know you're busy—"

"Ho!" a voiced boomed from far ahead.

Collin winced, the churning anxiety in his gut spiked with a sudden, strange urgency. Fergus had come to greet them. Of course he had.

The outbuildings fell behind, and the horizon straightened itself as they gained the flat yard of the old bailey. Collin felt the handle of the door bite into his hand and realized he had gripped it with bruising force, just as Fergus's grin appeared in the window.

"Welcome to Westmore!" he cried, pulling the door open with a flourish and nearly detaching Collin's fingers in the process. "My guid Lady Westmore."

Fergus wrapped his fingers around Alexandra's outstretched hand and swept her down from the carriage, setting her blue skirts swinging. Her eyes shone, sparkling with excitement.

"This is Fergus MacLean, my manager. Fergus, Alexandra Blackburn. My wife."

"I am at yer service," Fergus smiled, leaning over her hand. Collin stepped from the coach and into the man's shoulder before his lips could touch her.

He had forgotten to worry about this—his handsome, well-bred, dapper, witty friend. He'd forgotten to think of Fergus's charm and the unmistakable truth that, no matter how poor, he was the true son of a baron. The fourth son, yes, but certainly closer to Alex's respectability than Collin. The man had been raised as a noble.

Alex exchanged a few words with him, laughed up at his easy smile, reached out to touch her fingers to his sleeve. Collin glared at her hand.

"Come," he snapped, pleased when her fingers jumped away from his friend.

She nodded and moved them to Collin's sleeve where they belonged. He stared steadily ahead, not watching her as they crossed the yard and approached the simple wood door. He had wanted to see her face, her reaction, the first time she stepped into her new home. He'd wanted to watch for horror or disgust or resignation, or maybe for something good which he couldn't let himself hope for.

Now, he found, he could not bear to look.

Stone and fresh water—that was the smell that struck her when she stepped inside Collin's home. The keep smelled like the outdoors—clean and cool . . . cold, actually. A shiver took her, though she tried to stop it.

Dark as it was, she could barely see, but as she peered around she began to make out the sheer size of the room before her. The far wall was at least forty feet away, perhaps more, and the ceiling rose up to more than thrice her height.

Finally, her eyes adjusted, and she stared in astonishment. It was just like the paintings she'd seen of ancient castles. Several long wooden tables stretched out in front of the largest fireplace she'd ever seen. Did they roast whole animals in there? The table and benches took up the largest part of the room, and other sections were delineated by plush rugs set over the gray stones of the floor. No rushes were strewn about, at any rate.

A settee and chair hunched in one corner, looking strange and modern against the tapestry on the wall. In another corner, wooden stools and benches were scattered about a low table piled with leather and tools. An arched doorway led to another room that clattered and clanged with noise. The kitchen, no doubt.

Alex swung her head about, measuring the space and comparing it to her study of the outside walls. This was the whole of it. This and the kitchen, and the small door to her right that gave way to stairs.

Well, it was not much, but since Collin had not answered questions about Westmore and she had been too uncertain to press, she had arrived with absolutely no preconceived notions about her new home. She'd been rather afraid it was going to be above the stables. Oh, the stables he'd spoken of, just not the house. The keep. She did not giggle, though it was close. Perhaps she could order him a suit of armor and they could play at knight and maiden.

Lips twitching, she looked up to find Collin's face a cold mask. Her temptation to giggle faded. Of course, he wanted to know what she thought of it. Laughing in his face would not send the right message.

"Well, it's a bit cold in here, but I think if we built in some smaller rooms we could decrease the draft. Otherwise, it's perfectly lovely, isn't it? Will you show me the bedchambers?"

Damn, the man could be intimidating when he wished to. He stared down at her, studying her as if she were a snake that might strike.

"This is my new home, Collin. I should like to see the whole of it."

"Get it over with as quickly as possible?"

"Are you determined to be dark then? Let me guess . . . You were expecting me to gasp in horror at the primitiveness and run back to my life of luxury? If I'd wanted luxury I would have married the earl who proposed at my coming out."

"Primitive?"

"Well, it is primitive, isn't it? It needs a woman's touch. Luckily, you've brought one home with you."

Collin grunted.

"There is no reason that rooms cannot be added to this space. And windows too. And I think a suit of armor would be a nice touch." She winced when her joke fell on humorless ears.

"And where will I get the money for all these improvements?"

Oh. A sticky subject. Alex cleared her throat. She could afford to gut the whole place herself, but the man was as proud as a peacock and certainly more difficult.

A throat cleared behind her, rescuing her from an answer that would surely get her in trouble. "Mr. MacLean!" she cried too loudly as she turned toward him.

"Oh, 'Fergus,' if it pleases ye, milady."

She laughed at the teasing spark in his eye. "Fergus then, and you must call me Alex. It is not at all proper, of course, but neither am I."

Something rumbled in her ear, making her jump. Not an animal growling, though she'd thought to turn and find a giant wolfhound at her side. Just her husband.

Fergus gave her one last smile before shooting a frown at Collin. She saw the jerking shake of Collin's head before he took her arm and wondered what the men were glaring at each other about. There was some undercurrent there, but she forgot it immediately when she turned to find a short line of women stretching out from the kitchen door. The servants.

The first thing she noticed was the young woman at the left of the rest. She stood tall and straight and her smile could have cut glass. The housekeeper. She was far too young for the job, but there was no question who she was. The heavy ring of keys at her waist advertised her status.

"Rebecca Burnside," Collin stated as soon as they drew near. "My housekeeper."

"Mrs. Burnside," Alex offered, hoping the woman simply had a stiff smile.

"My lady," she crooned, curtsying deeply and still conveying a message of disrespect. She would be trouble, Alex could see that much immediately. And a new bride did not need that kind of trouble from the first day of her marriage.

"Mrs. Cook," Collin continued, needlessly adding, "the cook," as a sturdy, round woman curtsied.

They worked their way down the line—Bridey, the chambermaid; Jess, the kitchen maid; Nan, the little scullery maid who wasn't more than twelve. There were others too, Collin explained. Bridey had a son and daughter who often came to help. And several young men were about to help with the heavier chores.

Alex smiled and nodded to each of them, studying their faces for hostility or resentment. But they all seemed simply curious and a little hesitant. All except Rebecca Burnside.

The housekeeper kept smiling, smiled her damndest, as she ushered the others back into the kitchen. She turned back to face them when she stood alone in the archway, and the smile warmed when she met Collin's eyes.

"It's good to see you home, milord."

"It's good to be home, Rebecca."

Rebecca, was it? Alex's spine stiffened.

Fergus strolled around to stand at Collin's side. "Perhaps you should show her ladyship upstairs, Rebecca. I'm sure she's weary from her long journey."

The look she shot at Fergus was murderous. His smile widened. "Of course," she finally chirped, and slid past them all to lead the way. She did not acknowledge Alex except to call out "this way" as she hurried across the hall.

Hiding a sigh, Alex followed, then stopped to wait for Collin, but when she glanced back to him he was already turned to Fergus and deep in conversation. She frowned, hesitated, unsure if she should proceed or not.

Fergus met her eyes and frowned just as fiercely before nudging Collin with an elbow. Her husband spared her naught more than a quick look before he waved her on, and even his manager seemed displeased with the dismissal, his mouth twisting to a sneer. Collin shook his head and continued talking, not noticing that his wife was doing her best to turn him to ashes with her eyes. By the time she finally spun to follow the housekeeper, the woman's smile had blossomed to full-fledged happiness.

Alex bit back a nasty word and trudged up the stairs behind her, practicing her fiery stare on the woman's back. What kind of housekeeper could she be at her age? She couldn't be more than twenty-five. And she didn't look like a maid of any sort. Her skin was fine and pale as ivory silk, and her blond hair was swept into an intricate topknot that emphasized her long neck. If Alex didn't know better, she'd suspect Rebecca Burnside of being Collin's mistress, but she dismissed the notion out of hand. Collin was not a man to set up his doxy in his home, and he most definitely would never keep her after marriage.

A door at the top of the stairs stood open, and Rebecca hurried through, waving again for Alex to follow. She seemed averse to speaking to her new mistress. Did she dislike all English or just the one married to her employer? Alex narrowed her eyes and stepped into the room, determined to find out, but her curiosity about the room got the better of her and she spun in a slow circle as soon as she passed the doorjamb.

A large bed took up most of the space, high and wide and covered from head to foot in sable fur. Alex blinked. Sable. She took a tentative step to slide a hand over the throw. Oh yes, that was sable. My word.

Resisting the urge to rub her cheek against it, she pulled her eyes away and surveyed the rest of the space. Her dresser and wardrobe filled it. The shutters were thrown back on the one small window, but it was so narrow and deep that only the tiniest sliver of fading light shone through.

A door set against the right wall reminded Alex of Collin's description of the chamber, and she opened it with an anticipatory smile. Here was the turret room, round and cozy and furnished with a delicate table and chairs. There would be room here to dress and to breakfast. Hardly any light, but there were a few windows and it would have to catch sun at some point of the day. It was charming and suited her perfectly.

A small noise reminded her of the woman at her back, and Alex's smile faded. "You're a bit young for a house-keeper," she said, not bothering to look at her.

"Collin . . . Lord Westmore and I have known each other for years. He was happy to offer me the position."

Alexandra's jaw popped. She turned to sweep the woman with a cold look. "I'm sure we will be close companions then."

Her blond head inclined in the barest nod.

"I would imagine that Collin's letter was surprising."

"Yes."

"And I hope you were given adequate time to prepare for the arrival of a wife."

"Of course."

Well, the woman was not being helpful. She would have to solve the mystery later, though she'd bet her eyeteeth that Rebecca's dislike of her had nothing to do with England.

"Thank you, Rebecca. My maid's carriage should be arriving any moment now. She will lend any assistance I need. Please be sure that her room is ready."

"Milady." She did not curtsy or even nod her head this time, simply swept stiff-backed from the room.

Alex stuck out her tongue at the closing door, but forgot her annoyance when she turned back to the bed. The sight of that fur sent a shiver up her spine, and she wondered if she had time to strip off her clothes and roll naked over the bed before Danielle arrived.

Chapter 17

She rolled and slid and buried her fingers in the unbelievable softness. Then she fell asleep.

Her rumbling belly wakened her and the first thing she noticed was the presence of sunlight in the room—a clear shaft of sunlight that shot straight through the window and onto the closed door. Odd, hadn't it been almost sunset when she'd climbed up?

Air strained into her lungs on a wheeze as realization struck. Oh my God, she'd slept straight through her first evening in Collin's home. She sat up with a cry and whipped her head around, trying to make sense of what she took in. Her perfumes and powders, brushes and clips were laid out on top of the dresser. Her carriage dress had disappeared from the floor and a wrap and slippers were laid at the foot of the bed. Danielle had definitely made it to Westmore.

And what of her husband?

"Oh, no," she moaned in utter horror. Had he slept alone? No, the whole bed was rumpled, not just her side.

What must he think of her? What must everyone think of her? Surely Mrs. Cook had prepared something special for their arrival. Surely Collin had meant to consummate this homecoming in their new bed. Oh, why had they let her sleep?

Her mortification dissolved with a pop. Why *had* Collin let her sleep? Why hadn't he wakened her for her first meal in her new home? Why hadn't he at least roused her to make love to her in their very own bed? A growl was just working its way up her throat when the door swung open.

"You're awake, *Madame*."

"Danielle, what time is it?"

"Only eight. Shall I bring your breakfast?"

"I . . . I don't know. Why didn't you wake me last night? I should have gone to dinner, I should have . . ." She threw her hands high in exasperation.

"Your husband wanted you to sleep. He said you had not been sleeping well." Danielle's mouth quirked into a naughty smile. "Is this true, *Madame?* Have you been kept awake nights?"

"Yes, I . . ." She let her hands fall to her lap, let her anger fall away with them. It had been considerate, she supposed, to let her sleep through. She certainly had been kept awake nights—five nights in all. First, the two dreamy, endless nights in her cottage. Then they'd made good use of three inns along the way. Perhaps he could be forgiven his thoughtlessness. He had meant to be helpful.

All right. She would not ruin her first full day at Westmore with a petty argument.

"Is breakfast still being served below?"

"*Non*. The commoners have taken themselves off to their work."

"Danielle!"

"Well, it is terrible, is it not? Everyone gathers together to eat the same meal! Lucky for you that many of them breakfast in their homes in the village. I would stay out of there for luncheon if I were you."

"I believe they call it dinner here. And I have eaten many a dinner with laborers, if you'll remember."

"Pah. For you, working was an adventure. These people will be here night and day."

Alex slipped from the bed, turning over Danielle's

words. Was that true, that working had been no more than an adventure for her? She had felt she'd contributed something but, of course, she was too small to be effective at the manual labor. So even if she had improved her brother's holdings, her physical work had been no more than a lark, really. Perhaps she'd been deluding herself to think she'd been useful at Somerhart.

But here at Westmore . . . Here she could make a real difference. There was so much to be done, and she would start on it today.

"I will take my breakfast in the great hall, even if it is empty. It will provide me with inspiration."

"Inspiration to do what, *Madame?* Turn into a bat?"

"Danielle!" Her reprimand was ruined by the muffling effect of her chemise as the maid pulled it over her head. "This is our home now. I will not have you insulting it."

She raised her eyebrows in a French expression of disgust, but she held her tongue as she efficiently fastened up Alexandra's corset.

"Yes, there is much that needs improvement, but that will come in time. There are surely little things that can be added to make things more cozy for the winter. Then in the spring, we can build at least three good rooms into that space, that should not prove too expensive, though I do hope Collin will let me invest in some windows."

"But why?"

Alex cocked her head. "Whatever do you mean?"

"Why would you want to bother with all these improvements?"

"What?" The bodice of her gown blinded her for a moment. She came up sputtering. "Collin's home is a fine place, Danielle, but I can admit that it needs some work. I would not like to live year after year hidden away from the sun. What?"

Danielle continued to stare, nose a crinkle of confusion.

"Did the roads jar your brain, Danielle?"

"I don't understand, *Madame*. Bridey says the new

house will be ready next year. Why would you go to all the bother of fixing this one up? It doesn't seem worth it."

"What new house?" Before the words had even left her mouth, Alex felt a terrible foreboding, a sense of some deception. She remembered Fergus's questioning look and the shake of Collin's head.

Danielle's face had blanked in shock. She licked her lips. "The new house being built. Over the hill. It's lovely, they say." Her voice faded away.

"Oh, yes," Alex mumbled over the ragged beat of her heart. "That new house. Of course."

"*Madame . . .*" Her face was no longer blank; it had twisted to pained pity.

"Fasten the bodice, please."

Her eyes avoided Alex's as her fingers worked on the bodice, hands trembling against the soft wool gown. Or perhaps that was Alex's vision, jumping and twitching with rage.

The new house. The one her husband had neglected to mention. The fine new house they would move into next year. The house that everyone knew about but her.

Oh, she did not try to tell herself that it was a surprise. Her husband was not a man to plan surprises. She knew immediately what this was. A trial. A test of her character. He had not wanted her to see Westmore with the knowledge that it was but a temporary home. He'd wanted to see if she would be willing to live in a dark, cold cave of a home as befits the wife of a bastard. He had wanted to see if she would stomp her foot and complain and reveal herself for the spoiled bitch he'd once called her.

She should call his bluff, she thought, shoving her feet into the black leather slippers that Danielle held for her. She should march down to his stable and demand to be housed as befits the daughter of a duke. But she was in no mood to play games with him. She would sooner slap him than counter his move.

Danielle reached to run a brush through her curls, but Alex pushed her hand away. "It's fine."

By the time she'd gotten out the door and down the stairs, her breath was jumping from her chest, her heart trying to beat its way out. She flew past a young boy who watched her from his perch atop the second step.

A lovely day greeted her through the open door of the keep, but the golden smell of turning leaves only tightened her throat today. How could he begin things this way? How could he?

There was no one at the blacksmith stall and she doubted he would be hanging about the storage shed, so Alex stalked down the hill to the endless stables below. She spied him immediately, his wide shoulders straining at the worn seams of an old shirt. His movement was already so familiar despite that his back was turned. She could pick him out in the darkest of shadows as long as she could see him move, heartless bastard.

Fergus was with him and spied her first, raised a hand in greeting and smiled wide. The smile faded when she drew near.

"Um, Collin, my friend."

"What?" His voice floated from the darkness and pricked her rage.

"Ye've a visitor."

Alex stuttered to a stop as Fergus stepped far to the side.

"Alex?" His face turned toward her in the shadows of the stall. "I'll show you the stock after dinner." He had already looked away, already dismissed her.

"Um. Collin." Fergus inched farther away.

"What?"

"Ye may want to . . ."

"I think your friend is trying to warn you that I did not come about the damned horses."

He straightened, his head swung so that he could really look at her this time.

"I'm sorry I did not wake you last night, wife. You needed your sleep."

A warm flush of embarrassment crept up her neck to

join the blood that was already hot with anger. "I am glad I was not awake to hear any more of your lies."

Quiet seemed to drop over the stable like a shroud. Her husband froze, eyes too deep in shadow to read. Alex wondered belatedly how many others were about, knew she should care, and yet she could not muster the sentiment. If Danielle had not told her, if she had gone chattering about her plans to Rebecca or Bridey . . . Fresh anger flooded her veins.

"My maid informed me that we are to have a new home next year. *My maid.*"

The muffled sound of Fergus's boot against the dirt revealed his retreat. Collin set down whatever tool he held in his hand and stepped into the light.

Alex had expected fury or at least self-righteousness, but she saw only weariness in the lines of his face. "I meant to tell you."

"What does that mean, 'meant to'? We've been alone these six days."

He turned back toward the stable and jerked his head, prompting a young boy to scamper out and run down the road, grateful to be away from the fight.

Wonderful. He would likely repeat it all to his mother before the hour was out.

"Even the new house is not grand, Alex. I did not want to present it to you as such."

"Do not try to make it sound anything better than it is. You meant this as a trial. To see if I could be the wife of a poor man, a farmer. Well, let me make something clear to you, MacTibbenham Collin Blackburn, I *am* the wife of a farmer. And whatever regrets or doubts you have about me come too late."

"It is not that I doubt you," he lied.

"If you care to drown this marriage in falsehoods, I cannot stop you, but I will not stand here and listen to them."

Her hair whipped into her face when she spun to stomp away, the strands sticking to her lips, then to her tongue when she tried to push them out. A shadow darted behind the closest shed. Another eavesdropper. Lovely.

"Alex. Wait."

She managed a few more steps, but where was she going? To her new room in this strange house? What comfort would that be?

"Alex." His hands settled over her shoulders, light on her bones, tentative. So he should be.

"I'm sorry, wife."

Alex swiped a hand over her face to clear away the strands of hair and possibly a few tears as well.

"I'm sorry."

"This is the memory I will have now of my first day in your home."

Weight settled into his hands. She could almost feel him slump. His lips brushed her ear and she wanted to rest her back against him.

"Please. Will you walk with me?"

She hesitated, stupidly grateful that he felt sorry. He took her silence as assent and tugged her to his side, wrapping his fingers into her stiff hand.

"Come with me. I'll show you the new house."

Alex wasn't even sure she wanted to see his blasted house now, but she thought it might sound petulant if she said no. Nearly as petulant as she felt.

So, unsure how to react, she followed him, first staring hard at the ground, then glancing furtively about.

He led her to the road and along it where it followed the natural line of the shallow valley, curving 'round the base of Westmore's hill in a slow, wide arc. The hills were rocky and wooded, but a wide swath of green eased out in front of them as the road snuck between two low rises.

The closer they came to the green, the farther the meadow seemed to stretch. A small group of horses came into view, chomping steadily at the dew-wet grass as they wandered.

A minute passed, then five. Leaves crunched beneath their feet. Then she finally saw it. Collin's new home.

His hand fell away when she stopped to take it in. The

river-rounded stones of the foundation fit tight together like a puzzle. The gray stone rose up plaster walls to frame the doorway and to form the many chimneys. Oak timbers edged the rest of the long structure, and though it was only two stories, the gray, tiled roof rose so steeply that it seemed as tall as the hill that protected its north side.

It was lovely, large and yet so like a cottage it seemed as cozy as their trysting place in the woods. If she'd stumbled across it, she'd have thought it the longtime residence of a squire and his family if not for the flat black of the glass-less windows and the absence of wood-smoke tripping from the chimneys. In short, it looked like a home.

Tears burned her eyes. "It's so beautiful, Collin. How could you have kept it from me?"

"Do you like it then?"

"Of course I like it. What kind of person would I be not to?"

"I . . ."

Alex waited for something, an explanation or a denial, but he only exhaled—a sigh fraught with regret and frustration. His hesitance prompted a wave of tears and, in her weakness, she turned to him, the only one she wanted.

Pressing into his warmth, she dug her fists into his chest even as she leaned her face against his shoulder.

"I'm sorry," he whispered, folding her tightly to him. "It's nothing to do with what I think of you. It's just . . . This cannot be the kind of home you had imagined for yourself. It would fit into just one wing of Somerhart."

"Why are you so stubborn in this?" Alex huffed, then breathed him in, resisting the urge to put her teeth to his flesh. Anger and need warred within her and both wanted her to bite him. "I never spent a moment of my life imagining a husband or a home. I told you that. I had no dreams of a palace or riches. You are the only man I've ever thought to marry, Collin. Can you not understand that? And whatever you come with, that is what I want."

He smelled of work—horses and hay and man. Her

temper helped to rouse other passions, so that her belly jumped when he swept his hands over her back.

"Shall we go inside? It's not close to done, but I'd like to—"

"No."

"Oh. All right. The stables then. You asked to see—"

"No. Take me home, Collin."

"Home?" The stark lines of his face grew starker still. "To Somerhart?"

"To Westmore, you beast. To your bed."

"To my . . . Oh." He seemed to finally register that her burning cheeks were now hot with something other than ire, and his eyes narrowed. "Well." A new firmness rose to cradle itself in the softness of her belly. "Home then."

And after he'd taken her home, after he'd lain her body into that lush fur and sunk himself between her legs, Alex was able to set aside their argument.

He was a brooding man. She knew that, just as she knew herself to be hot-tempered and bolder than most men could bear. But she loved him for what he was and for what he accepted in her.

The first months could be rough going; Lucy had told her that just a week before. *Give it time*, she'd whispered. *Things have a way of settling into place.*

But they would not settle if she held a grudge over every slight and misjudgment, so Alex made peace with his test and vowed to wait for everything to fall into place.

"Jeannie Kirkland, ye blasted spawn of Satan, where the hell is my flask?"

Jeannie winced and clapped a hand over Alexandra's giggling mouth. She tried not to sneeze when the girl's black curls tickled her nose. "Shh."

They pressed closer to the wall, feet sticking out too far beneath the musty tapestry. But her brother stomped past them and down the hall till his boots slapped against the stairs.

They heard a faint shout of "Jeannie!" and burst from their hiding place in a cloud of dust and laughter. Jeannie tugged her new friend along.

"Come, Alex. I can't believe you haven't been up here."

They stole down a short hallway at the very back of Westmore keep and through a warped door at the end. A narrow stairway curved up, disappearing into the darkness.

Jeannie threw open a trapdoor and led the way into the starry night. The flask sparked silver in the moonlight as she held it high.

"The finest whisky ever made by man, lassie, and worth a king's ransom." She took a swig, grimaced, and pushed it toward Alex.

Alex took a sip and, though she didn't cough, she couldn't keep the rasp from her voice. "Fine. Very fine."

Jeannie laughed outright. "Liar. Don't worry, it gets better the more you drink."

She took another sip before she handed it back to Jeannie. Jeannie raised the flask again and felt the liquor burn a path to her stomach and upwards too, setting her eyes and nose tingling.

By God, she loved it up here on the parapets, had always loved it. The night bloomed above them in a swath of stars. The moon hung like a great belly in the east, surely too heavy to rise any farther. It was beautiful here, but cold as well. The whisky was a welcome warmth.

"So?" Jeannie drawled after another swig.

"So, what?"

"Ach, don't play dumb. How do you like being married to our Collin? My brothers kept me away as long as they could, but three weeks was too much for even them to bear. They were dying to meet you."

She and four of her brothers had raided the castle mid-afternoon, demanding to see the bride. The new Mrs. Blackburn had bubbled over with happiness to see them, but she fell silent now.

"Surely it's not so bad?" Jeannie prodded.

"No, it's not so bad. In fact, I think it's rather good."

"Mm. I always suspected the man would make an excellent bed partner."

Alex made a strangled sound, but Jeannie knew without a doubt that she wasn't offended. Growing up with brothers had a way of expanding a girl's horizons.

"Um. Yes. He is. Absolutely."

Jeannie thought of the bed she'd like to be warming and couldn't stop the sigh that fell from her lips.

"Did you . . . ?" Alex started. "That is . . . Did Collin never court you?"

"What?" That snapped Jeannie out of her brooding. "Oh, God no. We've known each other forever."

"But I would think, after so much time . . . You seem very close."

"Well, close in the way I am with my cursed brothers. We met when I was seven or eight and I suppose he caught me at a time when I was sick to death of boys. He was just a disappointment really. Another neighbor who wasn't a girl."

"And when you got older?"

"Hmm." Jeannie passed the flask back. "I willna say I've never noticed him, but I've been told my brothers are handsome—"

"Oh, yes."

"—So perhaps I was just exposed too young to braw, bonny men. It doesn't weaken my knees. Or anything else for that matter."

Alexandra sighed and wilted into the wall. "Well, he leaves me weak, I confess. Of course we've only been married a month now."

"And are you getting on?"

"Yes. Although . . ." Alex glanced in her direction, and Jeannie saw the pained tension in her face. "He is very dark sometimes. And the circumstances of our marriage—"

"What *were* the circumstances?"

"Oh, um. A bit of an indiscretion. My brother did not force him to the altar, but I doubt Collin would have thought of it if not for the . . . extenuating circumstances."

"Don't be so sure, Alex. He was quite fierce when he spoke of you."

"He spoke of me?"

"Oh, I caught him sneaking back into the ball that night with lilac petals in his hair." They both broke into giggles at the thought. "He was beside himself. 'Do not speak of this to anyone. She is a fine lady.' Needless to say, I was scandalized."

Alex laughed so hard that tears leaked from her eyes, and Jeannie grinned in delight, thinking of Collin tortured by love. The man had seemed to live like a monk before. But now . . .

"Really, Alex, I have never seen him so much as flirt with a lady. Do not doubt that he cares for you. Why, he stared at you tonight all through dinner!"

"I . . . Yes, but he seems *angry*, doesn't he?"

"He's just jealous. He didn't like the attention my brothers showered over you. And Fergus too."

Fergus, Jeannie thought. Fergus, who avoided her like the plague. Fergus, whom she'd spent so many hours watching from this very rooftop.

Alex leaned a little closer. "Jeannie, I couldn't help but notice . . ."

"Oh, I love him!" Jeannie cried, voice hoarse, rusty from the years she'd been waiting to say this very thing. "I love him, Alex. What am I to do?"

"Fergus?"

"Yes, Fergus. He won't . . . He won't hear of it. Says my father wouldn't consider accepting his hand."

"Would he?"

"No, that cold-blooded whoreson! He says Fergus has no money and no land and no hope of ever having either."

"Oh."

Jeannie pressed her knuckles to her eyes. "Alex, what should I do? It's been a year and I feel I'm going mad."

"A year since what?"

"Since he kissed me. Oh, he acts cold and indifferent now. But a year ago he caught me in the hall and told me to stop swishing about in front of him or he'd do something I wouldn't like. So, of course, I dared him to—"

"Of course."

"And, oh, it was lovely and, and . . . It was so *much!* He said he'd been wanting me so long and he couldn't stand it anymore. But then he stopped. And now he will barely look at me. And I've loved him for years!"

"Oh, he looks at you. But when he sees you watching, he turns away."

Joy leapt to painful life in her chest. "Does he? He watches me?"

"Absolutely."

"Why do men have to be such idiots? Why will he not just go to my father? Or better yet, kidnap me?"

"Don't ask me, Jeannie. I had to seduce Collin to get him in my bed. Oops." She clapped a hand over her mouth. Her other hand wobbled the flask.

"Seduce him." She thought of Fergus's kisses, thought of the way his hands had shaped her waist and drawn fire up her back. "Seduction. That might be the way then."

"I'm not sure that's a good idea. Collin resents it, I think. He holds it against me."

"Hmm. I rather like the idea though. And Collin will get over it. Don't worry."

Alex rubbed her eyes and sighed before thrusting the flask back to Jeannie. "Take this. I'm feeling a bit mushy."

Jeannie tipped it up for the last swallow and made herself set Fergus and her fantasies aside. "Do not worry over Collin," she said. "He's never been in love before, Alex. He is trying to find his way."

"In love? I don't think that's it."

"Of course it is. Give him time. He's a man who's used to hard work and discipline. He's no doubt scared to death. You'll see. And our whisky's gone. Shall we rejoin the boys?"

"I suppose. I rather like your brothers' stories."

"Well, just wait till later then. Collin keeps almost as good a whisky as my father."

They giggled their way back through the door and into the keep to join the men below.

For once, the great hall seemed stifling to Collin. He could see that it was not—his wife and all their guests were gathered in chairs pulled close to the fire—but he felt hot and restless. He wanted to get out, to stalk through the door and into the cold night beyond, but he stayed. He would not leave his wife alone with these men who grinned and winked and brought out the pink in her cheeks. These friends of his.

Collin had never winked at a woman in his life, had never even known he should, but Alex seemed to enjoy it. She giggled and laughed and chastised them for their naughty stories. And Fergus . . . Oh, Fergus she watched carefully, for what, he had no idea, but he did not need to know to find it insufferable. They weren't discussing land use, after all.

Still, he insisted to himself, Fergus was his best friend and the Kirkland men he'd known his whole life. And Alex was his wife, of course. He couldn't leave that aside. But he felt always uncertain around her, never knowing what to say now that they were man and wife. He did not know if he should discuss the horses with her and the business, or if he should turn over the finishing of the house to her. She responded with interest to everything he said, but she was so attentive that he did not know how to live with that either—a woman who awaited him every evening and seemed to want something which he couldn't provide.

Her eyes had grown wary over the weeks and, when she was quiet and didn't know he was near, she seemed smaller, deflated somehow. Perhaps she'd begun to realize that life as a farmer's wife was neither exciting nor glamorous. She'd been here three weeks and the Kirklands were the first visitors they'd had. And Collin had no idea how to entertain her, outside the bedchamber at least.

But Fergus—he seemed always to know what to say to her, how to make her smile or laugh or coo with interest.

Fergus had become her friend—perhaps her best friend, and Alexandra was unmatched in her beauty and sensuality. Collin felt mad with suspicion, and only more mad to know it was unfounded. He trusted her. Surely he did.

"Collin?"

"What?" He looked up to find Douglas Kirkland looking him over with a raised brow, while everyone else watched with amused expectance. Except Alex, who chewed her lip in discomfort.

"I asked how ye managed to escape being murdered by the duke."

His wife shrugged helplessly in his direction.

"The duke?" Collin felt his face darken.

"Well for God's sake, we're not so far in the wilds that we didn't hear the rumors. And why else would you two have married so quickly if not for scandal, Blackburn?"

"Oh, why else?" Collin growled back.

"It wasn't all that scandalous!" Alex's words came fast and too high. "Which is how he escaped being murdered, of course."

"We figured as much. Collin's well known for his upstanding behavior. God knows we never thought he'd be the one to steal a duke's bonny sister from beneath his nose."

The Kirkland men laughed uproariously, none noticing the look that passed between Collin and Alex. Collin nodded, glad they'd focused on him and not Alexandra. He tried to smile in her direction, but she had looked away already, still chewing her lip.

"Collin," James boomed into the now quiet room, "Will ye come take a look at my new mount? Damned if I can afford one of your get, but I think he's a fine one all the same."

He glanced at his wife to find her scooted forward in her seat to whisper secrets with Jeannie. Probably discussing the true story of the hasty courtship. He wondered what she'd told her new friend.

"Collin?"

"Aye. Let's go."

He made a conscious decision not to glance over his shoulder when he walked away. She would be here when he returned.

Chapter 18

She was missing, and where the hell had she gone? Collin glared over the room, probing dark corners with his eyes as if she might be crouched there like a hunting cat. He'd been gone not a half hour for God's sake, and thinking of her every moment and now she was missing. She and Fergus both. Only Jeannie and her brothers sat there—Jeannie in a snit over something and the men ignoring her.

Collin stalked into the kitchen without a word, anger already overriding his good sense. "Is my wife here?" Mrs. Cook and the two maids froze and frowned at him. There were no hidey-holes in the room after all. "Never mind."

He stalked back to the great hall, walking right past Jeannie's outstretched hand. He glanced toward the door, then toward the alcove of the stairway. Rebecca hung back in the shadows, one foot on the first step as she waved him over.

"Collin," she breathed, pulling him close. He tilted his head down, eyes straining up the stairs. "May I . . . ? I haven't known if I should speak of this . . ."

"What?"

"I do not think it appropriate that your lady should . . . Oh, I must hold my tongue."

"Speak, Rebecca." He was amazed that he could push the words out past the burning in his throat.

"It's just that I see them alone so often. I know they are friends, but they should not sneak off together like that."

"Sneak off?"

"I don't . . . Yes."

A smoldering fire flared to life in his chest. Oh, God. Let it not be so. His foot took the first step, and the other followed, though he tried to make it stop.

"No, not up there, Collin. Here." Her fingers made a hesitant motion toward the narrow door to her left. It had once led to a chapel and now led to nothing but a rubble-strewn portion of the yard. What business would anyone have there?

No business at all, some beast inside him crowed, *but pleasure.*

Collin jerked his head at Rebecca and she scurried up the stairs to disappear above. He wanted no witness to this mess. Bad enough if he had to see it.

His hand touched the door and flattened against the wood. Odd that he felt nothing beneath his fingers. The door swung open without a sound, revealing nothing but the trees beyond the yard and the stars above. Collin stepped to the threshold, hesitated.

A man's voice floated through the night. "No, Alex."

"But—"

"It canna be."

"Oh, Fergus. Why must you be so stubborn? I've seen you looking—"

"No!"

Footsteps crunched away, nearly running through the frozen grass. His wife cursed under her breath.

Collin reeled. *I've seen you looking,* she'd said. And hadn't she said that very thing to him? *I've seen you watching me.* Oh, and he had been. He had.

Please, God, this must be a misunderstanding. It must be. She was no harlot. She would not give herself to his best friend. She had been an innocent. A willing, loving woman, but an innocent nonetheless.

But not innocent, that beast inside him sneered. *A virgin, but not untouched.*

He stepped out to the frozen ground, quiet and careful. He could see her in the moonlight, turned away and staring toward the stables. And then Collin could see her in that meadow where she'd first lain beneath him, urging him on as he'd pushed up her skirts, spitting mad when he would not take her. And he could see her on their wedding night, kneeling before him like a damned fantasy, taking his cock into her mouth with a purr of satisfaction. And even on the trail where they'd walked in the forest, her face so demure and timid. *You're far bigger than*—Oh, she'd shut her pretty mouth then. Far bigger than who and how many, he should have asked.

"Collin!"

His name sounded jerked from her throat in surprise, but she walked toward him easily enough, a flash of white signaling her smile.

"What did you think of James's gelding?"

He could not crack open his jaw to answer.

"Fergus has gone home, so I hope you weren't looking for him."

"I was not," he growled, "but I found him all the same."

Her foot slid a little in the grass when she stopped. "What do you mean?"

"I mean, wife, that I was looking for you, and I found Fergus also."

"Oh, yes." Her hand rose to brush his sleeve, but it hovered in midair as if she could feel the rage radiating from his skin. "I wished to speak to him about . . . something."

"'Something.'"

"Um, is there something wrong, Collin?"

"I would say so, yes."

"What then?" The uncertainty had left her voice. Her words had gone clipped and short.

How dare she be irritated with him? "Do you think it is right that you steal out here with my manager and whisper in the dark?"

"I was not whispering."

His laughter sounded like metal against stone. She did not deny the sneaking out here, just the whispering. Very well, she hadn't really whispered. She'd pled.

"What is this about?"

"Well, let me ask you this. What was it that got you sent home from London?"

"I don't understand."

"What did my brother see when he opened that door on you and St. Claire?"

Her shadow drew itself up and stepped away from him. "Are you accusing me of . . . Do you think that Fergus . . . ?"

"I am only asking a simple question. I am curious as to your past. I spoke with two men in London who claimed to have kissed you, at least. I thought perhaps it was a hobby of yours. What else?"

"I . . . I did not kiss Fergus! I wouldn't even think it."

"No?"

"No! How can you ask such a thing?"

"Come now, Alexandra. You did much more than kiss St. Claire and he is no better than a dog."

"Collin, I am your wife." The sound of fear in her voice struck him like the snap of a whip. He stepped back from her, as if he stumbled from a dream. She had never spoken to him in fear. Never. He realized that his hands had gone numb with clenching.

"How could you think I'd be unfaithful to you? I've never . . . I've never given you a reason to hate me."

"Why were you hiding out here in the dark then?"

Her breath shuddered in her chest, just as he heard a curse behind him. "Jeannie?" Alex cried.

"Aye, sweeting." Jeannie's voice slid from goose-down to steel. "What the hell are you about, Blackburn?" She didn't brush past him so much as plow over him in her attempt to get to Alex.

"Come inside now, Alex, where it's warm. We'll leave your man here to cool down." Collin stepped aside to let them pass. "What did that beast say to ye, sweeting?"

The door closed behind them and Collin began to shiver. Was he a beast? Or was he the biggest fool in Scotland?

The wind, gusting and slapping against her face, burned tears into Alex's eyes as she waved farewell to Jeannie and the Kirkland brothers. She wished Jeannie would stay, wished she could hide behind her friend's anger forever.

Collin had slipped into bed late in the night, pretending that he believed her ruse of sleep. He'd slipped out this morning in the same manner, and had only just returned from his work to see their guests away.

The Kirkland carriage disappeared over the hill long before she dared to glance in his direction.

"It's cold," she murmured, and hurried past him toward the relative warmth of the keep. She felt him follow her through the door.

"Will you sit with me upstairs a moment?"

Her gut tumbled. She had no idea what to say to him, whether to rail or cry or hold her tongue. What could she say?

When he moved past her, disappearing up the stairs, she followed him up and into the circle of her sitting room.

"I accused you of something vile last night."

"Yes."

He stared at her, waiting for a confession, she guessed. She was tempted to give it to him just to see his eyes flare with whatever pain she could administer.

"I did not come to this lightly, Alexandra."

Oh, she was Alexandra now. Perhaps a "Lady Westmore" was coming.

"One of the servants said that you and Fergus disappear often together."

"One of the—? Who? Rebecca?"

"That doesn't matter."

"It most certainly does. That woman is a bitch. A bitch in heat where you are concerned."

"Don't insult her simply because she came to me with this."

"Oh, I can assure you I've insulted her many times in my mind before this."

"So she lied to me?"

"Yes . . . No. I don't know! What does she mean by disappear? We often go to the stables together. We sit in the hall and talk. Why do I even need to say this to you? I am your wife."

"As long as you can remember that, then we need never speak of this again."

"Collin . . ." Hurt clawed at the walls of her chest, tried to crawl out her throat as a sob. She felt stupid and angry and so confused. Should she be mad? Did he have a right to worry?

She wondered suddenly if one of the Kirkland men had mentioned that she'd followed Fergus out. Wondered if they had raised eyebrows at her departure. Her face burned at the thought. "I'm sorry." She nearly choked on the words. "I didn't think how it would look to our guests."

"That's all?"

"I did nothing wrong, Collin. Nothing." She thought of what Jeannie had said to comfort her the night before. *Tell him the truth. Make him feel a fool and he'll come to his senses.* The truth then. "Collin, it was Jeannie I spoke of to Fergus, why I searched him out."

"What about Jeannie?"

"There is an . . . an attraction."

"That's ridiculous. Fergus has known her since she was hardly more than a child."

"She's only two years younger than I, Collin. The girl knows what she wants, and Fergus refuses to acknowledge it."

"Then leave the man alone. And if you're speaking the truth . . . then I apologize, Alex. I'm sorry that I lost my temper."

She nodded, feeling like a stranger to herself, but a tiny ray of righteous anger shone through her muddled thoughts. "I want that woman gone."

"Rebecca?"

"She's been disrespectful to me since that first day. And to think that she has spied on me . . ." She could see by the razor line of his mouth that she should have waited to speak. Waited a week or two till this had passed.

"You want me to turn her out?"

"Yes."

"I have known her nearly twenty years. Her mother was a friend to mine."

"She does not treat me as she should, Collin."

"And where should I send her? Out to the cold to freeze? Her mother is dead and she has no family. Could I give her a reference at least, so she would not starve?"

"I don't care where she goes. She wants you, Collin! She watches you like a dog watches for scraps at the table. And she wishes me gone. That should be obvious now."

"What is obvious is her concern for me, as a friend. And what kind of friend would I be if I let you dismiss her? You have never lived as she has, Alex. You have never been hungry or cold or worried over anything more than which dress would flatter your figure most." He paused, and she thought he was done with his tirade, but he only drew a breath for the next attack.

"Rebecca is an excellent housekeeper. She works hard and she does her job and if she is shocked at your boldness, well then, I shall send away everyone who knows you, for who isn't?"

Collin slammed from the room, not caring that he left her heart bleeding in her straining chest.

A long day passed in heavy silence, and Alexandra was sure she would not sleep. But she had lain awake the night before, after all, and the world spun into oblivion as soon as she lay down.

A warm touch woke her to pitch black.

"I'm sorry, Alex." His lips moved against her back, his breath spreading hot over her shoulder blade.

She blinked her eyes open, but the dark soothed her

back to sleep within seconds. A heavy weight curled over her waist, Collin's hand curving to the shape of her body, and she sighed with pleasure.

"Shh," he whispered. "Sleep."

His mouth trailed kisses, his hand smoothed over her hip. Alex melted into the bed, liquid and warm, as his fingers stroked down to her thighs.

"You're so beautiful. Soft and wild as summer."

The length of his body pressed to her back, a world of heat against her skin. She couldn't help but stretch and sigh and burrow closer to him.

His hand slid over her thigh, he cupped her sex. "*Caitein*," he breathed.

She was dreaming, she thought, and sank further into the pleasure. She arched against him, pressing back until the hot brand of his cock burned her skin. He rewarded her by slipping one finger into her folds and stroking there.

"Ah!"

Collin's mouth whispered over her ear. "Shh," he said, even as he tortured her with pleasure. Her nerves slowly woke to a hum. His fingers slicked over and over her, teasing and circling until Alex whimpered.

It was lovely and too gentle, and she longed for more. She pressed her hand to his, trying to push him harder, but his fingers refused to obey, refused to stop the torment. She raised her leg and slipped it back, over his thighs. "Collin, please."

"Mmm." His chest rumbled with the sound. He ground his hips against hers. Alex arched and reached behind her to grip the back of his neck. Gaelic tumbled from his lips and he finally slid a finger deep into her body.

"Oh, God," she sobbed into the dark.

"So hot," he whispered on a harsh sigh. "So slick for me, Alex."

"Yes." She angled her knee higher on his leg, spreading herself for him, and Collin shifted his hips and pressed his hard length between her legs. "Yes," she moaned, mad with the feel of him sliding over her folds.

His hand cupped her again, holding her as he slipped back and forth against her. Alex fought back a scream of frustration. She wanted him deep and hard and ruthless, but he seemed bent on torture, merciless in his patience.

The darkness of the room pressed against her skin. Alex waited for the moment when he moved forward, then she tilted her hips and felt him slide into her body. Just an inch, just the head of his cock.

"More," Alex panted. "More." He slid a little deeper, stretching her flesh. She dug her fingernails into his hip, trying to pull him in. She wanted him to fill her until the pleasure grew to pain, wanted to burn with it.

"You consume me, Alex." Collin's words floated like a ghost in the dark. His fingers curled hard, almost hurting, and then he sank himself deep.

"Oh."

He slid out, then pushed harder in. Again and again, each thrust more brutal than the one before. Alex's body hovered on the edge of that sharp pleasure. Every stroke pushed a high moan past her lips. She dug her nails deep, urging, commanding him to be ruthless.

Collin obliged, finally. He wrapped his hand hard around her thigh and pulled her leg up and open. He drove into her. Alex threw her head back and pressed her own fingers between her legs. She'd barely touched herself when her spiraling pleasure broke open like a hot coal. Fire burned through her, sizzling over her nerves as she screamed and strained against him.

Collin thrust hard one last time, his cry echoing hers, sounds twisting together until they floated into the night.

"I'm sorry," he whispered. His breath cooled the sweat at her temple. "I'm sorry for what I said."

Alex didn't want to wake from her dream, so she only nodded and let the pillow catch her tears.

Chapter 19

"It is so lovely to meet such a beautiful new bride. Welcome to Scotland, Lady Westmore."

"Thank you, Mr. Nash."

New bride. Was she still a new bride? She did not feel like one. To think they had been married but two months. Was it supposed to get worse before it could get better? Lucy hadn't gone into specifics, but things were certainly not falling into place.

Her husband stood at her side amongst the bright gaiety, speaking comfortably, if not tersely, to those he knew. The Kirklands were more important socially than Alex had realized. Jeannie's father was not a lord, but his brother was an earl and the lot of them were rolling in money. The brother was not the only earl in attendance. The party would have been considered high ton even in London, for it was winter, after all, and not a time for idle travel.

The dancing had begun, but Alex did not move to join it. When she'd received the invitation, she'd thought of Collin's promise to learn to waltz but hadn't brought it up. She'd been afraid of his answer. If he'd said no, her feelings would be hurt and then she might lash out and break the fragile truce between them. So it had been for weeks—few words, uncomfortable silences. Whatever speech they exchanged was crouched in careful, polite phrasing. She felt they were circling each other and, when they finally drew close, she didn't know if they would embrace or strike.

Always aware of his presence, Alex felt his eyes on her and glanced up with a quick smile. He'd been lovely tonight, actually. His eyes had glowed at the sight of her in the dress she'd chosen so carefully. He'd swept the silver crepe with an appreciative look and had even come near to whisper compliments and kiss her neck. Alex shivered at the memory.

His lovemaking had not changed anyway. He still worshipped her with his hands and his mouth and all the rest of his wonderful body. But always in the dead of night. Always so late that she wondered if he slept at all. He would wake her with tenderness and need and speak Gaelic melodies into her ear as he slid his body into hers.

She had no idea what words he spoke, but they never failed to bring tears to her eyes. She'd asked Jeannie once, about one thing he whispered over and over again, though she'd blushed in horror of what it might be. *Maith dhomh*, he always murmured.

"Forgive me," Jeannie had translated for her, with a telling look, but Alex had said no more.

Forgive me, he offered her, in a language he knew she couldn't understand. What did it mean? She wanted to ask him, prayed that he wanted to try again at loving her. She had worked up her courage over the past few days, to talk to him during the long, private carriage ride to the Kirklands', but all that had changed this morning.

A youth she didn't know had come sneaking out of the trees to hand her a note as she walked Brinn along the edge of a forest. He'd handed her a slip of paper and, ignoring her questions, had slunk back into the firs.

Her stomach still clenched at the thought of it, and she glanced around as if she would see Damien St. Claire watching her from the edges of the crowd.

My Dear, he had written, *You are sleeping with the*

*enemy. How could you marry the very man who hunts your
lover? I demand restitution for your inconstancy.*

She would have scoffed at such a grievance a year ago,
even a few weeks ago. If he had tried to blackmail her
when she'd first come to Scotland, she would have gladly
set him up again, participated in whatever trap her husband
set to catch him. But not now. Oh God, not now. For he'd
known exactly how to threaten her.

> *The word in the Lowlands is that your husband is
> a jealous man, a man who in no way trusts you. How
> would he respond to a few stories about your past?
> How would he feel if I set the neighbors abuzz with
> tales of your talented lips? Could I adequately de-
> scribe the slick heat of your quim? I would dearly
> love the chance.*
>
> *Fortunately for you, my silence comes cheaply.
> £20,000. Do not deny me this or I will give your hus-
> band something to be jealous of. You have two days.
> Leave it in the place you received this note. Jewels
> will do nicely if gold is not at hand.*

He had not signed it. Why bother? There was no question of who had penned it.

So now she could not enjoy her husband's compliments.
She could not enjoy the party. She could not even enjoy the
way Collin had cradled her hand in his on the ride toward
Kirkland Hall. Instead, her stomach lurched each time she
looked in his direction, for she had finally betrayed him.
She had betrayed him the moment she'd received the note
and hidden it beneath her linens. She had betrayed him
when she'd spread her jewels out on the dresser and tried
to calculate the value of each piece.

She had lost all the certainty she'd carried with her
through life. She no longer knew who she was or how to
behave.

Fergus was her husband's best friend and so she'd

thought of him as a brother and treated him as such. It must have been wrong to do so. It must have been improper, for even Fergus avoided her now.

Improper. Always improper. Alexandra Huntington Blackburn was an unnatural girl. She had finally come to believe what her governesses had told her and what her Cousin Merriweather had screamed at her. Really, it had been obvious to everyone else. Why had it taken her so long to realize?

Collin turned her toward another introduction and she tried her best to be bright and lovely. She wanted to make him proud. She wanted him to watch her and see a lady and a wife. She wanted things to settle into place.

Why wouldn't they just settle into place?

Another gentleman approached her husband and, even in her musings, Alex blinked and stood straighter. The man had tears in eyes. She was quite sure she had never seen the like. The older gentleman took Collin's hand in a hearty hold, shaking his head as he did so.

"Lord Waterford?"

"We had to put her down, Westmore."

"What?"

"Devil's Drop. She snapped her foreleg right in half in a post hole. Just a week ago." His jowls trembled. "A damn shame, I tell you. Pardon the strong language."

"My wife," Collin murmured, placing his hand beneath the man's elbow. "A mare of ours," he explained, meeting her eyes and angling his head toward the library.

Alex nodded, cringing as the man pressed his hand to his chest.

"By God, she was a fine one. You should have seen her, Lady Westmore."

Still nodding, she watched her husband stride away, his head bent close to Lord Waterford, the better to hear the details of the accident. Her heart ached in sympathy as she remembered the pain she'd felt when her first pony had been put down, remembered looking into her sad, wise eyes and knowing they'd soon be lifeless.

Tears welled at the memory, and she blinked hard to force them away as a sudden weariness descended. It must be after one, hours past her normal bedtime, but the guests plowed on, bright and cheerful around her. Jeannie's smile flashed toward her through the crowd of dancers, drawing a quick lift of Alex's lips before her friend disappeared again, swallowed by the festive storm.

The relative quiet of the foyer beckoned, and she slipped past the milling people toward the realm of quiet conversations and murmured laughter. Relief cooled her warm cheeks for just a moment . . . The barest moment of calm before she saw him, before she watched in shock as his blond head came up and his eyes focused on her with narrow pleasure. Blond hair, cold eyes. But not St. Claire. Not the threat she'd half expected.

Robert Dixon. Heat returned to her cheeks like a gust of bellowed flame, and the feel of that blush only made the warmth prickle. He would look at her pinkness as a sign of guilt, when she felt nothing more than disconcerted. He would relish the thought of her embarrassment.

She watched him smile, watched his eyes sweep down to delve the shadows of her cleavage as he made a quick excuse to his companion and stepped away. Alex turned a foot, began to pivot, but pride stopped her from fleeing. She had no reason to run from this scrap of a man, she told herself as he approached, but she truly did not wish to speak to him. Not when his hazel eyes were so coldly lit.

So pride would not let her leave, but now, as he took his time approaching, it looked as if she waited for him, as if she gave him permission to join her. Her flat glare of disgust did nothing to dim his satisfaction or the curl of his lip.

"Lady . . . Westmore, is it now?" She pressed her lips hard together. "A pleasure to see you again."

She neither spoke nor offered a hand. A cut of the utmost dignity. It only served to brighten the amusement in his eyes.

"Come now. Aren't you happy to see an old friend from home? I insisted to Lord Bonnet that we attend as I was sure you'd be here."

"I think I made clear that you were not to come near me."

"A misunderstanding, I believe."

"How so?"

"How so?" He leaned in, eyes darting down her bodice as his lips crept close to her ear. "I can see now that you were only disappointed at my lack of persistence."

Alex inched to the side and did her best to look down her nose at a man taller than her. "Move away from me."

"Imagine my shock at finding out that the oh-so-demure Lady Alexandra had given herself over to no less an animal than an illegitimate Scotsman."

Her fan struck his elbow with a satisfying whack. "You go too far."

"On the contrary."

She felt the hot slide of his fingers curling around her arm, gripping too tightly, but she dared not pull away—two faces had turned in their direction. There was enough talk already about Collin's wife. She would not cause a scene over this snake's injured pride.

Smiling at the woman nearest her, she hissed through her teeth, "Unhand me."

"You'd give yourself to that scoundrel St. Claire and fall into bed with a damned stud farmer, but you turned me away like a supplicant, you little bitch."

"Let *go*."

"I hear tell that Blackburn is little pleased with you. Does he resent paying such a high price for ill-used goods?"

"Let go this instant or you'll regret it." Alex felt limp with shock when his fingers actually loosened and fell away.

"You're damned lucky your brother is a duke. You wouldn't be so—"

"Will you introduce me, Lady Westmore?"

Her husband's voice sounded so close that Alex jumped, spinning to find him only a yard behind her, his gray eyes flat. "Collin!"

"Yes."

She blinked, wondering if he'd heard, but no . . . He would be hot with rage if he knew. He stepped forward to join her and his eyes were positively icy when they swung toward Dixon. A thumping like a rabbit's heart took up inside her chest. What was she to say? Not the truth, certainly, not unless she wanted a husband on trial for murder.

"Um." A glance showed her Mr. Dixon's pale face. "Yes. Of course. Mr. Robert Dixon, this is my husband, Collin Blackburn, Lord Westmore. Mr. Dixon is a friend of my brother's."

Collin did not take the man's hesitant offer of a handshake. In fact, he looked at the hand so fiercely that Dixon yanked it back and gave no more than a murmured pleasantry before spinning away.

Alex's nerves hummed with anticipation of something dire.

"Are you ready to leave?"

"Yes!" she gasped and slid her hand over his hard arm. "Yes, let's go."

They slipped past the guests, Alex trailing behind his straight back, mind spinning for a way to deflect his anger. It didn't matter, really. She wanted to leave. And perhaps he'd only sensed her dislike of the man she'd been speaking with.

Her heeled slippers pinched her feet and provided no cushion against the granite underfoot as they hurried past the milling crowd. By the time Collin retrieved her cloak and called the carriage, she could do nothing more than collapse into the cushioned seat with a sigh.

"I forgot to say good-bye to Jeannie."

"Who was that man?"

"What?"

"Don't play dumb, Alex."

"Why are you angry?"

"I don't know, perhaps it has something to do with stumbling upon my wife in an intimate conversation with a man I've never met."

Her teeth ground hard together as she searched his face in the dim light of the carriage lamp, looking for a sign of . . . of something. Something that wasn't there.

"Was he one of your lovers?"

"What? Collin—" A hard shake of her head freed a spark of anger from all the guilt and self-pity she'd been hiding under. "That doesn't even make sense." She watched the frantic working of his jaw, the muscles that clenched and released, thrown into prominence by shadow. "Why are you asking me this?"

"Just answer the question."

"I will not! That question is not relevant."

"We both know you were no innocent when you came to my bed."

"I was a virgin!"

"Do not play coy."

"Coy? Am I speaking to an idiot? Why are you so suspicious? How could you ask me of lovers when you know you were my first?"

His eyes filled with harsh passion and his flat mouth thinned even further until the lips that had kissed her disappeared. "The first, yes. The first to have you there."

Her heart beat once, twice. Rage froze, crystallized with a suddenness that chimed like glass in her chest. "What?"

"You know quite well that there is more to making love than just sex."

Her teeth clattered together, a hard click in the quiet rumble of the space. Heart tearing, she worked words past her lips. "What are you . . . What are you asking me?"

"Just tell me who he is, and don't repeat that shit about him being a friend of the duke."

"No. *No*, I want you to tell me exactly what you mean. Put your ugly thoughts into words so we can both hear them, so you can finally taste them on your tongue."

"Alex—"

"No! Are you asking if I have ever . . . If I have ever taken that man *into my mouth?* Or, or . . ."

"Alex—"

"Or perhaps you mean something more vile yet? Perhaps you're asking me—*your own wife*—perhaps you're asking if I played at sodomy?" She watched with sick satisfaction as his body twitched. His eyes widened from their slits of rage and she thought she saw pain. Good. It couldn't begin to approach what she felt.

"What, did you think I didn't know about that trick? Perhaps there are other things I know that you're not aware of. I am a wee whore, after all." A throng of emotions played over his hard face, but Alex saw it all through a steady blur of hatred.

"You'll never tell me about your past, even when I ask."

"Oh, and how many women have you had, Collin? And what parts of their bodies did you stick yourself into?"

"It's not . . . You never asked. I'll tell you about my past if you like."

"No, I'm not a beast like you. What do you want to know? You want to know who that man was to me?"

"I just . . ." He threw his big hands up into the air before crossing his arms tight over his chest. "Yes."

"Well, let's see. Mr. Robert Dixon. Yes, I did kiss him, I remember that. He stuck his tongue into my mouth. What else? Oh, then he decided that I had granted him the liberty to do what he wished and he pulled up my shirt, dropped his trousers, and tried to have me."

She smiled at his sudden shift, smiled as he sat forward with a shout.

"Oh, yes. Of course, I encouraged him and I am a whore after all, so I can only be glad he was too much of a gentleman to give chase when I fell to the ground and crawled away, else I might have lost my virginity to a different bastard entirely."

Her eyes narrowed as his fist rose, but she did not cringe, not even when it swung toward her to pound on the roof of the carriage. "Turn this damn thing 'round!" He pounded again.

"Stop it," she growled, bouncing in her seat as they

shuddered to a halt. "Stop it. You have no right to play my defender now."

He closed his eyes. Opened them again.

"Sir?" a voice called.

Alex leapt to her feet and slid open the window. "Go! Drive on!" They drove.

"You cannot ask me to ignore him."

"I am not *asking* for anything. If I want to beg protection from a man, I will go to my brother and send him after *you*. You are the only man who has done me injury, my lord. You have revealed yourself." Her words stirred laughter in her mouth. *Revealed yourself.* She saw again the red jut of Dixon's manhood. A giggle escaped. The sound seemed to wound her husband. He cringed, rubbed a hand hard over his eyes.

"Alexandra. Wife. I'm sorry. I don't know why—"

"The same reason you always have, I suppose. Your suspicion of my very nature. Your hatred of me."

"Oh, God. I don't hate you. I love you. It is eating away at me."

"You love me?" Those precious words twisted from her lips like the vilest poison. "How dare you."

"*Caitein*, I'm sorry. I just, I feel mad with you sometimes, as if I have no control over my life."

Thank God for her anger. She could feel terrible things lurking beneath it, not yet revealed. Some piece of her had broken off in a jagged chunk that scraped and wounded. My God, could she never make a wise choice in her life? She had given everything to this man. Everything. And he thought her no better than a rutting cat, rubbing herself against every male in her reach. *Caitein*, he called her. *Caitein*.

"When I saw you with that man, and I knew there was something between you . . . Please, will you forgive me my words?"

"And what of your thoughts? Shall I forgive those also, do you think? A lot of forgiveness for how often you think them."

The familiar heat of his fingers took her hand and pulled her toward him. She yanked away.

"Don't. And don't speak anymore, I can't stand to hear it." She met his eyes dead on and saw a twinge of panic spark from their silver depths. "Tomorrow perhaps," she hissed when his lips parted, "when I don't wish to scratch out your eyes."

Looking away to fight that very temptation, she turned to the window, wide open to the cold night air. Her skin burned even in the cool of a hard frost, just as her eyes burned, dry and rough with the need for tears that would not come.

She was aware of his every move across from her—his gradual shift from anger to resignation, body easing back to slump against the seat; the occasional shift of his knee too close to hers. For some reason she did not want him to see her move, did not want to reveal even a breath to him. She was a statue, cool and rigid and utterly immune to his wild insults. She needed him to look at her and see nothing close to vulnerability.

Fighting even the rocking of the carriage, she thought her neck might snap at the next rut in the road. And perhaps that would be best for all involved, particularly her. What a mess she'd made of so many lives. This was what came of trying to do the right thing for once. At least when she did the wrong thing, she could expect the worst outcome, anticipate it and brace herself. But this . . .

Minutes passed. Then miles. The cold seeped into her as they rolled on, furthering her fantasy that she was made of stone. Smooth and hard and lovely, her skin froze in the caress of the bitter wind, and she hardened her mind as well, sculpted it until all her thoughts focused on the fascinating clouds of her breath escaping into frost.

Collin snapped the window shut with a crack and a curse and ruined that for her too. He leaned forward to rummage beneath his seat for a blanket, but the carriage was already tilting right, taking the hard turn that led toward home, no more than three minutes . . . maybe four in the pitch black of the moonless night.

Weight pressed her knee, drawing her eyes from their distance to see his hand on her leg. "We can't stay silent forever, Alex. Can we not discuss this?"

She stared at this hand, so wide and strong. So warm and deceptively gentle. She stared until he removed it from her person to clench it against his thigh.

A hot stove flared to life in her gut. She felt like herself again, like the self she'd hidden from him and his suspicions. Oh, and she had tried so hard to bury her hard-to-love boldness beneath layers of pleasantness, obedience. For him.

His hand rose again, hovering over her knee.

"Don't touch me." A sharp stop bounced her back against the seat. They were home. His home. "And find another bed tonight. I do not wish to sleep near you."

"Damn it—"

"Shut up." She darted out the door when it swung open, dragging her beautiful silver skirts against the carriage frame with not the least twinge of regret. She landed in a scrambling heap and pushed past the stunned groom to stomp her way up the stairs and into the gloom of Westmore.

"Send a glass of wine to my chamber," she growled at a sleepy maid and stalked toward her room. Perhaps he would sleep with Rebecca tonight. Perhaps this would be just the excuse he needed to fall between that bitch's thighs. And Lord help her if she dared to bring Alex's wine herself. She'd finally get the slap that she'd been begging for these past weeks.

Oh, things had gotten worse on that front, as if the housekeeper knew of the failed attempt to push her out. Now she didn't even feign deference. She spoke to the other servants in Gaelic even when Alex was in the room. She smirked at her when they were alone.

Oh, yes, Alex hoped she would be the one to bring her wine. She would find a new Mrs. Blackburn awaiting her sneering face. Alex's palm itched at the thought but, in the end, Danielle pushed through the door, glass in one hand and decanter in the other. She clicked the bedroom door closed with a jut of one hip.

"How was your evening, *Madame?*"

"Tiring."

"We keep farmer's hours now," her maid replied with a huff. The woman must have something against farmers, Alex thought as she turned her back to offer the tapes of her gown.

Danielle undressed her in tugs and touches punctuated by smothered yawns. She was too tired to chatter tonight, thank God, as Alex couldn't think well enough to reply to even the most inane conversation, and she certainly wanted nothing to do with pointed questions. When she felt the strong bands of the corset loose their hold, she pulled in a great rush of air and let it out with a shudder. The new ease in her chest seemed to free up a pain deep inside her.

"I'll sleep late tomorrow, Danielle. No need to rise until I call you."

Once alone, she found that the ancient latch slipped easily into place, locked for the first time in God-knew-how-long. Not for the last time though, not if she stayed in his home.

She did not cry as she slipped into bed. She did not cry one tear for him.

Chapter 20

A bright, cheerful sound floated to her ears, scraping her sleep away before she was ready. Again—a musical pinging, steady as a tolling bell. Horseshoes . . . Adam was forging shoes again. *Clang, clang, clang.* Those shutters kept nothing out.

Alex opened her eyes to the knowledge that her heart was broken. Sleep had dulled neither the pain nor the memory of its cause. Indeed, it had brought a new facet to its brilliant hurt. St. Claire's letter.

She no longer felt guilty at keeping it secret. Indeed, it had been a wiser deception than she could have guessed. *Tales of your talented lips.* She'd only thought of kissing and the dozen or so men she'd pressed her lips to.

Yes, she'd kissed Damien and even his best friend a time or two, and had thought herself well and truly scandalous. And how naughty she'd been to let Damien touch her in private places and how wicked to touch him as well, to let him press himself into her open hand, to enjoy the little whips of pleasure that touched her at her daring.

Three times she'd snuck off to let Damien teach her what it meant to touch and be touched. Three times she'd let him pull her into a secluded room and push up her skirts, let him spend himself into her hand.

She had thought these things too forbidden to reveal to

her jealous husband, and so she hadn't told him. But, oh, she'd had no idea the scenarios he would weave if left to his own devices. That he would think her capable of debasing herself to such lengths. She hadn't understood, but St. Claire had. Sad to think a murderer knew her husband so well. Perhaps they were all the same. All of them.

Alex pushed her aching body from bed and padded to the window to push aside the drapes and throw back the shutters.

The world moved on below her, people rushing to and fro. Horses ran in the paddock, heads thrown back to savor the bright cold of the day. A fine winter morning and no one the worse for her pain.

These people, these diligent, dedicated people . . . None of them needed her and half didn't even want her here. She had done something wrong or lacked something they expected from her. Just respect, perhaps, just the respect of their lord and leader. And the house servants followed the lead of Rebecca.

These people had jobs and families and why should they make room for a woman who could not even engender the respect of her husband?

She wanted to go home. To her home. She didn't belong here and she never would. She didn't even belong in her husband's bed.

"Bastard," she whispered. "Bastard." The fist that clenched her heart released, and the fingers that spread open inside her were tipped by claws. "You bastard." Her words were lost on a sob, a cry that had waited to escape all night.

Pain wracked her body, grief rode her soul. Her legs tried to curl up, tried to force her to the floor, but she fought it—fought it like she wanted to fight Collin. And she won. She suppressed the instinct to collapse. She forced her shoulders up and stalked to the door to throw it open and glare down the hallway to the swaying back of a girl with a broom.

"Send my maid," she bit out. "Now." Oh, the servants

would be whispering today, enjoying the novelty of outrage at her high-handed behavior. It was her parting gift to
them, the joy of justifying their dislike.

Alex turned the glare back to her room. Was there even
one thing here that she needed? Warm clothes. Coins for
food and shelter. What else? Nothing.

"*Madame*," Danielle panted from behind her. "What is
wrong?"

Alex spun, reaching past her maid's shoulder to slam the
door. Danielle gasped, alarmed by the noise and no doubt
by her mistress's face. Oh, she'd caught a glimpse of herself in the mirror—sunken, wild eyes and pale lips framed
by tangled curls.

"My lady, what is it!"

"I am leaving, but I need you to stay, Danielle. Can you
do that for me?"

"Stay? What do you mean?"

"My husband . . . My husband has accused me of being
a whore for the last time, do you understand?"

"*Oui.*" She paled, stepped away. "*Oui,* of course, *Mademoiselle . . . Madame.*"

"I am leaving. This morning. What time is it?"

"Nine."

"Nine, yes." Good. Dinner in three hours and he
wouldn't come home for that, despite that he was only
yards away. No, he wouldn't return till dark and she'd be
miles gone even if he did notice her absence.

"I'll need breakfast first. A lot of it and extra napkins.
Then . . . Then I'll pack just a satchel. Can you take it for
me, hide it outside the gate? I don't want the groom asking
questions."

"*Oui.* I'll go get the food, shall I?"

"Yes. And I will send for you as soon as I'm home, you
understand? I can't take you with, you hate horses." Her
voice broke on the last word and tears spilled over her
cheeks.

Danielle cried out and tried to reach for her, but Alex

pushed her hands back. "No, none of that. Get the food. I'll pack."

Her hands shook, but not one more tear fell.

Wool stockings. Wool scarf. Money. One of the plain dresses she'd worn for that long-ago tryst. An extra pair of gloves. What else? What else? There was room for the food and more, but she couldn't think. She stuffed in a candle, wondered how she'd light it. No matter. She would find an inn before nightfall.

Her knife. She pulled it from its hiding place under the bed and started to stuff it into the bag, then thought of St. Claire. He hated her now, and he had killed before. Alex eased the knife from the bag and stared at it. If he was watching the keep, if he followed her . . . Well, she'd do the best she could to draw his blood.

She set the blade on the dresser. She'd hide it in her boot once she'd dressed.

She couldn't think of anything else and her fingers twitched to do something, so she stripped off her night-dress and pulled on thick stockings, pantalettes quilted for warmth, a chemisette and a linen shift. She pulled out her boots, then spun around to yank another pair of stockings from the drawer. Layers. She laid her winter riding habit on the bed. Her fur-lined cloak and gloves. Another scarf.

A blanket? She rolled one as tight as she could and stuffed it into the bag. There, it was full. She could wedge a piece of bread in though. Some cheese and ham.

Danielle burst through the door, face blank with distress above the tray of piled food. Her eyes darted around, taking in the clothes draped across the bedspread, the bulging satchel.

Alex began sorting through the food before Danielle had even managed to maneuver it to the table. Salt stung the inside of her lip as she stuffed a piece of bacon into her mouth. A cut, she realized dimly. She must have bitten a hole through it sometime, trying not to cry. She didn't have that problem now. Her eyes were now dry as sand, barren as death. She wrapped food and chewed mindlessly.

"What . . . Where will you go?"

"Home."

"But . . . Take a carriage, *Madame*, please."

"No. I'm going now before he realizes. He would try to keep me here, try to do the honorable thing and apologize. I don't want his honor, his bastard replacement for love. I don't care to hear another apology."

"It is not safe—"

"Safer than staying here! He's likely to murder me some night when my eye falls too fondly on one of the grooms."

"But you're not . . . How will you find your way?"

"I remember the way. There's that town a day's ride from here, where we stayed the night."

As she stuffed the last of the roadworthy food away, her eye caught on Danielle's starkly drawn face. Her eyes were bright with a fear that Alex had never seen there before and her heart clenched at the sight.

"Danielle," she whispered, reaching to take her limp hands. "All will be well. I'll go home to my brother. I'll send for you and our life will return to what it was."

"But, *Madame*, you are married!"

"Pah." She let go her hands and reached for the habit. "Here. Help me dress."

Given something familiar to do, the maid sprang into action, muttering French in such a low tone that Alex could only hear the occasional punctuation. *Monster. Idiot. Beast.*

"Stay in the room as much as you can. I will not have you lie for me again and there is the occasional person here who'll ask after me."

"This is not a good idea!"

"I cannot make wise decisions even when I try, Danielle, so what is the point?" The last fold of her skirt fell into place, the cloak stirred the briar patch of her curls when Danielle swung it around her. She'd leave it unbound, it was warm that way, like wool batting.

"My boots!" she laughed, tucking the scarf around her neck. "What a madwoman I am, all bundled up with no boots on." She giggled again, watching Danielle's blond head duck low to slip the stiff leather over her foot. "I feel mad, you know."

"All the more reason to stop and think what you're doing!"

"Collin . . . He . . . I cannot even tell you what he accused me of. Even being a virgin was not proof enough, not for such an *honorable, decent* man. I will not live with a man who despises the very lust he avails himself of every night. He shames me, Danielle. He shames me at every turn. Am I such a shameful person, then?"

Her friend's eyes filled with the tears that Alex's body had ceased to produce. "You must not think such things. He is a fool. Have I not told you they are all fools? Write to the duke. He will come for you himself."

"No, I am sorry to leave you here, but I cannot stay another moment in his house. Take the bag. Perhaps you should wrap it in a sheet? I'll retrieve it outside the gate, where that grass grows so wild. Go."

And then she was alone. She slipped her sheathed knife into her boot and cast a cold eye around the stone walls of the room, skipping willfully over the items that spoke of her bed-partner. Not her room and it never would be. Leather slid over her fingers as she pulled on her gloves and turned her back on Collin Blackburn's bed.

The mare swung her head around in a sharp arc and caught Collin's chin with a thunk.

"Damn it." He dropped her foot, no doubt rewarding bad behavior with exactly the thing she wanted, but he couldn't seem to bring himself to care. It likely wasn't the worst hit he'd get today. At least his tongue hadn't been between his teeth.

Unfolding his stiff body, he rose with a grunt of true exhaustion. Uncertainty had kept him up all night. Uncertainty and guilt and the dusty cold of an unused bed. Not so unused now. He wondered when the maid would discover the rumpled bed. A week or two? Then again he might be moving in permanently; Alex's eyes had been that cold.

Stepping out of the shadowed barn, Collin's hands clenched to fists at the memory of her curls teasing the man's cheek. They'd looked so . . . involved. Tense in a way that bespoke an intimate past. He'd thought he might throttle him . . . And apparently he should have.

"Stupid prick," he muttered, meaning Dixon, but feeling the sting of the curse himself. Who was more stupid than he?

He'd felt the censure of Alexandra's gaze on him all night, as he'd twisted and turned in the rough embrace of pilfered blankets. Her eyes gone blank and depthless, a shield against his hatefulness.

"Damn your black soul," he growled, definitely meaning himself this time and not the startled boy who leapt out of his path. Pausing at the door to swipe his boots against the bale of hay he kept there to catch stable muck, Collin dug his fingers into the stiff muscles of his neck.

He had wounded her. Again. Perhaps unforgivably. He'd struck out in childish anger when she had needed his protection. God only knew what that blackguard had been saying to her—that rapist disguised as a pale English milksop. And the startled dismay he'd surprised from her face . . . that hadn't been fear of discovery, it had been helplessness as she'd stood in a crowded ballroom and tolerated the presence of her attacker.

His throat thickened with regret, with disgust at what he'd accused her of. Worse than that, really, for what if he'd been right? What if she had serviced a dozen men before he came along? Hadn't he been with a dozen women in his life? Hadn't he suckled and licked and screwed them and never thought twice about it? Oh, he was cruel, and wretched with it now.

He loved her. He loved her and he had abused her as surely as if he'd beaten her to the floor.

The walls moved past him and he was walking through the great hall, between tables still littered with the mess of dinner. Bridey's small girl worked her way 'round, stacking metal plates and cups. The meal was done then. Had she eaten?

His boots slapped the stairs as he bounded up, abruptly urgent with the need to see her. He smelled of sweat and horseflesh and no doubt she'd spit and slap at him, but he wanted to see her, wanted to dare an apology.

Her door fell open, unbarred.

"Alex?" A sound stirred from the turret room. A woman slipped into view, her blond hair a disappointment. "Danielle. Is your mistress about?"

Collin glanced stupidly around, as if she crouched behind the bed. The maid did not answer and when he looked back to her, she only returned his stare, though her lips twitched into a momentary snarl. Well.

"Ah, has she gone for a ride?"

"You could say that."

He felt a flicker of irritation and set it aside. "What does that mean?"

"You may figure that out on your own."

"Please don't growl at me. Just tell me where she is."

"Fool."

"What?"

"*Salaud*, she has left you."

"Left me? But—"

Danielle swung about, skirt and hair flying out in a wave as she stepped back into the turret room and slammed the small door behind her.

"Left me?" His brain seemed to creak under the pressure of the words and his eyes wove circles around the room, finally landing on her wardrobe. With one great lunge, he yanked the doors open and shook his head at the crush of dresses inside. Left him . . . No, she couldn't have. Her things were still here, her trunk still lurked at the foot of the bed. Her maid was sitting not ten feet away. She couldn't have gone anywhere.

No, she hadn't left. She was probably hiding in the turret room even as he stood here reeling.

"Danielle!" The door burst open under his palm with a sharp crack. "Damn it, is she here?"

But his wife was not in the tiny round room, only her maid staring at him past her tears. Danielle, crying? What was this? A shaft of ice pierced his churning gut. "What the hell is going on?"

"I told you!" She sprang to her feet to face him, a tear dripping from her chin. "She has left you."

"But all her things are still here. *You* are still here. Where could she have gone?"

That narrow shaft of ice split and widened. She had left him, run away. Left in the dead of night for all he knew. And where could she go with just the clothes on her back? Back to Kirkland Hall?

A suspicion struck him, terrible in its familiarity, and comfortable despite that. Fergus. Fergus who liked her so well and defended her and who hadn't yet shown his face today. Fergus who lived not two miles from here and was missing from his post.

Collin's hand shot out to grip the maid's arm. "Has she gone to him? Has she?"

Her face flushed and twisted into an ugly snarl as she reared back, pulling herself from his tight fingers. She did not answer his question. Instead, she drew herself up and spit full into his face.

Rage clawed at him, tearing his gut into ribbons, urging him to slap her, to punish her for the pain that ground his mind into dust. Frightened by the violence that stretched into his muscles, he growled at her wide-eyed stare and swung about to hunt down his wife and her lover.

By God, he'd been right. Right all along and she had actually made him feel sorry for her. His wife and his best friend.

But, no! his small, stupid heart cried. *No, there is a mistake.* And perhaps there was. He'd never really thought she could do this. He'd only been so afraid of it.

His vision darkened and he blinked around, startled by

the change in light. The stable. He was in the stable. A groom stared, eyes round with question.

"Has Mrs. Blackburn been here today?"

"Aye, sir. Off for a ride on that mare o' hers."

"When?"

"When? 'Round about ten. Maybe before."

"Ten this morning?"

"Ahh . . . Yes, sir." The man's eyes rolled to meet briefly with the boy mucking out the first stall.

"Saddle Thor. Quickly."

Collin's mind worked itself into knots while he waited, examining the possibilities. Fergus's house first, but they couldn't be stupid enough to stay there. Of course, Collin usually stayed busy all day between the horses and the new house, so perhaps they'd counted on a few more hours of secrecy. But surely this was all a misunderstanding. He'd go to Jeannie's. Likely Alex was there. And it would sting to have to retrieve his woman from a neighbor, but he would deserve that. He'd deserve it for expecting such terrible things from his own wife.

He blinked again and there was Thor, held by the worried groom and tossing his head in impatience. Ten minutes to ride to Fergus's home and then he would know.

The ground passed beneath his feet, tumbling nearly as fast as his flailing soul. *Don't be there*, he found himself praying. *Don't be there. Please, Alex, don't be there.*

Thor flew down the road, bursting up over a hill and back down the other side, neither horse nor rider sparing a thought for the danger of such speed. A gust of wind caught them at the next hill and slowed their pace for a moment, a cold hand that forbore snow and ice. The road wound down then, slipping them into a valley and out of the force of the breeze.

He could see the house from here, could see the curl of smoke from the chimney and the low bench where he'd passed many a summer evening over a glass of whisky. He could see the apple tree and the window below it that looked in on Fergus's small room and his bed.

Dread closed his throat.

Thor slowed, winded already from being run cold, and Collin guided him to the left, down the narrow path and closer to the place he did not want to be.

"Don't be here," he whispered into the smoke-spiced air and drew the horse to a stop.

Knees weak and body nearly too heavy to catch, Collin slipped to the ground. The door opened to him—the third door today that he'd suspected of hiding his wife. And there was the fourth, just to his left. A narrow square in the wood and daub wall. It was firmly closed, and why would that be? Why close a door against the home where you lived alone?

Pain spiraled tight, rising from his gut to his throat and squeezing everything in-between to ruin. The room was only two steps away and he had to do this.

The first thing he saw, the first thing that carved itself into his brain, was Fergus's long, tanned arm—a swipe of skin and hair that curled over the gentle hill of someone sheltered beneath the quilt. Collin's eyes followed the curve of the blanket, swept down the bed to see another of Fergus's limbs—his leg, naked and bent and thrown over one tiny female foot that snugged against his calf.

Something fractured in the quiet of his chest, a concussion of silence that nearly broke him.

"*You are a God-damned traitor.*"

A sweet female gasp assaulted his ears as the bed shuddered.

"You can have this woman if you want her, but you will *not have her on my land.*"

Fergus sprang naked from the bed. His fierce snarl fell to blank shock at the sight of Collin looming over his bed. "Jesus Christ, man, what the hell are ye doin' here?"

Collin's vision blurred, swirled, until the world was a jumble of Fergus's nude body, and his own rising fists, and the trembling shape of a woman hidden in her lover's bed. "*Druis.*"

Fergus's face burned crimson, or Collin's vision turned

red, he couldn't tell which. "She is not a whore, you bastard spawn of the devil, and I'll kill you if ye say it again."

Collin barked in disbelief, reaching for the quilt instead of his friend's throat. "You'd dare to defend my wife when she lays in this very bed, naked and filled with your seed?"

The blanket felt like paper beneath his hands, so light that it floated halfway across the room with the tiniest jerk. The roar in his head was his own blood or Fergus's growl or the sob of the woman he'd bared. His mind tripped, lurched, just as his body did, just as he saw the nude length of a woman who was not his wife, just as his chest caught Fergus's shoulder and his body fell back.

Breath burst from lungs caught too hard between the floor and the body that fell upon him.

"How dare you?" A hand fisted in his hair. "How dare you come into my home and . . . and—"

"Where is she?"

The hand wrenched. "Get out."

Fergus's weight left him and he felt himself pulled to his feet by his scalp, but the pain couldn't penetrate his shock. "Where is my wife?"

"God damn ye, man, are ye mad?"

A blink brought his friend's face back into focus, revealed the rage in his eyes and lips a line of white in his beard. Collin's eyes rolled and swung past him to catch on the sight of Jeannie Kirkland, crouched and hiding herself behind the paltry shield of a pillow clutched to her chest. She stared, horror-struck, breath panting out between her lips.

Collin's hands hung limp at his sides even as he saw the open hand fly out to crack against his cheek.

"There is a lady present, ye daft prick, and you'll leave this moment or I will dig your eyes from your head."

Collin turned, stumbling when Fergus yanked the quilt from beneath his feet and pulled it back to the bed. Murmurs, fierce whispers flew to his ears, but he couldn't begin to decipher the words. Nothing here made sense to him. He walked from the room and out into the platinum day and stood, waiting.

Five minutes must have passed before the door creaked open behind him, perhaps another five before he turned to stare at the stony face of his best friend.

"I've lost my wife." The words sounded hollow in his ears.

"You do not deserve her."

He did not wince. His face felt slack with the truth of it. He did not deserve her, and wasn't that the problem?

"Did you really expect to find her here?"

Fergus's voice had grown so solemn that it drew Collin's gaze back to his face. He no longer looked hard with anger. No, grief had softened his eyes to a terrible sadness. Collin was shocked at the prickling behind his own lids.

"I did not want to."

"But you thought ye would."

"No. No, I didn't, and that is why it killed me to see . . . to think I saw her . . ."

The door swung out to reveal a red-haired bundle of rage, her chin impossibly high above a stiff neck. She rushed forward to grasp Fergus's outstretched hand and stared at Collin through slitted eyes.

"Jeannie," he croaked.

His name was a curse on her lips.

He glanced to Fergus, back again. "What are you about here?"

Jeannie growled and Fergus tucked her tight beneath his arm to glare. "You'd best see to your own business, Collin, if you're able. It seems to me you have your hands full without bothering yourself with my woman."

"Your woman?"

"Aye."

"Her father will not approve."

"I am right here," she snapped. "Do not speak around me."

"I am aware that her father willna approve. Why in hell else would she be here without a priest's blessing?"

She pushed away from him in irritation and Collin

watched her, studying this girl who was like a sister to him, and sighing with a sudden weariness at the whole damned world. "I will speak to him," he finally said.

"*I* will speak with her father," Fergus barked, and her face brightened even as she shook her head.

"You're both mad. And what are you about anyway?" Her eyes drilled into Collin. "Finally driven your bride away, have you?"

He felt his lip curl, felt his teeth clench in a snarl of frustrated rage. Fergus said her name as a warning, but she pulled away from him and glared in return.

"He has broken her heart, can't you see that? Can't you?" Her jade-green eyes swung back to him, and Collin fought the urge to close his own, to shut out the truth. "You and your stubborn pride. When did you last see a light in her?" Collin swallowed the roughness of her words. "She is your wife, and your responsibility extends further than keeping her under your thumb! She should have left weeks ago."

"Jeannie," Fergus murmured, his voice not a caution now, but a plea.

Tears glinted in her eyes, but she stepped again out of her lover's reach. "She loves you, Collin. She thinks you a good man. And you have made her something less than she was before she met you."

"Jeannie, stop."

The urgency of the words reached him from a buzzing distance, past the thought of Alex's eyes, eyes like blue joy until the daring had slowly seeped away from them. He thought of her laugh and of his helplessness as it had come less and less often and never with him. She smiled so easily with Fergus and that had been the start of it—seeing her more happy with his friend than with her own husband.

Jeannie pressed her face into Fergus's shoulder as his hand stroked over her hair, slow and gentle and steady, just what a man should be for his woman and everything that Collin had not been for his wife. He watched Fergus breathe her in and whisper into her hair, watched as she drew strength from him and grew steadier. He felt shame to see them together, to see their love given with no hesitation. He had been too weak to risk that with Alexandra.

"I'm sorry." Lurching toward Thor, he was stopped by a hand on his shoulder before he could mount. He pressed his forehead against the warm strength of the stallion's neck. "I'm so sorry, Fergus."

Jeannie watched Collin's bowed head and fought back tears. She wanted to go to him as Fergus had, but she was still too angry to offer comfort.

"Shall I come with ye?" Fergus asked him. Collin did not raise his head.

"No, it's my own mess," Jeannie heard over the growing wind. "Tell Jeannie that I'm sorry. Tell her I'm happy for you."

Her heart lightened at his words, then threatened to fly away when Fergus spoke. "Will you stand up for us then? Even without Kirkland's blessing?"

As Jeannie walked toward Fergus, Collin eased his head away from the great black stallion. "You would ask me?"

"Aye. You're like a brother to Jeannie and to me." Fergus's arm fit around her shoulders as if he'd always rested it there, or had always wanted to. "And every family must have a mad one about. You can be ours and we'll be glad to have ye."

"Ha. Fine then. If her old man doesn't kill you, I'll host the wedding myself." Collin pulled Fergus into a rough hug, then turned to Jeannie.

"I'm sorry if I caused you any shame, Jeannie," he offered, voice breaking. He pressed a light kiss to her forehead. "I hope you can forgive me."

"'Tis not I you must worry about, you great lout."

"I know."

He swung into the saddle and raised a hand before wheeling about. Fergus's "Godspeed" was lost in a thunder of hooves. "Good luck," Jeannie added quietly.

They watched until his hunched shoulders disappeared over the hill.

"I should go with him," Fergus murmured.

"No, he must bear this burden alone."

"Still . . . He's near broken."

"He will be fine if he can catch her. And you have your own burden to worry over, Fergus MacLean."

She watched his jaw angle into a smile before he looked down at her. "So I do." The love in his blue eyes spread heat over her skin and through all the places he'd touched during the night. "I canna offer you anything more than a wee cottage and a warm bed, Jeannie."

"Fergus—"

"But I pray it's enough, because we'll be wed within the fortnight, and here is where you'll stay."

"Good," was all she managed before she began to cry. Her lover cursed her for a fool before he carried her back to his warm, welcoming bed and compromised her one more time for good measure.

Chapter 21

Nothing was the same when Collin walked through the doors of Westmore. The comforting bustle of the great hall stuttered to a halt as soon as his shadow fell over the floor. People—his people—stopped to stare at him with wary curiosity. She was not here, he knew that without asking, just as he knew she was not at the Kirklands'. No, she had not run to a friend to wail and whimper. She had not flown somewhere to wait for him to follow. She was gone. Gone to her own home, no longer willing to fight for a place in his. And she should not have had to.

He did not bother cursing himself for a fool and a bully. He would not grant himself the release of self-flagellation. His guilt would not ease her. He could only change, could only redeem himself.

Ah, God, he loved her. He admired her and feared her, truth be told. But he had never wanted to hurt or break her. He'd only meant for the fear to cease its endless scratching at his gut, only needed to stave off the inevitable end of his good luck. At least he did not have to fear it anymore. She was gone. The suspense had ended.

The servants and workmen who'd gathered stood frozen under his lost stare. Some had begun to show grimness, a few sported smug mouths. He had no idea what he should say, if anything.

"My lord! Collin . . ." Rebecca pushed past a house-maid, her cheeks in high color. He watched as she hur-ried toward him, face smoothing itself into sympathetic concern. "Do not worry yourself over such as her."

A vibration thrummed over his nerves as he pulled his eyes from the curving edge of her lip and swept the room-ful of faces.

"Did anyone see her leave?" Eyes widened, darted back and forth. One young boy flushed and looked hard at Collin's belt. "Ben?"

The boy blinked and his nose seemed to wrinkle into his brow.

"I saw her." Rebecca's words rushed into the quiet room. He did not look at her, could not stand to. He knew what was coming, knew now what Alex had tried to tell him and what he had thrown back in her face.

"She snuck out to the stables this morning while you were at the new house and took her horse north, Collin, over the hill. I often see her ride that way, so I thought nothing of it."

"North. And Ben? What did you see?"

A lump jumped visibly in the boy's dirty neck as he swallowed. "I . . . I saw that Frenchie maid o' hers hide somethin' in the grass, and then her ladyship come out and fetch it. But she didn't go north, sir. She headed south at a fast trot. 'Twas a big bag she hitched up out o' the meadow and she tied it right up behind her."

"When?"

"Hours ago. Long 'afore noon."

"South, hmm?"

Rebecca's shadow jittered on the floor at his feet. Ben was wise enough to keep quiet. She was not. "Where is your man, then?" she hissed. "Where is Fergus?"

A gust of wind blew through the open door behind him, scattering leaves into the hall with the smell of snow. Snow.

"I want Thor watered and packed for a week on the road.

And you—" He slashed Rebecca's face with his gaze. "You are to be gone from this house when I return."

When his hand flew out, gasps filled the room, one woman cried out, but not Rebecca. She glared daggers into him as he tore the circle of keys from her apron and tossed them to Mrs. Cook.

"She gets a fortnight's pay and nothing more."

"You are a fool! Fergus is not the only one she meets," Rebecca hissed as he started to turn away. "There's another man. I've seen him in the woods. He says that your fine wife is nothing more than a whore who tricked you into this marriage. I cannot stand to see you brought low, Collin!"

"What," he ground out, "do you mean, there is a man in the woods?"

Red rose to her cheeks. "He is a gentleman, not some beggar. He says he was a friend to you and that you parted ways over that doxy."

"*His name.*"

"John."

"*John.*"

Rebecca took a step back. "I only wanted to help you, Collin."

Collin reached out and snatched her wrist into an iron grip. "What have you done?"

"Nothing." She tried to pull away. "Nothing! I only met him three days ago. I was to make sure that you were occupied tomorrow, so that she could go to meet him. And then . . . Then be sure that she was caught sneaking back in, be sure that you saw the evidence of her infidelity."

"My God, you would send my wife out to be *raped?*"

Rebecca sniffed, "Hardly," but then began to claw at her wrist. "Collin, You're hurting me."

"I . . ." Collin tried to loosen his fingers, but he could not feel them. "I should beat you for this. Beat you like the spoiled child you are. If she comes to harm . . ."

He let her go and watched as she stumbled away. "But I am as much to blame. More. Do not be here when I return or you will regret it."

The crowd parted before him. He stalked toward the stairs to take them two at a time and was bounding back down in minutes, armed with winter cloaks and blankets, his pistol and dirk and a small bag of gold.

The hall had emptied, though a frantic murmur filled the whole house like the swell of pigeons in a barn. But Collin's soul stayed quiet. It had nothing more to say to the likes of him.

Something dripped from the tip of her nose and plopped to her sodden cloak. Tears or melted snow—she no longer had any idea. Self-pity had set in about the same time as the wet snow and she had since descended into depths of misery the likes of which she'd never imagined. Why had she not stopped at that dark cottage she'd spied through the gray mist? Why had she not turned back?

Brinn snuffled behind her and nudged her arm, but Alex ignored her, resenting the horse's damned delicate leg that hadn't held up past the first patch of ice.

They hadn't passed an occupied home since the start of the bad weather and only one rider had overtaken them. She hadn't even met the man's eyes much less asked assistance. His muttered, sing-song cursing had reached her long before his mule had drawn even.

Clouds parted above her for a bare moment of palest moonlight. The sliver of moon would provide little light even on a clear night, but during this snow . . . It wasn't nearly bright enough to warn her of the ice that sent her feet skidding.

Her own scream scared her more than the fall. She was so cold that she barely felt the pain in her knees, but frustration overwhelmed her and she knelt in the cold and wept.

Another mistake, this flight. Another misstep in her life. My God, she was only twenty. How many bad decisions were still ahead of her? When she got to Somerhart—*if* she got to Somerhart—she would do best to avoid the outside world entirely. She would hide in her room during parties to avoid lecherous men. Visit convents for holiday to keep her body cool. And perhaps if Hart married, she would simply retire to her cottage and transform herself into a crazy spinster.

A memory danced behind her closed eyes, of Collin standing above her, face fierce with pleasure.

No, not her cottage. Never her cottage. One of Hart's lesser holdings then. One that employed no men. She would be the crone with wild hair and wilder eyes, the woman who trailed a path of half-feral cats and the smell of pipe smoke.

Pressing her hands to wet eyes, she pictured herself old and alone, something she'd never done when she'd been so determined not to marry. But now she understood what that would mean . . . to be alone. To never feel a reverent touch. To never stroke her belly and wonder if it quickened with life. And it never would. No, she had bled not a week ago and now there would not be a chance of holding a tiny babe to her breast.

Her bones shivered, a deep rumbling of cold that vibrated weakly at first, then strengthened to something more . . . a pulsing. Stronger then, and Alex wondered weakly if she were dying there in the snow. Her heart stuttered over the rumble of her bones. Metal clinked.

A rider. Someone on the road behind her.

A whine of fear escaped her throat. *It can't be St. Claire*, she told herself. Not in this weather. He wouldn't dare breaking his precious neck for her. Her fear didn't ease.

She tried to push herself off the ground, but her legs felt thick and stiff as trees. How long had she knelt here?

Brinn blew a hot breath against her neck, her teeth closed around a snarl of Alex's curls.

"No, Brinn. Come on, we have to move. Please." She batted the damp warmth away and rocked to her knees. Still no word from her legs, and the trotting horse was nearly upon them. "Move!" she whispered and crawled toward the ditch. She pulled Brinn's reins with her and felt her follow.

Five feet of road scraped beneath her knees in a space of seconds, and Alex felt the dirt give way to crunchy grass just as the air stirred with a rider's passing. He didn't slow, didn't see her in the black night and, luckily, did not career into Brinn's hindquarters. Relief slid over her, spiced with the terror that she had lost a chance for help, but her first instinct had been to hide and she could not change that now.

Just as she relaxed, a jerk on the reins pulled her off balance. Brinn strained forward and her sharp neigh pierced Alex's ears just after the mare's intent cleared the fog of her owner's muzzy brain.

"Shh. Quiet!"

Brinn whinnied again, happy and eager, calling after the disappearing horse. Alex heard a snort of a call from far ahead and squeezed her eyes shut in denial, even as her heart gave a pitiful leap. *Saved!*

The rumbling slowed, stopped altogether. Vacillating wildly between relief and horror, she listened to the muffled clop of hooves.

Another hard snort from the horse ahead, a joyous reply from Brinn. It was then that a paralyzing thought crept into Alex's mind. *No.* It couldn't be. Even with the setback of Brinn's injury he could not possibly have come after her yet. No.

The silhouette of a huge centaur loomed out of the black. The silver moon peeked out and flitted its light off a buckle.

"Who's there?"

Her soul fluttered at the sound of that voice and a weight pressed against her tongue. Brinn's reins slipped from her fingers and the mare pushed away to nudge her favorite stallion. Alex refused to do the same. She only tucked her arms close and wondered if Collin might miss her in the dark.

"Alex?" The word conveyed a dozen things, the strongest of which was fear. "Alex, where are you?" He slid from the saddle and his boots crunched closer on the ice. "Alexandra!"

This was not how she'd planned to meet him again, curled up and freezing wet. She'd woven a scene of sorts, but the confrontation had taken place in the elegant drawing room of Somerhart, beneath the painting of her beautiful mother. She had planned to injure him with her scorn, to send him back to Scotland with the knowledge that she neither wanted nor needed him. She had definitely not planned on hiding in the grass at his feet, hoping he might just stumble past her.

Her paralysis ended when his knuckles brushed against her hair, and only her pride kept her from falling to her face and weeping. She fell, instead, to her backside, a grunt of shock rushing from her mouth even as his fingers reached to cup her chin.

"Alex?"

"Keep your hands to yourself."

"Alex, love, are you hurt?"

"No!" she protested, denying so many things at once.

"What are you doing here then?" Collin hooked his hands under her arms and pulled her up onto numb legs. Oh, she tried her best to stand, wanted so badly to press him back and stand away from him, but her legs did not respond to her wishes. They simply folded until her body lurched into his.

"*Caitein*," Collin gasped, catching her, pressing her into his chest. "What have you done to yourself?"

Those damned steady arms of his wrapped around her, held her like something precious, and stole her hatred away. Tears warmed her cheeks as she fell into the scent of him.

"You're wet through." Lifting her, he set her down near Thor, still taking all her weight as his own. She didn't protest the treatment until she felt her cloak fall away and the freezing wind against her damp dress.

"My cloak!"

"Shh." His hands unwound her scarf and set to the buttons of the riding habit.

"Don't." She meant to curse him, but her jaw occupied itself with chattering teeth together.

"You can't keep these things on. Just a minute and we'll have you warm again."

Her skin burned cold, then colder still, until only her shift and boots still covered her icy flesh. She felt something dry fall over her, then a heavier warmth that settled on her shoulders with delicious weight. Collin scooped her up and curled her body into his, hands chafing over her back until her shivering gentled.

"Is Brinn lame?"

"Yes."

"Thor's worn out. We'll have to go slowly." Scooting her up to perch on the front of the saddle, he mounted behind her and draped her over his lap, pulling another blanket tight to her legs. She was so warm by then that she noticed the twinkle of lights ahead, just over the push of a hill. She was just thawed enough to prickle with anger.

"The inn?"

"It's just there. A mile or so."

They hadn't ridden a minute when a break in the trees revealed the warm glow of a nearby cottage. She was back in civilization. She hadn't needed his help at all. "Let me down."

"What?"

"I don't want your help. Let me down."

"You haven't any clothes on, Alex."

"The better to negotiate a fair price for the room."

His laughter spurred her anger and she struggled to free her fist from the blankets and pummel him.

"I've been an ass."

"Yes."

"A terrible husband."

"It seems we've had this conversation before." That silenced him for a few seconds. Her legs began to ache as her blood warmed them.

"So we have."

"I am going home, Collin. We will both be happier."

"I will not. But if you would hear me out, if you'll talk with me this night, I will let you go in the morning. If you still wish to."

"Really?" She couldn't keep the shock from her voice, though she managed to disguise the sharp hurt. She had never imagined he'd give his blessing, no matter that he did not want her as a wife. But he sounded resigned to it, as if he too had realized that he couldn't stand her.

"We'll speak then," she forced herself to say. "Tonight." More than her legs ached now. Her jaw hurt, her throat and her heart. She could not want him and yet she did. Could not bear the thought of loving him, yet there was no stopping it.

The wind died a little as Thor walked them toward the inn. An owl hooted above their heads. Alex turned her face toward Collin and smelled sweat and horse, wood smoke and wet. And she smelled him, her lover and husband. His scent made her weak and heavy and her heart swelled with pain.

Why could he not love her?

"What happened to Brinn? The ice?"

"Yes. She slipped and started limping right off."

"How long have you been walking then?"

Her shrug shifted his arm. When he resettled it, he pulled her closer and she let him. Just this last time, she told herself. She had missed this so much.

The sound of his heart lulled her, gentling the strain in her throat until she caught herself rubbing her cheek against him. The arm that supported her back tightened and snugged her firmly into his embrace. When he leaned down to press a kiss to her hair, she found herself cocooned by his body.

Bastard.

I am only chilled, she told herself in pitiful defense. *I must be kept close.*

And you have always been weak for him, the broken part of her heart replied. *Always*.

A full minute passed before she could gather the strength to push up, to straighten her spine to a semblance of independence. One of his arms fell away, and then they crested the hill and there was the inn, lights and raucous laughter a clear beacon in the cold.

It seemed to take a damned eternity to arrange for food and hot tea, to see to Thor and wrap Brinn's knee. By the time he got back to the room, Collin had begun to fear he'd find himself alone, abandoned again. But his wife was there, bundled into bed, her beautiful face lit by a glowing hearth. She was warm again, he could see, even beginning to sweat a little so that tiny curls stuck to her temples in black rings. He wanted to set his mouth there and taste her. He did not.

Instead he stood, back to the door, and watched her sleep. Just this was a relief—to be in the same room with her. This was what always frightened him, that her mere presence felt like a blessing. How could he live easy with her when she might leave at any moment? When she might grow tired of him or take ill and die? How could he turn to her for his happiness when he could not control her?

Well, he had no choice. He needed her. It calmed him just to admit it.

Knuckles rapped hard on the door behind him and stirred her from her doze. She watched with wide eyes as he let the serving girl in, and they stared at each other over the girl's busy work.

"If you would bring my bag," Alex said as soon as the door closed again. "I have a spare dress."

"Of course."

She juggled the blankets around a little until he realized she wanted privacy and turned away. It stung to see her hide her body from him. She was not a modest woman. Had he given her that shame?

When she rose from the bed, he followed her lead and sat at the square table to eat roast duck and pudding. They both passed up tea for ale and drank in silence till the mugs were empty.

"Rebecca is gone," he finally spit out and could not tell by her frown if he'd begun well or not.

"Run off, you mean?"

"No, I turned her out. I came to see what you tried to tell me."

"Where will she go?"

"Somewhere she'll cause less trouble, I'd hope." The awful silence descended again. She did not appear moved by his gesture. "Let me be honest—"

"Please."

"I came to find you today, to apologize, to explain myself. I wanted to tell you that I understood, finally, why I'd been acting so . . . so . . ."

"Jealous?"

"No. More than that. I've been a brute and a coward. I've hidden my fears behind a mistrust of you. And I wanted to explain why."

Her eyes watched, giving nothing away. "Why?"

"Because I love you and it scares me to death."

Her mouth opened, closed. She breathed in. "Do not—"

"Wait. There is more. And I'll tell you the whole of it before I ask your forgiveness.

"I came to find you, to make amends. And when Danielle told me you'd gone, my first instinct was to suspect the worst."

"The worst?" Her words were thick now, and harsh. "You mean Fergus?"

"Yes." Collin wanted to look away from the hate darkening her eyes. "I came to offer a promise of trust, but given the first opportunity, I turned back to jealousy."

She tensed as if to leap up, so he rushed on. "I did not really believe I'd find you there, Alex. I didn't. It was more a terror that it could be so. It always has been."

"Of course you believed it." She stood and stalked to the

window. Though he followed, he gave her the space she wanted.

"No. I have never truly thought you unfaithful or untrustworthy. I've just hidden behind that. I know this, because when I went to his home, when I saw him there in bed with a woman, I felt such disbelief that I could not even hate you. All I felt was shock and pain and the sureness that I was dying."

"But why, Collin? Why do you always suspect the worst of me? Only because of my past? Because I welcomed you to my bed?"

"No, Alex. God, no. Your past . . . If that were true then your maidenhead should have cured it. It's not you. I just . . ." *You are better than me*, he wanted to say. *You will realize it someday*. But his throat closed the words off and he could not force them out. His silence spun her around.

"What? What is it, if it's not my nature that gives you such fear of me?"

"It's . . . You did not choose me, Alexandra."

"What do you mean?"

Collin could feel his fingers shake as he shoved them through his hair. "This marriage was simply the least of two evils for you. Me or another scandal. You would not have chosen me as a mate."

"Collin . . ." Her lips curved in a fierce frown. "That's ridiculous. I chose you. I lured you to that cottage—"

His sharp gesture cut her off. "You chose me to lie with, not to marry."

"But—"

"Sleeping with a common bastard is one thing, but even you said you wouldn't deign to marry one."

"I . . . I didn't!"

"You did. When I accused you of trapping me into marriage."

"Oh, for God's sake, you were yelling at me."

"So?"

"So, I was mad! And speaking of mad, your explanation

is completely ridiculous. All those suppositions apply to you more so than me. You had absolutely no choice at all."

"Of course I did."

"Oh, how so? Marry me or take a bullet to the head? Live with shame the rest of your life? What kind of choice is that? But I wanted you, Collin. I wanted you so much that I married you knowing you didn't want that."

He stared, jaw sore with tension, and began to feel the smallest stirrings of hope. "But you are a lady, the daughter of a—" He blocked the little fist she threw at his chest. "What?"

"I love you, you idiot. I love you."

"But . . . But why have you never said so?"

"Why have *you* never said so?" Tears glittered in her eyes, magnifying the blue hurt.

"You had too much power over me already."

"What power?"

His bark of laughter cleared the thickness from his throat. "You rule my body, my soul."

"You barely even speak to me!"

He dared a step closer to her, dared to reach out and take her clenched hand. "I'm sorry, wife. Truly I am. I never meant to treat you so badly. I just . . .

"Nothing in my life excited me anymore until I brought it to you. A mare pregnant, a sale—the magic was all in the anticipation of telling you about it, and I thought . . . I thought you must leave me some day. Go back to your real life and leave me with nothing. I meant to keep my pride, at least, since you had my heart."

Collin was sure he'd seen nothing more beautiful in his life than her face then, at that moment, softening into tenderness for him. Her fingers reached to smooth a curve over his brow.

"I love you, Collin. I only left because you pushed me so far away. I'd thought I could make you love me, but I couldn't seem to manage it."

He caught her hand and pressed it hard to his mouth, felt

her fingers curl to cup his jaw. "Come home, *caitein*," he whispered into her skin. "Come home with me, wife. Please."

She did not answer his plea.

"I want your help. I want your help with the money and with the manor house. You and Fergus can share an office even, in the new home. I won't blink an eye, I swear."

"Truly?" She laughed at his nod. "And you won't let me be lonely anymore?"

"Never," he moaned, and kissed her, breathing all his fears and needs into her mouth. "Please forgive me."

"You'll take meals with me? Every day?"

"Yes." A kiss.

"And you'll let me work in the stables?"

"Aye." Another.

"And I may wear my breeches?"

He froze at that, lifted his head. "Ah . . ."

Her soft giggle nearly brought tears of relief to his eyes.

"*Maith mé duit*," she murmured, her hands urging his head closer again.

"What?"

"*Maith mé duit*. I forgive you. Didn't I say it right?"

"Christ help me, I'll never keep a secret now." Her hands pulled him down and he opened his lips to her stroking tongue before he pulled away again. "Mmm. That was easy. I'd no idea you were such a soft heart."

Distracted by the feel of her round bottom in his hand, Collin neglected to block this punch, and her fist, small as it was, turned out to be much sturdier than his left ear. His soft-hearted wife seemed quite satisfied with his howl.

Chapter 22

Alexandra had never felt so buoyant, so happy. Even when she'd handed over Damien's letter to Collin . . . Even as she'd watched him curse and scowl and mutter vile threats of retribution . . . she'd had to work hard at seriousness. His foul mood did not make her cringe or pout. She was happy.

Her heart had flipped quite acrobatically when Collin looked up from his third reading, gentled his features, and apologized for "putting her in a position of believing that little prick's threats." In short, he understood. Truly.

And now even Collin had relaxed, riding abreast of her borrowed nag, though his eyes roamed the trees ahead and his hand stayed close to his pistol. Brinn tagged along quite happily behind them, naked back twitching beneath the midday sun. Collin and Alex did not speak but snuck dozens of smiles at each other, until she was hard-pressed not to giggle at each touch of his eyes.

She felt like a bride, finally. Like an innocent girl just stripped and stroked for the first time. She actually blushed at the thought.

Collin growled from her left. "Are you thinking of last night, wife, or the night to come?"

She let her laughter free. "Both."

"And what about this afternoon?"

"This afternoon?"

His wolf smile was back. Alex squealed like a cornered lamb when his long arm shot out and plucked her from the saddle to ride his lap instead.

Thor danced sideways under the strange weight, and Alex reached in panic for a handhold. She found one—a perfect one—and felt the huge expansion of Collin's chest as her fingers tightened convulsively.

"Shit," he gasped, a croak of pleasure and alarm.

"Sorry!" she squeaked, releasing her grip.

"Just glad you didn't fall off and take it with you." The words were strained, but he composed himself enough to grab her hand and tuck it back into his lap. "Not so tight this time, lassie."

She wiggled her hip against him, easing closer to his growing length. Thor shied again. Collin bit her neck. "Mm."

"I don't think Thor appreciates the weight," he murmured, lips sliding over her skin to her ear.

"Mm."

"He's tired, probably. Needs a rest."

"Yes."

"There's a stream just ahead. A clearing. And we must stop for lunch."

"Perfect."

And so their day went.

They were not three miles from Westmore when Alex shook her head to clear away the haze of languid satisfaction. "It was Jeannie in Fergus's bed, I hope."

"And how could you know that?"

"Instinct." Her eyes flew to his and away again. "I did not know she'd been to his bed."

"He says he will ask for her hand."

"Oh, Collin! That's—"

The world slipped, shifted under her, spinning till it hit her face. The whole of the earth seemed to have landed on her chest and she could not draw a breath past the weight.

"Alex!" Hooves danced near her head. She saw Collin's

face above her as he slid from the saddle, saw him look to the horse, saw a stream of blood flowing from the gelding's chest. Then a pistol clutched in a fist fell from the sky and her husband dropped away, disappearing from her vision.

Air flooded suddenly into her stunned lungs. "Collin," she coughed when she had enough air to exhale. She could not roll her eyes far enough to see him, so she forced her cringing body to push to the side. Shadows swam before her like fish darting through water.

"Greetings, Lady Westmore. What a pleasure to see you again."

The shadows melted together to form a man.

"I do not appreciate being ignored, my dear. Lied to *again*. But perhaps this is for the good. Your husband is better leverage than a threat, after all. And if you refuse to turn over the money, I will simply rid myself of the underlying problem."

"Damien?"

"Oh, my name still sounds so lovely on your lips."

She searched the road at his feet till she found her husband, still and bloody. "What have you done?"

"He is only unconscious."

"But . . . Why?"

"I warned you to leave the money. Imagine my disappointment when I found you had left without paying me."

"I didn't . . . I meant to return with it."

"Oh, what a pretty liar you are. No, you meant to leave your brutish husband; however, I did not worry. I knew he'd retrieve you, animal that he is."

"I have the money, the jewels. I'll turn them over."

"Yes, you will. Or I'll slit his ugly throat."

"No! You can't—"

"Come, let's get off this road, shall we? I've a campsite just off this trail. Too bad he's too heavy to lift."

He turned away, busied himself with rope and the horses. Alex tried to heave herself up and managed to raise her chest from the ground.

"What a pity. Your face will swell. We shall have to say he beat you. That is in keeping with his nature, is it not?"

"No," she mumbled and folded her legs beneath her. If she could stand, perhaps—

St. Claire bent over her, pulled her wrists up and tied them together. Even the barest try at resistance set her arms shaking.

"You're not going to vomit on me, are you? Good." He patted her head. Alex blinked at the swarm of dots before her eyes. "I will help you to mount. If you try to escape, you'll come along behind your husband."

She realized, in a sudden rush of horror, what he'd been doing with the rope. Collin lay on the road, hands limp and tied above his head. The rope bound him to Thor's saddle. He was to be dragged.

"No!" Her eyes rolled again, taking in every jagged edge of every rock that jut from the roadside. They found the small hint of a trail and the litter of branches and tree roots across it. "No, you'll kill him."

"Oh, it's not far. And I can't possibly lift him. A moment, please." He held up an elegant hand to stop her words before reaching for the trailing rein of the injured horse. She was thankful for the moment to think, thankful till he led the horse a few feet into the brush and slit its throat.

A sob and a rush of bile choked her.

"What?" St. Claire scoffed when he returned. "Was I to leave it limping about for anyone to find?"

Alex stared at his bloody hand as he wiped a crimson streak over a handkerchief. She bent over to be sick, but the wave of nausea passed.

"All right, come along. Into the saddle."

By the time he'd dragged her to her feet and led her to Thor, she'd begun to beg. She had no thought of pride or will, she only wanted Collin alive. "Please," she pled. "Don't do this."

"For God's sake, shut your mouth. You always did talk too much."

She pushed up, tried to straddle Collin's saddle, and nearly tumbled to the ground.

"Here. Let me help." His hateful hands pushed up and under her skirts, shoving dress and petticoat to the tops of her thighs. "That should be easier. Taken to wearing drawers, have you?"

She shivered and made herself swallow her cries when his fingers edged underneath the drawers, and she sat forward in the saddle to keep his hand from exploring further. Still, he traced over her, touching flesh still tender from her husband's attention.

"He's been at you already, has he?" The touch lifted from her, thank God. She watched him wipe his wet hand over her skirts, horrified to see the red crescents of horse blood under his nails. "Punishment for running away?"

"No."

"Was he rough with you, Alex dear?"

"Shut up."

"Perhaps you like it rough. I wouldn't be surprised."

"Keep your hands off her, you filthy whoreson."

A little scream leapt past her lips, part joy that Collin was alive and part horror that he would antagonize their captor.

"Ah, Blackburn. Happy to have you join us. Hope you can keep your legs under you." With that, he led Thor to his own horse and mounted, leading Brinn as well.

Alex twisted and stretched, trying to guard Collin with her eyes, as if her gaze could keep him safe. He had pushed to his feet, thank God, and stumbled behind them on the trail, blood dripping down his face. She prayed fervently, prayed he would not fall to his knees and be dragged. The trail would shred his legs, and Brinn crept close behind him, hooves like stones waiting to crush.

Thankfully, the trail had grown over with vine and brush and slowed them to a careful walk. Collin tried to catch her eye, but he could not look away from his feet for long and Alex could not think well enough to interpret his brief stares.

The smell of crushed fir needles overwhelmed her suddenly, the scent sharp and acrid in her nose, her mouth. She had to turn away from Collin to lean over Thor's neck and retch. She heard the harsh pant of Collin's breath even over her own sickness.

"Almost there," St. Claire called cheerfully a few moments later, voice conveying his absolute pleasure with the situation.

Alex's stomach heaved again, but she forced back the sickness. She must push past the blackness that crept into her vision. Collin could not get them out of this alone.

The sun shone ahead of them, lighting a clearing. The grassy circle was so eerily picturesque that she wanted to weep. A lovely place, and terrible.

This was where he had camped, next to a stream, beneath the shelter of a solitary tree. The sun would warm the air during the day; the tree kept out the wet. It was perfect.

St. Claire led them to the far edge and tied the horses, seeming at ease under Collin's watchful glare. At ease, but not unaware. The click of a cocking pistol snapped through the air.

"Do not move, Alexandra. Blackburn, you come with me."

Collin bit out a Gaelic curse, straining against the jerk of the rope in St. Claire's hands.

"I have your wife at my mercy, bastard."

Collin snapped the rope, pulling free. "We both know you are not planning to let her go."

"*Au contraire.*" The gun rose to stare at Collin's chest. "She will return to Westmore to retrieve her jewels. If she refuses or tries to bring help, I'll kill you."

"Do not listen to him, Alex. He'll kill me anyway."

"Silence! Walk to the tree now or I'll cut off one of her pretty ears." The knife he'd used to kill the horse appeared suddenly in his hand. "She could still function quite nicely *sans* earlobe, don't you think?"

"Collin. Don't. He won't hurt me."

St. Claire's chuckle iced her nerves. Collin met her eyes,

then walked to the tree, wrapped his hands behind him around the trunk. "Don't come back, *caitein*."

"Very good," St. Claire crooned, following to tie Collin's wrists in a tight knot. He pulled a handkerchief from his coat pocket with a flourish and stepped around the tree to face him. "Can't have you distracting her," he grinned and stuffed the fabric into Collin's mouth. Another length of rope secured the gag and pulled his head against the bark.

"You don't look much like your brother, you know. Must have been the peasant blood that made you so large."

"Why are you doing this?" Alex asked again, desperate to distract him from whatever he meant to do to Collin.

"I need the money, of course."

"But why did you start this? Why did you kill John?"

"I didn't mean to kill him. I only meant to break him. The killing was an impulse, though perhaps not a smart one. I simply couldn't resist."

"But why? Why?"

"Oh, so many reasons, really. He had everything I wanted—money, his father's title, the friendship of every damned buck in school. Still, he stole from me. First that blond whore at The Priory . . . pulled her right from under my nose when he knew I wanted her. He stole my money, though he had too much to spend. Goaded me into playing too deep, then threw my notes back in my face to show everyone I couldn't pay them."

"He was only being kind!"

"Do you know nothing? He may as well have slapped me in the face right there in the club. And then he did it again, the little fool. Turned over his hand with that mew of pity. You should have seen their faces. Oh, they loved watching that.

"I wanted to kill him then, but I didn't have the nerve, not yet. But everyone knew he was in love with you, so I stole you from under *his* nose. A whore for a whore."

Her temper flared, finally, worming its way from beneath her fear and injury. He had killed John for a petty slight, an imagined insult. He had lured her to that room, had set her on that desk and faced her toward the door so that John would see her naked thighs and busy hands as soon as he turned the doorknob.

"You're a coward," she growled as he left Collin and approached her. She regretted her words almost instantly. Her eyes fell on the rope binding Collin's hands. She couldn't goad him on, couldn't give him the excuse he wanted to hurt them. If he let her go, surely she could do something . . .

"Come down and visit with me, beautiful."

He reached up and yanked her off the horse, letting her fall to her knees before him.

"I don't know that I'd call myself a coward."

He pulled her, dragging her toward her husband. Collin's eyes drilled into her, demanding she obey him. But she wasn't stupid. She knew he planned to kill them both.

"I'll admit to being cautious. For example, it would have been easy enough to swive you, to truly ruin you. You were certainly itching for it." She tried not to moan in disgust. "But I did not wish to bring down the wrath of a duke on my head. It was a near enough thing as it stood, but I counted on you to protect me; everyone knows your brother indulges you. Perhaps he was the one who had you so primed, hmm? Was big brother after you in the nursery?"

"You're vile."

"Mm." He stopped in front of Collin, pulling her to face her husband as he pressed his chest against her back. One hand held her to him, the other rose to cup her chin, angling first one way, then the other, as if offering her for examination. Alex studied Collin's face, memorized it.

"And I am still cautious, so this is what we'll do. When we leave here tomorrow morning"—*Tomorrow*—"I will release you to go to Westmore. Your dear husband and I will move on to new environs. Wouldn't want you leading a hunting party back to us, would we?"

His hand slipped from her jaw to her neck. His fingers caressed her skin. "You will leave the money somewhere convenient for me, but—listen to me now—Blackburn will not be with me when I come to fetch my prize. Do not think to ambush me or you will never find out where I've hidden him."

"But you will not hurt him?" She felt her voice shake against his fingers. Collin's eyes flared.

"Oh, no. I give you my word as a gentleman."

She nodded, ignoring the silver fire that leapt at her. "Don't hurt him."

"I won't." His hand crept lower, playing over her collarbone, flicking aside her wrap. "Not if you cooperate."

Nodding again, nodding past the lump in her throat, she felt the hand cup her breast and jerked her eyes from Collin's scarlet face. The thickness of her wool habit proved a paltry defense to the sensation of a killer's fingers pinching her nipple.

Collin roared past the gag in his mouth. Alex closed her eyes altogether, and felt a tear creep down her face as Damien's hand crept lower still.

"We have the whole night to kill, my sweet. Shall we pick up where we left off those years ago?"

"Yes," she choked. "Yes. Anything you want. Anything." Her muscles shook, but she forced herself to let him touch her, forced herself to lay her head back against his shoulder. When his hand pressed against the juncture of her legs, she bit her lip until it bled, then curled her fingers over his to cup them to her.

"Oh, yes. I shall enjoy your *cooperation* immensely. Does this excite you? To do this right in front of his eyes? I can see that it does."

Alex couldn't speak. If she opened her mouth she would begin to scream and she would not be able to stop. It wasn't just this violation, this horrible fear. It was the terror that if she looked she might find Collin's eyes full of rage, full of hurt and betrayal and the sure knowledge that she was a whore. But she had to distract St. Claire.

"Your husband had good reason for his jealousy."

St. Claire's laugh was warm this time, burning the delicate skin of her neck.

She nodded as he jerked a handful of her skirt up. His hand snaked beneath the fabric and pressed between her thighs. "You've always been so wonderfully easy to excite. Right here, eh? Right in front of him?" His tongue traced a wet line up her neck to her ear. "A fantasy of yours, maybe?"

Despite her intent, there was no stopping her body's reaction when he pushed a cruel finger into her body. She jerked away and shook her head, biting back a sob as she tripped toward the far side of the clearing. St. Claire's laugh followed behind her, not quite covering the hoarse sound of her husband's cry.

Alex faced the trees and began to undress.

Warmth dripped down Collin's thumb, then more as he pulled desperately at the ropes that bound him. The blood slicked the knot, so he pulled harder, pulled till the bark of the tree scraped and tore at his skin, pulled till his arms threatened to pop from their sockets. His hands would not come free.

Oh, God. Her eyes. Her eyes. He had watched them dull and fade, had watched as she decided to sacrifice herself for him. And she could not save him, couldn't she see that? St. Claire would kill him as soon as she disappeared toward Westmore, and she would blame herself. If St. Claire let her live.

Collin stilled, pressed his back to the tree, straining to hear. The man had stopped laughing. What the hell was he doing?

There. A whisper of sound. Collin's mind tumbled, sending rough fragments of pain flying and crashing in his head. He should have resisted, should not have fallen for that monster's threat to cut her. Maybe he wouldn't have done it. Maybe.

"Are you playing shy?"

Collin froze.

"Take off your shift. I never did get to see you naked."

A pause. He heard his wife's voice, couldn't make out the words over the blood in his ears.

"I can't wait long enough to build a fire. Later though."

"Please . . . the cold."

"Now."

Footsteps. Rustling. Alex's panting breath.

Collin felt frozen and constrained, ready to burst past his skin. Oh, God, no. Oh, please, no. Not after all the terrible things he'd said to her. Not this.

St. Claire's voice whispered urgent commands, then he heard it. A grunt, a moan. Alex's sharp, sobbing cry.

Collin screamed against the rag in his throat, roared until his voice cracked and died against the linen. *No. No. No.* He arched off the tree, pushed with his feet. He felt blood drip from the wound on his head and trickle from his hands. He collapsed against the bark and sobbed, helpless and dying inside.

A branch snapped to his left, springing open his eyes and jerking his head to the side.

Alex.

Alex. She stood, limp and sightless, blood covering her white shift in a swath of gore. Collin shook with terror and cried out. My God, it hadn't been enough to rape her, the man had killed her too. He'd killed her. Why?

She took a step toward him, then another, blood dripping from her sleeve. Her eyes blinked and saw him. Then Collin spied the dagger, so covered in red it had been invisible in her bloody hand. The dagger he'd reminded her to put in her boot just this morning. He pushed his feet beneath him and stood, sliding his body up the tree.

"Collin," she breathed. The knife flew in a low arc from her hand and she rushed forward to throw her arms around him. "Collin."

He tried to curl into her, to cover her with his body, but the ropes held him tight. The absence of his arms seemed to wake her, and she jumped away, falling to her knees in the grass to scramble for the blade.

A high cry flew from her lips and she jumped to her feet, dagger caught in her fist.

He felt the pull and tug of her sawing at the rope, then his head fell free. Then his hands.

"I killed him," she whispered into his chest as he wrapped her tight against him.

"Thank God, Alex. Thank God. Are you hurt?"

"I killed him," she repeated and her head came up, eyes on his. "I didn't want—"

"Don't ever say it. Never. I know. I know. *Tha gaol agam ort, caitein.* My God, I love you."

His legs gave way, and he carried her to the ground with him.

Epilogue

The bride blushed like a virgin, pink face clashing horribly with her beautiful red hair.

"I can't believe I'm married," Jeannie whispered to Alex just before her husband took her hand and led her down the aisle to the church door. The guests began to crowd the aisle, fighting to get outside and pile into waiting carriages for the drive to Kirkland Hall. Jeannie's father had relented after all, though not easily. The groom had worn a black eye to the ceremony.

Alex felt her fingers pulled into a strong hand and beamed up at her husband. She softened with such love that she nearly melted. Instead of falling upon him like the starving wanton she was, she settled for brushing a hand over his brow where a jagged cut was healing.

What a ragtag wedding party they were. Fergus with his black eye, Collin with the head wound, and Alex herself, with the ugly yellow shadow of a fading bruise spread out over her cheek. Only Jeannie had looked pristine, glowing in a pale gold gown. She'd been lovely.

Alex felt the stares of dozens of eyes on her and Collin. She could hear the muted roar of their whispers. Everyone knew what had happened, or thought they did. A man had been killed, after all. Authorities had been dispatched to Westmore to clear up the question of murder.

But their avid eyes did not bother her in the least. She beamed and walked down the aisle at Collin's side and even he smiled, a satisfied curve of his lip that would wag tongues for weeks, she didn't doubt. The unhappy couple had suddenly bloomed into newlyweds. Alex laughed into the bright cold sunlight as they stepped from the church.

"Do you think anyone would notice if we took a short drive 'round the country? For the air, of course."

Alex rolled her eyes. "Since we are second only to the bridal couple in interest . . . Yes. Yes, they would notice."

"Would you care?"

"We'd better not." She couldn't keep the mourning from her voice. "I shouldn't like to take away from Jeannie's day."

"But I missed you last night."

"Poor husband," she sighed. He had not understood in the least why Jeannie had wanted Alex to stay in her bed-chamber with her.

"She is not a virgin!" he'd cried the night before. "She's not lying there in fear of the marriage bed."

Alex had mumbled something about feminine appre-hensions and natural modesty, then she had rushed to Jean-nie's room to giggle and gasp and compare illicit experiences. Both men had emerged with high marks.

She did not mention this to Collin as he handed her into the carriage. "Just a few more hours, Collin, and we'll be home. I promise to make you forget about your lonely night."

"I'll hold you to it," he growled, but still could not banish his smile. He was so different now that she wanted to cry out her happiness to the world.

The only regret that tainted her happiness was her lack of guilt at Damien's death. Perhaps she was unnatural indeed, to feel nothing more than thankfulness that they were both alive and well. Jeannie had scoffed at the idea and the Kirkland brothers had patted her back. Fergus had done nothing more than pull her into a long, tight hug.

And Alex knew that Westmore was finally her home.

"By the way, husband . . ."

"Yes?"

"Jeannie asked me to pass along a message to you."

He raised a brow.

"She says that you must stop blushing when you speak to her and that you may consider it payback for the time she spied on you at the River Tweed."

His face paled a bit, his quirk of a smile faded.

"You've seen naked women before, Collin."

"Well, my God, she's like a little sister to me."

"Not so little, eh?"

"Jesus, Alex!"

She laughed. Laughed until she cried and fell into his pride-stiff chest. Laughed until his arms came around her, finally, and he kissed her giggles into soft sighs.

"*Caitein?*"

"Hmm?"

"Your punishment will not wait for tonight, I'm afraid."

"Punishment for what?"

"Laughing at your lord and master. Just the sort of dis-respect that calls for a spanking."

Her squeal could not be contained by the thin walls of the carriage. Wrens startled from their nest in the chapel tower and shot across the sky above the swiveling heads of every person still in the churchyard.

She would never be a lady. She knew that just as surely as she knew the whispers of "scandalous" and "shameful" would not disappear just because the carriage wheels began to turn and masked the sound.

She would never be a lady, or not a proper one at any rate, and that was fine. Because she was a farmer's wife. And her farmer had fallen in love with her in all her bold, unnatural glory.

She laid her head on his strong shoulder and smiled, looking forward to the quiet ride and the lively wedding breakfast and the night they'd spend alone . . . And won-dering all the while if she really could tempt him into that spanking once they reached home.

Please turn the page for an exciting sneak peak of
Victoria Dahl's next historical romance,
coming in 2008 from Zebra Books!

Chapter 1

December 1844, outside London

The storm had passed only hours before, blanketing the countryside in half a foot of snow. Moonlight and torch flame glittered and sparked off the icy garden, and the sight called to Emma Jensen through the hard cold of the window. Nature had reclaimed the tamed bower, swept in and buried the pathways, softened the stark angle of hedges cut to precise corners. This garden, painstakingly shaped by man, now lay hidden under gentle hills and deep drifts of snow; and Emma wondered how it would feel to be so effortlessly smothered. So still.

Her deep sigh fogged the glass and blanked the stark scene. Straightening, she glanced back to the bright whirl of the ballroom. Boredom had set in, and when she grew bored her mind turned to useless melancholy. Her life was not so bad, after all, or someday wouldn't be.

"Lady Denmore!"

Emma angled her chin, set a smile on her face, and turned toward the half-drunk voice.

"Lady Denmore, your presence is greatly desired in the hall."

"Why, Mr. Jones, whatever for?" Emma forced the words to come light and pretty.

"Matherton and Osbourne have arranged a race and they wish you to start it."

A distraction. Good. Emma smiled more genuinely and took the arm the thin young man offered, leaving behind the cold escape of her daydream.

Giggles and loud voices filled the cavernous front hall of Matherton House. All heads were turned toward the sweeping staircase and the impossible sight at the top. There, perched atop the landing, were Lords Matherton and Osbourne, peers of the Realm, each crouching down to sit on what looked to be huge silver platters. The men, once seated, began to slide gingerly over the Persian runner, easing themselves closer to the edge of the top stair.

"This is a race?" Emma laughed, but she didn't let her amusement distract from a quick study of the men. "Fifty pounds on Osbourne."

The noise around her paused, as if the whole room drew a breath, then exploded in a flurry of betting. Emma took the bottom step with a smile, meaning to climb to the top to start the race, but a loud shout stopped her.

"Ho there! The starter can't bet on the race!"

Emma only shrugged and stepped aside with a flourish of her hand, letting another woman take the starter's position, a woman not so cursed with the need to gamble on the outcome of every contest.

A moment passed, then a handkerchief dropped and the men burst from the landing, gaslight glinting off silver as the trays tilted. They shot down the stairs with surprising speed. Emma gasped—everyone gasped—and the crowd parted in the face of imminent danger.

She almost closed her eyes, afraid to see the crash that surely awaited both men—but she did have fifty quid riding on this. She watched the men fly down, watched as Osbourne's greater weight proved its advantage. She nodded in satisfaction as Osbourne shot past her perch, then grimaced as he crashed with drama, a cacophony of metal and wall and groaning man.

The crowd dispersed almost immediately, back to their drinks and gossip, and Emma wound her way between the guests, working toward Osbourne to see how he'd fared. Matherton, she saw, had already righted himself and stood laughing with his friends.

"Osbourne," she called past a small crowd of attendees. "Are you injured?"

"Just my elbow," he wheezed.

"Oh, Lord Osbourne," Emma sighed at the sight of his flushed face. "Tell me you haven't broken it?"

"No, no. Just banged it up a bit."

"Thank God. Lady Osbourne would have my head if I'd encouraged your injuring yourself."

"Mine as well."

"Come, my lord, let's see if there is ice—"

"Henry!"

"Oh, no," the earl breathed.

"Oh, no," Emma echoed. "Well . . . If Lady Osbourne is coming to help, I'll just leave you to her care."

"But—"

"Henry! Have you lost your mind?"

Emma ducked away, not willing to be caught between a tipsy old man and his loving, outraged wife.

Mr. Jones caught her arm and presented her winnings with a grin. Seventy pounds. Not as much as she'd hoped for. Her reputation for good hunches had begun to cut into her profits, as people often bet *with* her instead of *on* the wager. Luckily, the tables still proved profitable.

Tucking the bills into her glove, Emma craned her neck, looking past the soggy smile of Mr. Jones for Matherton. She spotted him moving away, toward the card room, waving friendly acknowledgments to those he passed. Emma followed, though she was waylaid for a moment by an agitated Lady Matherton who was sure her Persian carpet must have been damaged. After much patting of hands and sympathetic murmurs, Emma edged away from her hostess and moved swiftly toward the card room.

She couldn't help but smile when she spied the familiar shock of white hair glowing in the dim light at the end of the hallway. Lord Matherton would play the wounded party well. No doubt he planned to accuse her of treachery and betrayal for placing her bet with Osbourne. Perhaps she would let him win a round of *piquet* to help heal his wounded pride.

Emma drew a breath, meaning to call out to him, but just as her lips parted, he stepped aside and revealed the face of the man he spoke with. Emma froze. Someone plowed into her back.

"Oh, my dear girl. I'm so sorry."

Emma steadied herself against the wall as a man tried to help her stand upright. But she didn't take her eyes off the black-haired stranger just ahead. "No need to apologize, sir. 'Twas my fault, after all."

"Still, I should have been watching . . ."

"No, I'm sorry. Shouldn't have stopped like that." She finally glanced to her collider. "Admiral Hartford, that man looks familiar—the one with Matherton—but I can't place him."

"Oh." The admiral's eyes widened, then slid back to her with a sympathetic smile. "That, my dear, is the Duke of Somerhart. A committed bachelor, I'm afraid."

"Somerhart," she murmured, feeling the name on her lips. "Oh, yes. Of course. Somerhart. Thank you, Admiral."

Emma spun on her heel and retreated, hurrying back to the front hall, then around a corner to the ladies' retiring room. She darted into a corner that had been curtained off and sat hard on the padded chair.

A *duke*? She would never have believed it.

Had he seen her? And if he had, would he know her?

"Of course not," Emma breathed. It was ridiculous to think so. She'd only met the man once and that had been . . . What? A decade before? Yes, she'd been nine at the time.

He couldn't know her. He'd probably forgotten her that very evening.

Still, the whole of her plan rested on this charade, this lie of being the widow of the tenth Baron Denmore, and if Duke Somerhart did remember her then the game would be up, for she could not have been married to her own great-uncle.

She'd planned on at least another two months before doubts began to surface. There were few fashionable members of society from their county, and none who'd arrive before the season. She needed just a few more weeks . . .

Emma sat up straight and looked into the wall mirror. No, the duke would not know her. Her brown hair had been dark blond then, and she had certainly filled out in important places. Also, she was not wearing a white nightgown and braids. She was unrecognizable.

He, on the other hand, had been etched into her mind the first moment she'd seen him, stepping from his shadowed space on the wall.

"Hello, pet," he'd called as she snuck down the wide hallway, trying desperately to get a peek at one of her father's strange new parties.

By God, he'd scared the devil out of her, his voice like a ghost's, floating from the dark. Then he'd come into the light and Emma had gaped.

"What are you about so late?" he asked, voice soft and low. Emma thought he might be an angel. He was far prettier than any of her father's other friends. But did angels wear red waistcoats and smoke cigarillos? "You should be in bed, kitten."

"I, I . . . I wanted to see the dancing. I can hear the music from my bed."

His eyes, pale sky-blue, swept over her, from her braided hair to her bare toes, and his beautiful face turned sad. "This is no place for you. You shouldn't come down to your papa's parties, all right? Best to stay in your room."

"Oh," she breathed, amazed at the kindness of that

voice. He was an angel, the most beautiful creature she'd ever seen. Emma eased one foot back, meaning to turn toward the servants' stairs, but his eyes stopped her, blue warmth closing her throat with something hopeful.

She drew a breath. "But . . ." When she leaned forward a little his mouth quirked up into a smile, but the smile blurred when her eyes pricked with tears. "But someone has come to my room."

"What?" She'd thought him enormously tall, but he drew himself up taller. His pretty mouth hardened and thinned. "What do you mean?"

Emma took that step back. "I don't . . . My, my room. Someone came in last night. While I was sleeping. I don't want to stay there." Her cheeks flushed hot at the burn in his gaze. "He kissed me."

Something hard and terrible stole over his face. Emma gasped and meant to spin around, but his mouth gentled with a twitch and he reached out one hand to curl her fingers into his.

"I'm sorry." He crouched down and offered a small smile. "You are certainly pretty enough to want to kiss, but only a husband should do that, you understand?"

"Yes, sir."

"And no one has hurt you?"

Emma shook her head.

"All right. Is there a lock on your door? Yes? You go back to your room then, and lock the door. Then put a chair under the handle. Do you know what I mean?"

A nod this time.

"Do that whenever your papa has a party. And do not try to spy again, pet, all right?"

"Yes." And she had fled. And though she hadn't ceased her spying, she'd nursed an infatuation for that nameless man for nigh on four years. Then she'd forgotten him. Until now.

A duke. A rather notorious duke at that. Not known

for his kindness. And still the handsomest man she'd ever seen.

Well, there was no choice; she could not accomplish her goal by sneaking nervously about for the next few months. If her plans were in danger, she needed to know now. So Emma forced herself to her feet and went to meet her old protector.

"Ah, the traitorous Lady Denmore!" Lord Matherton boomed, eliciting a husky laugh from a woman somewhere behind Hart's back.

Hart turned toward her and let his eyebrows rise in surprise as he looked her over. It wasn't often one met new women at a ton gathering, and certainly not lovely young matrons.

"I can't think what you mean, sir," she laughed, her hazel eyes sparkling. She glanced at Hart, then away just as quickly.

"How could you do it, Lady Denmore? Put money on another man?"

She reached a gloved hand out and touched Matherton's sleeve. "I am deeply wounded, my lord. Surely you can see that I had complete confidence in you. I thought only to salvage Osbourne's pride, fully expecting you to trounce him."

Matherton snorted. "You, madam, would do the country a great service if you were to offer yourself as a diplomat. Words flow so prettily from your mouth that it matters not in the least if they are true."

She laughed again, and Hart took in the sound with pleasure. What a bedroom voice she had, soft and rich. It didn't quite match the rest of her. She was pretty in a mild way, certainly not exotic.

"Lady Denmore, may I present the Duke of Somerhart? Your Grace, this lovely woman is Baroness Denmore."

He watched her curtsy, her dark lilac skirts crumpling a bit. Those hazel eyes crinkled in a smile as he took her hand.

"Lady Denmore. A pleasure. And no 'Your Graces,' if you please. Just Somerhart."

"You do not employ your title, sir?" she teased.

"Oh, I make full use of it. To the extent that I command how others may address me."

"Ah. A man heady with his own power."

Hart smiled, watched her full lips curve in answer, and wondered quickly if her husband were in attendance. If not . . .

"Madam," Matherton interrupted, eyes darting toward the open doorway to his left. "I believe my table awaits me. May I leave you in Somerhart's care?"

"Certainly. I will, however, be in to take your money soon."

Hart smiled at Matherton's sigh, happy to be left alone with this appealing woman. "Shall I escort you to your husband?" he drawled.

"Ah. I am a widow, Duke Somerhart. The *dowager* Baroness Denmore."

Hart blinked, surprised by both the information and his gaffe. "My apologies." This girl was a *widow*? She looked no older than his baby sister. "And my condolences for your loss." His mind began to tick through the history of the Denmore line.

Baron Denmore. He had known the ninth Baron Denmore, that lecherous, perverted drunk, but he'd died years ago. Hart had no idea who'd inherited the title. No one of his circle, certainly. A servant passed, and he plucked two glasses of champagne from the tray.

"Have you been in London long?"

Her pink mouth smiled at the glass he urged into her hand. "No. Not long."

"And will you be staying with us through the season?"

She glanced up at the word "us," a flash of surprise lighting her eyes. She recognized his flirtation. Good. He did not like obvious women. He was a man of subtle tastes and subtle actions, or he was now at any rate.

"For a little while, certainly," she murmured before raising the glass to her lips.

Hart's eyes widened as he watched her, this modest young woman, drain a full glass of champagne and pop it back into his hand.

"Thank you. A pleasure."

And then she spun away and disappeared into the card room, leaving behind the faint scent of citrus and one startled duke.

Chapter 2

Crystals glinted in her hair, caught by the flickering gaslight as she glanced at her cards. Hart glanced too. "Split," she murmured, and placed another bet.

She was good at the game, *Vignt-et-un*, had been winning steadily since she'd sat down a quarter hour before, but she seemed distracted now . . . bored, glancing toward the whist table even as she played her hand.

"What do you know about this Lady Denmore?" Hart asked of the man next to him.

Lord Marsh chuckled. "Ah, she's a tempting bit, isn't she? Married to an old man for a year and now she's free to pursue more interesting interests."

"An old man?"

"Yes, Baron Denmore must have been seventy at least, a recluse, and she no more than nineteen when they married. She'd never even been presented."

Hart's mind turned over the possibilities. "And who introduced her to London?"

"Ha! No one. She arrived in *October*, of all times, and still in mourning. The Mathertons were practically the only people left in town. And the Osbournes, of course. She's rather become their pet."

Hart watched her collect her winnings and rise. She

made her way immediately to the whist table, inviting several of the men already playing to wince.

"She's an accomplished player, I gather?"

"Mm. That coward Brasher is already fleeing the table. See the men tremble at her feet."

Hart allowed himself a small smile. The men were, indeed, unhappy to see her. Lady Denmore, on the other hand, was all gracious good humor. "She seems a woman who enjoys taking risks."

"Indeed," Marsh grinned. "And I am hoping that will translate to other habits as well. Did you get a good look at that mouth?"

Hart pressed his lips together. He knew his own reputation with women, but it was just as well known that he preferred privacy above all else. He disdained to speak of women like whores on the bartering block, just as he expected not to be evaluated like a stallion on parade.

"Well, old man," Marsh continued, oblivious to Hart's anger, "I do believe I'll join the play. Perhaps I can divest her of her coin and move on to other trade."

Lord Marsh approached the table, and when Lady Denmore looked up, her eyes slid to meet Hart's. They widened as if the sight of him surprised her. Odd, considering he'd followed her into the room. She blinked, a strange flutter of her lashes, and turned away from him to glare at the cards she'd been dealt.

She reacted to him almost as if she knew him. Perhaps it was only his reputation that made her so nervous. She was a country miss, after all, despite that her voice gave one visions of tumbled sheets and sweat-damp hair.

A seventy-year-old husband. Hart shook his head and pushed away from the bookcase he'd leaned against. She stiffened when he passed her table on his way to the door, her awareness of him tempting him to stop and stand over her shoulder . . . but he walked on.

She was a bit young for him, perhaps. But he preferred widows, after all, and he was presently unattached. Still, well-bred, proper innocents rarely offered up much excitement in bed, unless one counted declarations of love as exciting. Hart did not. Not that he'd had much experience with innocents, but one did hear things.

He moved at a quick pace toward the ballroom, ignoring the dozens of people who tried to catch his eye as he passed. Being a duke was very much like being a prized stud, and as an eligible duke . . . He suppressed a cringe of disgust even as he spied his quarry at the edge of the dancing.

"Osbourne," he started, planting himself next to the old gentleman.

"Ah, Somerhart! On your way into town?"

"Yes. Lady Matherton was kind enough to offer a room so I wouldn't have to fight this damned snow."

"Well, thank God none of the new crop has arrived. If it were April you'd be awash in eager mamas."

"As you say. By the way, I made the acquaintance of your friend Lady Denmore."

"Ah, where is Emma? In the card room, I suppose?"

Emma. "Yes. The men cower in fear."

"As they should. By God, she's livened things up for us this winter. Taught me a thing or two about whist, I can assure you. Do you play brag? Do not go betting your estate on a game with her. She will divest you of more than your pride."

Hart smiled at the man's hearty laughter. "I was not acquainted with her late husband, Denmore."

"I wasn't acquainted with Denmore either! When I knew him he was plain old Mister Jensen. He never expected to inherit the title, you know. We ran about town together long ago. I hadn't seen him in . . ." Osbourne shrugged. "Must have been fifteen years now."

"Really? So you had never met Lady Denmore?"

"No, no. Denmore had become garden-mad in his old age. He had no time for hunting or balls. He had ceased to even write letters." Osbourne's bushy eyebrows lowered. "I cannot imagine his interest in a young girl like Emma, but duty comes along with the title, I suppose. Still, they must have got on well. She knew all the old stories about me—some I wish she hadn't, I can tell you that." His chuckle turned to a sigh. "She speaks of him with great affection."

"Of course."

Something of his doubt must have cooled Hart's voice, because Osbourne turned to glare at him. "I daresay she knew him even better than I, and she'd only spent a year or so in his house. She's a fine woman and she was clearly a fine wife. A bit wild for games of chance, but that's the extent of it. A good girl."

"I didn't mean to imply otherwise. She seems quite lovely."

"Hmph."

"How is your arm?"

"Damned thing aches like the devil, but I can't let on. Lady Osbourne is not pleased."

"Well, you seem to be good at charming her out of these piques."

Osbourne flashed a reprobate's smile. "That I am, young man. That I am."

Emma left the table abruptly, startling the other players. She still had twenty pounds in the pot, after all. But better twenty than two hundred. Her thoughts would not bend to her demands and kept careening away from the game to a certain black-haired gentleman.

Glancing about the hallway to be sure he'd gone, Emma hurried toward the music room. She hadn't been prepared for him, not up close. She knew now why'd she'd thought him an angel that night. He was beauty and power and mystery. Those ice-blue eyes framed by black lashes. That lush mouth and careful control. And he was tall, just as she'd remembered, tall and impossibly elegant.

He hadn't remembered her, and she should have felt

relieved, not nervous. But he'd flirted with her. And she'd flirted back.

Unwise and reckless as ever. She thought she'd learned her lesson.

The music room was crowded with women, and Emma had to weave her way through the door. But the suffocating heat proved bearable when she heard the name she'd hope to hear.

Somerhart. She felt an urgent need to know something about this man, and as luck would have it, the whole party seemed abuzz with excitement at the duke's appearance.

Emma had heard things about the famous duke. "Winterhart," they called him. Or Hartless. But she'd never paid attention, not realizing she knew him. And now . . . now the things she heard were like a veil of sadness over the fantasy she'd once created.

Oh, she had woven quite a hero out of their brief meeting. Yes, he had been at her father's house, a place well known for its unsavory assemblies, but he had left after their encounter. Emma had hounded the housekeeper for information and learned little—just that a man had left Denmore that very night after having words with her father. So she had excused his presence there. He'd likely had no idea what kind of party it was; and, upon learning, had confronted her father. Perhaps he'd even threatened violence before leaving in outraged shock.

It hadn't seemed a fantasy at all, when she'd imagined it ten years before. It had seemed definite. The actual scenario. He might have even thought of coming back to check on her, to save her from her life.

But . . . no. No, of course not. The man was pretty, but he was no angel and never had been. The easy gossip confirmed that. Emma plucked bits of it like low-hanging fruit as she strolled through the crowd. *Cold. Cruel. Ruthless.*

And lower voices whispered other words, tales of his past that did not match his present. Decadent and wicked. Shameless and insatiable.

He was no pillar of morality, no upstanding gentleman. It seemed he had attended many scandalous gatherings like that in his youth, though he was more circumspect now. Quieter about his pleasures, but still in pursuit of them. He was a reprobate, just like her father, so why had he bothered with defending a little girl?

"He must be *sans* lover," Emma heard Lady Sherbourne whisper to a friend. "He only ever makes an appearance to troll for a new bedmate." The woman spoke derisively, not noticing the way the other lady perked up at the words. "No doubt that Caroline White displeased him with her indiscreet prattle. You know why he despises indiscretion, of course."

The other woman nodded thoughtfully, then turned keen eyes on Lady Sherbourne. "Did you ever actually see the letters?"

Emma leaned closer to hear the friend's reply. Her efforts failed. She caught only the word "shameful."

Was he looking for a woman to warm his ducal bed? He had flirted with her, watched her. Emma felt a swarm of sparks float up from her belly, heating her chest and setting off a buzzing in her head.

Hot damn.

She did it on purpose—a hint of cleavage, the curves of her magnificent breasts always draped in some kind of soft material, her clothing perfectly fitted to a waist he knew he could nearly span with his hands. Any further than that he never went, honest to God, not unless she was walking away from him. The last thing he could afford, under any circumstances, was to get mired in the fantasy land of Suzi Toussi's hips. She was just too damned important, his secret weapon.

"Stargate?" she said, repeating the word he'd dropped between them like a small atom bomb. "Sure, Buck. I remember Stargate, the Defense Intelligence Agency's experiments in remote viewing, the psychic spies, the ones trying to gather intelligence using ESP."

She, at least, could say it with a straight face. That was the great thing about Suzi, her smooth coolness. She was always gracious, always unfazed, always somewhat imperious.

Okay, he paused and backed up to his last thought. She was always *damned* imperious. She knew the effect she had on men—which was the point, the reason Christian Hawkins had recruited her five years ago to do a piece of contract work for SDF, Buck's unit of black-ops shadow warriors based in Denver, Colorado. She'd done good, damn good, so they'd used her again, and again, and again, until information gathering had become a sideline for her, if not exactly a full-time job.

Marsh Annex, Washington, D. C.

Elegant.

The woman sitting across from General Richard "Buck" Grant in his office absolutely, positively owned the word—lock, stock, and barrel.

It was impossible for a guy to keep his eyes off her, so Buck didn't even try. What he did do, what he always did, was try not to let his gaze drop below her chin. If she was fascinatingly beautiful from the neck up—and she was—then she was nothing but trouble with a capital T from the neck down.

Dangerous, dangerous territory—he let the thought cross his mind with just the slightest downward glance.

CAN'T GET ENOUGH OF THE
STEELE STREET GANG?

*Buckle in for more hot cars
and sizzling suspense with*

BREAKING
LOOSE

BY TARA JANZEN

Coming from Bantam Dell in August 2009
Read on for a sneak peek inside. . .

ABOUT THE AUTHOR

TARA JANZEN lives in Colorado with her husband, children, and two dogs, and is now at work on her next novel. Of the mind that love truly is what makes the world go 'round, she can be contacted at www.tarajanzen.com. Happy reading!

box, revealing a one-of-a-kind Nikki McKinney creation, a gold band with platinum inlaid wings and a diamond set in a swirl of sapphires.

"Too smart to say no," she said softly, taking the ring out of the box and slipping it on her finger.

"I don't think we should wait, no long engagement or anything like that. I think we should just get married."

She glanced back up from the ring, a small smile on her face. "Sounds like you got that part right."

"Yeah." He figured he did, and he kissed her again.

She pressed herself against him, getting even closer, her mouth so hot and sweet on his, and he could instantly see where this was all going to go, with her legs straddling him, and him being so much in love with her.

"I'm glad we're not going to be on YouTube," he said after a while.

"Yeah, me, too." She kissed him again, with his ring on her finger, and it was all so perfect, cold snowflakes coming down, hot steam going up, and Esme the Wonderful on top.

He pulled the small jeweler's box out of the pocket and showed it to her, and his mind went blank. Just like that. Completely blank.

No, he thought, no, this couldn't be right. He'd had it all worked out. He'd sweated over it, practiced it, memorized it, just the right words. Something about . . . about love, and life, and forever—sure, something about all that, except better, with a part about how wonderful he thought she was, more wonderful than anything else, and a small part about kids, maybe? What had that part been like?

"Honey? You look confused," she said, and when he shifted his attention back to her, she was grinning at him.

"I had this all planned out." It had been so perfect. "But I can't quite remember how it went."

"You mean your proposal of marriage, where you tell me you can't live without me, and we'll work out all the logistics, because in your heart you know we'll both be happier if we're together, even if certain sacrifices have to be made? That part?"

"Yeah." He nodded, grinning back at her. "That part, but there was more."

"You mean the part about how much you love me, and that you can't imagine finding what we have together with anyone else?"

"Yeah. That part," he agreed, settling back against the hot tub and just enjoying the view. "You're pretty smart, aren't you."

"Valedictorian of my senior class," she admitted.

"Smart enough to say yes?" He opened the